hold my Breath

a novel by
GINGER SCOTT

Copyright © 2016 Ginger Scott

All rights reserved.

No part of this book may be reproduced in any form or by any electronic or mechanical means, including information storage and retrieval systems, without permission in writing from the author. The only exception is by a reviewer, who may quote short excerpts in a review.

This book is a work of fiction. Names, characters, places and incidents either are products of the author's imagination or are used fictitiously. Any resemblance to actual persons, living or dead, or events is entirely coincidental.

Ginger Scott

ISBN: 0996873473
ISBN-13: 978-0996873475

For anyone who has ever had to fight through their demons.

PROLOGUE

Will Hollister

My coffee is sour. It isn't sour enough. Nothing is ever quite sour enough.

And bitter. I crave bitter.

I need to hold something harsh in my mouth, swallow it down, letting it slide away pieces of me from the inside, sip by sip. That…*that* is what I crave. It isn't the taste or the buzz or the high or low left in the wake. It's the torture. I crave the torture.

I deserve the torture. For wasting time. For being the one who *gets* to waste time. I'm not sure if I'll ever quit feeling like that completely, but I promised I'd try.

I haven't had a drink in three hundred and sixty-six days. Yesterday marked the anniversary of when I told the world I was done giving up. Or maybe it was the world that told me. Every day since has been a decision—go back to bottom or keep clawing. That's why everyone is here today. The real reason why. Nobody would care if it weren't for the bottom I hit, and for the horrible road that led me there. They're all here because I fell a great distance to land at their feet. They're here for my story—*for my pain.*

Will Hollister, *a loser to root for.*

"It's a lot more crowded than I thought it would be. That's good, yeah? I think it's good. Definitely…good."

My uncle Duncan sounds out of breath, and he grunts as he wedges his wide body into the small frame of the chair next to me, milk from the last sip he took of his coffee still fresh on the tips of his overgrown and graying mustache. I hand him a napkin. He squints at it, not understanding.

"You're wearing half-and-half," I smirk, my lips falling back to the flat line that rules my face.

"Oh, right…sorry," he says, taking the napkin from me and running it around his mouth, chin, and cheeks.

This is his first press conference. It isn't my first. Not even close. It *is* the first one I've had in a long time, but the ones from a few years ago are still fresh in my memory. They were like a media-frenzy boot camp—nothing can be as tough as those were. My uncle is nervous enough for the both of us. He's also a bit of a mess. Not like me, where things are all messy on the inside, but rather…disheveled. His hair is a white tuft of a comb-over; his short-sleeved button-down permanently stained with a touch of grease near the pocket. He's a watchmaker, and he's always carrying a few small tools in his breast pocket. I don't think he owns a single shirt that doesn't have evidence of his trade spilled on it somewhere.

I'm about to answer a barrage of questions from every major news media outlet in the country, as well as a few others, about my miraculous bid to be on the US Olympic swim team, and the only man I have in my corner doesn't even know how to swim.

"You have a speech or somethin' prepared?"

I glance at him and shake my head *no*, folding my hands together in my lap and working a pop from each knuckle only to start back at my thumbs and go through the routine again.

"Will…" he says. I barely hear him as I mash my lips and breathe in through my nose, my focus drifting in and out on the crowd growing in the room. I'm pretty sure we're over capacity. Maybe a fire marshal will show up, throw a few people out. I can only hope.

"Will," my uncle repeats, this time a little more forcefully. I cup my knees and exhale, turning to look him square in the eyes. He tilts his head forward, his wire-rimmed glasses sliding down the bridge of his nose as he peers at me over them. "This is the easy part. Just give them what they want. Give them *you*. Everything else will come out in the water…just like it always does."

I hold his gaze and search his eyes hoping to steal an ounce of his conviction.

"Evan would have handled this so much better," I say.

"Maybe," he shrugs, and I wince a little at how easily he agrees with me. "But no one is expecting you to be Evan, Will."

"They're expecting a miracle," I say, giving my attention back to the crowd, the row of cameras lining up and the glare of the hot lights making me sweat. "I'm pretty sure I used up all of my miracles by now."

"I think maybe you've got one more left," he says, patting my knee twice with his heavy hand. I have no idea how he does such delicate work—his fingers are fat and his palms enormous. I guess the Hollister men have a habit of doing things they aren't supposed to.

The sound of the crowd begins to even out, becoming a hum in my head while my eyes scan slowly around the room. I wore a royal-blue polo shirt because I wanted to look patriotic—I wanted to look ready and irresistible, ripe for the team. The collar is tight and now I wish I'd worn the green one. I glance down the row I'm sitting in, nothing but khaki pants and pretty skirts and dresses covering honed muscles. I recognize almost every single swimmer, and my mouth starts to curl. Everyone here is an example of discipline until you get to me. I'm in suit pants desperate to be laundered and a scratchy polo shirt that I had to iron the hanger indents out of this morning, and discipline is the *last* word that will get tossed around in any of my headlines.

Disaster-in-the-making.

Embarrassment.

The Wrong Hollister Brother.

My mouth frowns at that last thought. More than any of it—more than the questions I know are coming about my drinking, about my fall from grace, about the tragedy that *is* my life—the fact that I know everyone in this room, including myself, wishes it were Evan sitting in this chair instead of me is what burns the most.

And then there's *her*.

Maybe deep down, a small part of her wishes Evan were sitting here, too, but still…

Maddy takes the last seat on the end of our row, the farthest chair away from mine. She tucks the pink skirt of her dress under her knees, crossing her ankles under her body as she laughs at something the guy sitting next to her says. He's a much better suitor for her. Yet even knowing that…

Her dark brown hair slides down her arm and obstructs her face from my view. I watch her anyway. I wait.

She is why I'm sitting here. She's why I keep going. Maybe she's why I picked myself up from bottom in the first place.

She is the last person I should be swimming for, but she's the only one I want to.

None of that matters the second her brown eyes open on mine.

One more miracle, my uncle says. He has no idea that I used that last one up, too—and she's sitting two-dozen feet away from me.

CHAPTER 1

Six weeks earlier

Maddy Woodsen

I don't think anyone has sat up here since the last time I waited for the Hollisters to drive through the trees and pull into the gravel parking lot outside. There's a layer of dust on the windowsill thick enough that it practically looks like fur, and the window has a yellow film permanently burnt on the outside from where the sun hits it all day long.

A spot on the glass looks like a handprint, and I reach up to press my fingertips along the matching marks. The fit is exact. The print is mine. Four years old, but still my hands are the same.

I've known the Hollister boys since I could swim, which in a family like mine pretty much means *birth*. My father, Curtis Woodsen, won the gold in the fifteen-hundred freestyle in back-to-back Olympics two decades ago. It was the same Games my mother, Susan Shephard, won the gold in the one hundred and two hundred. My parents were made for each other. They wanted me desperately. After two lost pregnancies, I was their third and final attempt at having a baby. I wasn't supposed to survive. My mom's uterus was "hostile" according to the nine different doctors she sought care and help from to conceive me. But her insides weren't hostile—they were…competitive. Like her. Like *me*.

I took to the water fast. I won young. I broke records, and I made them proud. This place—they built it for me…and it brought me Evan.

We were both sixth graders when we officially met, though I'd known of them from school. My parents had just opened the Shore Swim Club here in Knox, and the Hollisters were the first family to join. I remember my dad shaking hands with Mr. Hollister, their forearms flexing with their grips, competing even in this. It didn't take long for their pissing match to send me and the two Hollister boys into the pool for a sprint. I lost to Evan by two strokes, and Will beat us both by a full body and a half. He should have; he's two years older.

Every weekday evening began this way—the Hollister boys came to practice early, and we raced. I won twice over the seven years we sprinted in that water, and when Evan's body caught up with Will's in size, the race between the two of them was always close and could go either way. We trained hard; we laughed harder. We were close, more than family maybe. The three of us wanted things—wanted to win, to push ourselves.

We pushed each other.

Sitting up here in the attic office and waiting for them to arrive were some of my happiest memories. Only twice I sat in this window box seat without feeling joy—four years ago, when I knew their car would never come again, and today, when I know it's only going to be one of them…the *wrong* one.

"Maddy, their plane only landed an hour ago. I doubt they'll be here for another hour or so yet." I startle hearing my mother speak behind me. "Sorry, I guess it is kind of quiet and eerie up here."

"Like ghosts," I say, my words soft. I didn't mean for that to be aloud.

My mom breathes in deep enough that I hear it. She does it on purpose, a way for her to tell me she thinks I'm being dramatic without really saying the words.

"It's not going to be as strange as you seem to think it will be. You haven't seen him in years, and you two were so close. Somewhere, deep down in there, you've missed him," she says. I close my eyes and breathe out a tiny laugh, then twist enough on the small window seat to see her. My eyes don't bluff, and her head falls to the side when she reads my expression. "Maddy…"

"You have no idea how it's going to feel for me to see him. Quit pretending you do," I say as I stand and turn my back completely from the yellowed glass.

My eyes meet hers and our glares match, neither of us flinching. Eventually, my mom's focus falls to my chin, and she sucks in her top lip hard. She's frustrated with me, quite literally biting her tongue to keep herself from engaging.

"You shouldn't waste your time by the window is all. It could be hours," she says, spinning on her heels and gripping the doorknob. She steps through and pauses short of closing it completely. "It isn't Will's fault he survived."

My eyes flutter to a close again, and my chest burns. I hate her honesty. Perhaps because I've never mastered it.

She's right, of course. Every single word out of her mouth is truth. But I still don't know if my heart can handle seeing Will Hollister, and I think maybe there's a part of his heart that can't bear to see me either.

Too many reminders.

Too much that's familiar.

Too much…Evan.

Somewhere along the way, Evan Hollister and I fell in love. It happened both slowly and all at once. Will left for college, leaving only the two of us to train together in the evening hours. The first time my father left us to swim our laps alone, Evan kissed me. He said he'd been waiting to do it for years, only he lacked the courage. He kept kissing me every day since, until he no longer could.

We both went to Valparaiso together, an unpopular choice Evan made not following in his older brother's footsteps and going to State. I'd gotten into Valpo, though, and Evan came for me.

For me.

I got used to him doing things for me. Coming *home* to me. Until one day, he didn't.

The Hollister family loves to fly. Evan's dad, Robert, had been flying since he was a teenager, probably before he could drive. He had his own plane, and when life got boring, he piled his family inside the cockpit and they took off to see parts of the country. I'd gone with them all…many times.

There was no reason that the Hollister plane should fall from the sky, but that's exactly what it did on Christmas Eve four years ago. Nobody had to call. A plane crashes onto a country road outside of Knox, killing three on board, and leaving one to fight for his life—that makes the news everywhere in the country. Tragedy…pain and loss. Those are the things that lead at six o'clock.

My eyes were seeing the pictures just as friends and relatives were starting to fill our house with news. I had hope that it was a different plane for almost an hour—as if it could be any other plane. When that was dashed, I began hoping that the one fighting for his life was Evan.

It wasn't.

It was Will.

I didn't want it to be Will, but at the same time…I did.

I keep that thought buried deep, and I've never said it out loud.

I haven't seen Will since days before the crash, which means…years. He was still in a coma when we buried his parents and brother. His body managed to come through the crash virtually unscathed. His head took severe trauma, however. My parents went to see him when he finally awoke, but I couldn't bring myself to visit. They're too much alike, he and Evan. I just couldn't bring myself to see something that was a near match, but not the same, when I looked him in the eyes. It's the differences that would kill me.

Once Will was released, he moved to Michigan to live with his uncle and complete his rehab. He came back to Indiana a few times—for friends, I guess, and handling his parents' estate. My dad used to try to tell me about it, and at first, I listened. I actually almost felt a kick in my heart for happy news that Will was improving. But the resentment always took over. It made me feel ugly because I knew it wasn't fair. I still know it, and I still feel ugly, but I can't help it. It's like a sickness, guilt is the only salve.

So I live on a perpetual edge, held up by guilt and the dull ache forever left in my heart because I loved a boy, and fate stole him away from me.

It took me a year of counseling, and my father begging, to get back into the water. It was another year before I remembered how to win. And for the last six months, I've started to feel like I can remember how to breathe—how to live without the weight and the constant feeling that something important is missing. I'm going to swim for gold. This is the year. I've reemerged, remembered, and I'll finally be able to consider peace.

Then my dad had to fuck it all up with one phone call.

Will wasn't looking. He was fine training on his own, working out with coaches in Michigan. Clearly, whatever they were doing for him was effective because, despite falling thousands of feet to the earth in an aluminum tube—that at some point caught on fire—he was back to winning freestyle sprints in the pool. He didn't need my dad. We didn't need him. Yet, he's somewhere on the goddamned sixty-nine highway, barreling southbound right for me, and I can't hide up here forever.

Eventually, I'm going to have to look him in the eyes.

And eventually, it's going to hurt like hell.

I'm not sure whom I'm really angry with. My dad for making the deal. Will Hollister for wanting to walk the same path as me. The universe for throwing us in the water together again. Robert Hollister for forgetting one small check in a series of thousands—a critical error that would doom his legacy.

Almost completely.

It doesn't matter, because I'm too far in now. I want to win. The competitor in me is back, with the hunger of a thousand dragons. And Will Hollister is just going to have to be okay with the line I need to draw between us. I can't get close to him. We can't be friends. There's too much Evan there. It will only slow me down.

I move back to the small bench seat and let my forehead fall against the glass, ominously close to the hand print, and eventually the boring wait lulls me to sleep. The crack of a car door slamming shut startles me awake. Before my mind can catch up to reality and realize I'm not dreaming, my eyes see Evan standing in front of a black sedan, his arms stretched above his head, his hat pulled low, and his shirt rising enough I can see the bronzed muscles on his stomach. My arms tingle and my face rushes numb with a single blink.

"Ghosts," I whisper to myself.

I watch Will walk to the back of the car with a white-haired older man. When they disappear behind the lifted trunk, I leave the window seat and the small attic office, pushing the door closed behind me. I can hear my parents in the lobby, so before anyone calls my name, I grab my keys, walk through the women's locker room to the pool and leave through the gate on the side to where my car is parked along the alleyway. I crank the engine and look in my rearview mirror. The driveway is clear for me to back out, but I know I'll have to pass them all as I leave unless I wait long enough for them to move inside. After five or six seconds, though, I decide that saving face isn't as important as running away. I shift into reverse and back out without ever once looking to the side. When my wheels hit the gravel driveway, I turn hard to pull away. I'm not strong enough to avoid the mirror as I go, though, and I catch a final frame before I disappear through the thick trees around the road. They are all watching me, and everyone looks surprised to see me leave.

Everyone but Will.

Will

Maybe it's good the first time I'm seeing Maddy it's the back of her head as she runs away. She *is* running away, too. Some things never change, and Maddy has never liked the twist that conflict does to her guts. She always outruns that feeling.

I only caught a glimpse of her profile before she ran her fingers through her dark hair and let it fall along her face, shielding her from us. That glimpse was enough, though. This thing I'm doing—it's going to be harder than I thought it was. Being here…I don't know if I *can* be here.

"Well, you sure travel light, Will," Curtis Woodsen says, pushing the trunk closed and turning to face me, one of my two bags in his hand.

"I didn't want to overpack…in case…" I pull my lips together tight for a flat smile, exhaling through my nose.

"Planning on washing out already? That's not the Will I knew," Curtis says, his eyes crinkled with the pull of his lips on one side, like he's looking at me and evaluating what he has left to work with.

Not much, Curtis. There isn't much here at all.

"I've just learned to keep my expectations out of the equation is all," I say, hoisting the straps of my stuffed duffle on my shoulder and following Curtis through the familiar front doors of the Shore Swim Club. I reach my right hand up out of habit to tap the top of the doorway as we pass through. I used to have to jump to reach this spot.

"Expectations aren't much different from goals, Will. And I know you've got goals. That's why you're here," Curtis says over his shoulder. I barely hear him through the rush of memories that pound me with every blink of my eyes. This is definitely going to be harder than I thought.

"Goals?" His hand is flat on my chest, and I shake away the demons.

"Huh? Oh…yeah. I just keep them simple. Sorta part of my therapy—one minute at a time, one step forward, then another," I say.

Curtis twists his lips and studies me for a few seconds before his mouth curves into a smile and his heavy hand pats my chest twice.

"Well, sounds to me like you've got hundreds of expectations then…maybe thousands. They're just all lined up." His chest lets out a raspy laugh as he turns and continues to the steps that lead up to the small apartment area and business office.

"Oh there's a line, all right. And I'm constantly standing in it," I say. He laughs out hard, but since he doesn't turn around, I don't bother to smile. I wasn't joking.

Curtis holds the door open near the end of the hallway, and my uncle and I walk in front of him into the wood-paneled room that smells of old towels and chlorine. The carpet is a green mesh, made for wet feet and cheap maintenance.

"It ain't much, I know, but it's still better then you all trying to rent something for a couple months. Just didn't make sense to me," Curtis says while I survey every piece of the place I'll call home for the next several weeks.

"Oh, it'll work just fine. Thanks for putting us up," my uncle says, reaching his hand forward and gripping Curtis's for a tight squeeze.

"Well…I guess I'll let you get settled. Keys are on the dresser. They work on the main door and this one," he says, jiggling the knob for the small apartment door in his right hand.

I hold them up and nod in acknowledgement, then push the keys into my pocket. I look toward Curtis, but not directly in the eyes. His gaze stops short too, and we both stare into a nothingness between us for a few seconds before he breaks the silence.

"Right, well…I guess I'll see you bright and early tomorrow. We hit the lanes at five," he says, and with a quick wink, he turns and pulls the door to a close behind him. I push it the rest of the way in until I hear it click, but something about the way my hand looks against the grain of the door holds me in my spot. I am literally swimming in memories, and even the good ones—like the way my hand looks right here, right now—feel like gravity pulling me down from my insides.

"I think you should take the bedroom," my uncle begins, but I cut him off.

"I'm good on the couch," I say, lifting the golden cushions and tossing them on the floor before pulling up on the bed frame. "It folds out, and I…I've slept on it before."

It's actually the last place I want to try to close my eyes and sleep, but my uncle is in his sixties, and I'm not making him sleep on something that I know will have him crooked and unable to stand by morning.

"I'm sure," I say when I see his concerned expression. I lift his bag and carry it to the small bedroom, setting it on the twin bed pushed up against the wall. Honestly, when he sees this room, he won't feel like he got the better end of something. He just got the *other* end.

Our eyes meet as he moves into the room, and he chuckles at the tight fit. I nod and let my chest shake with a laugh, too.

"I guess I'll unpack then. I'm going to need to set up the desk with my tools if I want to get anything done while we're here…oh damn. I think my toolbox is still in the car," he says, patting his hands in search of the keys.

I pull them from my pocket, along with the ones for our room, and tell him, "I got it."

"Thanks, Will," he says, unzipping the top of his travel bag.

I leave my uncle to his things and run down to the car, grabbing his small toolbox from the backseat floor. My uncle brought a few special projects with him to stay busy and keep up with his business while we're here in Indiana. Just a few antiques he's been trying to get working again—one a wrist watch, one a pocket. He didn't need to come, but I didn't fight him very hard when he insisted. He's the only family I have left, which means I'm also it for him. We're a healthy kind of codependent, I think, because we definitely need each other. He's also the only person who saw me at my worst, and I feel a little less like I'll fall with him around.

When I come back inside, I lock the front door and flip out the lights. The sun is setting, and for the first time in days, I feel like maybe, just maybe, I'll close my eyes and find a few minutes of actual sleep. I tuck my uncle's tools under one arm and take the steps two at a time, but I halt when I see the opened door opposite my temporary home. It isn't fully opened, and there isn't a light on, but I know for certain that it was closed when I ran outside.

"Uncle Duncan?" I say, pushing the door lightly. I hear papers spill onto the floor a second before my palm finds the light switch on the wall. She's nothing but wild hair buried under her hands as she crouches down in front of the desk. She lets go of her head, and soon her hands are rushing to gather spilled papers around her feet. I set my uncle's tools down and hurry to help her.

"I got it," she bites out.

I stand with the few pages I managed to pick up before she stopped me.

"I thought you were my uncle," I say, my free hand moving to the bridge of my nose. My brow pulls in tight and I hold my mouth open, unsure of what to say next. I decide nothing is probably the best for both of us.

The more Maddy rushes, the more the papers slide free from her hold, but I let her work through it, eventually laying a mish-mash of ledgers and receipts into a disorganized pile on the desk.

"My mom will sort it out. Just," she says, her eyes coming up enough to see the papers in my hands. She grabs them and adds them to the stack. "Just leave them here for her."

My lips are still parted, my words caught somewhere in my throat. Of everything, I knew this would be the hardest. This place, the drills, her dad, the water—it's all going to be hard. But seeing Maddy...

I can't move my gaze up no matter how many times my mind screams at me to be civil, to pretend that none of this is strange or hurtful. I'm stuck on her hands, the way she's balling her fingers into fists, the way her nails are filed down low—for speed. *Every piece of a second counts.* Maddy swore she was the fastest girl in the pool when she was in junior high because she was the only one without giant nails dragging through the water. My lips betray me and quirk a smile at that memory. She must be looking at my face, because the second my mouth curves, she tenses and grabs a phone and set of keys from the desktop near the papers.

"I only came in here because I forgot my phone. I have somewhere I need to be," she says, rushing past me. She has nowhere to go. I could always tell when she was lying.

"Yeah, me too," I say, surprised at my own voice. My eyes widen a little and my pulse picks up. Maddy stops at the doorway and turns her chin just enough that I catch a glimpse of more of her profile. "I have to be...over there," I say, gesturing to my new home on the other side of the hall.

Her fingers drum once along the wood of the doorframe, and she grunts out a tiny laugh before she flees down the hallway and steps, slipping out the back door just like she used to when we were kids. I hear her car motor start up soon after and watch the shadow of the lights move along the windows that line the alleyway. When I hear her car hit the gravel, I let my head fall back and I bring my arms up over my eyes. I breathe in long and deep, holding my lungs full. She's even more beautiful than she was the day before I ruined her life.

This is going to be hard. I want to quit already. But I can't, because—whether she remembers it or not—I promised her I wouldn't.

Never.

CHAPTER 2

Maddy

I saw this thing on the Internet. It's a series of videos of these junior-high boys flipping half-filled water bottles on things, landing them just right, then running around with their arms in the air as if they've accomplished something amazing. My best friend Holly sent it to me, sort of as a joke.

What you're doing can't be half as hard as this.

That's what her text said. It made me smile, because how stupid is a water-bottle stunt. Then I spent the next hour trying to get my damned water bottle to land upright on the floor. I just stuck it, and I refuse to pick it up now because that was really, really hard. I even threw my hands up when I did and let out a whoop—all alone, in my room, at sunrise. I whispered the whoop. And then I mimicked the sound of a roaring crowd.

Hats off to the water-bottle flippers of YouTube.

I miss Holly. I miss the late shift, and putting in stupid hours just trying to get ahead. I miss eating dinner out of the vending machine and talking about the cute doctors that I never really want to notice me, but that bring me some sort of feeling of normalcy—like maybe, just maybe, I'll kiss a man again someday.

I took a sabbatical from the UV Mercy Nursing Program. When I get back, Holly will be on staff, and I'll still be a senior. Damned fear of regret, though—it's a powerful thing. I lit up the NCAA my junior year. All of those times when I was too slow didn't matter now that I was faster than everyone. I was fast enough when it counted—fast enough to swim for gold.

Fast enough to swim for my father.

My dad runs one of the most elite training camps in the country. Four years ago, the US team came through here on their way to glory. It isn't so much the pool, which is fairly dated, or the location—it's my father that makes it the best. This year, he aims to be one of the coaches. I'm his ticket, and I'm all right with that because I couldn't imagine going with anyone else in my corner.

Will…I guess he's the wild card. Or maybe he's the insurance. If my dad can make him a winner too, then there really isn't a better choice to head the team against the world.

The pound on the door is harsh and fast. I've been up for more than an hour, but it still startles me as if I was roused from a dead slumber.

"Rise and shine. We've got some serious conditioning to do," my dad says, his voice trailing off as he moves down the hallway.

"I'm up!" I yell, my voice sounding defensive, like a teenager rather than a twenty-three-year-old who's had her own apartment and knows how to pay her bills on time.

I glance at the water bottle on my floor then push it over on its side with my foot.

"Half as hard as this, huh?" I chuckle to myself.

I grab my packed bag and slide my feet into my flip-flops before opening my bedroom door. My mom ordered a mattress so I wouldn't have to sleep on the futon now residing in my old bedroom. It's an odd mix of things that used to define me in this den-slash-guest room my mom transformed the space into the second I signed a lease near the university. It didn't make sense to spend the money on a place while I was here, especially since it's temporary, so for the next few months, this time warp is my home.

Dad is already in the driveway with the car engine running, and my mom is holding a power bar out for me to take along with one of her special drinks.

"I can drive myself," I say, ripping the bar open and taking a bite before leaning into her and kissing her cheek.

"Yeah, but he likes this idea of you and him doing this together. Humor him. Underneath that tough-guy persona, he's scared shitless," she says with a wink.

My mouth tugs up on one side.

"Fine," I sigh, feigning frustration with a roll of my eyes.

"Good girl. Now drink your shake. You're going to need the energy," she says, shoving the smoothie into my right hand. It's green, and her shakes make me gag, but they seem to do the trick.

I tilt the glass and take a big gulp, turning before she sees my disgusted face. My dad has his music on when I get in the car, and I'm hit with a second whammy—ABBA's greatest hits.

"Are you and mom trying to make me quit?" I ask, raising a brow.

"What? Who doesn't like ABBA?" he says, turning the music up and singing along, off-key as always. I shake my head and smile, looking out my window while I force the rest of my drink down, chasing it with what's left of my protein bar so I have some hope that I don't burp the awful flavor up over the next four hours.

When we get to the club, a few other cars are in the lot. I know most of the swimmers. A lot of them aren't really ready for this, but one or two have a shot at some of the distance trials. There's only one that I'm interested in, though. And by interested, I mean interested in avoiding.

Will's already warming up when I pass by the glass doors to dump my things in the women's locker room. It's going to be impossible not to look at him. I came to terms with that fact sometime around three in the morning. I'm going to have to get used to looking at him; I need to become numb to the similarities. Only now that I'm here, at the pool, faced with the reality of actually looking at him, I'm not so sure I'm strong enough.

I sit on the bench and let my head fall back against the metal locker door behind me, pulling my phone into my palm. I text Holly.

I think I made a mistake.

That's the thing I love most about my best friend; I can be raw and honest with her. She's one of a handful of people I've always been able to cut through the bullshit with and get right to the heart of things. The other two people were Evan and Will.

My phone buzzes with her response.

Don't be a pussy.

I laugh out loud.

Okay.

After tucking my phone away, I push my locker closed and grip my goggles and cap tight in my hand. It's just a pool. Fifty meters that I can cross in seconds. *My lane—I see nothing but my lane.* I remind myself of the words my father used to tell me when I got nervous before a race when I was a kid, and it works for the few seconds it takes me to walk to the pool's edge.

And then nothing will help. Nothing could ever help, or ever will help this. Will is standing on the opposite end, dripping from warm-ups, his body strong and similar. His hair wet…and similar. The blue of his eyes…piercing.

Similar.

The same.

There are maybe a dozen other athletes around—splashing and chaos between us—my father whistles, orders to begin, but we're both locked in the past, and I just can't seem to tear my eyes away. The hurt is almost good. It reminds me that something real was in my heart once, and as much as I want to run away from it, in this moment, I also want to hold onto it. I want to remember what exceptional felt like so I make sure I never settle for less. I wonder if exceptional comes along twice in a lifetime?

I wonder what this feels like for him? I wonder if the hurt is the same? Will and Evan were more than brothers; they were best friends. One ended and one began. I breathe in deep and let my chest feel full on the air and those thoughts, and I finally look away, bending down and splashing water on my arms, dunking my cap and goggles before getting in.

The water is my home, and I manage to do as my father always told me for the next few hours. I focus on the lane. I count my strokes, and push my capacity. I breathe and then hold my breath. I dig my arms into the water, and I kick and push. By the time my father blows the whistle for us to stop for the day, I'm spent—more than I have been in years. It takes me a few attempts to pull myself from the pool, and as I'm about to push my elbow into the ground to lift myself, I feel a hand wrap around my bicep and steady me until I can find my feet.

I don't look at him completely. I knew it was Will's touch the instant I felt it. It's the only thing that doesn't really remind me of Evan at all. Will's hands—the size, strength and tenderness of their movement—that was always something unique to him.

"Thank you," I say, smiling, but again, not at him. I move to the bench near the women's locker room entrance and work my cap from my hair, toweling myself dry while I try to ignore the panicked thumping in my chest as I see Will walking toward me in my periphery.

"We have six weeks," my dad says. Most of us sit at the loud boom of his voice, some of us on the ground. Will leans against the metal pillar several feet away from me, and I sneak a glance when his attention is on my dad.

He looks like Evan.

"Trials are going to be like nothing you've ever seen. Some of you," my dad pauses, dipping his head to catch my eyes, "are going to have major targets on your backs. You're the ones to beat. And the people chasing you are going to swim the race of their lives, faster than they're capable of, running on adrenaline alone."

His words soak in, and I know that as tired as I am from today, I still didn't empty my tank. I need to give more, because I'm going to have one shot at clinching this. There is no *next* meet. There are trials, and today…I was distracted. My gaze drags along the ground to Will's feet, then his legs, then his body. I can almost sense what it feels like to run my hands along his chest, around his back, to his neck, the wet ends of his hair, his jaw, his mouth. Not him, but...*almost*.

"Tomorrow we add an hour in the evening. Even for the sprinters. Distance is good for your lungs, and we all need bigger lungs. I'm going to turn you all into fish. Now go eat something real for breakfast," my dad says, reaching down and pulling a small granola bar from the hands of one of the younger female swimmers. She shrugs as he tosses it in the trash and heads inside through the men's locker room.

I don't mean to look, but my eyes just go to Will. He's packing up his things, his jaw working and his eyes hyper focused on the small space directly in front of him. He's trying to become invisible...*to me*. My chest grows heavy, and my gut twists. I'm not being fair to him, blaming him because of his blood—because of who he reminds me of. He can't help that any more than I can help the fact that my past is forever connected to his brother. But him being here...it's also stirred other feelings—the kind twisted up in memories and adolescence. I don't like the guilt that comes with those feelings.

But that...*that's* not Will's fault, either.

I linger, my fingers tingling with doubt while my mind second guesses what I'm about to do, but I know that I can't keep going like this. If Will and I are going to swim in this pool together for the next six weeks, we can't do it with the weight of the past drowning us. We need to find our way back to our younger selves—to the kids who used to dare each other to swim across Peterson Lake in the dark. We need to be pushing each other, not pulling the wrong way.

"You want breakfast?" My question squeals from my mouth, my voice cracking. My teeth bite down on my lower lip while I stare at the wet pile of towels on the ground between us.

"I could eat," he says.

His voice.

"I...I rode with my dad, so..." I glance up and our eyes meet briefly before I blink away again.

"I can drive," Will says.

I nod slowly and remind my mouth to make a smile as I look up again.

"I'll meet you out front," I say, every word rehearsed in my head a millisecond before I utter it. Will doesn't respond right away, but his eyes don't seem to be as skittish as mine. He holds his stare on me, and his mouth is curved in a sincere hint of a smile. I've missed him.

After a long second, he nods and tugs the men's room door open, disappearing inside and leaving me alone under the covered patio. I look out at the water, the surface smooth—no breeze to make ripples. My insides are the exact opposite.

My father is talking with two of the younger swimmers as I walk out to the main lobby. He's holding one girl's arm out and splaying her fingers, then cupping them.

"Grabbing the water, are we?" I say through a closed-lipped smile. My dad's expression reflects mine.

"That's how it all started with this one, you know. She was always coming in second. It was like this curse we just couldn't seem to break until I told her she needed to grab more water," he says.

"I'm really excited to be swimming with you here…I'm…I'm a fan," the girl says, shaking her arm out and flexing her fingers in and out like she was just instructed. I reach down and grab her palm, squeezing it lightly, but with enough muscle to live up to her idea of me.

"I'm nothing special. I'm excited to be swimming here with you," I say, pausing and tilting my head, waiting for her name.

"Amber," she says.

I repeat it and smile, and I can feel her grip grow a little stronger just before she lets go. Confidence is a funny thing. The slightest sentence can be either a rocket or a missile to self-esteem.

My dad always keeps the negative away from ears, especially young ears. Even now, as the two girls leave us alone in the lobby, he waits for the door to close to tell me what he really thinks.

"She's not ready. She'd get eaten up at trials. But…she can train. She's young, just graduated high school. Maybe…maybe in four years, if she sticks with it," he says, turning to me, our eyes locking.

I nod, grateful that my father spares me of the negative, too. It doesn't mean I don't think about it, though. And in a way, that's almost worse. I bet there have been times when my dad has thought I wasn't ready, or that I was lucky to win. He would never say it, but I know better than to believe he's never thought it.

I'm about to let my dad know I don't need a ride when Will steps through the men's doors, his eyes settling on both of us.

"I just need to run my things upstairs and we can go," he says, holding up his bag. His gaze darts between my father and me before he moves to the stairs, leaving us alone.

"We're…I thought maybe it would be good to…breakfast. I invited him for breakfast," I stammer.

"Good," my dad responds quickly. Both of us are watching the empty stairwell, waiting for Will's return, and several seconds pass without a sound from his door or his footsteps.

"I just don't want there to be any distractions," I start, stopping when I sense my dad looking at me. I turn to meet him.

"I think it's good, Maddy. You two need to talk. You've always been good teammates…and friends…" my dad says.

"That's what I was thinking," I say after a sharp inhale.

My dad nods, and eventually we both look back at the steps again. They remain silent, but I can hear the sounds of drawers sliding in and out upstairs followed by a few muffled words. I wonder if I should invite his uncle?

"Will is an important part of this," my dad says, catching my attention. I twist my neck and pull my lips in tight, waiting for him to elaborate. His brow is heavy, and his eyes seem to be lost somewhere else entirely, but eventually he shakes his head and breathes out a short huff through his nose, turning to me and patting both of my shoulders twice before squeezing them. "He'll never make it past trials, though, so just…don't torture yourself more than you need to."

My father finishes speaking just as the door creaks upstairs, leaving me alone with just one more dose of his brand of honesty. I force my wide eyes to normal before I face the stairs, and then I remind my mouth to smile again when Will walks toward me—gray T-shirt, faded jeans, hair dark from being wet, not the normal light brown, and a scent that is, of course, familiar.

"Ready?" I ask. He looks at me with pause, and my chest tightens because for a brief second, I think he must know—he must have heard my dad or read my face. That hint of suspicion in his expression fades quickly, though, and soon his keys jingle in his palm and his head gestures toward the front door.

"Or would you rather climb out through the back, maybe hop the fence in the alley?" he says. I stop walking, and he spins to walk backward, the left side of his mouth tugged up in a teasing grin. I purse my lips and say something I haven't said in years.

"Careful, Will Hollister. You don't want me to remind you what it feels like to lose to a girl again, do you?"

My chest opens up and my lips stretch into a smile all on their own as Will's head falls to the side and his eyes narrow on me. *Familiar.*

"You. Wish." he says, his mouth careful with every word, uttering them nice and slow—just like he always has.

Were this the past, now would be the point when I would rush past him, and he'd grab my stomach and toss me in the air, each of us pulling on each other in our battle to be first. But this isn't the past, and while my legs itch to run, my heart doesn't have it in it. So instead, I chuckle and shake my head. Will turns to walk forward again, and his smile falls just a hint as he does. I think maybe he's disappointed I didn't follow through.

Will is an important part of this.

My dad's words echo as I wait for Will to open the car door. I'm starting to wonder if the whole reason my dad agreed to let Will train here, at home, was because of the push he hoped it would give me.

My arms begin to tingle again, and my legs grow restless at the thought.

Rocket? Or missile?

Will

I can't help but take the fact that she looked at me—we made actual eye contact—as a sign that things are going to be okay. The single percent of optimism left in me holds on to it. I'm not naïve enough to believe that we can pick up right where life ended for us without ever having a conversation about what happened, about Evan, about my coma, about the shit reality that is my life and how it bled into hers. But at least she's willing to be alone with me, and that's…that's not something I thought would happen ever.

Even with damp hair, denim shorts, and a T-shirt, Maddy Woodsen is still the most beautiful girl I've ever met. She's never smelled like anything other than lake water or chlorine, yet somehow those two things have only ever been able to remind me of her.

We don't talk during the short car ride, and when we get to the diner off old sixty-six, near Pigeon Creek, we both sit still, our eyes forward on the faded-blue doors, the sound of cars whooshing by behind us.

"I haven't eaten here in years."

I'm the first to break the silence. I can hear her breathe, long and slow. I hate how hard this is for her. I hate how hard *everything* probably is for her. That's why, no matter my urges, I don't need to say any more than she truly wants to hear.

"I come here sometimes with Dad. Or…at least since I've been back," she says, her hand finding the lever for the door. She pushes it down and climbs from the car; I wait for her door to close before I exit, needing that brief second of time in a space all alone to remind myself that I'm here for her.

She's waiting in front of the car when I step out, her hands stuffed in her pockets while her feet kick at the loose gravel on the ground. I hate how uncomfortable this all is, but I guess that was always inevitable. That's why we both stayed away.

"You still at Valpo?" I ask, knowing she is. I look her up all the time.

Not...stalking, just...shit, I guess it's stalking.

"I am. Last year of nursing school, or, it would have been. I took the year off, for..." she stops, holding her arms out to her side, her mouth offering a crooked smile. I gesture for us to walk forward, and her hands slap against her thighs as she drags her feet forward, still kicking the gravel.

"You had to, Maddy. This is your year," I say.

"You sound like my father," she says through light laughter.

I hold the door for her, and when she walks inside, she moves her hair from the opposite shoulder to the one facing me. She's still putting up shields.

The hostess holds up two fingers, and I nod. We both follow her to a booth near the kitchen entrance, and I wait for Maddy to pick what side she wants.

"Coffee?" the woman asks.

"Please," we both say in unison. She bites her tongue, her cheeks raised with her smile, and I breathe out a small laugh.

The silence is never far away, and when the hostess leaves, we're instantly back to avoiding eye contact and busying ourselves with straightening the condiments on the table, checking our phones and wiping away lost salt granules from the table top. I start to regret agreeing to come, only because I see how hard it is on her. When she looks up and our eyes catch and hold on, *I regret nothing.*

"I'm sorry I'm being so..."

"It's okay," I break in, shocked she's even going here. I swallow hard and hold my breath, hoping she doesn't retract everything and go back to awkward silence. This conversation is too necessary.

Another minute passes while we look at each other. The waitress delivers our coffee and tells us she'll be back in a minute to take our order, and I break away long enough to tell her "fine" and smile.

"I miss him," she says, her eyes leaving mine as soon as she says the word *him.*

"Me too," I say, stopping there. *Only what she wants to hear, and nothing more.*

She chuckles to herself and adjusts her posture on her side of the booth, tucking one leg under the other before leaning to stare at me, her mouth crooked, curious.

"How'd my dad get you back in his pool, Will?" she asks.

Not the direction I wanted our conversation to go. I wanted to air out things with Evan, all the shit I've done and been through, but again, all of that would be for me. We'll do this her way, under her direction. It's fine.

"Actually, I called him. I'm getting old," I say, and Maddy laughs, sliding her hands forward on the table as she leans. I itch to touch them, but I don't. "Twenty-five is old in swimming," I add, my lips twisted.

"So's twenty-three," she chuckles.

"Nah, twenty-three's right where you wanna be," I say, stretching one arm out along the back of the booth and twisting to match her. My muscles ache. I'm nowhere near in the condition Maddy is, and I broke myself trying to keep up with her today. I knew I would—*that's why I had to come here to train.*

"You all ready?" the waitress asks. I raise a brow to Maddy, and she furrows hers, holding up a finger.

"You go first, then I'll be ready," she says.

"Short stack, side of bacon," I tell the waitress. When I look back at Maddy, her hand is on her forehead.

"That was really fast…ummmm," she flips through the pages of the menu, like she isn't going to get what she always gets, what she's eaten every single time I've ever had breakfast with her, which numbers maybe into the hundreds. "I don't know…I guess…uhhhhh…"

I only catch it because I'm watching her manically turn the pages of her menu. Her hands are shaking with nerves, and the more she rushes to pick something to eat, the bigger those trembles become. I reach forward and push her menu flat, causing her to look up at me, so I wink.

"She'll have the oatmeal, topped with apples and cinnamon, and a side of bacon," I say.

The waitress waits for Maddy to look up and nod, confirming it, then tucks her pen behind her ear and tears our ticket off on her way back to the kitchen.

"What if I wanted something different?" she asks.

"Since when have you *ever* ordered anything else at this place," I smirk.

She purses her lips, but they betray her and bend into a smile. We both settle into our seats more, and before the silence can win again, I fill the void, continuing to answer her last question.

"I only have one more shot at this, and I know I'm a long shot, but I kinda think maybe I'm better than some of those other freestylers heading to Omaha. I just had to see it through, and if I was going to go, I wanted to be my best," I say.

She studies me, her arms folded over her chest, and I'm relieved when a refill comes for our coffee so I can give my attention over to the creamer and packs of sugar.

"You were always my dad's favorite, you know," she says. Her words hit my gut like a heavy-handed punch. I can't help but feel like that's a lie—only Maddy has never lied to me.

"I'm pretty sure *you* are your dad's favorite," I say, the only answer I can think of that doesn't head down a dangerous path.

"Oh, I can assure you I'm not," she laughs.

I laugh with her, blowing the steam from my coffee and sipping, the heat stinging the tip of my tongue.

"My dad's glad you're here. I can tell," she says. I glance over the rim of my cup and her eyes look uncertain. She's never lied to me, but that doesn't mean she always tells me everything. When I called Curtis, I could sense the hesitation in his voice. He's always been in my corner, even after the accident. But he also loves his daughter, and I know he had to be worried about what my presence would do to her.

"I'm glad I'm here, is all I know. Nothing's ever quite felt like home," I say, leaving out the unsaid things—*since my family died.*

Our food comes quickly, and for the next ten minutes, we both eat and make comments about how "nobody makes better bacon" and "coffee tastes a million times better with whole milk." We talk nonsense, like acquaintances, and the world feels right for just a moment. I know it can't last, though. My phone buzzes with a message, reminding me of one of the biggest reasons it can't. I glance at it enough to know who it is, then I tap the auto response, hoping that the person who sent this just assumes I'm busy in training. These worlds cannot collide right now. They can't collide at all. And I just need the universe to give me six damned weeks.

CHAPTER 3

Maddy

That ease in conversation—it left the second Will got a text message. He said it wasn't important, and it probably wasn't, but that disruption was enough to bring everything that is our reality right back to the table. The wall between us is back. It was never really gone, but it was nice to know that, for a few minutes at least, I could ignore it.

My father is spending the day at the Swim Club. My mom is at city hall. She's a councilmember in Knox, and her passion is rebuilding the city's youth programs and parks. Unfortunately, she's the only councilmember under the age of sixty-five, so she's usually the only one willing to put in the extra hours to make calls for grants and sift through research from staff. The mayor applauded her when she made the commitment publicly, but also told her she'd be working on it alone.

"I've already done this for my kids. It's your turn now," he said. Never mind the fact that her kid—*me*—is all grown now, too, so that argument really doesn't hold much water. He's just making an excuse to be lazy.

With both of them gone so much, it leaves me here in an empty house. It's been good for my training because I run or binge on Netflix while I pedal on my dad's stationary bike during the middle of the day. I can't call Holly until odd hours because of her classes and hours at the hospital, but we'll text sometimes.

Idle time is my worst enemy today, though. Maybe it was seeing Will, talking with him. Or maybe this is just one of those things I've needed to do for a long time. Closure comes from a lot of acts. That's what my therapist drilled into my head before I quit going. No amount of therapy is going to heal the wound left behind when the love of your life gets ripped from your heart, but maybe I can get some relief from it for just a little while. Perhaps closure is a thing.

My mom's step ladder is barely tall enough, so I end up stepping on the lower shelves of my old bedroom closet to steady myself enough to reach the dusty box, still taped shut, pushed high near the ceiling. A layer of dust cascades down on my eyelids when I finally reach it, and I wipe my face with my shirt as I cough my way back to my mattress bed.

Mom wouldn't let me throw these things away. I hated her for it, but I'm sort of glad right now. I might change my mind when I rip the tape away and look inside, though.

I dig my dull nail into the taut tape along the edge, near the lid, sawing for almost a minute and finally making a tear that rips completely. I flip the lid without giving myself a chance to back out, and I'm hit with the worst immediately. The photo on top is from Christmas Eve. It's one of those small Polaroid ones. Evan is cradling me, and my head is slung back with laughter. His handwriting spells out TRUE LOVE ALWAYS on the bottom. He liked to tease me with things like that, like our love was out of some high-school yearbook or some teen-movie special. He ran out of room for the ALWAYS, so there's an arrow pointing to the back of the image where he finished writing the word. I laugh as I turn it in my hand and read it. I also wipe away my tear.

I breathe in deep and hold my lungs full, my eyes focused on the layers of photos, notes, and memories in the small shoebox in front of me.

"Closure, huh?" I whisper to myself, lifting the next few photos and spreading them out on the sheets in front of me. The feeling that rushes over me is not what I expected. I don't cry, other than that initial tear, and I don't feel a shock or surprise or pang at seeing these photos. I feel the same dull ache that's always there, constantly there, and with every new photo or note or memento I pull from the box, nothing changes. I think it's because I see every single one of these memories in my sleep. They're with me always. And seeing them laid out before me in the flesh, it's just more of the same.

As I pile the photos back into the box, a thought occurs to me. My smile—it's so bright. Every single photo of us as a couple, my teeth practically glow. I hold the one of me laughing in my hands, close to my face, and I can almost hear the sound I made. Before I realize it, I'm smiling at the image. The ache is there, but the visual—it's made me happy. I am glad I didn't throw them away.

I slide my fingers along the mattress and pick up the last few pictures left out. One image catches my eye, so I leave it to the side, putting the rest away. I don't recognize this one, but I remember the day it was taken. I don't know that I ever really saw the photo, and I'm not sure how it got into this bunch, but my chest starts to thump rapidly looking at it, almost like I'm…nervous.

I'm pretty sure I was fourteen, and Will…he's sixteen. I know it because this was the summer he grew. The Hollister boys blindfolded me and took me down to Peterson Lake to see their surprise, and they didn't pull the cloth away until my hands were wrapped around the scratchy rope and my feet were balanced on the small piece of wood fused to the bottom. They'd always talked about making a rope swing, and they finally made it.

I was nervous on it, unsteady on my feet, maybe a little untrusting of the wood that had been singed into the rope. The fall wasn't far, but it was enough to leave me frozen. Will promised to take my first swing with me. Seeing the way his arms wrapped around me, his hands dwarfing mine on the rope while his body cradled mine a breath before we both kicked off and swung our way into the icy, crystal-blue water, brings back the rush of feelings I had that day—that moment.

Will always felt older, even older than he was. Maybe it was the way his body had changed. Or perhaps it was the fact that I was fourteen and growing more curious about my body, feeling things. Puberty is a twisted bitch, and I'm sure it was at work then, too. When Will held me, he didn't let go—not even in the water. And I remember it as if it was just minutes ago, because at the time, I didn't want him to let go. I didn't want him to let go at all. And when he did, I got scared because feeling something like that, for Will Hollister, wasn't how my story was supposed to go. He was older, and my crush had always been on Evan.

None of that explains the beating in my chest right now, though. My hand trembles holding the photo, so I grab my wrist with my free hand.

"Stop," I tell myself.

I pull the lid onto the box and climb the ladder, leaning to put one foot on the shelving system as I slide the box back into the darkness and dust. I leave the photo of me and Will out, though. I'm not done looking at it, and that isn't okay.

Will

My stomach is so tight I don't think I could even convince my muscles to help me throw up if I wanted to. My left knee has been bouncing for the entire drive back to the club; I race into the driveway with enough force that my wheels spin out a little on the rocks.

I'm not sure why I'm in such a hurry. There's no deadline for anything, and having to look Curtis in the eye before I take off isn't going to be a pleasure. Hell, I should have driven slower and maybe he'd have been gone for the day.

I push the gearshift back into reverse, but I'm not fast enough to escape his attention. Curtis holds up a hand, waving hello while he holds the front door open for a group of young swimmers and their parents.

I gnash my teeth together hard and plaster a smile on my lips while I mentally repeat the word *fuck* over and over again. I don't like confrontation. Avoiding conflict is half the reason I'm as miserable as I am. If I'd embraced it, once—the important time—I wouldn't be carrying half of the misery that I walk around with every minute of the day.

But I can't change who I am, and I'm a lying chicken shit.

Curtis holds the door open for me while I lock the car and jog up the front walkway, mentally running through every possible excuse I can give. His reaction is going to be terrible regardless of what I say, but not nearly as awful as it would be if I just spoke the truth.

"You remember being that young?" he says as I step up next to him. I turn and look at the young bodies wrapped in towels all making their way to idling cars.

"I don't think I was ever that young," I say.

I feel Curtis looking at me, so I hold my attention on the last kid, watching as his mom dries off one leg and then the other so he can push his feet into a pair of socks. I can tell by the look on the kid's face that the last thing he wants is to put socks on, but he's still too young to be defiant. I'd say he's seven, maybe eight. *Hang in there, buddy. When you're twelve, you can decide about your damned feet on your own.*

"You were that young," Curtis says, drawing me from my trance. I squint one eye and look at him. "You were a lot better of a swimmer, and maybe twice that kid's size, but you were still young, Will. And oh my god were you a pain in the ass!"

I wince on instinct, but when Curtis starts to laugh I relax a little.

"You and your brother would come in here, and I swear to god the volume of life in general would go up about a million decibels. Maddy…she didn't know how to scream, I don't think, until she met the two of you," he says, holding the door more open and urging me inside. I step in, and he follows, clicking the lock behind us, and flipping the main sign around to show the business number and open hours.

"Maybe we wouldn't have been half as loud if that girl of yours didn't provoke us mercilessly. I seem to remember a certain phrase she'd say, something about 'if only we could learn how to swim like a girl?' She always said she learned it from her dad, but…I always gave you the benefit of the doubt," I say, smirking at the man I've always admired as much as I'd feared. My stomach still churns with my rapid pulse, but my body is getting used to the rhythm. Nerves are a funny thing—eventually, they start to enjoy the rush of adrenaline.

"Oh, I said it all right. Whenever Maddy would catch on to something faster than you two," he chuckles.

"Well, that wasn't fair. Girls are smarter, and we were two blockheads," I say. He pats my arm and nods, agreeing with me. We both laugh, but mine…it's a lie. All I can think about is how I'm going to say what I need to so I can *do* what I need to.

"You and your uncle settling in okay?" he asks, and I feel my palms start to sweat because I know I'm going to have to say something soon.

"We're comfortable, yeah…thanks. Honestly, I think you could set my Uncle Duncan up in a closet and as long as he had a desk, a magnifying glass, and a decent lamp, he'd be happy for days," I say, not happy that Curtis has started to walk up the stairs toward my room and the business office. I follow him, my hand sliding along the railing, gripping with each step as if I have some power to anchor us where we stand.

"He seems like a good man. Your dad…" he stops midsentence, his feet faltering on the last two steps. I can see the apology on his face as he turns to look at me.

"It's okay. It's honestly nice to hear people talk about him," I say. Curtis grins and nods once, but I can tell he doesn't believe me. I'm going to need to get better at lying, and fast.

"I'm sure it is…" he says, chewing at the inside of his lip for a second. "I was just going to say that your dad, he always said nice things about your uncle. I guess they were pretty close?"

"Sort of. I mean, we saw Uncle Duncan on holidays and stuff, but he and my dad were pretty different. Duncan likes being alone," I chuckle, nodding toward the shut apartment-room door where my uncle has been happily holed up with his gears and tools since I woke up for practice this morning. "When we'd get together, though, it's kinda like each would get a little of the other's personality. My dad would quiet down, and Duncan would cut loose."

"Kinda like you and Evan, I guess," he says, his eyes still apologetic.

"A lot like us, yeah," I say, my mouth closing tight because we need to stop talking about Evan.

We both pause in the middle of the hallway, my hand on my door and his on the office door—awkwardness comes with every breath. His face contorts in twitches, the same as mine, almost like he's trying to muster up the nerve to say something, too, and we both end up opening our mouths in unison.

"About tomorrow…" I start.

"Breakfast go all right?" he says over me.

"Sorry…" I hold up my hand. "You first."

"Oh, no, it's okay. I was just making sure breakfast went all right is all. I know Maddy's been…" he begins, but stops, pressing his lips in a tight line, his brow furrowed in thought while he tries to define his daughter's feelings and behavior for me. He doesn't need to. Of everything, that's the one thing I understand.

"She's working through things. Me being here, it reminding her of Evan…I get it," I say.

Curtis begins to nod.

"She's trying," he says.

Our eyes meet, and my drumming pulse stops for just that second.

"Breakfast was good," I say.

Curtis smiles, and I know that I have to say what I need to now, while he's relieved.

"Listen…I uh…I've got something I need to deal with, and I hate to ask, especially now, and I know it looks bad on the second day of training camp and everything, but…" I make the mistake of looking him in the eyes again, and I see the mix of suspicion and concern. I hate it, and my mouth starts to taste the acid from my stomach.

"Are you…slipping…Will?" He asks me with his head cocked to the side, and it reminds me of the way every doctor and therapist has looked at me over the last four years. It's such a rehearsed gesture when they do it, feigning genuine concern, and even though I know Curtis is looking at me with nothing but the best intentions right now, it still kicks at my nerves.

"I'm fine. Really, I promise. I just need to take care of an estate thing with my uncle in Indianapolis. It's just easier if we drive to the city rather than me waiting for the lawyer to come down here. I'm just afraid I won't make tomorrow's sessions, but I swear I'll put in the work. My uncle can't drive alone, not all that way. I'd really like to put it off, but I just…it has to be done now."

I breathe out a long sigh through my nose, resting my weight against the door I'm dying to disappear behind, while Curtis sizes up every word I just said. Not a single bit of it was true, and I'm honestly a little impressed with myself. It's going to be a bitch to sort through the details if I ever need to embellish on or reference this lie again. I'm still not certain Curtis quite believes it as he moves his gaze from me to the floor, but he looks up again with his hand out, as if to shake. I reach for his palm and grasp it, the weight removed for barely a second before it comes crashing down on me again with the feeling of the apartment door opening behind me.

"Will, geeze louise…I didn't know you were out here. You scared me," my uncle says, one hand on his chest, the other out in front of his face, palm open to catch the eyeglass he lets fall from his eye. "I guess I've been concentrating in my own little world."

"We didn't mean to distract you. Sorry, Dunc," I say, stepping forward into our room with him. I give my uncle a glance, my eyes widen, and his narrow, trying to understand my silent message. I hope to God it's enough.

"You know, I have a watch…it's an old family heir loom. Thing hasn't worked for years, if you wouldn't mind taking a look at it?" Curtis says.

My uncle's ears literally perk up.

"Absolutely," he says, his fingers rubbing the edge of his eyeglass, flipping it around in his palm with nervous excitement. A new puzzle brings my uncle immense joy.

"Perhaps when you two get back tomorrow. After the estate thing. I can hang around after the afternoon workouts, or come by tomorrow night and drop it off with you," Curtis says.

My uncle's head tilts a fraction, but before he responds, I see him put it all together—my nonverbal plea, the lie he's just heard.

"That'd be good. In the evening, when we get home," he says, essentially repeating everything Curtis said.

"Wonderful," Curtis says, smiling as he turns to the office door, gripping the handle and pausing before stepping inside. "If you guys need any help, you know…getting in and out of the city, or with documents or something, just let me know. I'm no lawyer, but I know a lot of really good people."

"Oh, I'm sure we'll be fine," my uncle says, again, his answer vague.

"Okay, then. I guess I'll see you Wednesday, Will. I'll know if you skipped that workout, too," Curtis says with a wink.

"There won't be any doubt, sir," I respond, holding a thumb up until Curtis finally disappears behind the office door and my uncle closes ours, turning to face me slowly.

We both stare at one another for a few seconds before my uncle speaks.

"I'm guessing she needs something?" he asks.

"Yep," I nod.

My uncle pushes forward from the door, moving to the small desk he's set up with his tools and light, his eyepiece landing on the wood with a heavy thud before he grips the armrests of his chair and lowers himself down.

"You didn't tell him the truth." My uncle doesn't ask. He doesn't have to.

I shake my head to affirm his statement.

"Didn't quite know how. I think it's probably easier for them all to just have this certain idea in their heads," I say, kicking my shoes from my feet as I walk. I stop at the edge of the sofa and tug up one corner, flipping out the bedframe. I collapse on the pile of messy sheets and rub my face into their coolness, wishing I could erase a lot of things by doing this.

"It's always easier to walk around life believing in bullshit," my uncle says. I twist my neck, my face flat against my bed, and I stare at him. He's not looking at me anymore, instead lost back in one of his projects.

"What time are we leaving in the morning?" he asks, his hands holding tweezers steady while his neck cranes forward, his eyeglass already back at home between his cheekbone and brow.

"Five," I say.

"Dibs on showering first," he says.

I lie there for the next several hours and watch my uncle work. He hardly moves, and I'm inspired by his level of concentration. I don't think I have ever focused on something so minute—on the details and the parts. Maybe if I did I'd start to understand how things work. Maybe I need to take his magnifying glass and press it against pieces of my life.

And maybe if I hold it there long enough under the sun, I can just set all this shit on fire.

CHAPTER 4

Maddy

Will didn't make practice today. Morning and afternoon.

It's all I focused on during my entire swim. I was off. Everything about me was off. The fact that Will wasn't here threw me off, which is screwing with me even more because I didn't really want him here in the first place for that very reason. His presence was supposed to throw me, not his absence.

I asked my dad where Will was, but he didn't have a real answer.

"He said something about estate papers, having to drive his uncle to the city. I questioned it at first, but his uncle backed it up. Seems legit," my dad said.

That's the thing, though. I never thought it could be anything more than something simple until my dad put that idea in my head. Then I lost focus. As much as I've tried to pretend that I don't think about Will Hollister, because it's a direct line to thinking about Evan, I do think about him. I have for years. Every time I read something about the State swimmer who blew it his senior year—the guy who drove his car into a tree just outside the city because he has, as the newspapers put it, *a death wish*—I thought about Will.

And I worried.

And then I hated him…just a little. He was the one spared, and here he was—wasting it. The last time I saw him in the news, in a short local spot that referenced the talented former swimmer and brother of the late, great Evan Hollister, he looked like a bum. His unshaven face poked out of an ill-fitting suit while his uncle walked him up some courthouse steps to deal with an extreme DUI. That was a little over a year ago, and I swore I would quit thinking about him, quit worrying.

He's still in there, though. He's always been in my head, rattling around. This nagging worry, this source of resentment—a symbol for all of my worst parts. It wasn't fair that I begrudged him for his self-destruction. He was suffering, too. I just hated him for making it all so public. I didn't want to see it, because no matter how much I worried about Will, in the end, all I was left doing was mourning Evan.

Yet here I am—worrying about him again.

I pull my phone into my lap and lean back into the deck chair, looking out on the quiet pool lanes of my parents' swim club. It's peaceful here at night. I like the quiet.

I've been waiting for Will to come back for about an hour, but now, with each minute that passes, I begin to feel more and more pathetic. It's clear that he wasn't lying. At least, his uncle is gone, so it seems reasonable that they did, in fact, go somewhere together. I still crave proof, though.

I send a short text to my friend to ease my whirling mind.

I think I need to get a job.

I wait for Holly to respond, and when my phone buzzes with her call, I'm happy. She speaks the second I answer.

"Why would you want to do something crazy like that?" she asks. I can hear the beeping noises around the nurses' station behind her. I miss those sounds.

"Because…" I sigh, sliding lower in my lounger, pulling my knees up and swaying them side-to-side. "I have too much idle time. I swim all morning, then I work out. Then I watch shows about tiny homes, tree houses, biker life…Neilson should really hire me. I'd be a great ratings representative."

"I don't think Neilson ratings work like that," she says, stopping to crunch through a snack.

"You on a break?" I ask.

"Yeah. Slow night. Not that I'm complaining," she says.

Our conversation goes quiet for a second. It feels nice, like I'm sitting there next to her, watching people so we can make up stories about them later. Holly and I are comfortable with our quiet. Introverted soul mates.

"So…" she says finally. She doesn't finish. She doesn't have to. I know everything the *so* implies. Holly knows my sad story, and she was with me when my dad called to tell me about Will coming to train. Holly was the only person I could truly rant to and not sound like a heartless bitch. I told her that I didn't want to see his face because it reminded me of Evan's, and that I hoped he washed out right away or changed his mind. She never once judged.

"He's still here," I say.

She crunches something again. It sounds like celery.

"Oh," she says, through a full mouth.

More silence.

"I'm actually at the pool right now waiting for him. He never showed today, and…"

"And you're afraid something bad happened to him," my friend fills in.

I breathe in deeply and let the air escape through my nose.

"I think maybe I am," I say.

"He isn't Evan," she says. They're words I need to hear.

"I know. That's what worries me. Evan would never have missed a practice. Not for anything in the world. And Will has a history of…"

"Missing life? Yeah, you said that before. But don't let his shit stick to you," Holly says.

I chuckle, because she has a way with words.

"I miss you," I say.

"Awe, hon…I miss you more. There's a new doc. He's…well, frankly, Maddy, he's fucking delicious. Like, he has me eating celery and shit because he's all about nutrition, and I want him to notice *me eating celery*," she says, punctuating with one more crunch.

I knew it was celery.

"He's probably married, Holly."

"Nope. Checked. Double checked. Asked," she says. I can hear her moving, and the sounds in the background start to fade, which means she's probably heading to the break room to throw away her trash and get back to work.

"I can't believe you asked," I say.

"Someone had to, and I've sorta become the outspoken one. It's my thing here now. I have a thing," she says.

"You, the outspoken one. Shocker," I laugh.

"Bite me," she says, and I hear her locker slam shut in the background. "Call you tomorrow."

I chuckle to myself after she hangs up, but it only takes a minute or two for me to feel lonely again. It's strange how I can crave the quiet but miss the noise all at once.

Before tucking my phone back in my pocket, I check the time. It's almost nine, and if I want to get my ass up at four to show up here again, I should give up on this rescue mission I seem to feel obligated to carry out. I straddle the chair as I stand and tuck my phone into my back pocket just as the sound of tires on gravel hits my ears.

By the time I slide the back door open, Will and his uncle are unlocking the front. I stand, half inside, half out, while Will's uncle takes a heavy-looking messenger bag from Will's shoulder. I step inside and meet them at the bottom of the steps.

"Maddy, I'm not sure how well you remember me, but I used to come to some of your meets…when you all were kids," Will's uncle says. "I'd come down from Michigan for the summers?"

I reach forward and grasp his hand, smiling.

"Duncan, of course I remember you. I'm glad you're here with him. This one…he needs eyes on him at all times," I lean in close, smirking. "Can't be trusted."

Duncan laughs at my joke, but it fades quickly. Will watches my eyes the entire time, only allowing a slight smile.

"I'm gonna head up to the room. Long day for me, but Maddy...I do hope we get a chance to catch up sometime. I'm looking forward to watching you two swim. I always loved watching you race," Duncan says, squeezing my grasp on his hand once before letting go.

"I'll be up later. I've gotta get my workout in," Will says, his eyes leaving me for only a second.

"No matter to me. I'll be asleep in about thirty seconds," Duncan says, his hand waving over his shoulder.

When the door shuts, Will leans back against the wall, his thumbs looped in his pockets and his eyes paused just below mine.

"You're here kinda late," he says, and his gaze flits to mine for only a beat. He's nervous.

He's guilty.

"You missed. I wanted to make sure you were taking this whole thing seriously," I say, falling against the opposite wall and folding my arms across my body.

Will's mouth tugs up on one corner just before he pushes off from the wall and walks past me and through the back door.

"If you want me to pee in a cup, Maddy, all you need to do is ask," he says.

I open my mouth to argue that's not why I'm here, but before I can utter a word, Will's hands reach above his head and he tugs the black T-shirt he's wearing up and over his head.

"What are you doing?" I ask instead.

"I'm getting my laps in. Promised your dad I would," he says, his feet working to kick off his shoes before he pulls one heel up and slips away a sock.

"Will, it's nine at night. You're swimming again in..." I pull my phone from my pocket to help me with the math as I look at the clock. "Less than eight hours. You're going to exhaust yourself."

"Better than not trying," he says, unbuttoning his jeans and sliding them down without hesitation. I turn to the side and bring my thumbnail to my teeth, shielding my eyes with my other hand.

"Maddy, you've seen me in my underwear more than any girl I know," he says.

His words make me shift to look at him again, but the moment I do, my eyes grow wide and my face heats up at the sight of him. There's something different about seeing him like this—not in his training suit, but just...like a man. He's toned, hell, ripped even. His muscles make that perfect parallel down his stomach and into his underwear, which hug his hips and legs like only the world's greatest pair of boxer sport briefs can. I cover my eyes and turn again quickly.

"Yeah, I know, but it's different when you're scrawny and fourteen. I'll leave you to it," I say.

"Suit yourself," he says. I take a few steps to the door, and my heart is pounding in my throat, when Will baits me. "If you're afraid to lose to a boy."

Goddamn him.

I hear the water splash, and I wait a second before turning to make sure he's submersed. When I face the water, he's treading in the center lane, a dozen yards out, moving backward. The deck light is only bright enough to see his profile.

"I've got nothing to prove to you, Will Hollister," I say, taking more steps forward until I'm at the end of the deck.

"Yeah...I know," he says, splashing as he pushes backward a few more strokes. "But I have a mountain of shit to prove, most of it to myself. Racing you always brings out the best in me, but it's okay."

The water moves with his strokes as he swims slowly to the other side. I watch as his form fades until the only evidence he's in the pool at all is the ripples left in his wake. He doesn't move for several seconds, and I know he's waiting at the edge, watching me.

"Shit," I say finally, kicking my sandals to the side.

"Ohhhh ho ho yes! I knew you couldn't handle walking away from a challenge," he says through cocky laughter.

"Turn around," I yell.

"Oh I am, don't you worry," he says, nothing about his tone sounding honest.

"Will, you better turn your ass around or so help me God…" My hands are frozen on the button of my shorts, my arms and legs tingling with adrenaline.

"I'm turned; I'm turned! Pinky swear," he says.

He's never broken a pinky swear. Not with me. Shit, I'm really going to do this.

I tug my shorts down fast, then flip my T-shirt over my head, leaving my clothes in a pile by my shoes a few feet away from the water.

"You're in my lane. Move over one," I say, sitting on the edge and feeling the water. The heater hasn't been working great, so the temperature is a little cooler than I'm used to.

"If you want the center lane, Maddy, you're going to have to earn it," he says, and I can tell he's facing the other way by the way his voice echoes off the back wall. I stop swishing my legs in the water and look up, squinting in his direction.

"I *always* swim in the center lane, Will. Move. Over," I grit. It's a stupid thing to pick a fight over, but aggression has always been my friend in a race, so I let myself be childish.

"Tonight you don't," he says, and I hear the water splash with his movement. "And if there's something you don't want me to see, you better get your ass in the water now, because I'm coming back."

Will

I catch her body slipping into the water just as I turn and begin swimming to the other side. I have no idea what I'm doing, and I know that my motives here—they're dangerous. I should leave her alone. I should have just gone upstairs and changed and come back down when she left, but something in me just sort of acted.

She was here waiting for me. If anything, she was told the same story

I told her dad, and yeah…maybe she didn't believe it and figured I'd gone to hit up some bar, ditched my responsibilities to drink away my sorrows—like I've done in the past. None of that takes away the fact that she was still here, though. That she was waiting. Whether it was just to see me or to check on me, she was here for me. Not Evan, but *me*.

I look up for my last few strokes and see her holding onto the side of the pool, both arms stretched out along the deck, her chest puffed up defiantly and proud. Her absolutely perfect breasts both sexy and strong underneath a blue silk bra. It's no different from the swimsuits I'd seen her in for years, but yet somehow, just knowing that this garment is not meant for the water makes it appealing as fuck. I swim up next to her, gripping the side.

"Nice suit," I smirk.

Her eyes narrow. She nudges her head to the right.

"Get in your lane, buddy," she says. Her lips are tight, almost smirking, but not quite.

"I told you, you're going to have to earn it," I say.

I watch her breathe in, her eyes locked on mine, as she considers my challenge. I could easily just swim five feet to the right, but something about this feeling makes me not want to be so accommodating. It's a rush—and I've always had a problem saying no to rushes.

"Fine. We'll swim opposite. Go back over there, and when I say go, you give me your best two hundred," she says. Her lip always gives her away. Maddy Woodsen has always had swagger, even when she was a kid. Her right upper lip is her tell, though—it lifts like Elvis's when she's holding a pair of aces.

"You go over there. I just swam back here, and you need a little warm-up anyhow," I say.

Her brow falls and she huffs out a "fine." I wait until she's maybe fifteen yards out before I change the terms.

"And five hundred. I'm supposed to be making up for missing. Two hundred won't make a dent on what I need to get in," I shout. Maddy stops mid-stroke, twisting then treading in the middle of the pool.

I can see enough of her to know that her mouth is flat again, lips probably pursed, and her nostrils are likely flaring. I can read the silence between us, and I pissed her off. My mouth curves because God, I love pissing that girl off. I've missed it.

"Fine," she says, louder than the time before. "You better be all right with getting lapped."

"It's on, sistah," I say, splashing water over my face and head before stretching my arms one at a time.

"Like Donkey Kong," she yells back through her own splashing and stretching. I chuckle at her because she's cute. This whole scene is such a bad idea, and if I were half the man I'm pretending to be, maybe trying to be, I'd call this whole thing off now and tell her to just head home, that I have work to do. I'd be cold and avoid her just like she did the minute I arrived. But she let me in—and then, there's the rush.

God, I love the rush.

"You call it," I shout, lifting myself to the deck and shaking out my arms in front of my body, searching for more blood flow—any edge I can get.

I can barely see Maddy climb out on her side, the shadows of her arms and legs mimicking mine. She's not going to make this easy, but I also know that she doesn't have a shot.

"You ready?" she yells.

"Born ready, Woodsen. Bring it!" I chuckle.

"Take your marks," she yells.

I breathe through my nose, my heart starting to race faster while I blink once at the water below me. I'm coiled and ready, like a runner waiting for the gun, and when Maddy shouts, "Go!" I hear her hit the water just as I do. For exactly two strokes, I think about her body gliding in, her form and discipline—and then the new me takes over.

I grab water and pull while my legs kick hard, my shoulders rotating in a perfect rhythm with each pound of my palms against the surface. I am a machine, and this is what I've been trained to do. I spent a year finding myself again, and nothing could seem to bring back my speed, until I learned to use the weight of everything in my life to my advantage.

My arms dig harder, and my mind forgets that there are nine more laps to go as my body flips and my feet kick against the sidewall. I never even felt her pass, but I know she did because a quick glance shows that she's once again heading toward me. I dig harder, and I forget it all again—I hold on to nothing but the pain. I hear the hum of the plane, I hear my mother's screams; I hear my dad telling everyone it's going to be all right, that he can land us. I hear the explosions, the impact, the sirens, the beeping of hospital machines.

I flip.

My arms move faster.

I feel Maddy pass me to the right. I can tell I'm ahead.

Each time my feet hit the wall, they push harder. Each time my hands punch the water, they pull my body faster. With every stroke she takes, I take two. My lungs work in sync with my heart, my head swivels when I need air, my mind mentally calculates how long it will take until I reach the wall again, and I count—five, four, three, two...*spin.*

My body moves so fast and my mind focuses on what fuels me so intently that I don't realize what's happened until I feel Maddy's hand brush my leg as I push off the wall and spin. I twist and startle in the water, the wave of my wake washing over me while I grab at the rope and push water from my eyes.

"What's wrong. You okay?" I say, breathless.

"You went a hundred too far, Will. You beat me already," she says.

My chest rises and falls, my lungs trying to claw their way back to normal from the ragged abuse I put them through. I stare at her, and her expression looks like pity.

"Don't," I finally say, swimming to the edge next to her. I move to lift myself from the water, but her hand finds me again, her touch on my bicep soft, but arresting.

I look at her touch and then into her eyes. She pulls her hand away, reaching instead for the rope behind her. She doesn't speak for several seconds. She doesn't have to.

She and I—we never really needed words. That's why we stayed away from each other. You can't hide how fucked up you're feeling when the other person can read it all over your face.

"Thanks for the race, Maddy," I say. I lift from the water and pick up my clothes, shaking away enough of the water to step inside without leaving a slippery trail. I leave the door opened a tick behind me, but I don't wait for Maddy to get out and leave. We're done here.

We probably should have never started.

CHAPTER 5

Maddy

He doesn't even look tired.

Will was early to training, most of his warm-up laps done before my fingertips hit the water. I'm dragging today, and I know it. My dad knows it, too. He just doesn't know the reason why.

I left here last night early enough to get a decent night's sleep, if only my eyes and mind would have cooperated. I laid awake until almost three, and I honestly think sheer exhaustion was the only thing to knock me out. Without it, my mind would have kept working to make sense of Will's behavior...*of my own.*

"Do it again," my dad says the second I lift my body from the pool. His mouth is flat, and he's painted with disappointment. My chest hurts because I don't like it when I make him act like this—like a *real* coach.

"Yes, sir," I say, mimicking his tone. It doesn't help my case. His glare drops and his eyes narrow, that flat line on his mouth moving into angry territory.

I dive in and begin my strokes to the other end, a swimmer's equivalent to running away. I get to the other side and push off to return, but my eyes catch Will and my dad talking. My strokes get sloppy, and without realizing it, I stop in the middle of my lane, reaching for the rope. My dad's eyes swing my direction, so I pull my goggles down and act like I'm adjusting something until he looks away.

The second their conversation breaks, I start my swim again, and I don't stop for a dozen laps. It isn't my muscles making me slow today; it's my head.

"Okay, ladies and gentlemen. Today is about speed. We're going to sprint today, probably until your arms feel like they're going to fall away from their sockets. Today is all about getting a good start, and all about nothing but you and the wall over there, and getting there as fast as you can. So hydrate, shake out whatever might be holding you back today," my dad pauses, his eyes moving to me, "and then get on the blocks, ready to go."

Amber, the girl I met the first day, waits for me near the bleachers, her bag wedged next to mine. I admire her spirit—but small talk, and being an inspiration or team leader or whatever—is kinda the last thing on my *possible* list right now. My mouth closed tight, I manage to show her a smile as I snatch my water bottle from the side pouch on my bag.

"I love sprinting. I hope I don't embarrass myself," she says.

I hold her gaze and smile with my eyes while taking a drink. I have to manage one motivational minute. Amber seems sweet, and the turmoil in my head isn't her fault.

"You won't. You wouldn't be here if you did anything embarrassing in the water. Remember, it's all about *personal* bests. Don't worry about what any of the other swimmers do."

Wow, that wasn't half bad.

"It's *you* I'm worried about. I watched you swim at Nationals last year," she says, looking from me to her feet over and over again. "You're pretty much the reason I'm here. I pushed myself enough to make it into this camp. I honestly don't even care if I make the team from here. This is *so* enough."

She laughs nervously before drinking more water and looking the other way. I've never really had a fan before, and it feels nice and awkward at the same time. I sort of feel responsible for her.

"How old are you?" I ask her. Her eyes dart to me.

"Eighteen," she swallows. That means she's a new eighteen. Probably fresh out of high school.

I glance from side-to-side before leaning into her.

"Come back here tonight, after practice. Be here by nine," I say, the right side of my mouth twitching.

"Oh….kayyyy," she says, her eyes worried, but a glint of excitement in them. I remember when mine looked that same way when the older swimmers took me to The Flour Mill the first time. A perk of growing up here in Knox, the person working the door always knew someone who knew someone who let them in when they were too young.

I leave Amber wondering, and on that fun edge of nervous and excited that I'd give anything to go back to. I take my spot on the blocks, and I wait while the other lanes fill with girls, too. There's enough of us for two heats, so at least there will be a rest between sprints. The guys line up behind them, enough to fill every lane, and Will has decided to take one, two away from mine. He's clearly avoiding me, after near skinny-dipping last night. That was a stupid idea. I got caught up. I wanted to remember how it felt to be that girl, who had that feeling in her chest like a guy might just want her. I let myself forget who it was I was letting look at me. Will did, too, until something else entirely took him over. The way he moved in the water was almost desperate—like he was fighting for his life.

Maybe he was.

I glance to my right to see Amber take lane one, and I wink at her, smirking when I turn back to face the water. She'll learn quick—drink fast, grab your lane, because that first one? You're never going to win from there.

Fifties are my favorites—always have been. My mom liked them, too, and when I'm in my lane, focused on nothing but one arm after the next, the wall, the touch, the kick—it's seconds where I get to be her, just for a little while.

My dad calls us to get set, so I stretch my arms out, shake away my nerves and take my position, my fingers itching to go the second I anticipate the sound. That's the secret to a great start. You have to feel it, otherwise your opportunity to be first will pass you by.

The instant my dad's breath hits the whistle, I'm coiled, and when it sounds, I'm off. My body slides through the water, my feet kick and I find my zone. Kick, pull. Kick, pull. I repeat and push myself to make each series faster until I feel the familiar home of my palm on the smooth tile at the other end.

My smile takes over my lips, and I throw my arms over the ropes, breathing hard and pushing my goggles up to see how I did. My father's standing on the other end, his arm raised over his head, one finger up, and Amber squeals, covering her mouth before looking at me with nothing but sheer elation all over her face.

I bluff. I smile tightly. She'll think I took it easy, probably. She'll let these initial seconds pass; she'll exit the pool, then we'll all climb out of the water and catch our breath to do it all over again. She'll think I gave her a gift, but I didn't. I lost. I lost because someone was faster, and when I turn my body as I lift myself from the water, both my father and Will are looking at me like something terrible just happened.

It did. And I have exactly four minutes to fix it.

The next heat of girls takes to the pool, and I'm assaulted by the sounds of cheers of encouragement. Funny how I can't hear a single thing when I'm the one in the water. I watch the girl in my lane work. She comes in first easily, and she barely pants as she climbs onto the deck next to me. Her eyes hit mine, and I swear I see pity in them.

Will's group swims next, and as much as I tell myself not to watch, my eyes can't seem to move away from his body. This time, I block out the sounds, and I focus only on his form. He's loose, but somehow, even from far away, I can tell that every muscle in his body is prepared for war. He grips the blocks and his head rises, eyes forward and looking ahead to the next several seconds, like he's traveling through time. My dad's whistle startles me, I'm so buried in the visual, and I miss most of Will's entry into the water, his body gone under the surface in a blink. When he rises, just like last night, his movements are smooth but urgent—every stroke more like an attack. Hands pound and fight through every stroke, almost as if he's more machine than man.

He wins easily, and as I step up to the blocks again, I watch the swimmers near him offer congratulations. Will stands there expressionless, swinging his hand in their direction to tap knuckles only to be polite. His eyes remain on the water, like he's searching for something underneath. I should be doing the same thing, only I can't stop looking at him.

We sprint for nearly an hour, and I lose my first three heats, each race getting tighter, until fatigue takes down my opponents and nobody can keep up. I have them in stamina at least. It doesn't make me feel any better, and it doesn't erase the crease between my father's eyes—the ones that tell me he thinks something's wrong, too.

Something is wrong. My head is all fucked up because of Will Hollister, just like I knew it would be. Yet, every time I pull myself from the water, he is the first place every ounce of my attention goes. I study him. I look so hard that for the first time since that day on the rope swing, when he was on his way to being a man and I was still a child, I notice all of the little differences between Will and Evan Hollister. Where Evan was polished, Will is rough. One brother quiet but always in control, the other loud as he pounds and kicks, absolutely nothing about the way he moves in the water in control at all.

My dad doesn't say a word when I exit the pool. He talks to a few of the other guys, but Will and I are left alone, as much physical distance between us as we can both put there. I can tell he's actively trying to stay away just like I am. Something happened last night—we got too close to the center of both of our pain.

That can't happen again.

I slip into the locker room and change, glad to have driven myself here this morning. My T-shirt and shorts are on in minutes, my hair clipped in a wet twist on the back of my head, and my phone is held in my hand to text my best friend so I can avoid talking to anyone on my way to my car. Amber manages to catch me before I sneak away unnoticed, though, and

I feel her hand brush along my arm, stopping me mid-step through the front door. I turn to look into her anxious eyes.

"You…you said nine, right?" Her brow is pinched slightly, and I know it's because she beat me, so she assumes I must hate her now.

Part of me does, but not really. Just the immature, ego-driven part that doesn't feel like admitting that nobody beat me today but myself.

I give Amber a closed-mouth grin as I nod.

"Nine," I repeat, leaning forward. "And…wear something nice, with comfortable shoes."

"Right. Okay, great…I'll…I'll be here," she says, adjusting the straps of her bag on her shoulder. I wait for her to take a few steps backward before I continue through the lobby door, my phone gripped in my palm.

Please say tonight is your night off.

By the time I get in my car, my phone dings with Holly's response.

Define night off. I'm not working, but I have a paper due Monday, and I haven't even started.

I turn the engine and push the volume control on my stereo down to zero. My head is noisy enough on its own; I can't handle music right now.

I'll write your paper.

This is a lie. Holly knows it, but I need to work my way up to begging her to drive two hours to help me sneak an underage swimmer—I wish I had never talked to now—into the club that led to the loss of my virginity.

You hate papers. You'll just put it off until I'm desperate. This is a trick.

I laugh for a second, then lean back in my seat, my phone propped in my hand against the steering wheel. I need to get her here.

I sort of invited one of the new girls out for "initiation."

She writes back quickly.

Well that was dumb.

I wait for more, but she ends it there. I need something that will make this irresistible for her. I need to up the stakes.

And Will is coming.

Lie, lie, lie! My words send before I'm able to think about what they really mean, and when I look at them, I gulp out loud.

What time?

My head falls to the side against my window and my eyes glance out to see everyone finding their way to their own vehicles. He won't show up, and we'll be gone from here before he sees us. I'll just tell her he changed his mind.

I text her nine and tell her to meet me at the club, then toss my phone in the center console before clicking my belt and staring long and hard at the back of the black sedan parked in front of me. My stomach hurts like I'm guilty of something, and the more seconds that tick by, the more symptoms I seem to come down with—my head hurts, my eyelid twitches, palms are sweating.

I pull my phone out to confess, to tell Holly never mind before I chase after Amber and make up a different lie for why I have to cancel, when the tapping on my window makes me jump in my seat, clutching my phone and both palms against my chest. Will winces, squinting one eye in apology as I slowly roll down my window.

"I thought you saw me, sorry," he says.

I shake my head *no*, my heart still pounding too hard for me to talk.

"I…" he stops, his eyes locked on mine while he sucks in his top lip. He shifts his weight and looks down, pushing his hands into the pockets of his jeans. When the wet strands of his hair fall forward into his eyes, he pushes them back, leaving his hand on his head for a few seconds while his focus remains on his feet.

"It's okay, Will," I step in for him.

His head lifts and his eyes meet mine, his smile crooked. He nods slightly, then looks down again, a sad laugh escaping his throat.

"You know it's not," he says, only glancing up to me for a beat before looking down again.

I watch him wrestle with himself, with the demons in his own heart and mind. He shakes his head and draws his mouth in tight again before pulling his hands from his pockets and resting them on the edge of my window.

"I'm just sorry, Maddy. Last night…I wanted to tell you that," he says, his fingers sliding from their grip and falling back to his sides as he takes a step backward.

This time, I'm the one who can't look up all the way. My mouth works independent of my best judgment.

"I'm meeting Amber here at nine. In the lobby. I'm taking her to the Mill. You…" I swallow once, fast. "You should come."

I peer up, somehow not surprised when my eyes meet the perfect blue of his. A second or two passes before he smiles faintly.

"Probably not a good idea," he says, turning his wrist over and tapping along a small tattoo. From here it looks like a series of lines, almost like a sketch-drawn barcode. I don't know what it means, but I understand enough from his tone that it's probably a symbol that reminds him of his worst self, *avoiding* that self.

"Right," I say. "Bars probably aren't a great idea."

His lip ticks up in a silent laugh.

"Like a sparkler at a gas station," he says.

I laugh quietly with him, nothing about any of it really funny. It's the sad kind of truthful laugh that fades away with regrets and weakness.

"I've got some things I need to do, anyway. I'm not sure I'd make it back in time," he says.

"More estate things?" I ask.

My question is innocuous but there's something about the way his eyes snap to mine. His mouth parts, but he doesn't speak right away. When he finally does, it's strange, like he's repeating some line he knows will work and not beg for questions. He sounds like he's lying.

"Just more papers."

He shrugs, his mouth shut tight. His eyes dare mine for a few seconds, a half smile plays out on his lips, and I feel questions swirling around my head. This estate should have been settled four years ago. Even things that could come up—the unexpected, like debts—would be dealt with by now. Four tax cycles have passed. Either something else has gone wrong with it, like maybe Will drained it all in a few short years, partying hard and driving fast, or he's not dealing with his family's estate at all. He's dealing with—*or doing*—something else. And if his recent past is any indication, those other things aren't going to be good for his swimming, and the risk is also there for my father and this club.

"Papers," I repeat the word, "or…whatever."

His eyes flair a touch, so I hold his stare long enough to force him to respond. He takes a deep breath and backs away a step from my car, a slight shake to his head, like he's warning me not to dig too deep.

"You always shot straight with me, Will," I say, a tightness taking over in my chest.

"I did," he says, his eyes blinking twice, his mouth closed tight. I note the careful choice in words, the past tense.

"You shooting straight with me now?" I ask, my pulse now constant.

Will sucks in his top lip, his hands finding his pockets while he puffs air from his nose, his head down as he laughs silently. He cocks his head to one side, his eyes leveling me. I'm sick because I want to know, and I'm praying for him not to say anything.

"I'll see you Monday then, I guess," he says.

We stare at each other for a few more seconds, my hand poised on the button for my window. Will nods one more time before I push it, and I watch him in my rearview mirror as I drive away. I look at him for as long as I can. He never moves. He never tells me a thing.

Straight shot my ass.

Will

It's a little over a two-hour drive to Indianapolis. Without Uncle Duncan in the car, I make it just under two. It's noon when I roll up to her house, right in time for lunch. The van is out front, and I'm glad to see it there. At least one thing I've helped Tanya with has gone right.

I sit at the edge of the driveway for a few minutes thinking about Maddy, but looking at the doorway to my real responsibilities. I'm taking on too much; I know I am. But Tanya's the one who convinced me to compete again. She said I needed to do one thing for me. And at least while I'm training in Knox, I'll be able to drive to her house to help with things rather than having her save them up for whenever I can get myself to make the trip. Flights...they're still hard for me.

I kill the engine, and the front door opens. She's wearing sweat pants and a large State T-shirt, her blonde hair twisted in a knot on top of her head. She looks exhausted. I'm not helping enough.

"Thanks for driving in, Will. I'm really sorry. I know you were just here, but I didn't expect the lift to come in so quickly. I tried to figure it out, but some of those parts are so dang heavy," she says.

I grasp both of her shoulders and slow her down. She closes her eyes and exhales, her shoulders slumping. She blinks them open, and this close, I can really see the circles around them.

"I don't mind driving here at all. Ever. Okay?"

She breathes in again, holding it for a second then huffing out stress that I know will begin rebuilding again in seconds.

"Okay," she says, a forced smile stretching into her cheeks.

"Show me the equipment," I say.

Tanya leads me through the living room of the small two-bedroom home, and we pass through boxes of medical supplies and stacks of clean towels, linens, and a few baskets of unfinished laundry. She glances at me sheepishly when I have to step over a pile of more clothes to get into the kitchen.

"Sometimes it's hard to keep up," she says.

I look around at the state of her house. She looks buried in life.

"Maybe I should come stay here...just for a little while," I start, but she laughs to herself and reaches for my hand, squeezing it.

"I'll catch up, Will. You can't come here and drive to train every day," she says.

I chew at the inside of my cheek, my mouth tasting of guilt as I nod and agree with her. She's right. I couldn't keep up with training at the Shore Club if I lived here. Doesn't mean it's not the right thing to do, though.

"At least let me hire you some help? In-home care, or a nurse, or..."

She holds up a box labeled LIFT MECHANISM, interrupting me before I can continue offering solutions that will never be enough to fill in for everything she needs. What she needs is me…here…full time.

"How about you figure this out instead, and then I'll get Dylan up, and we can try out this whole van thing with his new power chair? You do that, and we'll call it even," she says, looking up at me through her lashes.

I shake my head and take the box in my hand, pulling out a booklet that unfolds into pages of tiny-print instructions. I drop the box to the floor and begin to read, rubbing the back of my neck wondering if I'm smart enough to even know where to begin.

"See, you do this, and we're even," she laughs, stepping around the laundry pile toward her refrigerator.

"For once, Tanya, I think that sounds fair," I say, glancing at her then back down to step one of 178.

"Coffee?" she asks.

"Lots," I say.

It takes me a little more than two hours and six phone calls to my Uncle Duncan to get the lift mechanism working and attached to the van. For such a small part, it serves an incredibly enormous function. We test it on our own a few times before moving the electric wheelchair down the hallway to Dylan's door.

"He's just napping. He gets so tired, and we had therapy this morning," she whispers.

I push the door open slowly, and Dylan doesn't stir until I kneel at the edge of his bed and grab his hand in both of mine. My touch startles him, but the second his eyes focus and he realizes it's me, he begins to squirm and moan with excitement. His fingers fight against their rigidity, and I force mine into his, massaging his impossible muscles and joints, wishing I knew how to make things okay for him.

"How's the new therapy going?" I ask, leaning forward and pressing my head to Dylan's. It calms him when I do this; it always has. He smiles, and I can see he's grown another tooth. "Hey, buddy," I whisper to him.

"It's hard to tell. We've only been at it for three days or so. But you know Dylan; he's up for anything," she says.

"He is," I say, smiling.

His hand comes loose from my grip, so I lean back on my heels and let Dylan work to steady himself. His severe cerebral palsy has kept him non-verbal, but the doctors we met with a few days ago told us we weren't too late to be aggressive with speech therapy.

"What do you say, Dylan? Wanna take this new chair and van for a ride?" I ask.

"You'll need to help him in, but he's already figured out the forward and back. He doesn't steer very well, though, so I keep it on the lowest speed," she says, while I lift his small, struggling body into the seat.

"I'm good at patching walls. I broke a lot of them roughhousing when I was little," I chuckle.

"You and Evan? Hard to imagine," she says.

I laugh lightly to myself before giving all of my attention over to Dylan. Tanya was right about his comfort in the chair, and he begins to palm at the controls quickly, his fingers finding the right switch, sending the chair forward. He bangs the corner of the doorjamb only once on his way out and manages to get down the hallway without much trouble. The ramp I built during my last visit seems to be able to handle the weight of the chair, and within a few minutes, with Tanya's guidance, he's moved himself to the open door of the van.

It takes us several tries to line him up just right, but the first time the lift raises him, Dylan begins to hoot loudly and clap his curled hands. I hold a fist to my mouth and pull Tanya to my side, letting her cry at the sight of her son finally being able to go for a ride in something safe. Until now, she's been carrying him to the backseat of her old car and laying him down, strapping him in with the belts and avoiding major roads, hoping she wouldn't get in an accident. He'd gotten too heavy for her to carry, and I finally convinced her to let me buy some of the things she so desperately needs. As far as this takes her, though, she still has so many hurdles to overcome. The more times we practice with the lift, the more the weight of it all hits my chest, and the more guilt I feel for letting her do this alone.

We get Dylan back inside. He watches television in the living room, and I sit with Tanya at the table, finishing the pot of coffee she brewed. I slide my empty cup on the table and pry hers from her hand, holding on to her small fingers.

"We could make this work. Let me stay here. We'll just see how it goes," I say, my eyes pleading with her.

She runs her thumb across my knuckles and turns my palm over in both of hers, running her fingers along the lines tattooed on my wrist.

"I count twelve here, Will. That's amazing. I'm so proud of you," she says. I look down at my skin, the last line still pink around the edges.

"I got that last one a little early," I grimace.

"You could put a hundred on your arm now. I know you'll make it," she says, her eyes tired, and her smile struggling to stick around. If she believes in me so much, I don't understand why she won't let me help her now.

"So then, let me stay," I say.

She stares at me for several seconds, maybe considering it. But just as she always does, she cuts me off.

"We both know it wouldn't work," she says. "You've got big things to accomplish, Will Hollister. And I'm the one who decided to be a mom."

Her words cut, and the taste is bad.

"You weren't alone in that," I say, standing and following her to the sink with my cup. She laughs lightly, turning into me and taking my cup with one hand, patting my chest twice with the other.

"Sure am now," she says.

I step in beside her, taking my cup back from her hand and rinsing it before lifting up a few of the other things piling up in the sink. She wraps her hands around mine and mouths "stop."

"At least let me do the damn dishes, Tanya," I sigh.

She shakes her head *no,* cuts the water, and hands me a towel to dry my hands with.

"I have to do this on my own, Will. You won't be here all of the time to pick up the slack when I get tired…"

I start to protest, but she holds up a hand.

"And I don't want you to be. I want to know I can claw my way out of holes on my own. And it's nice to get the practice in while you're just a phone call away," she says.

I hold her gaze, daring her to budge, but I know she won't.

"Okay," I finally say, tossing the dishtowel on the only open counter space nearby and pulling her in for a hug. Despite how exhausted I know she is, she never once broke down in front of me. The only thing that makes her cry is pride in watching her son achieve something.

"Go make that team, Will," she says against my chest, her hands patting around me. "And when Dylan learns to talk, he'll bring his gold-medal winning uncle in for show and tell one day."

I roll my eyes at her and laugh, backing toward the kitchen door to leave through the carport.

"I'll settle for a participation ribbon," I say.

"Dylan would be just as proud," she says.

I nod, because she's right. He would. He's probably the best Hollister who ever lived.

I am walking the path of a series of bad ideas. If there is a wrong call to make, I seem to be powerless against taking it. It's a sign of how unready I am—yet another thought that I'm conveniently ignoring. I can hear the voices of every counselor I've had over the last four years all collectively screaming at me to stop, not to swim in temptations, not to add weight to my already drowning soul.

It was eight thirty by the time I got back from helping Tanya, and my uncle was sleeping in the old, beat-up lounge chair in front of the television—some History Channel show about the first modern irrigation ducts built in the West on loud enough to hear the occasional muttered word. I was lulling myself into ignoring that itch deep inside, trying to focus on the regular pattern of his breathing, when a photo flashed on the screen of a line of girls, all standing in a canal, the skirts of their dresses tied up around their thighs as they bent forward to wash their families' clothing. The one in the middle—she looked like Maddy.

Or maybe she didn't at all. Perhaps I was just waiting for the slightest resemblance to put the rest of the pieces already in my imagination into place. I could have closed my eyes just then and I would have seen her. She was everywhere…waiting.

Visiting Tanya and Dylan didn't make me want Maddy any less. If anything, it made me want her more. It made me resent my brother more—for leaving me with his lies. Maddy looks at me and still sees him, she sees the man we all kept on a pedestal. So many times, I've wanted to tell her the truth about who he really was, what he did. But that would only crush her. And maybe she wouldn't even be able to look at me at all then, and that…I can't go back to that. I missed her too much.

I can keep the secret. But I can't avoid getting close to the fire. Temptation and I have always been codependent.

I dig through the suitcase I'm living out of and find my long-sleeved black shirt. I put on the antique watch Duncan gave me for my birthday and look long and hard at the man in the mirror. I shave quickly and look at him again. I recognize him sometimes, and parts were familiar tonight. There's enough of the *good* Will to push the lesser man out the door and down stairs to the front lobby—where I sit now, my back against the doors leading to the pool, my elbows on my knees, and my eyes intent on the front door and lights from the car pulling into the parking lot.

The window I have to escape is small, and it grows shorter every passing second. My legs stretch and my muscles remind me that they're strong enough to stand, to run before Maddy gets her key in the door. My ears hear the lock twist. I don't move, and when she steps inside, the look on her face breaks everything left that was strong inside of me. She was hoping I would be here.

"Hey," she says, her voice a raspy whisper.

She shuts the door quietly then turns to face me again, her arms folded over her chest. There's a slight sway to her hips, and I laugh to myself because she's not going to let this go.

"You get done with all of that...*paperwork?*" There's a little bit of gloating to her tone, like she's caught me. I'm sure she thinks I've done something bad, or screwed something up that requires the help of lawyers. I'm fine with her thinking that. It's so much better than the truth, and if I can protect her from that, then I'll keep playing the role of the high-profile Indiana screwup.

I bring my hands up to my face, rubbing my cheeks for feeling to mask my reaction.

"Yep," I say. "All done."

I keep my answer short, and she shakes her head, *tsking*. After a few seconds, though, her arms finally fall to her sides, and her posture warms. She's still irritated with me, and I know this isn't the end of her prying, but for now...I have a break.

The closer she comes, the more the dim lights from the Swim Club lobby catch her profile. She's not wearing anything special. It's a black sundress falling just above her knees. I'm not looking at the dress though. I'm looking at her bronzed legs, the curves proof of her discipline every day of her life for the last decade. As I stand from the ground, I take in her golden shoulders, the way her hair is swept up in a twist, her neck long and soft. The front of the dress is modest, but the line along her chest traces every curve the way I've dreamt of doing with my hands. I look at her shoes last, lines of strappy leather that wrap around her feet and ankles, heels tall enough to make her look closer to my height, though I know she's not. These aren't her normal shoes, and I know she wore them hoping I'd see them. The message they send is nothing but temptation—the greatest weakness I've ever had, too—*wanting her*.

"You look absolutely nothing like that girl I snuck into the Mill all those years ago," I say, my steps slow as I approach her, enough of my wits with me to stop before I get too close. If I breathe any of her in, I will drown.

"Same girl," she says through a sideways smile. I hadn't forgotten how she sometimes talks out of one side of her mouth. I *had* forgotten how much I liked it.

"Taller shoes," I say, raising my eyebrows and glancing down her legs. She turns one foot into the other.

"First chance I've had to wear them," she says, laughing softly. "I'll probably be barefoot within the hour."

Mental pictures of her leg in my hands, my fingers unbuckling her shoe, sliding it away before my hand runs up her calf, under her knee, to her thigh. I bite the tip of my tongue and smile at her joke, stopping myself before I think too far.

"When's the rookie showing up?"

Maddy pulls her phone from a small purse slung around her body.

"Ten minutes. I…got here early. I didn't want her to have to wait outside," she says.

I nod once and hold her gaze, reading her until she looks away. *Did you come here early for me?* I watch her profile, and the way she avoids looking at me straight on fills me with a twisted sort of hope because I shouldn't want this, and probably even more so, neither should she.

Her head falls to the side eventually, and her mouth twists in a crooked smile while her eyes scan down to my shoes.

"Pretty much first time I've worn these, too," I say, kicking the toe of the black leather into the ground.

"Does this mean you've changed your mind about joining us?" she asks.

I pull my lips tight and breathe in through my nose, a tiny pause to make sure I'm really going to follow through before I nod and meet her eyes again.

"Well, here's the thing. This new me…he makes an excellent designated driver," I say, shifting my weight, my hands pushed deep in my pockets again, my right hand gripping my keys.

We both turn when there's a soft knock at the front door. Maddy didn't close it all the way, so it slides open in the middle of Amber's knock.

"That's probably good, Will, because I'm pretty sure I'm drinking," Maddy says, her voice quiet and her words just for me. Her shoulders are raised, and I hear her exhale as she steps away from me and reaches her arms out to hug the young girl who still looks up to her—even though she beat her today. Maddy has never been good at losing, but she's gotten better at grace it seems. I know that's why she invited this girl out tonight, to keep herself from turning her into an enemy, even though on some level, she has. She won't beat Maddy again, and I bet my old friend shows up nice and early Monday just to make sure her muscles are primed and her starts are the fastest.

"I wore pants. I hope it's okay; they're all I have with me. But my top is nice. Does this work? Will they let me in?"

Maddy slides her arm through Amber's, smiling at the young ball of nerves wearing gold glitter, blonde curls and a shirt that falls down one shoulder.

"You'll be fine. You look great," Maddy says, looking over her shoulder at me as she walks back out to the parking lot. Her expression is sad, and I know she wanted me to see it. She's wishing she wasn't going to a place with so many memories, and she's mad at herself for being drawn there. She could have taken this girl out to any of a dozen different bars, but instead she chose this one—the one place that's significant. I draw in a full breath and feel the burn of it in my chest. Whatever that face she made meant, it's exactly what I feel, too. I think probably there just aren't words for it.

I start heading to my car when Maddy stops in the middle of the lot.

"My friend Holly's coming. I see her lights at the end of the street. We can take her car," she says.

I put my keys away just as a lifted Jeep Wrangler barrels into the lot, sliding to a stop in the rocks a few feet away from us. I raise my brow and look at Maddy.

"I'll be sure she knows you're our designated driver," she says, smiling on one side of her mouth.

"Or maybe, I just drive no matter what, because…" I stop, pointing to the dust still settling behind her giant tires.

Maddy chuckles, opening the passenger door for Amber to climb inside. I wasn't kidding about driving. I have a feeling my control issues are not going to remain in check if I'm going to be in the back seat while this Holly chick drives. I round the Jeep and hold up a hand at the driver. She has short, red hair and freckles along her nose and cheeks; she begins laughing lightly to herself while she rolls down her window.

"No thanks, I don't need valet," the chick says before I even get a word out. She's mouthy, and kinda funny. The old me would really get along with her, but the new me doesn't like being called a car parker.

I purse my lips and step closer to the window, holding on to both sides.

"I'm Will," I start.

"I figured," she shrugs, nodding over her shoulder for me to get in the back.

"Uh, yeah…" I chuckle then hold out my palm. "I'm your designated driver tonight."

She puckers her lips and narrows her gaze on me then looks down to my hand and back up again.

"I ain't drunk yet, Will," she says.

"You sure about that?" I ask, my brow raised. I'm teasing, but not really because fuckin' wheelies, man!

Holly holds my stare for a second, then breaks into laughter, slapping my palm.

"Get your ass in the back, Will," she says. "Dude, Maddy. You didn't tell me Will was so funny!"

I exhale and yank the back door open, meeting Maddy's eyes on the other side as I climb in. I thought hanging out in a bar around endless alcohol was going to be the tough part about tonight, but it turns out the drive there is what's going to do me in.

"You were right about him being cute, though," Holly says, peeling out of the lot before my belt is secure. The moment my buckle snaps into place I look across the seat; Maddy is staring out her window, her hand squeezing her neck on my side, hiding her face. Right now, Holly could drive me off a fucking cliff and I wouldn't notice.

We get to the Mill in one piece, and I take my eyes away from Maddy for the first time in several minutes. My heart switches gears the instant I do—the rapid beating from hope and flattery turning into a free fall inside my cavernous, empty chest as my eyes take in the tall, white towers of the club.

The silos used to be a working flour mill, but when we were all in high school, an investor bought the property that had sat vacant for years and turned the warehouse into a country bar night club. They play a little bit of everything, but the big draw is the bands that slide through town and stop here without warning. Knox is off the beaten path, but this club is packed every Friday and Saturday night with kids from colleges hours away and high schoolers pretending they're old enough to get in. They come for two reasons—super stars take the stage and are close enough to touch, and parents tell their kids to stay away because the Mills is about nothing but sex.

That last reason is what always got me here. Acres of land surround the dance floor that bleeds outside, lights strung above. The groves are thick, and the pathways wind around for more than two miles. The mood is romantic—stars, crickets, and the nearby hum of sweet music. Plenty of places to get lost with some girl and bury yourself inside of her for the night. I only did it twice. Maddy did it once. With Evan. That was the night after I found out they were dating. I haven't come back here since.

I shake away the memories and follow the girls inside, trailing behind them and wishing more with every step that I had stayed home. When we step through the tall doors along the side of the silos, the music hits my ears and drowns out most of my thoughts. My hand runs along the old barn wood out of fondness, and when I look forward, I see that Maddy's is, too.

We find a high-top near the patio, half inside and half out, and Holly and I take the seats while Maddy leads Amber through the growing crowd toward the bar for what I sense will be the first of many shots. When she promised to bring me a water, I felt Holly's eyes dart to me; she hasn't let up her scrutiny yet.

"Is that like a training thing? No drinking on the job, or whatever?" she asks.

I step from the stool enough to reach into my pocket, pulling out my wallet to fold it open. I slide it toward her, the photo that reminds me of everything that's at stake covering up the rest of the article about how lucky I was to walk away alive.

"I drove my car into a tree, so no…not really a training thing. More of a…lucky-to-be-living thing," I say, sliding my wallet back to my lap, folding it and putting the memory away. I mouth the word "twice" to myself, but Holly catches me. She doesn't ask, which means she knows the story. I smile with tight lips and breathe in through my nose, folding my arms on the table.

"You ever been here before?" I ask, wondering if Maddy's been back since Evan's been gone.

Holly glances around, pulling her purse strap from her shoulder and setting her bag in the center of the table.

"Nah, but I always wanted to check this place out. I grew up in Gallworth, so the drive was always too far. I wanted to drag Maddy here, but we were too busy with class and the hospital, and she had swimming," she says, shrugging. "Not sure I could get her to come here, anyhow."

We stare at each other for a few seconds, and I can tell by her quiet expression that she knows all of Maddy's story. If only she knew the parts only *I* know—the secrets that almost touch her, but so far haven't penetrated.

"Probably not," I finally say, standing from my seat to pull Maddy's out when I see her and Amber walking up with small glasses and a bottle of water.

She sets the shots in the center of the table and then hands me my bottle. I twist the cap and hold it out in front of her before tipping the water back to guzzle half of it down.

"Ah," I say, running my sleeve over my mouth, "hits the spot."

She breathes out a laugh, but pulls her lips in tight before mouthing "sorry" and gesturing toward the table full of drinks.

"I'm good," I lie.

I'll never be good. But I'm strong. And feeling numb isn't as important as being present—not anymore, at least.

I step away from the table while the girls do shots, and I eventually find my way to the line of orange trees near the dance floor outside. I step between two of them and walk along the irrigation trough until I get to the sidewalk. They've added lights and a few benches near the walkways, which is probably a good idea. I smirk at a couple in the distance making out on a bench. The deterrent of a spotlight can only do so much.

I walk around for a few minutes, noticing everything that's the same, and all of the things that are different. When the memories start to hit me too hard, I cut back to the tables near the outdoor bar. A band has started playing, and the dance floor is filling up with girls in denim skirts, boots, and tank tops that are too tight and hang too low. I smile thinking about how that used to mean heaven to me.

"Still a *boob* man, I see," Maddy says behind me.

I chuckle and lean my head to the side, turning enough to face her. She has a beer in her hand, which probably means she's going to vomit later. I tap it and raise one brow, and she shrugs before taking a drink.

"I told you I was getting drunk," she says, turning back to face the dance floor. I watch her tilt the bottle back again, swallowing. Her eyes are smoky, and some of her hair has started to fall away from the twist, grazing the back of her neck.

"To be honest with you, I've never really been much of a *boob* man," I say, my eyes still mesmerized by her perfect profile. She laughs, and I love the way it makes her move.

"Bullshit," she says.

I don't answer, and eventually she turns to look at me, squinting.

I cross my heart, and she purses her lips, leaning her head in doubt.

"Swear to god," I say. "I mean, don't get me wrong. I like them," I say through a guilty smile, chuckling. She nods like she's caught me in a lie, then glances back out on the dance floor. I watch her for a few more quiet seconds, and then I do something completely stupid.

"Your hair does this thing when you wear it like that. It sort of tickles the curve of your neck, right…here," I say, reaching up and drawing my finger lightly along the few inches of skin from her jaw down to the strap of her dress. My eyes move to hers, and I catch her looking at my finger against her skin a second before her eyes flit to mine. I breathe in slowly and pull my hand away, pushing both palms in my pockets again. "Anyway…just…I notice other things. That's all."

I can feel Maddy staring at me long after I turn my attention back to the people on the dance floor. When the band finishes a song, I hear her take a deep breath, like she's about to speak, but we both startle when Holly jams herself between us, slinging an arm around both of our shoulders.

"I didn't come here to stand, kids. I had a guy throw up on me at the hospital yesterday and am spending tomorrow cramming out a paper. Tonight, we dance!" She lets go of us and reaches between us toward Amber, who shimmies forward in her high heels, laughing and drunk already.

"You better take it easy on her. She'll be passed out within the hour if you keep going at this rate," I laugh.

Maddy takes a long swig from her beer, then reaches over to set it on an empty table.

"Yeah, probably. Sucks to be the rookie," she laughs, looking at me for a brief second, her smile falling when she looks back out to her two carefree friends on the dance floor.

Couples are starting to form, and the fact that Maddy and I are standing close to the dance floor begins to feel weird. She points over her shoulder, toward our table, and I nod, but when she turns, I reach out to grab her arm, stopping her.

"Actually…" My head tips down, my eyes at her waist. I glance up into her surprised expression and shrug, letting my hand slide from her arm until I'm holding an open palm in front of her. "Whataya say? I don't think I ever actually got to dance with you."

Her brow bunches and she looks out at the people dancing under the strings of lights. She cups the back of her neck, and her eyes come to me again.

"You...dance?" she asks.

I close one eye, and wrinkle my other brow.

"I mean, not in a while, but yeah. I can handle the two-step," I say, starting to feel silly holding my hand out for her to take. She looks at it again, then back up to me, finally taking my palm and smiling on one side of her mouth.

Her fingers are tiny in my grasp. I don't know how they're so lethal in the water, and I'm careful with them as I turn and lead her to an open area on the outdoor patio. My pulse quickens when I realize I have to turn and face her, and my other hand needs to hold her close. I thread my fingers through hers, our hands held at shoulder height between us while my other hand moves nervously to the curve of her waist.

I sway forward and back in rhythm with the rushing fiddles and guitar, and I concentrate on keeping this exact, arbitrary amount of space between our bodies for the entirety of the song. I don't realize how rigid my muscles are or how long I've been holding my breath until the song ends and the couples around us all break away from each other to clap. I let go of her hand and turn to the side, clapping loudly, my palms sweaty and my chest working to catch up on air.

Maddy leans into me.

"You *barely* know your way around a dance floor," she says. I wince and look at her. "It's okay. Your brother never danced either."

My lungs grow tight, and my heart stops for a second. The light in her eyes dims.

"Let's take this next one nice and slow," the lead singer says into the mic.

Maddy shrugs and turns to leave the dance floor, and I do something stupid...*again*.

"One more chance," I say, reaching down and wrapping my fingers around her wrist. She turns into me, and I catch her, this time holding her close enough to feel her gasp. I swallow away my nerves, our foreheads so close they almost touch. She peers up at me through her lashes as I reach down, grabbing her other hand, before dragging them both up to my shoulders. "I'm not a bad dancer. I was just nervous."

I clench my fists, hidden from her view, before forcing myself to run my fingertips along her hips, wrapping them around the small of her back, bringing our bodies even closer. With nowhere else to go, Maddy's head falls against my chest, a perfect fit under my chin—and the last hold on her hair slips loose. I bring my hand up to sweep her hair over her shoulder, and I feel her take a sharp breath again when I do, so I stop, moving my touch back to her waist.

I can feel her relax with every step we take, her body resting against mine, depending more on me, until the singer reaches the chorus and I'm finally holding her like she's where she's meant to be. I look around at the world from this view. Her friends have each found partners, and strangers enter and exit the dance floor. Nothing has changed, yet somehow, just by holding her, everything feels different. My heart is slow, the storm inside calm. It's time to be brave again.

"Evan never took you dancing?" I ask.

Her shoulders tense, and I let my eyes fall closed. There is no room for us unless we can find a way to live with talking about my brother.

"He didn't like the attention, he said. We'd go out, but usually we'd sit at the bar, or maybe shoot pool," she says. I notice the way her cheek feels against me when she talks. I breathe in deep—a blend of citrus and coconut radiating from her skin. I swallow hard, and I know she feels it. Her shoulders grow even more tense.

"I bet you kicked his ass at pool," I say, opening my eyes and scanning at our surroundings. It was a pool game that lead to me breaking open their secret. Evan and I were playing here, and Maddy was hanging out near our table with a few of our old friends from high school. Evan lost the game, and I played the winner. Maddy disappeared, and a few minutes later, he followed her. I probably already knew, but I just had to see it for myself. I let the guy playing me win, and I went for a walk. I found them in the dark, and after embarrassment faded, I pretended I was happy they were together.

I adjust my hold, and the feel of her strong back under my fingertips forces my eyes closed again. Without even thinking, I let my lips fall forward against the top of her head. I don't kiss her, but I want to. She must feel me, because she shifts against me, turning her head to the other side, gaining distance between my mouth and her body. I suck my top lip in and bite it hard.

The song breaks for a guitar solo, and I count the seconds, knowing that she's going to slip away the moment everyone in here begins to clap. I won't ask her to dance again. I won't torture myself or push my luck. But I'll remember this. As bad of an idea as it is, I'm glad I did it. So many painful memories woven into this place, I needed this one good one. It might just be the best memory I have out of everything in my life.

I feel her shift in my arms, and when I pull away slightly, Maddy's chin pushes into the center of my chest, her eyes blinking slowly while she looks up at me. Two shots and a beer are about to talk to me right now. I smile softly and nod.

"That was a much better dance," she says.

I chuckle, tilting my head back to laugh before bringing it forward slowly, resting my brow against hers. My eyes look down at the curve of her lips, lower at the line of her jaw, and even lower at the swell of her breast under the soft black cotton of her dress. A heavy breath escapes me.

"I make you nervous?" she asks.

I don't answer right away, instead closing my eyes and swallowing again. I don't even care if she can feel it. I drag my hands up her body to her neck until I'm cradling her head in my palms, my fingertips flirting with her hair along her neck and my thumbs caressing her jawline.

"That's what you said…before. You said you didn't dance well because I make you nervous," she says, her words coming out slow and sleepy.

My mouth smiles against the top of her head, and I give in, opening it enough to press a kiss against her, hoping only the strangers are our witness.

"Yes, Maddy. That's right," I say. "You make me incredibly nervous."

CHAPTER 6

Maddy

I'm a happy drunk. Always was.

The first time I went to a kegger with the Hollister boys, I took over the DJ duties, and apparently, I played nothing but the Beastie Boys *Licensed to Ill* album over and over again. It's because I know every word. Because when I was eleven, Will Hollister locked me in his tree house and forced me to listen to it until I admitted I liked it.

I love that album, and it's all his fault.

No Brooklyn rap at its best this morning, though. I spent the night swaying to country songs in Will's arms, and at some points, my mind tricked me—*I thought it was Evan.* I would look up and realize it wasn't. It hurt, but it was also okay.

And so, I would drink more.

I'm not sick now, but I am not well. I can tell it's not morning any longer. My head is pounding, and I'm still wearing my black dress. My face is sweaty, and my hair is sticking to my cheeks and mouth. My tongue feels…dry. I chew at nothing and push my body over, stretching my arm out to feel for my friend Holly, for Amber. I'm alone.

I slide down my mattress, my dress sticking to the quilt tossed over it, and when my knees find the floor, I manage to slide the dress up and over my head. I crawl on my hands and knees to the closet, and I pull down the cotton shirtdress, sliding it over my body, but leaving the bottom pooled around my waist because I'm too miserable to stand just yet.

My back finds the comfort of a few stacked boxes, so I decide to spend the next thirty minutes waking up right here, just like this. I consider crawling back to the bed and forgetting about heading to the club when my door pops open. My mom carries a stack of fresh towels and my latest round of laundry, folded into perfectly neat squares. I smile at it, or at least, I think my face is smiling. I'm not entirely sure because I can't be certain that I feel my lips right now. I bring my hand to my mouth and rub it, relieved when I feel my touch.

"You're a mess," my mom says after setting my basket of laundry on the mattress. She picks up last night's dress and a few other items I've left on the floor, then rolls them into a ball and tucks them under her arm as if she's going to drive them to the end zone. She's pissed. I can tell by the way her hand is on her hip.

"Don't look at me like that," I moan. I let my head roll to one side along the soft cardboard behind me.

"Like what? Like my daughter is throwing away the most important thing in her life?"

I blink a few times before lifting my head to meet her waiting stare. She is *not* blinking.

"I'm not throwing anything away. I just wanted to blow off some stress last night, maybe show the new girl a good time," I say, pulling my knees in. Step one to standing.

"You also showed her what it feels like to throw up in a stranger's toilet," my mom says, lips pursed and weight shifting, jutting out her other hip.

She's *really* pissed.

I scrunch my face.

"Amber got sick?" I ask.

"Yeah. Your friend Holly took care of her. She drove her back this morning to get her car. Told me to tell you she'd give you a call later tonight," my mom says, moving to the doorway.

"Where...was Will here? He...he drove us," I say.

My mom stops at the door, her back to me.

"I didn't see him. Your dad said he walked home last night, though. Your father heard you all come in and offered to drive him, but Will refused," she says. She tilts her head to the side, glancing at me over her shoulder just enough that our eyes meet one more time.

I was wrong. She isn't pissed. She's disappointed. Whole different emotion. Whole lot more guilt.

I wallow in my self-made misery for another thirty minutes, eventually tying my hair up and getting changed into my swim suit, sliding on my cut-off shorts and favorite flip-flops.

My mom is at the table, reading through what looks like a set of planning documents.

"I'm heading to swim," I say.

I pause at the other end of the table. She looks up at me, pushing her black-rimmed glasses down her nose, and nods. We both glance at the top of each other's heads, our brown hair twisted into knots. I smirk as she chuckles.

"You're more like me than you care to admit," she says.

My lips pinch in as I fight against my smile, eventually giving in and grinning.

"I hope so," I say, walking around the table and kissing my mom's cheek when she gives it to me. "Try not to piss off too many lobbyists today."

She groans and turns her attention back to the pile of documents, and I run my hand along the table's edge as I head to the door. My father and I pass one another, and he stops on the stoops as I rush past him, his arms folded across his chest and his keys dangling from his thumb.

"Don't worry. I'm going to swim. Always getting faster," I say, waving over my shoulder without turning around.

My dad's not as forgiving as my mom, and if he was here when we came home, he probably has a good visual on how off my game I was. As long as I don't let any of *that* carry over in the pool, he'll get over it. I just need to avoid talking about it until he sees me swim again.

I get to my car and don't look his direction until I can see him in my rearview mirror. He's still standing in the same spot, one hand on the side of his face. We haven't been coach and athlete in a while. When I went to Valpo, my dad let them take over the reins completely. He said it was good for me, and he was right. But now we're both in this position where we need to navigate back to those old roles, only we've both changed a lot since the last time we were in them. My father has to think about more than just me. I have to think about myself. We're both still trying to figure out what's in the middle.

I flip through a few radio stations, settling on the local news on my way to the club. Every song makes me think of something, but local sports and traffic seems to empty my head, and that feeling is welcomed. Will's car is in the same place it was last night, and Amber's car is gone. I pull up to park next to Will, but I wait with the air running, my eyes glazing over as I stare at the weeds and brush along the gravel drive.

One thing became abundantly clear last night—Will's company makes me feel just a little bit better. It's also the reason I feel worse, but the scales seem to balance somehow when he's around. I missed him. *I missed us.*

Taking in a deep breath, I force myself to step from my car, unlock the clubhouse doors, and climb the steps to the office area. I'm quiet as I pass Will's door. The office one is wide open. My heart jumps when I see Duncan at the desk, but not enough to cause me to gasp or scream. I knock softly on the doorframe to get his attention, and he looks up, dropping his eyepiece into his palm when he sees me.

"Maddy, hello," he says, smiling and rolling out the chair so he can step closer to me. He reaches for my hand with his free one, and when he grasps it, he squeezes nice and hard. "What a nice surprise. I hope you don't need the office. The light in there wasn't bright enough, and I'm so close to getting this damn pocket watch to work again."

"No, no. I came for Will, actually," I say, shaking my head lightly at the sound of my admission.

Duncan's expression softens and his head falls to the side with his smile.

"It's nice to see you two reconnecting," he says.

A heaviness hits my chest with his word choice, but I shake it away with a quick breath.

"Yeah…he was always a good friend," I say.

Our eyes lock for a few seconds, and I squirm a little, feeling as though he's studying me…reading me.

"He's awake. Watching some movie or something. Go on in," he says eventually, his eyes still narrowed enough that I feel exposed, like he knows more than I do about me.

"All right," I smile, my cheeks suddenly red.

I turn my attention back and forth from Duncan to Will's door, the old man watching me all the way. I'm half expecting Will to pop out and scare me and them both to have a good laugh over it.

I knock lightly.

"Go on in. Really. He'll just think you're me knocking," Duncan says, waving his hand forward. *Pushy old man!*

I nod, twisting the knob and pushing the door open slowly. Will's leg is slung over the couch, and I can see his messy hair tussled in all directions, peeking out from the top of the armrest.

"You hungry for some lunch?" His voice sounds groggy, and I think maybe he's been napping.

"Duncan said I could just come in," I say.

Will sits up quickly, his head popping up and looking over the back of the sofa. He's watching some old car-chase movie, muscle cars squealing around tight corners on the TV screen.

"Hey," he croaks.

I hunch my shoulders, a warm feeling crawling up my neck the longer he stares at me.

"I wanted to see if maybe…you wanted to swim?" I ask.

He continues to stare at me before shaking his head and running his hand through his wild hair. He twists on the sofa, his hand searching for the remote and finally pointing it to the TV to turn it off as he stands.

"Swim…uh…yeah. Sure, I could get some work in. Just…" he babbles, spinning in place and pacing, as if he's trying to somehow make this space he's in look better. As if he needs to impress me with the spare room my family's put him up in.

"I wasn't thinking laps, really. More…" I pause, pulling the photo of me and him on the rope swing from my back pocket and holding it out for him to take. When he grabs it, I move my hand to my forehead, instantly embarrassed that I'm suggesting it.

"Wow," he says, leaning into the back of the sofa and pulling the photo closer in both of his hands.

"We don't have to, if you don't want to. I just thought…I don't know. I haven't been there in a while, and my mom says they might tear that swing and tree down, and…"

"I'd love to go," he says.

I look up into his waiting eyes, his expression serious.

"Yeah?" I ask.

Will's eyes linger on me before falling back to the image of a better time—a simpler time. He nods.

"Yeah," he says.

He looks back up and hands me the photo.

"Give me a minute to change. I'll drive," he says.

"I'll meet you outside," I say, leaving before he encourages me to wait here. This room is too small to be in with him right now. I need to learn how to survive the wide-open spaces in his presence first.

I wait for Will by his car. He finally steps through the front door, locking it behind him. He's wearing light-blue swim trunks and a white T-shirt, nothing like the skin-tight suit he trains in every day. Somehow, I notice more of him like this, though. He runs his hand through his hair, pushing his gray State hat on before he unlocks his car and we both get in.

"It smells new in here," I say, noticing how spotless everything is.

"I think they spray that smell in every rental. It's not bad for the price, but I miss my Bronco," he says.

I smile as I buckle up and Will pulls us out onto the roadway.

"You still have the Bronco," I say, fondly.

He turns to me, his mouth rising on one side.

"Fucker barely runs, but I'll never sell it," he chuckles. I laugh with him.

Will bought that truck with the money he earned mowing lawns in Knox one summer. He had these big dreams of rebuilding the engine, fixing it up. By the time he graduated high school, he had only managed to buy the thing two new tires. His parents refused to let him drive it to State, calling it a deathtrap. It sat in their garage for years. Will must have kept it when the house sold, after…after they died.

"I'm glad you kept it," I say.

I look to him, watching his profile as he chews at the inside of his cheek, his eyes focused on the road and his nostrils flaring with his breath. Eventually he nods.

"Me, too," he says.

Will turns onto the country road that leads to the lake. It's about fifteen minutes from this point, and I spend the first few listening to the rumble of the tires on the beat-up roadway, cattle grates buzzing the rubber every couple miles.

"What made you pick nursing?" Will asks, breaking the comfortable background noise. I shift and sit up tall in my seat.

"I'm good at taking care of people…I think," I say, closing one eye and looking at him. He laughs and meets my gaze.

"I'll agree with that statement, Maddy. Yes…you are in fact good at taking care of people," he says.

"Thanks," I say, bringing my hands into my lap, twisting them. "I don't know, I guess it's the only thing that I felt was a good fit for my skills. I don't want to run the Swim Club. I watched my dad struggle with the books for too many years, always just barely eking by. And my mom's into this whole local government thing, which…gah…sounds so awful to me."

"Oh, I don't know," he says. I pinch my brow and face him, twisting in my seat as he glances to me a few times. "I mean, yeah…the politics part is pretty gross, but your mom seems to genuinely want to improve things and enact change. It's kinda noble, really."

"So is beating your head against a wall," I laugh out.

Will's forehead furrows and his mouth hangs open before he laughs hard.

"Beating your head against a wall is *never* noble," he says. "That's just stupid."

I shrug.

"Seems a lot like local politics to me," I say.

Will laughs again, smiling at the winding roadway disappearing into the thick cluster of trees ahead.

"Yeah, well, it's better than delivering newspapers in Michigan in the thick of winter," he says.

My tongue pushes into the corner of my mouth and I bite it as I watch him and wait for him to elaborate. He eventually glances my way and shrugs.

"I needed a job with benefits, and there aren't a lot of people hiring a marketing guy—a few credit hours shy of a bachelors—with an extreme DUI record that made most of the papers in the Midwest, thanks to the footnote about a potential recreational drug problem."

I know my eyes widen, but I try to keep my reaction in check. Will still turns away, though. I wait for him to say more, and when he doesn't, I ask.

"Was it true?"

His mouth falls into a tight, straight line, and his eyes scan the roadway, moving from mirror to mirror before pausing to look at me at a four-way stop, our last turn before the lake. Will sighs and slides his hands to the center of the steering wheel, leaning back into his seat and letting his head roll to the right, peering at me.

"Some of it," he says.

I wince, and he reaches over and brushes his arm against mine.

"I said *some,*" he repeats. I hold his gaze and take a deep breath. "My drinking got dangerous. And I tried some things, maybe ended up hanging out with some people I shouldn't have. I'm not the first wannabe athlete to be caught smoking pot, though. And the other things…I tried, but only once or twice. Nothing felt as good as Jack Daniels."

"Until the tree," I say.

He nods and lifts his eyebrows high before swinging his body forward again to turn the car toward Peterson Lake.

"You *are* an athlete, Will," I say, just as the water begins to come into view. His forehead wrinkles and he glances toward me. "You said wannabe, but I just wanted to make sure you knew that you were different. You actually *are.*"

He chuckles bashfully, slowing the car as we clear the thick trees.

"Thanks, Maddy. But I'm nothing, yet," he says.

We both exit the car and walk toward the water's edge, thick layers of leaves caked along the shoreline. The rope is tied around the tree's trunk, and my eyes follow the length up high to the thick branch several feet above the surface. The sight of it makes me smile, and when I turn around to share this moment with Will, I find him making the same face.

"It's exactly the same," he says, kicking his shoes from his feet.

I smirk, and kick mine away too, pulling my arms through my shirt and tossing it to the ground quickly, catching Will's attention.

His head cocks in suspicion as I unbutton my shorts and slide them down my legs, stepping out of them cautiously, gaining a few feet on him before he gets what I'm doing and tosses his shirt to the ground.

"Last one there…" I shout through laughter, running barefoot along the water's edge, up the dirt hill, Will close behind me.

"You are *not* going to be the first to swing from that tree, Woodsen. You don't even do it right!" he teases.

"Sounds like *loser* talk to me," I shout back, darting through trees and clawing at roots to pull myself up the small bluff holding the trunk of the swing's tree.

My footing slips, and soon Will passes me, laughing over his shoulder and winking as his toes fling mud all around me.

"Oww!" I shout, sitting down and turning to lift my foot in my hand.

"Maddy, what's wrong? Are you okay?"

Will climbs down a few paces to lean on the hill next to me, and as soon as he's resting his weight on his knee, I push against his shoulder and lift myself up, sprinting by him again.

"Ha ha, sucker!" I yell, pumping my arms and legs hard the rest of the way to the rope. I tug the end and begin unwrapping, but am not fast enough to beat Will completely. His hands cover mine as we both manically battle to take control over this piece of our childhood.

"I got here first!" I giggle, pushing one of his hands away only to have to fend off the other.

"Doesn't matter. I'm the superior swinger," he says.

I lean my head back and laugh hard.

"You're a swinger, Will Hollister? I had no idea," I say.

He purses his lips, and my chest shudders with my amusement.

Our arms tangle, and we both try to hug the rope, my feet struggling against his to steady the small peg of wood at the bottom. Eventually, we're both locked into one another, and I let out a heavy sigh. There's no way I'm going to be able to cut him loose, and there's no way he's going to give up and let me have the first swing. We never let the other one win at anything, not even the shit that didn't matter.

"Fine, we go together," I say.

Will's eyes hit mine.

"Fine!" he shouts, pulling my body in close to his and pushing away from the ridge of the hill before I have a chance to truly prepare myself for any of it.

"You son of a…"

My words fade into a scream as we sail above the water in a huge half circle. I scrunch my eyes closed and hold my breath as Will tugs my hands free of the rope, our legs kicking together while his arms hold onto my body tightly as we fall toward the water, the cold hitting us in a rush, knocking the wind from our lungs—muffled screams quickly silenced under the water.

We fall deep into the blue, bubbles fizzing along our arms and legs as we break free and kick our way back to the surface. I cough when I taste air, and Will howls, flinging his arms back into a backstroke, kicking his legs hard and splashing water into the sky.

"Wooo whoo!" he yells, his voice echoing around us.

I gasp and tread water, my arms and legs working hard to find warmth for my chest.

"That was so much better than I remember!" he says.

"Ye…yeah…so so so so so…."

My teeth chatter.

Will chuckles, swimming back to me, reaching his arm out for me to take. I grab hold and let him pull me in, my only focus on catching my breath until suddenly I can breathe, and my attention becomes fixed on the feel of his hand on the place where my suit is cut low along my back. His warmth on my skin. His legs kicking with mine, to hold me up. His head resting against mine. His breath…ragged. My eyes falling to his mouth, my lips quivering, his parting. His tongue resting between his teeth. Shivers.

"We should go," I say. My hand finds the center of his chest and pushes.

Will doesn't fight, quickly letting go of his grip on me. I kick and swing my arms a few times until I see the shoreline come into view through the murky water. Righting myself, I walk up the rest of the way, pushing my hair back from my face, twisting it and wringing it out. Debris from the ground sticks to my feet and legs, so I pick some of the larger leaves away before bending down and grabbing my T-shirt. I slide it over my head, and it sticks to my wet suit underneath.

I don't turn to watch Will walk up the shore, but I hear the crunch of the leaves under his feet as he steps closer, and from my periphery, I see him lift his own shirt in his hands. I pick up my shorts and feel in the pockets, panic hitting me unexpectedly when I don't feel the photo inside. My eyes begin to dart around, and I turn in circles until Will's hand wraps around my arm, causing me to look up at him.

"Here," he says, his eyes on the photo of a much younger me and him. I look down and take it from his hand.

"Thanks," I say. "It must have fallen out."

He breathes in slowly.

"Must have," he says, his voice quiet, but the swallow that follows is loud.

I stand frozen while he moves to a large stone, sitting and pulling on his shoes. I choke on everything eating me up inside, coughing as I step into my shorts, keeping the photo in my hands to protect it from getting wet.

"You ready?" Will asks, his eyes moving away from me the moment I look at him.

I nod, even though he can't see me. He doesn't wait to hear my words and begins to walk up the slope to his car.

This walk isn't as hurried. There's nothing to win at the end of this journey. If anything, I would be running away.

We both climb in quickly and buckle our belts. Before Will shifts the car in reverse, he turns the radio on, stopping at a classic-rock station. The Eagles tell us to *take it easy*, Bruce begs for glory days, and by the time John tells us a *little ditty about Jack and Diane* I start to laugh uncontrollably. Will turns his head just enough, curious.

"Even the classics want to make me crazy," I say, not really to anyone at all. Will turns back to the road. He doesn't respond, and after a few minutes, I quit smiling about it. Nothing about it is funny anyhow.

We ride the rest of the way without talking, and my hand reaches for the handle, ready to rush toward the safety of my own car, the second Will's tires grip the gravel of the club house driveway. When he pushes the car into park, though, neither of us move. Will's hands run along the steering wheel, and he leans forward, folding his palms on top of one another, resting his chin on them, his eyes staring at the building where we first met.

So many years ago.

I leave my hand on the door latch, but my eyes center on Will. My mouth itches to frown, the taste inside acidic. Nothing is fair, and I hate this confused feeling. I don't understand why I have it. My pendulum swings from missing him, to feeling relief that he's here, that he's *home*, to wanting to hit him in the chest so hard that it empties the air from him. I want him to hurt, just like I hurt. And I'm terrible for wanting it, but that's our thing…we're honest with each other, aren't we?

"Why did you leave Indiana?"

My voice breaks the silence, but nothing follows. I breathe. My chest in and out. My pulse quickens.

"You transferred to Michigan with one year left. You never came back here. You were…*gone*."

Will's body rises with a long slow breath, and his head rolls to the side, his cheek flat against the back of his hands, his blue eyes opening on mine.

Crystal. Honest.

"I couldn't be here…because you were here," he says.

I swallow hard, sucking in my lip to keep it from trembling. It's both what I wanted to hear and what I dreaded. His words make me afraid and angry. Through it all, he never looks away. I force myself to stare right back through him. I read him. He couldn't possibly have been more sincere with what he just said, and it breaks me.

"Why did you…come…back?"

My breath grows heavy through those last two words. My chest hurts, and fear starts to snake its way around my body. Will's eyes remain fixed on mine. Seconds pass before he finally blinks. His head shakes the tiniest bit, and I know it's coming.

It's going to hurt. There's a slant to his eyes. A souring. Regret.

"Because you were here," he says.

The same honesty laid bare before me, my heart drops to the depths of my chest, and my head grows light. My mouth begins to water with sickness, and within seconds, my forehead rushes with heat.

"No," I say, breaking our stare and pushing hard on the door handle, rushing from the small space I was trapped in—with him—to my own car nearby.

"Maddy, wait!" he yells. I hear the sound of his door slam closed and his feet pound along the ground, so I walk faster.

"Let me go, Will," I say, fumbling with my keys, clicking the unlock button just as I reach for the door. I open and slip inside, trying to close Will off.

"Maddy, stop. Just…please, Maddy," he says, grabbing the car door just as I try to shut it.

"Let go, Will. I shouldn't have come here. You and me, we need to focus. This…digging up the past, and all of these memories, it's…none of this is good for either of us, Will. Just let me go, and let's go back to being friendly in the pool. I'll root for you, Will. But that's it. I can't…"

I stop when he kneels down just outside my door, his hands taking mine, grappling and pulling them toward him. My eyes sting with tears, and I lose my grip on everything. I give over.

I'm weak, and I don't care.

"I can't do that, Maddy," he says, his hand lifting my chin, his thumb swiping away a tear. He leans forward, sitting on his knees in the gravel, until his head falls to my lap in the driver's seat and his arms circle around me. My hands shake as they hover above his head, his hat on the floor of my car, near my feet. I'm locked, fingers rigid, afraid to let myself touch him.

"You're the only thing that doesn't make me want to drown," Will says, and my hands fall softly into his hair. My lungs fill at the touch. "I think I came here knowing that you were my only shot at peace."

My fingers thread through the wet strands, and Will twists his head in my lap, his rough jawline scratching my leg, his lips opening enough to catch on my skin, pausing until he pulls them closed in a kiss. His head rolls more, and his mouth brushes against my thigh again. I feel the chills all the way up to the back of my neck.

"Maddy," he breathes my name against my skin.

My hands fall deeper into his hair, my hold stronger. Will's hands move around me more, one sliding under my legs, bringing them toward him, outside the car, while his other hand holds the center of my back as he crawls closer to me, his body rising between my legs. His mouth kisses along the fringe of my denim shorts, then up to the waist band, until his teeth grip the bottom of my T-shirt and his hands slide to my hips, his thumbs hooking underneath the fabric and lifting my shirt up and over my body, tossing it to the passenger seat behind me.

Will rests his knee between my thighs, and I arch back over the center console while he moves over me, his mouth now pressing a kiss into my swimsuit-covered ribs, then the center of my chest. My fingers glide into his hair more, then down his chest as he rises above me, his forehead falling against mine as his eyes close. He shakes his head and parts his lips, almost as if he wants to say more, but before he can stop himself, before I can resist, his mouth covers mine completely, and the weight of his body falls into mine, every curve of my body scorching with the heat from the hardness of his.

Will's lips caress, and he pulls my bottom lip between his teeth, applying sweet pressure that bends me against him and makes me want more. My hands circle to his back, and Will leans into me, pressing his hard erection between my legs while his right hand drags up my body, his thumb grazing along my breast and nipple on its way to the taut, wet strap digging into my right shoulder. Will's fingers wrap around it, and I press into him, wanting him to keep going, the only way I can give him a sign because I'm too much of a coward to use my words. I don't want to hear myself say I want Will Hollister. I don't want to know what that means, what it says about me and the kind of girl I am. But I don't want him to stop touching me, either.

Will begins to drag my strap over my shoulder, and our eyes meet just as fate steps in to stop us from something irreversible. Something we'd both probably regret, even though his eyes right now are telling me otherwise.

I bite my lip, and Will lays his head flat against my chest, and we remain motionless—*soundless*—until we hear my father's car door slam closed—our bodies hidden by Will's car parked between us. My dad's steps slow, and I take a sharp breath through my nose, the sound of my heartbeat deafening in my ears. Neither of us breathes again until we hear the main door for the club open and close.

We lay still for another full minute. Will is the first to move, his arms lifting his body, his head falling heavy against me, like a magnet pulling—not wanting to let go.

"I'm so sorry," he whispers.

My hands slide away from his hair, and he backs out from my car, from me.

I let him go.

CHAPTER 7

Maddy

"See, now *this* is precisely why I didn't ask you to write my paper. Look at me—spent the night out, still got up at a decent hour and *bam*...wrote that fucker in a single day," Holly says. She turns the shopping cart down the next aisle and sweeps six bags of chips from the edge of the shelf into our cart.

"I cannot fathom how you are a healthcare professional," I say, putting two of the bags back.

"What? They're baked?" she says, reaching for them behind my back and putting them back into the cart.

"Baked *flavored*," I correct.

Holly left her phone at my parents' house, something we discovered when I sent her half a dozen texts after the lake with Will, only to have my mom carry my friend's phone up to my room and hand it to me. Luckily, I didn't say anything incriminating in text, because now that I'm an adult, my mom has no qualms about blatantly sticking her nose in my business.

I also seem to have lost the desire—or perhaps the courage—to share what happened with Holly. Talking about it, even with her, makes it a thing. And I have to see Will for five more weeks of training, and *things* make getting my work done in the pool hard. *Things* also make sleeping hard. And…well…functioning gets hard, too.

"You know, the fact that it was so easy for you to bounce back from, what was it, *seven shots of tequila?* That sorta points to a bigger problem…perhaps," I say, sucking my bottom lip in and holding my breath, waiting for her reaction.

"First of all, it was eight. And second of all, it means I have a very high tolerance, like a super power. And it also means that you're a pussy," she says, the grocery clerk at the line we just entered shooting his head up the second that word leaves her lips. Holly just winks at him, her lips puckering a hint, which makes the old man reach up to loosen his collar.

"That's, like, the second time you've called me a pussy in a week," I say, my cheeks a little hot from the stares my friend has earned us. *I'm feeling it, too, old man, though for different reasons.*

"You know, the fact that it's so easy for me to call you a pussy sorta points to a bigger problem, perhaps." My friend shoots me a sideways glance as she delivers her dig, then takes one of the chip bags off the conveyer belt and hands it to our now-mortified grocery man. "Scan these real quick, pops. I'm starving."

"You are too much. I see why I'm your only friend," I say, rolling my eyes and tapping my credit card against the pay machine.

Holly laughs with a full mouth.

"Yet you keep coming back, babe," she says.

"I know, I know…which probably points to a bigger problem, yeah, yeah," I say, squeezing the bridge of my nose and closing my eyes tight.

We finish buying my week's-worth of protein bars and super fruits, and my friend's sack of junk food, then climb back into her Jeep to head to the Swim Club for a few hours of workouts. Needling one another is just our way, and I can tell Holly misses my company just as much as I do hers. She could have just turned around and headed back to the apartment we used to share near campus, but instead, she asked if I needed any help. What she meant was *company*, but Holly and I don't like using words like that—words that denote love and attachment. Even for our friendship, and even though we both feel it.

I don't use those words because I'm afraid anyone I say them to will be marked for a tragic death. Holly doesn't because she was raised in the foster system and doesn't believe real love exists. Together, we're a pretty cynical duo. This is also why neither of us has a lot of friends. But we do have each other.

Holly pulls into the Swim Club lot, and I know she's parked next to Will's car on purpose. Just seeing it brings a rush of heat over me, one that starts at my thighs and slides up my body until it leaves my lips with a tingling sensation. I can still feel him—feel our mistake.

"You two seemed to be getting along really well the other night," she says.

I shrug, avoiding her eye contact and lifting my two grocery bags from her back seat, trying not to engage. I think I've gotten away with it, too, and then *bam!*

"So, has he *always* been in love with you? Or is that a new thing?"

Her question knocks the air from my lungs, and my steps stutter as I round the back of her Jeep. I know my eyes are wide. I know my lips are tight. I can feel it.

"Right, so…new thing then, huh?" she adds, smirking.

I pinch my brow and suck in a short burst of a laugh, acting, then keep walking to the main lobby.

Preposterous. Impossible. Ridiculous. Ludicrous. I'm saying that and a dozen other similar words with the expression I give her. Meanwhile, though, I can't say that I haven't asked myself the same question. Yesterday's kiss was not something that happens because of a place or circumstances. I may suck at romance, but I know when a kiss is more than physical attraction and hormones, and Will's touch was almost forbidden—a scent of longing traced on my body everywhere he'd been.

I wanted it.

I walk straight through the lobby to the small kitchen and shove my two bags into the little space left in the fridge around my dad's cases of water and energy drinks. I hear my friend crunching behind me, and I turn to see she's brought her bag of chips in with her along with a neuroscience book.

"You sure you can get your studying done out here?" I ask, leading her to the back door, and eventually the deck. Funny how I missed her, but now I kinda wish she'd go home, and take her blunt honesty with her.

"Yeah, I can study anywhere. Besides, I'm sorta hoping Will's gonna show up, and then I can get a real case study out of this thing," she says, popping a whole chip in her mouth and wrapping her lips around it slowly, grinning at me as she chews.

I stare at her while I slide out of my shorts, shaking my head and not understanding.

"Ya know, cuz you're probably going to have a nervous breakdown and all, from him being so in love with you," she says, laughing out bits of chip through the last few words.

I bend down and scoop up a handful of water and fling it at her, causing her to flee to a chair.

"I'm pretty sure you're going to fail your neuroscience labs," I say, turning my back on her and moving to my favorite lane to stretch and splash water on my legs and arms.

"I know that's not how neuroscience works, Maddy," she says, her tone full of sarcasm. "I was just making a clever play on words. You don't need to be such a pussy."

"Stop calling me pussy!" I shout, this time kicking water at her, the sprinkles pelting the spine of her book as she shields herself with it.

"Quit being one," she says, sticking her tongue out at me then shoveling more chips into her mouth, crumbs literally falling everywhere.

"You're like Cookie Monster," I say.

"Yeah, well Will Hollister's in love with you," she says.

I jerk my head to face her, glowering, which only makes her laugh harder, spilling more crumbs on her chest. The only way to escape her barrage is to dive under water, so I go in cold, and my muscles pay for it for several strokes. Eventually, my body warms up and my movement becomes steady. No matter how fast I swim, though, I can't seem to outpace my friend's words. They invade my head, probably because a part of me was starting to let the same thoughts unravel.

Is Will Hollister in love with me? Has he always been? And, more importantly, why do I hope so?

Will

When I was little, maybe five or six, I would spend hours over the summer watching my Uncle Duncan work in his shop. Mom and Dad always shipped us up to Michigan for two weeks near the end of July. Two boys, two years apart, our brawls could get taxing when we were home all summer. They had a break when I was in school, even when Evan was still too young, but summers dragged. My mom would begin to use the time-out chairs more and more often, and pretty soon, we'd find ourselves on the train headed up to Grosse Pointe.

Evan always spent his time playing with the neighbor kids, or making cookies and shopping with our Aunt Maggie. All I wanted to do was help my uncle, though. He had a special stool he'd made just for me, a little higher than normal, and it allowed me to lay on my hands with my head low to the table so my eyes could watch him maneuver tiny gears into place, setting them in motion with the smallest sparks.

"You remember what I used to tell you?" he says, jarring me from my trance. I'm no longer the young boy who could barely reach the table, but I am the man whose legs are too long to fit at the same small desk as my only remaining relative, and I still love to watch him work.

"You said if only the heart could be fixed like this," I say. "I always thought it was weird," I chuckle. "When I was a kid it made me think that you were Frankenstein. I used to tell Evan you kept bodies in the basement."

My uncle shakes with silent laughter.

"You always were a little shit," he says.

My eyes focus on the end of his tweezers, the tiny clip held open by his steady hands as he slowly lowers it to the table, dropping the pin in place just as he frees the gears from their hold with his other hand. The task seems impossible, and success seems futile, yet I hold my breath to listen with him as the tiny machine begins to work.

Tick. Tick. Tick.

"Best goddamned sound in the world," my uncle says, his muscles relaxing as he pulls his glasses from his face and switches off the headlamp he'd been wearing on his head.

I shift my eyes from the watch to my uncle.

"Can I?" I ask, wanting to see it up close.

"Yep. Just don't turn it over. If those suckers fall out, you're going to have a crime scene to clean up," he laughs.

"Got it," I breathe out a laugh. Careful, I take the watch into my hands, pulling it close, my eyes transfixed on how every tiny piece plays a part.

"You still sticking with that plan of yours?" he asks.

"Not sure what you mean," I say, my attention on the tiny grooves where one wheel meets the other, the shine of the metal, new parts helping old.

"That one where you think you don't deserve anything, and where that girl I hear swimming out there doesn't deserve the truth?"

I look up fast, and my uncle grabs my hands, closing my palm and easing it toward him.

"Don't drop my masterpiece just because you can't handle my frankness," he says, prying my fingers open slowly and taking the watch back into his own palm.

"Sorry," I say in a quick breath. I blink a few times, still a little stunned from his statement and unsure how to respond. I pinch my brow and move my eyes to his. "I don't think she deserves the hurt. This has nothing to do with lies and truths. What does it matter now that Evan's gone? The least I can give her is a happy memory."

"You really think that's what's best for her, do ya?" he says, leaning back in his chair and folding his hands behind his neck.

I think about all of the possibilities, her finding out, me telling her, Evan getting the chance to tell her. No matter how I play it out, Maddy thinking she was Evan's one and only is always the best...*for her*.

"Yeah...I do," I say.

I watch my uncle work for a few more minutes, but the urge wins over, and soon I'm tugging my shirt over my head as I stand and tossing it on top of my pile of clothes on my way to the bathroom. My favorite suit is dry, so I slip it on, grab a towel from the stack Maddy's mom left for me and head back through the door before I have a chance to change my mind.

"Suddenly have the urge to swim, do you?" my uncle chuckles.

I glare at him as I pass, and it only makes him laugh harder.

I don't realize Maddy isn't alone until I hear the pool door click closed behind me. Her friend Holly is sitting in one of the lounge chairs, a book propped up on her thigh with one hand, the other knuckle deep in a bag of Doritos. She looks up at the sound of the door, staring at me for a few seconds before her lips give way to a lopsided smirk.

"Hey, Maddy," she says, pulling a chip from the bag. She points it at me, then glances to her friend who has just stopped on the opposite wall to catch her breath. "You've got company."

There's a long exchange between the two of them, and I'm starting to feel like I was the subject of some high-school-style bet.

"I can come out later to get my work in. I didn't know you were here," I lie. I hover at the edge of the deck by the chairs, not really wanting to leave, when I feel her friend kick me with her toe, against my leg.

"You're welcome out here, Will. I'm the one she wants to leave," her friend says, shooting Maddy a glare.

"It's because you keep calling me a pussy!" Maddy shouts.

My lip tugs up, and I laugh quietly, looking down at my feet before moving my eyes to Holly. She shrugs.

"She's right. I do," she says, looking back to her friend and cupping her mouth to make her voice come out even louder...as if that's possible. "Because you're acting like one!"

I can't hear Maddy sigh, but I can tell by her shoulders and the way they rise and fall while she holds on to the pool's edge that she is.

"You know she doesn't like it when people underestimate her," I say to her friend, laying my towel on a nearby table and kicking off my slide shoes.

"Just trying to bring out her best," Holly says, holding her half-eaten bag of chips out for me. I shake my head *no* and rub my sore abs.

"Trying to bring out my best," I laugh.

Her mouth curls as she shrugs, and her eyes narrow, her expression shifting to flirtatious. "Yeah, well…it's working for ya," she says, eyebrows waggling.

I thought I was too old to blush, but Maddy's friend may just be the female equivalent of the stereotypical construction worker, and I feel pretty damn objectified.

"All righty," I say, eyes wide as I stretch my goggles in my hands and turn my attention to the pool. Maddy's soon approaching my side of the pool and is about to touch the wall, so I step quicker, kneeling by the edge to force her to look at me on her touch. She slows when she notices me, her eyes masked by her tinted goggles, hair tucked under her cap. My brother used to say that all swimmers look the same when you gear us up, but Maddy doesn't look like anyone else at all—even masked and ready to compete. Her cheekbones are always a little higher, her lips a little pinker, and I'd recognize her form even under the deepest waters. She's perfection.

"I thought maybe we could sprint together. I know it's always easier for me when there's someone in the lane next to me," I say. I could not possibly be more transparent, and I hear her friend breathe out a laugh behind me. The more seconds that tick by without Maddy's response, the more see-through I become.

And by sprints being easy, I mean I just want to be near you because I literally cannot get your taste out of my mouth.

I start to stand, but before I make up an excuse to leave, Maddy gives me a slight nod.

"Cool," I nod back.

She swims a few slow laps while I stretch and warm up, and when I twist to the side, I notice her friend Holly is now chewing on her pen cap, her legs folded in the chair while she stares at me. I wonder if Maddy told her about yesterday?

I do my best to ignore her, but every time I glance her direction, I'm met with her eyes, and a wry grin that she flashes, like I've been caught.

"You, Evan and Maddy…you guys were close?" she finally says after locking eyes a dozen more times.

"We were," I answer quickly, turning the opposite way and stretching an arm that is already limber and loose just to avoid looking at her more.

"Was it always *Evan* and Maddy, or did you and her…ya know…like, date or anything?"

My head cocks and my mouth hangs open, my stomach tightening as I think of the best way to deflect this, when Maddy steps in before I have to.

"Will is two years older than me, Holly. It would have been weird," she says.

Weird. I nod to agree with her, but as I get in the pool, I stay under water for a few extra seconds just to mouth the word to myself. *Weird.* I guess she didn't say *gross*, so weird is better, but I never really thought of the idea of a me and her as weird. Two years when I was a senior and she was a sophomore would have been difficult, yeah, but…no…a *me and her* has always been far from weird.

When I resurface, I hear the middle of her friend's response.

"I was fifteen and he was five years older than me, and I didn't find it weird at all," Holly says.

I twist to look at Maddy, and she just opens her eyes wide and shakes her head at me, urging me not to dig deeper.

"Holly was a little…*advanced*…in high school," Maddy says.

"Fuck high school. I was advanced in junior high," her friend says, her book snapping closed as she stands. "I really should head home to study, Maddy. Maybe Will can take you home? You know…when you two are done with whatever…*this is?*"

Holly waves her hand above us, her lips pinched like she's holding in a laugh. I see what she's doing, and as much as I appreciate that she's trying to force Maddy and me together…*alone,* I'm getting a vibe from my other side that alone time isn't exactly wanted. Unsure how to answer, I turn to Maddy for a sign, some expression that gives me a clue, but Holly—my unrequested wing-woman—doesn't give me time.

"Great, okay, well…call me later, Mads. Will, as always, been a pleasure. Keep avoiding carbs and making those abs look super sexy, would ya?"

I can only laugh to myself when her friend leaves us alone, and I let my face fall forward so I'm looking at the water.

"I'm pretty sure that falls under sexual harassment," I chuckle.

"You have no idea how much worse that could have been," Maddy says. I meet her eyes, and she widens them. "We used to do this thing after big tests. We'd each take turns picking how we'd celebrate. I'd make us splurge and go out to some fancy dinner, or maybe go dancing."

I raise an eyebrow, kinda guessing where this is going.

"Strip clubs," she says, and my chest shakes once with my laugh. "Every. Single. Time. She has a stack of ones on hand, like, always. Seriously, the next time you see her, I'll show you her wallet. Ones. Filled with ones."

"Wow," I mouth, stretching forward while my fingers grip the edge of the wall. "You…went to these clubs with her?"

Maddy's head falls to the side and her eyes scowl.

"I'm a big girl, Will. I can go to a strip club if I want to," she says.

"No, yeah. I get that. And I'm fine with them. Young men need a way to earn their way through college, you know?" I say, doing my best to keep a straight face before Maddy splashes water at me. I splash back a few times, but when it causes her to put more distance between us, I stop.

She looks down into the water, folding her arms along the ropes and lifting her legs up until her toes break through the surface. I smile at them. Even her fucking toes are cute. The quiet grows a little uncomfortable, and I'm hit with the need to make some kind of move.

"I didn't really come down here to swim," I say, lifting my head just enough to peer at her.

She kicks her toes, making tiny splashes in the water.

"I know," she says out of one side of her mouth. Long seconds pass, and I watch as she chews at her lip. In my mind, I swim the few yards between us, back her into the wall, and tug her hair free from its cap while I taste her lips again. Holly kept calling Maddy a pussy, but she has no idea.

"I shouldn't have let it happen..."

"I'm sorry for yesterday..."

We both talk over each other, freezing mid-sentence, our eyes locking just before our lips curve and our smiles reflect one another's.

"Sorry, you first," I say.

She shrugs.

"Kinda sounds like we were both saying the same thing," she says, the right side of her mouth curled into a wry smile. My head falls to the same side as her smile, and I study her, hoping that at any minute she'll change her mind, say something that's just a little better than wishing yesterday never happened. She doesn't, though, so I nod, accepting this place we've met at in the middle. I don't like it, and I won't be able to live with it. But for five more weeks, I can bear it.

"So you wanna sprint?" I ask, dipping my goggles into the water and sliding them on. Business it is, then.

"Probably should. I can't be anything but the first girl to the wall again. Makes it kinda hard for your dad to push for you to make the US team when you lose to a girl who literally just got her braces off," she says.

"She's not that young," I laugh.

"No, I'm actually being serious. She told me at the Mills. 'Let me take out my retainer before we do the next round of shots,' she said, to which I responded, 'You have a retainer?' And then she smiled, all bright-white teeth, tapping her fingertips on the front ones. 'Just got the braces off a month ago.'"

Maddy's lips purse and she blinks slowly while I laugh.

"Maybe she had to wear them for a really long time," I laugh, lifting myself up to sit on the pool's edge. Maddy does the same, then turns to her side, sliding her goggles up enough that I see her eyes.

"Either way, she's still a lot younger than me, Will," she says, letting out a heavy sigh. Her eyes hold onto mine; I see the subtle difference in her expression with each passing second. Her mouth falls flatter, her eyes become sullen. She breathes in deep again, letting it escape in one heavy blow. "And losing to her scared the shit out of me."

I look down to the place where my hands meet the concrete, then to my feet still in the water. I let my legs circle once, and I think about how impossible it is that I'm even here, that I'm even breathing. Maddy's my motivator, even though she has no clue. Maybe, just maybe, I can find the old Will deep down inside me somewhere. Maybe I can find the guy who used to motivate her to win—even if it was just by pissing her off.

"Seems like this would be a good time for me to make a bet with you, then," I say, standing to my feet. I laugh to myself, still not entirely sure about what I'm about to propose. It will buy me more time with Maddy, though, and torture or not, I still want those moments with her outside of competition. I've had enough to remember what her friendship feels like now. No going back.

"Your bets have never been anything but trouble for me, Will Hollister," she says, looking up, keeping her eyes trained on me while she pulls her legs in and stands.

"We're not eleven, Maddy. I'm not going to dare you to drink vinegar or write LOSER on your forehead in marker. I'm thinking we need a more mature type of motivator," I say.

"Like?" She looks at me with one eye closed more than the other, her hand on her hip.

I smirk, and mentally thank my wing-woman Holly for giving me such a great idea.

"I give you a full body-length lead, and if I still win, then Friday, you have to take me to the strip club," I say, trying not to smile too broadly while her eyes narrow under her consideration.

"And if I win?" she asks.

"Then you get to pick the place we go on Friday to celebrate. And I have to pay the bill—no matter what," I say.

Her eyes flash at my suggestion, and her lip twitches upward on the right.

"Do we have a bet?" I extend my hand, daring to step forward a few paces. My pulse kicks up with a mix of adrenaline and desire. This was very clearly another bad idea—but the moment Maddy lifts her hand at her side and meets me halfway, I forget about my moral compass and readjust my definition of what's good and what's right.

"Two body lengths," she says when our eyes meet.

I squeeze her palm, loving the fact that she squeezes back with equal force.

"Fine, two," I say, and she nods.

"I'll set the sensors," she says, leaving me to shake the nerves from my limbs behind her back while she moves to the control box and flips on the timers.

She comes back to stand next to me; we both put on our best game faces. My lips hurt trying not to laugh, but I hold my eyes on hers and do my best to sneer while we both swing our arms then slide our goggles into place. I wait while Maddy readies herself up on her blocks, and I step up next to her on mine, bending down, and holding the front, relaxing my back and testing the sway of my legs as they move back and forth.

"You call it," Maddy says, her head turning to me while she reaches up with one hand and points her finger at my face. "And you better not cheat. If I find out, I'll do something really shitty to your shampoo bottles when you're not home. And you know Duncan would help me."

I pull in my brow and laugh out a breath.

"This sounds like something you and my uncle may have worked out in advance," I say.

"That's for me to know, and you to worry about. Now call the damn race, Will," she says, turning forward again, her hands both steady on the block. "And don't swim like a pussy."

"No, ma'am," I chuckle.

I crouch again, swallowing down my nerves. I'm not worried about winning or losing. I'm worried about making shit messy.

"On your marks," I say, my eyes falling closed, my heartbeat ratcheting up quickly.

"Get set," I say, holding my breath for a full second. My last chance to turn back is right now.

"Go!" I shout, giving over to fate. Whatever will be will be, and whether this is a good idea or bad is something I have to see through to find out. But at the very least, Maddy is going to swim fast, and she's going to find her spark. I'm going to give it to her, right…*now*. My fingers hit the water, and I dig in hard, making up ground. I feel the wake of her kick, the trail of her best.

Maddy is swimming fast, and she's never going to lose to Amber again. I'm making sure of it, because, good idea or bad, in about six more seconds, she's going to lose to me.

CHAPTER 8

Maddy

My purse is loaded down with ones—stacks and stacks of them. Tonight will be the best sixty bucks I've ever spent, and Will doesn't see it coming.

He beat me when we raced. I have to admit there was a small piece of me—the tiger living within—that thought for most of the distance I had a shot. But Will's just too big. His arms dwarf mine; his body length is dominating even to other men, and the power he brings with every stroke sounds like thunder in the water. I lost by a little more than two seconds, and two seconds in the water, in a fifty-meter sprint for your life, is a *really* long time.

I thought about those two seconds all night, and I brought them with me to workouts on Monday. I held onto them when we took the blocks again for more sprints. I obsessed on them every single time we raced this week. And today…*today* I clocked in just under twenty-four seconds in my fifty. More than a personal best, if I can swim that time in competition, better it by one less stroke, I'll take the world record.

When I saw the time, the first person I turned to wasn't my dad—it was Will. It's been Will all week. It's been Will since the moment I first saw him again. Wrong or not, he makes me faster. He makes me happy. And this rekindled friendship that has grown by leaps and bounds this week, just because of some stupid bet, has made me happier than anything has in years.

The routine isn't very old, which I guess doesn't make it much of a routine, but for the last four days, Will has invited me out for lunch or coffee after our morning training, and he's always waiting for me to show up before he puts in his laps at night. Not once have I told him I was coming, and not once has he asked if I was. It's this weird understood agreement we never discussed that I'd be here when the sun sets, and he'd be here. I'm not sure how long he waited the first time, but the smile that stretched across his face when I showed up to join him took me back to the old *us*, and I think that's why I keep coming. I like making the trip back in time.

I like making Will Hollister smile.

I find my favorite old chair in the club lobby—the one with the chenille arms that I can draw doodles on with my fingers—and pull my legs in, my hands wringing the dripping water from my hair while Will changes upstairs. My father walks in from the pool with two men wearing dress shirts and pants, with sunglasses on their heads, but ties left out of the wardrobe. It's clear they're here on business, probably sponsorships, so I sit up tall and prepare myself to help my dad close the deal.

"Here she is," he says, walking the two men who look more *Wall Street* than *Indiana swimming hole* over to me. I stand, wiping the excess water from my palms along my dry shorts before I reach out to shake their hands.

"Maddy, I'd like you to meet Craig and Allan Cumberland."

I swallow, recognizing their names instantly. Their name—Cumberland—is printed on the label of every swimsuit I own.

"Nice to meet you," I say, careful to give each of them the perfect handshake. My eyes glance to my dad, and we communicate silently. This visit, it means dollars.

"That was some sprint out there. Your dad tells me it was on world-record pace," the taller one says. I'm not sure if he's Craig or Allan, but I do know that this is not the time to ask. I'll pretend I know and plan to consult Google images later.

"Oh, uhm…thanks. I'm sorta trying not to think about that part," I blush.

"She's lying," my dad says, leaning into the shorter one and covering his mouth while still talking loudly. "It's all she's thinking about."

My eyes rush to my dad's, and I smile on one side, shrugging.

"He's right," I admit.

"Hard not to think about something when it might actually be within reach," the shorter brother says. "I get it."

I give him a tightlipped smile and nod.

"The Cumberlands were actually talking to me about maybe having you and Will sit down for an interview or two under their sponsorship umbrella?" my dad says. I arch a brow and look from the brothers to my dad and back.

"Why Will and me?" I ask, knowing. It's Will's story, and then how I fit in with it all.

"Only if you're comfortable," the brother nearest to me says, his hands falling into the pockets of his expensive pants and his smile shaded by the stubble around his cheeks and chin. I don't answer, because I'm finding it hard to evade, to not be honest on this one. I don't mind being interviewed when it's about me, my training, my wins and losses, but this will be about Will. And Will won't want to dig up any of this. My eyes meet my dad's and he takes over.

"We'll work on setting something up, here at the pool," my dad smiles.

My brow furrows, but my pulse races up my throat, and I'm paralyzed from it. Within a breath, my dad is already showing the Cumberlands through the door, just as Will climbs down the steps. He's smiling—the smile he makes for me lately—so I choke down the scene my dad just led away, and talk myself into forgetting about some interview that *might* happen.

He takes the last few steps quickly and approaches me with such ease that, for a second, I think he may just keep walking up to me until his arm finds its way around me and his lips find their way to my neck. He stops two feet shy of my daydream, though.

"Miss Woodsen," he says, rubbing his hands together like a greedy banker in a Dickens novel.

Here we go.

"I believe we have a bet to settle, yeah?"

He cocks a brow and tilts his head, a lock of wet hair falling forward onto his forehead. I stare at it for a second, and my lip ticks up on one side betraying the fact that I notice this small bit of sexiness. It's not the only thing I've started to notice. Yesterday, it was the way his shoulders push the seams of the long-sleeved T-shirts he wears and the bronzed color of his chest, and the way I can see the roll of his collarbone through the V-neck of his shirts. The day before, it was the slight difference between both of his eyes, one a little green, one a little blue.

Monday, though, might have hit my heart more than anything else I've observed about the oldest Hollister brother. He was walking in alongside my father, and I was trailing behind. Neither of them knew I was there. My father didn't ask him a question, and there was no reason for him to suck up with flattery. His words, they were genuine—admiration. He told my dad I was the hardest working person he'd ever met, and he wished like hell he had an ounce of my talent. I stopped just outside the door and let it close between us, and I waited for almost ten minutes after.

I waited, thinking about his words—and how much I felt the same about him.

"Oh we have a bet, all right. Come on; let's get this thing over with," I say, rolling my eyes and slinging my purse over my shoulder as I spin on my heels for the door.

Will chuckles behind me, and I'm glad he can't see the smug look on my face. He's about to wish he'd never made that bet. At the very least, he's about to wish like hell he'd lost.

"I'm driving," I say.

After we drive for an hour making small talk about practices and the other people in the training camp, Will starts to get antsy. His right leg begins to bob up and down. Every time I glance over, my eyes catching his movement, I notice he's also chewing on his thumbnail. At first, I think it's just his hormones getting ready to take in all of the bare tits he can stand, but when I make a turn onto the next highway, headed for Indianapolis, his nerves start to ratchet out of control.

"Are you all right?" I ask. Sparing glances at him, each time my eyes take in a picture of a man falling apart.

"Yeah, I just…I didn't know we were going this close to the city for this. I mean, there are joints near the county line, maybe half as far," he says, his brow creased and his eyes constantly scanning his environment.

I laugh lightly, trying to lighten the mood.

"Will, I lost fair and square. I'm not taking you to some county strip joint. Nothing but the best for you, my friend," I smile and wink. He mimics me, but his laugh is fake—it's masking a whole bunch of other shit going on inside his head right now.

I focus on the road for the next few miles, but the closer we get into the city, the more fidgety Will gets, and eventually, I pull off onto a side road, into a gas station. I stop kind of hard, and Will's hands fly to the dash.

"Jeeee-zusssss!" he shouts.

"Will, what's going on?" I ask.

His eyes meet mine. We enter a faceoff that lasts almost a full minute before Will breaks, a heavy sigh leaving through his nose. His hands cover his face, the butts of his palms pressing into his eyes.

"I just have a lot of history in Indy," he says.

I pull the corner of my mouth in tight, squinting at him.

"Why would you have history in Indy?" I ask, the answer hitting my mind almost the second I finish my question. "Ahhhh…"

Will's hands fall away from his face and his eyes open on me, his eyes wide.

"Will, it's not like it's a secret," I say.

He nods slowly.

"Oh…kay…" His lower lip puckers and his eyes close a little more on me.

He doesn't want to talk about any of it, and I get that. But his mistakes were pretty public, and they're the reason my dad and those sponsor investors want to roll him out for interviews. Will's a great story—and he'll get their brand plenty of airtime, as long as he can behave.

"This is where you had your accident. When you hit the tree. It was in Indy, off this highway," I say, not hesitating with my words. I need to convince Will that his car crash isn't something to be ashamed of. It was his bottom—or very damned near close to it—and the Will I've seen the last few days is a man on his way up. This Will is far from bottom.

"I get why you're antsy, is all. If it helps," I say. He's looking down at his lap, but his head slowly rises until his eyes meet mine, the worry lines deep in his forehead, his teeth clamped tight, fighting against his urge to disagree with me. The tension washes from his features slowly, and eventually his lips fall closed into a tight smile, and he nods.

"Thanks for understanding," he says, almost a whisper.

I'm not sure why I reach for his hand, but when my fingers touch his, what happens next is instinctual as our fingers weave together, and Will brings my wrist to his mouth and presses a soft kiss against me. I let him keep my hand until he's ready to let go, and after a few seconds, he turns in his seat and clears his throat while I check my mirrors to back out of the parking spot at the gas station and retrace my path back to the on-ramp.

There's no use trying to fix the quiet left behind after that, so we ride the rest of the way to Foxy Tails in silence. I notice Will's restlessness seems to be much less, though. As hard as that topic was to broach, I'm glad I did.

The pink sign and the swinging tail come into view after a few more miles. I exit the highway and find a spot in the very crowded parking lot. I've actually never been here, but Holly recommended it. Will has no clue what I've done—and he remains in the dark until the man in the three-piece suit that checks our IDs at the door winks at Will and swats his ass with his palm.

"You said strip club, but you didn't say it had to be girls," I say through a half smile.

Will's eyes widen. I wait at the entrance while he spins in a half circle, pausing for a few seconds to take in the *Magic Mike* knockoff performance happening on the center stage, then turning more to see the men dressed in chaps, barely-there jeans, and G-strings waiting in chairs for the line of women all fanning themselves with dollar bills.

I'm a little nervous for his retribution, but as he turns to face me, I can tell he's laughing, his hand on his cheek and his mouth twisted in a smile that only says defeat.

"Well done, Maddy," he says, pointing a finger at me and shaking it. He chuckles more. "Damn, just...well done."

I laugh, too.

"We can go," I say, satisfied enough with the fact that I tricked him. "I won't make you stay."

"Oh no," he says. "You brought the play money, right?"

I tilt my head, one eye closed more than the other. "Yeah," I say.

"Then let's go play, Maddy. We're celebrating you getting faster," he says, his arm reaching around me and pulling me close as he leads me through screaming women to a small table near the main stage.

I slide up on the stool and pull my purse over my body, resting it on the tabletop in front of me. Will drags it toward him, gesturing with a quick nod, asking my permission to open it. I nod *yes*, and he reaches in, pulling out the cash, then fanning himself with it like the women we'd seen when we walked in. I laugh so hard my head falls back, but when I look forward again, Will is closer, and his eyes are serious. My smile starts to fall, but he presses two fingers on my lips and leans in toward me, his forehead almost touching mine. He slides the stack of ones across the table to me.

"You know how I feel about competition, Maddy. I'm willing to earn it," he says, grabbing my hand and pressing it against his bare abs while he lifts his shirt up with his other hand, gripping the bottom with his teeth.

My eyes flash when he rolls his hips. He pushes my hand along his body, and I flush with heat—incredibly aware of the path my fingers take along every ridge, ever tip, every searing piece of flesh until my fingertips hit his waistband. Will lets his shirt fall from his teeth, his lips curving into a devious smile as his body quakes with quiet laughter.

He was joking with me, which, in so many ways, is the Will I crave. But I felt those few seconds throughout my entire body—between my thighs, in my chest, and along my tingling lips. That one small practical joke brought back the feel of Will against me, his mouth on mine, his tongue on the inside of my leg, and it takes more strength hiding that from him right now than it does to swim the fifty in twenty-three seconds.

With little hesitation, I fan out the ones in my hand and blink at him, as if I'm unfazed and bored by his performance. I reach into the center of the stack with my thumb and finger, pulling out a single dollar, and then I reach forward and tuck it in the neck of his shirt, pressing it flat against him while my eyes meet his and his laughing comes to a pause.

"I'm gonna need change for that," I say.

His eyes are on the place where my hand rests against his chest. For a brief second, I think maybe he's flashing back to that moment of weakness, too. His lip curls, though, and his chin lifts as he slides from his stool, backing away from me toward the bar.

"You got it, darlin'," he says. "Two waters, coming right up."

I wink and nod, a little proud and a little guilty that he's drinking water in a place that serves alcohol. He wanted to come here, though. Well, not *here*, but booze flows at any strip club. You have to be a little drunk, I think, to let go of the inhibitions that make it hard to enter these places in the first place.

But not Will Hollister. Not *this* Will Hollister. He walks away with his head held high, nodding to half-dressed men as if he knows them, not a glimmer of redness from being embarrassed. He owns this strip joint, just like he owns the water.

Kinda like he's starting to own me.

Somehow, my prank turns into one of the best afternoons I have had in ages. Will and I both grade the performers on their dancing, and we decide to give the biggest tips to the guys with the least amount of coordination. We dub our mission the Maddy-Will College Fund, and by the end of our afternoon, we've earned ourselves a fan club of male strippers, some who actually run over to give us hugs goodbye before we walk out into the hot parking lot, orange-lit from the setting sun.

We don't speak about any of it until we're in the car for a few miles—then, out of nowhere, we both burst into laughter, the uncontrollable kind that tears up in our eyes.

"You do know, that small guy at the end was also named Will, right?" I glance over at him, his body relaxed and his mouth stretched into a smile that makes his eyes crease with happiness.

"Why do you think I gave him the rest of the cash? I gotta take care of my Wills, darlin'," he says, putting on a drawl to his tone.

"You're his pimp now, are you?" I tease.

Will pulls his right leg up, propping his foot on the seat and leaning into the door, his elbow resting on his knee while his teeth hold onto his thumbnail. All the while, he smiles. It's the sexiest thing I've ever seen.

This lighter mood continues for most of our drive, and we talk about the old days—when there were three of us and we were all young and stupid. We talk about hiding in my dad's storage closet at the club until he had to put something away, just so we could scare him. And we reminisce about holidays at the club—swimming on Thanksgiving, even the year when we couldn't get the pool heater to work. The only time we give pause is when we mention Christmas, but neither of us falls into the trap of thinking about the one *worst* Christmas. We don't go there; we stay in the light, and we laugh about Evan and we laugh at ourselves. It feels like it should, until Will's phone *buzzes*.

We're close to the club, maybe five miles out, when he pulls his phone from his back pocket, tilting it just out of my view. He silences it immediately, and begins to put it back in his pocket, so I dismiss it. Until it happens again. Another *buzz*, and suddenly everything about him changes. Over and over, his eyes shift to me briefly while someone calls.

"It's okay…if you need to take that," I say.

I watch him in glances. He stares at the phone intently, his mouth shut tight as he takes a deep but short breath through his nose. His eyes fall shut, and I look back to the empty highway ahead, determined not to make this into something.

"Hey," he says. It's a familiar answer, his voice soft and warm. I wonder if I called him, if that's how he'd answer for me. I feel stupid for wondering this.

"What did they give you as the cause?"

I look over at his question, his arm still propped on his leg, but his thumb is pressed on the bridge of his nose, his eyes shut while his hand cups his phone against his ear. Whatever is being said on the other end isn't good news—that much is clear.

"Okay," he sighs.

"Everything all right?" I whisper. He turns his head to me and his lips paint a fake smile while he nods. I recognize it—we both made it to each other a lot before today, before this past week.

"No, it's all right. You can call anytime. I want to know."

He's quiet for several seconds, listening to the other end, his thumb again pressed into his forehead.

"Okay. Yeah…I'll talk to you tomorrow," he says, ending the call and dropping his phone to the pocket on the opposite side of me.

I pull us off the highway, onto the exit for the main road through town. We're minutes away from the club, and I'm not sure if I want to press the gas to make them fly by, or if I want to coast and draw this out.

We're stopped at the light to turn, the car's cabin echoing with the sound of the blinker. My heart starts to match its rhythm, and I feel my stomach knot and give with my uncertainty.

"Are you sure?" I ask, timid.

Will's head has fallen against his window, his attention lost to something far away.

"Will?" I speak a little louder. My voice booms amid the silence.

"Huh?" He turns to me, shaking his head then rubbing his hand down his face. "Oh, no…it's fine. Just…a friend of mine's kid. I'm sort of the only person they can call."

A friend. *They*. He means *her*, but he's just not saying it. I think all of this in a span of a single second, and then I bury the suspicion, and the weird tinge of jealousy that comes with it, because I don't need to carry that weight. Will and I are friends, and if that's what he wants me to know, then that's where I'll leave this conversation.

His mouth forms a thin, unconvincing smile, and I pretend to believe it, whispering, "Okay," before turning toward the club. Will moves his leg back to the floor of my car, and his hands fold in his lap, his thumbs beating against one another in a nervous battle counting down the few minutes we have left together in this car. When I pull in to the club lot, Will wastes little time, pulling his belt loose before I stop, and opening his door the moment I push my car into park. I'd considered coming back inside with him, talking more, but the sweet feeling of our conversation has soured. I almost can't wait for him to shut his door so I can pull away as quickly as he exited.

I watch his hand grip the door's edge, swinging it a few inches more open, then more closed. His back is to me as he pauses, and his fingers wrap once—twice—against my car doorframe. He bends down, enough that I can see his profile, his sideways glance meeting my eyes and hitting them with a dose of something just shy of sorrow until his lip ticks up on the left.

"You know, you really are beautiful when you laugh, Maddy," he says, my body feeling as though morphine has just rushed down my spine and along every single nerve. His eyes soften more, the smile making it to the other side of his face. "It's exactly how I remembered it."

I blink when the door closes, and I move both of my hands to the top of my steering wheel. But I keep my eyes on the other Hollister brother. I watch him walk all the way inside, and I wait until I'm sure he's made it up the stairs, to his uncle, where there is nothing but space and building and wooden doors and glass between us. Barriers—a dozen various barriers—including the solace of my car.

"You're beautiful, too, Will," I whisper, my lips barely parting with the words. I wanted to see if I could say something I was feeling for him out loud, no matter that nobody could hear it.

I push the gear into reverse, and I drive home happy. I'll judge myself for letting Will inside my heart later. For now, I like him just where he is.

CHAPTER 9

Will

Dylan's seizures are getting worse. They're hard to predict because of how difficult everything is for Dylan. He can't communicate, other than some limited arm movements and sounds that can't quite form words. Tanya's found a doctor at the Cleveland Clinic willing to evaluate Dylan's case. The problem is getting there. Dylan doesn't exactly travel light. A plane ride makes the most sense, because that much time on the road wouldn't be good for either of them, but this isn't really something Tanya can do alone by plane, either.

I knew it when she mentioned it to me, told me about the correspondence she had with the doctor, the tentative appointment. She'd never ask me to go—to help. She's desperate for me to, though. She just can't bring herself to ask. I get that. It's an independence—or perhaps stubbornness—I possess, and maybe it's why I decided to admire her instead of blame her or be angry with her when I found out she had Evan's child.

I woke up early this morning, finished my laps and sat by the pool while the sun rose, spinning my phone in my palm until I was sure that I couldn't live with myself not helping her and my nephew. She cried when I insisted I would come, and I told her to keep the appointment. It's next week, which means I'll miss workouts Thursday and Friday. Which means Curtis might cut me from trials. It hurts like hell, but it's a possibility I can live with, because not helping Dylan would be far worse.

I've spent the last two hours sitting in the same place, on the top row of bleachers at the far end of the pool, trying to talk myself into undoing it all. I don't think all of the time in the world would get me to do that, though. I give in to the ache settling into my lower back and legs, and I climb down from my perch to make my way back inside.

My uncle is hard at work at his desk when I enter our room, a small cloth wrapped around a sharp tool, his eyepiece focused, and his headlamp on. He's so meticulous.

"You actually *clean* the parts nobody sees?" I ask.

He looks up at me, one eye squinting while the other holds on to the magnifier.

"I do when it means something will keep working for years to come. Seems lazy not to put in that little extra bit of effort," he says, looking back down and returning to work.

I step back and tilt my head, feeling a little put in my place.

"Right," I say, nodding and chewing at the inside of my cheek. "I'll brew a new pot of coffee then. Do my part."

"Sounds good," my uncle growls.

I laugh silently to myself because despite my uncle's slight frame, portly belly, and thinning hair, he can still wear the confidence of a tough guy when he's right. And he is…right. It does seem lazy not to go the extra mile.

I fill the pot with water and slide it into place, pressing the two-cup option. My uncle pulls out one of the mismatched wooden chairs from the small card table we've been eating our dinners at. I lean against the counter space where the fridge and coffee pot are housed and fold my arms, preparing myself for more words of wisdom, when he slides the watch he's been working on across the table. The band is polished platinum, and the face is antiqued, but also a style one doesn't find any more. I slide it closer and pull it into my hands, admiring his work while the tiny second hand makes its pass around the dial and the exposed gears underneath work in unison.

"It's remarkable," I say, holding my hand out to him to take it back.

"It's yours," he says.

My brow lowers.

"It was your dad's, Will. Our dad gave it to him when he went off to college, as a gift. Your dad wore it for many years, but then it stopped working. I always promised him I'd get around to fixing it. Took a little longer than I planned to, I guess," my uncle says. He chews at the corner of his mouth while his eyes stare at the treasure held in my palms.

"Dunc, I don't know what to say…"

I turn the watch over, the date engraved on the back instantly recognizable.

"It was their anniversary," my uncle says.

I smile, barely.

"I know," I say, quietly.

I trace the cold metal rim with my thumb.

"Should be set to the right time," he says.

I nod just as the sound of the coffee beginning to drip kicks in. I swallow and turn to face the pot, holding the watch carefully in my hands, unable to take my eyes off it.

"Thank you, Duncan. This…it means a lot," I say.

My uncle's chair slides out, and soon I feel his heavy hand pat my upper back twice.

"I know it does, Will. That's why I had to finish it. You needed to have something of his that meant something," he says.

Slipping my hand inside, I fasten the band around my wrist, the fit almost perfect. When I twist my wrist, there's a faint sense of recognition—my arm reminiscent of my father's, and I smile again seeing that. When the dripping coffee finishes, I pull the pot from the machine and fill both of our cups, setting my uncle's on the center of the table to cool while I add a shot of milk and a sugar packet to my own.

My uncle takes his in his hand and drinks, not even bothering to blow away the steam. Hot and black, exactly the way it was made. Even the way he takes his coffee matches his personality.

"That sweet girl we both love has been sitting over there in that room for the entire morning," my uncle says, jarring me out of my trance and jolting me enough to splash coffee onto the leg of my swim shorts.

"Shit!" I let out, setting my mug down and blotting the spot with a towel. It's hot, but I'm pretty sure that's not what I'm swearing about.

I toss the towel into our sink, and leave my mug on the counter, walking over to the door, but stopping and pacing back into the small kitchenette. I follow this same pattern three more times before my uncle chuckles.

"Did she come by while I was swimming?" I ask.

My uncle pulls his lips in, his eyes laughing at me while he shakes his head *no*.

"She's just as bad as you are. She'd rather sit over there, in the dark, than come in here and have a real conversation," he says.

I open my mouth to ask another question, but then his words settle in, so I close my mouth and take a sharp breath in through my nose.

Straight. Black. Hot. Honest. Just like his damned coffee.

I turn back to the door, but I don't move. Frozen here in limbo.

"You gonna go over there and talk to her? Or are you gonna crack the door open and spy?" my uncle asks in a gravelly voice as he passes by me, his hot coffee in one hand and the TV remote in the other. I twist my lips at his back as he passes.

"I just don't want to interrupt something. Maybe she wants time alone," I say.

"Or maybe you're just a chicken shit," he says, not waiting for my response as he clicks on the late morning news and kicks his feet up on the oak coffee table, settling deep into the cushions. He'll be napping as soon as that cup is drained, caffeine or not.

I think about flipping him off, but I can't even do it behind his back because the old man is right. I am a chicken shit.

I slip into the bedroom to change out of my trunks, not bothering to hang them since they're dry from sitting around in them all morning, and I pull on my cargo shorts and the gray, long-sleeved thermal that I've worn so thin, it's actually cooler than any of my T-shirts.

Yesterday with Maddy was the closest thing I've had to normal in a long time, and we were at a male strip club. There was a small window on our drive home when I thought about asking her on a legit date. Every bit of me wanted to kiss her, but more than that, I wanted to feel the entire thing—the chase, the small little favors like holding her door open. Then Tanya called, and shit just quit feeling like I deserved more than I had already gotten out of life. I still have more I need to give to get myself back to even.

Maddy needs to understand why I'm going to be gone Thursday and Friday, though, so I roll my shoulders and pinch the bridge of my nose, squeezing my eyes closed and cracking my neck to one side. You'd think I was heading out to the dumpsters behind the schoolyard for a good old-fashioned ass kicking.

Maybe I am.

I leave our makeshift apartment, and pause for only a second before pressing my palm flat against the office door, pushing it open enough to slip inside. She had left it open the tiniest bit, and I wonder if she was hoping I'd notice when I walked upstairs the first time. I wish I had.

She's sitting in the window seat, her knees pulled up to her chest, her arms holding them in place. Her hair is messy waves, the way it looks when she just lets it dry after swimming, which means she probably got here early. She's been waiting here for a while.

"Hey," I say, my voice light, not wanting to scare her.

She turns slightly, her chin falling to her shoulder, but not far enough for her eyes to meet mine.

"Hey," she says, leaving her head in its place for a few long seconds before turning back to stare out the window.

I walk closer to her, rounding the desk behind her and sliding to sit on top of it, pushing a few of the tools my uncle has left here to the side.

"You working on your dad's books or something?" I ask.

She laughs lightly.

"I never want to see those books," she says. "I bet they're a nightmare. Receipts stapled to margins, arrows pointing to expenses, moving them from month-to-month. This place is an IRS treasure trove."

I look around, layers of dust on binders stacked haphazardly in a nearby bookcase, each marked with a year in black Sharpie on the spine.

"Your dad used to swear up a storm when he worked on that crap up here," I say.

Maddy turns her head again, her eyes moving to the same bookcase I looked toward. Her shoulders rise with a short laugh, and I see her mouth curve on the right with a smile.

"He sure did," she says. Her chest rises slowly, her body moving as she breathes in deep, then exhales. "My mom does it all now. Mostly on the computer. They just like to store things up here."

"You still come here to hide, I see," I say, holding my bottom lip between my teeth, worried that I overstepped with that statement, about *hiding*.

Her head waggles from side-to-side, and she adjusts her posture, leaning forward and pressing her head against the glass.

"I guess. I just always liked to watch the world from up here," she says.

I study her. I look at her so long that minutes pass, neither of us saying a word, and when Maddy finally speaks, it hits me dead center.

"I used to watch you. You and Evan, but mostly...if I'm being honest...I looked at you when I came up here," she says.

My throat tightens, and I let my head fall forward, looking at my dangling feet above the wooden planks of the floor.

"You can't see the pool from here," I say.

"I know," she says. The silence that follows makes me think she's done, but after several seconds, she says something I've ached to hear since I was sixteen. "I'd wait to see if you were coming to practice, too. It was the only place I could look at you like a part of me really wanted to."

My jaw works side to side and I hold the back of my tongue between my teeth, trying not to be a chicken shit. My eyes close, and I keep my head down.

"And how's that?" I ask, every breath I take after the question hurting my chest.

The short silence that follows is filled with her breathing, my heart pounding, my fingers gripping the edge of the desk hard, my soul hoping.

"Like maybe I should have fallen in love with you instead," she says, the last word escaping with only a breath, barely audible, but enough that I heard it perfectly clear.

"What are you saying, Maddy?" I ask, lifting my head to find her looking at me over her shoulder.

She shakes her head, her forehead dimpled with worry and confusion. I'm sure I look the same. All it takes is for her tongue to pass lightly over her bottom lip for me to slide from the desk and walk over to her, coming as close as I can without touching her.

"I don't know what anything means anymore, Will," she says.

I shake my head.

"Evan was my whole life. He was the plan, and I know..." she takes a sharp breath, a small sob escaping her chest. "I know he was planning on marrying me, Will. I even think he was going to ask. Before you all left that night, he wanted to talk."

My eyes grow heavy, and my heart stills completely. She couldn't be farther from the truth, and this moment—it's literally breaking me into two halves. I want to protect her, but I also want her more than I've ever wanted anything in my life. How can I keep saving her when every greedy bone of my body wants her for my own?

"My being here," I say, moving my hands to my pockets and forcing my feet to slide a step away, to give myself distance from temptation. "I haven't made anything better for you, and I'm so sorry, Maddy..."

"No, that's not it," she says, her body turning until her legs fall to the floor.

Her hands reach for my wrists, and I grow weak, letting her pull them from my pockets and bring them close to her, my body following. She turns one hand over, her thumb running along the metal of the watch I'd just been given, and I watch her eyes react to it. It's obvious it's old, and there's a part of her that suspects it was probably my father's. I can tell by the reverence with which she admires it. She looks up at me slowly, her cheek falling against one open palm, and the pleading look in her eyes undoes me. My hands move into her hair, and I step closer, gently coaxing her to stand, her chin resting on my chest as I lean my head forward and brush my nose against her, my mouth grazing her cheek, my eyes closing as I inhale.

"What is it, Maddy?" I whisper into her ear. "If I haven't made things worse, then what? Tell me?"

Her hands fall from my wrists to my chest, her fingers slowly grasping fists full of my shirt. I watch her face fall into me and her mouth part, her lips touch my chest, kissing lightly and trembling in-between.

"You've made everything clear. You've made me feel whole, like something was missing for the last four years, and now that it's in place, I'm stronger," she says.

I reach down and lift her chin, and her eyes open on mine as I do.

"I meant what I said yesterday, Maddy," I say. "Your laugh…your smile? It's just as beautiful as I remember it. As beautiful as…as I always thought it was, even if it wasn't mine to admire."

Her eyes widen with a flare at my confession, and I know by the way she breathes that she understands the truth barely hidden behind those words. I've wanted Maddy since she dared me to beat her when we were kids racing in the pool. I've wanted to kiss her since I wrapped my hands around hers on the rope swing, and I know in my gut that I loved her first. I loved her more…and I loved her first.

I breathe through my nose, holding on to the quickly losing battle my conscience is having over what's right and wrong—what would be a betrayal and what is just life, continuing on. The longer I look into her deep brown eyes, the clearer everything becomes, until the choice is no longer a choice, it's just something I have to do.

My hands slide around her body slowly, and my eyes hold their gaze on hers, waiting for the cue that tells me to stop. When it doesn't come, I lift her up so her body is flush with mine, and I spin around and set her on the desk, her hands not once letting go of their grip on my shirt.

Her bottom lip quivers, and I press my finger to it, stepping away just long enough to push the door closed completely and lock it. We don't need anyone walking in, making either of us question whatever happens in the next several minutes.

I walk back to her quickly, and her mouth opens in a way that I know she's about to doubt what we're doing. I can't let that happen, because it's poisonous, and it will halt me before I can just see…I need to see if this is real, if she feels this, too.

Without pause, I reach through her hair, threading my fingers through the strands, and tilting her head up just enough that her lips are waiting for mine to cover them. I kiss her hard; she leans back with my force, her hands falling to the desktop behind her to catch herself.

"I won't let you fall," I say against her mouth.

She tilts her head just enough that our eyes meet. A breath. Two. Her hands move from their careful place to my neck, and the second I feel her fingers in my hair, I taste her mouth again. My hands move to her back, and when she arches I groan at the feel of her breasts against my chest.

I let her lead, with everything, content to have this, to kiss her raw and memorize every curve of her mouth and bend of her back. Her hands fall down my chest, though, reaching for the bottom of my shirt and lifting it up and over my head, her fingers retracing their path down my chest and abs to the button on my shorts. She grabs the waist of my shorts and pulls me closer, until my dick is pressed to the center of her legs, and the heat that radiates sends me to a place I don't think I'll have the power to come back from.

She's wearing a thin, black T-shirt that I lift up easily, taking the black bra underneath away with it. My hands roam along her shoulder blades, the curve of her back and to her arms, but I keep my eyes on hers, almost afraid to look at this much of her. I know I'll never be able to forget any of this, and if something goes wrong, which isn't far from likely, I know the further in I fall, the more painful every memory will be.

Maddy's hands trace along my shoulders and down my arms until she weaves her fingers with mine, and she pushes me away enough that I have no choice but to see all of the girl—every bit of her that I have dreamt of for years. Her hair tickles along her shoulders, barely falling down her front, the length not quite making it over her breasts. Her nipples are hard peaks, and I hunger for them.

"Goddamn, you're everything I thought you would be, Maddy. You're more," I say, her eyes hazing with my words.

Her mouth curves up on the right, just slightly, and she holds onto my hands as she lowers herself back to the desk, arching the second her shoulders hit the wood, her head falling back until her hair cascades over the other side of the desk.

I let go of her hands and lay my palms flat against her bare stomach, my fingers aching to travel both directions, my cock so hard that I think I might break through the zipper on my pants. I indulge and lean forward, letting my hands travel up her ribs slowly, counting the deep breaths she takes in anticipation of my touch, teasing her when I meet the curve of her breast and taking my time arriving to the very tips. When my thumbs graze over her hard nipples, she whimpers, her body squirming and her back arching into me, begging for more pressure.

"You want more…here," I say, leaning over her and taking one of the peaks into my teeth, holding on with light pressure while my tongue passes over her skin. I draw it out until she arches again, and then I suck hard, leaving her nipple pink and raw.

I stand tall and cup her breasts, letting my fingers tickle down her body, to her stomach, slowing as I pass over the band of her cotton shorts, then over the gray material until my thumbs hover just over her center.

"Or do you want more…" I pause, pressing my thumb against her, feeling how swollen and wet she is through her shorts. "Here?"

"Oh god," she cries, and I rub her harder, her hips writhing on the end of the desk, her body wriggling to get closer to me.

I kneel in front of her, between her knees, hooking my fingertips in her waistband, sliding her shorts and the silky panties underneath over her hips, then down her thighs. I close my eyes once and breathe in slowly to force myself to take my time, to make sure I'm aware of any signs she gives, any hesitation I sense.

My hand starts at her calf, sliding slowly up her leg, over her knee and the inside of her leg until I reach the place I just was. I glance up to her body, one hand held hostage by her teeth gripping her knuckles and the other a fist on the wood of the desk until her fingers open and flex. I press my thumb against her, stroking her slowly, her body responding with my rhythm. I let my finger dip inside once, holding my place for a few seconds so she can adjust, until I feel her body relax as she rocks her hips to take me deeper. I lean forward, and I taste her with my tongue, feeling how ready she is, tasting how badly she wants me—wants this.

Unable to hold on to slow, I stand and unbutton my shorts, dropping them to the floor and taking my cock in my hand, stroking it while I stand before her bare naked body, splayed open and ready for me on an old wooden desk. Papers have slid to the floor, my uncle's tools have fallen—her beautiful body amid the mess we've made. I don't have anything with me. This…*this*…is not something I have done for several months. And this time is different, it's more. I rest my hand against her pelvis and step forward, sliding my tip along her soft folds, teasing her until I'm coated in her, until nothing less will do but burying my dick deep inside her.

"I don't have anything, Maddy. If we keep going, it's going to be…"

"I'm on the pill. I'm fine, I trust you," she pants. Her eyes open on mine and her hand falls away from her mouth, her lips a bright pink from the rough kisses I left behind. I hold myself at her entrance, uncertain, but so goddamned ready, until she bites her bottom lip and nods slowly, her eyes closing just enough and her lip curling in the anticipation of pleasure.

I move forward and fall into her, splitting her and pushing so deep that her body moves along the desk, so I grip her shoulder hard and she wraps her hands around my arms.

"Oh god, Will. More of that, please!" she begs, so I pull out of her completely and then enter her again, this time ready to hold her against me while I push forward. Her legs fall open even wider, and her body arches.

"Yes!"

I slide out again, grabbing myself and waiting, watching her eyes flutter, her mouth pant, and her breathing grow ragged until I fuck her again. I move my hand under her back and I pull her body close so I can suck her breast while my dick moves in and out of her. I push hard, and I bite her nipple raw, then I move to the next, turning and lifting her body with me so I'm sitting on the desk and she's straddling me, her knees on either side while her body lifts up and down, riding me.

I grab her ass, my fingers gripping her skin so hard I might leave bruises in my wake, but I hold on anyhow, moving her up and down on my cock, the pressure building while we both chase this feeling that's better than any high, than driving drunk and racing no one. This is what I've been missing, this is what was supposed to be—Maddy and me, we were the right fit. This can't be wrong. It's too perfect…too right and too good.

"Jesus, Maddy," I growl into the small of her neck, her hair sticking to my damp skin, her body moving hard and fast while she slides up and down. My hips meet her rhythm, and I push into her, the force growing with every move, until we both press our mouths against one another's necks to stifle the moans and cries that we can't help but make from a release so desperate and hard that it leaves us both shattered when our bodies collapse on the desk.

Maddy falls against me, and I pull her up, turning us so I'm lying on the desk and her body is on mine, her perfectly toned machine of a body completely wrapped in my arms and legs, sticky from our sweat and our sex.

I feel regret knocking against my heart. I feel it threatening to creep into my head. I see glimpses of faces—of Dylan, of Tanya…*of Evan*. I push them all away, bury them deep, and I gather Maddy's hair into my palm, pressing my lips against the side of her face.

"I need you to stay, Will," she says. "No matter what…if you lose, if I lose. If this gets hard, whatever this is. I need you to stay until we figure it out. And even then, I just think…"

She lifts her head, and I cup her face in my hands, her eyes locking on mine.

"I think I just need you to stay," she says.

I stare at her for several seconds, holding my breath, my mind racing with all of my demons, and with everyone else's demons, too. I fear none of it is possible. I'm going to break her heart. Those demons—they'll destroy her. But I can't give her up. I need her to stay, too. Even though I can't promise it; even though I shouldn't, I say exactly what she needs to hear. I let myself believe it for the breath it takes to speak.

"Okay," I say, bringing her lips to mine, kissing her softly, then closing my eyes as her forehead rests against mine. "Okay," I whisper again.

I may have to break this promise, but for right now…for right now, I mean it.

CHAPTER 10

Will

My fingers have been fumbling with these damned cufflinks for about twenty minutes. I'm about ready to toss them down the hall, down the steps, maybe go down there and kick them out the door and into the pool.

"What's wrong with you? Come here and give me your damn arms," my uncle says, dropping the newspaper he's been reading before waving me over to the sofa.

He slides his glasses to the end of his nose and jerks both sides of my sleeve a few times, lining up the slits. When he loses his grip on one end the first time and swears under his breath, I chuckle.

"Not so easy, is it?" I say.

"Well it would be if you wore a shirt that fit. This one's too tight for your arms, and the cuffs aren't sitting in the right spot," he says, jerking them in place again.

"Nothing fits me right. I have big arms," I say.

"Yeah, yeah…show off," he says, pushing the pin through and twisting it. He drops his hold on my wrist and curls his fingers asking for the other.

"Thanks," I say, admiring the flat, silver circles he fastened.

He glances up at me, smirking just as he twists the other one and pushes my hand away.

"Don't mention it," he says.

I walk over to the counter and put my watch back on, taking a minute to soak in how my hands look with my father's cufflinks and watch. My uncle gave me the links this morning, telling me I could keep them too. I may never wear them again, but I want them all the same.

"So where is this fancy dinner thing?" my uncle says, stepping up behind me and holding my jacket out. More tight shit to shove my arms into.

"At the Woodsens'. Maddy's mom thought it would be nice to have everyone over, sort of a team-building thing I guess," I shrug.

Curtis showed up yesterday minutes after Maddy left, and I only heard half of the words he said, because my head was too busy trying to process what had happened with Maddy, and whether or not her dad saw her leave or passed her on the way out. Even though he probably would just assume she was here swimming, I knew she wasn't. And the memory of us was so vivid I felt like he could see it in my eyes.

I focused enough to get that we would have this dinner, there were some sponsors he wanted a few of us to meet, and that he was lining up some interviews. I told him I'd have to think about the interviews, but when he left, I got the sense my thinking wouldn't factor into whether or not they happened.

My uncle straightens the collar of my shirt and the shoulders of my jacket, brushing along the arms and front and pulling spots where things just look crooked. I own two suits, and the other one was the one I was arraigned in. That makes this one luckier, I suppose.

"You spent a lot of time with Maddy yesterday," my uncle says, one eyebrow higher than the other. I lower one of mine, glaring at him.

"And…" I say.

"And…a lot of time probably gives you enough time to tell that girl the things she needs to know," he says.

I scowl, stretching my arms and testing how far I can bend them in this woolen straight jacket. I stuff my wallet in my coat pocket and circle our small apartment for my keys, finding them and giving my uncle one more glance as I head for the door. He follows me out, waiting in the hallway, letting me get a few steps away before giving me one more thing to feel tormented over.

"You don't owe anyone, Will," he says.

I stop, my head slumps forward, and I think instantly of all the people I *do* owe.

"I mean all of them, too, Will. You don't owe Tanya. You don't owe Dylan. I know you have a big heart, and you're trying to do what's right, but don't let it get in the way of giving yourself a little joy, ya know? You've earned it, son. This life is over in a blink. Don't spend so much of it punishing yourself over something that wasn't even your goddamned fault in the first place."

I take his words in for a few seconds, then turn, my gaze rising just enough to find his righteous one.

"Hard to think that way when they're all gone, Duncan. That's all," I say, turning and leaving without another word from my uncle.

It takes only a few minutes to get to the Woodsen home, and Maddy's mom is out front greeting a couple who pulled along the curb right before me. I push my car into park and check my mirror, looking myself in the eyes for a last-minute gut check. I need to talk to Curtis today about taking Thursday and Friday off, and I know I'm going to have to give an explanation to Maddy. I won't lie, but the entire truth can't happen either.

There's a loud knock on my passenger window, and my pulse doubles simply seeing her face. Maddy's bent forward, her hair falling over one eye, her shoulders bare from the white dress that's only held up by thin straps. Goddamn, she's an angel.

I roll the window down.

"You comin' in? Or you just planning on joining the party from out here?" She giggles and turns her head, looking at me sideways, and it does something unexpected to my chest—it fills it full.

I unlock the door, and she opens the passenger side, sliding in to sit next to me, pulling the rest of her long dress in between her feet before shutting the door and swinging her eyes my direction. I lean forward and fold my arms on the wheel, my head on my hands looking at her.

"I hate parties," I say.

"Me too," she says, the words coming from one end of her mouth. I smile seeing it, and she blushes. "What?"

"I have always…*always*…loved the way you talk," I say.

My heart races again. Maddy looks down at her hands in her lap, and I worry for a second I've made her uncomfortable. She bites her lip, though, and a smile hits her mouth on the side closest to me just before she glances at me with her head cocked at an angle, and I'm instantly glad I said what I did.

"Think we can just skip it? Hit the gas, drive to…I don't know…Chicago? Spend the day on Lake Michigan? Go to some museums. See the Cubs!"

Her eyes are wide, and I almost think she's serious until she sighs and falls back into her seat.

"Probably not, huh?" she says.

"Probably not," I say, motioning out the window where her dad is standing a few yards away, his arms folded and his eyes watching our every move.

"He likes you, Will. Don't be nervous," she chuckles.

I pull the key from the car and push my door open, sliding the keys in my pocket while I round the back of the car and meet Maddy just in time to take her hand while she exits my car. I'm playful with her fingers, and we both look at our flirting hands.

"I don't think he'd like me very much if he knew all of the things I want to do to you," I say quietly.

Her fingers keep playing along with mine, and I hear her swallow. I chuckle and hold my arm out for her to take, and she looks down, her cheeks red as she slides her arm through mine, her hands wrapping around my bicep and forearm. I lean into her, urging her to look up at me.

"A thousand parties," I say.

She quirks a brow and squints. I lean in close enough to whisper while we walk.

"I'd go to a thousand parties if I got to walk in with you on my arm," I say.

Her head falls against my shoulder, and her hands squeeze where they hold. I feel strong enough to survive anything.

Maddy's mom, Susan, has joined Curtis just outside the door while we walk up, and their expressions couldn't possibly be more different. Susan's eyes look a happy kind of surprised, and Curtis looks like he wants to take me out back and dispose of my body in the alley. On instinct, and perhaps a little out of self-preservation, I slide Maddy's arm loose from mine and let her go when we reach the door.

"Will, I haven't seen you enough. I'm so glad you could come today," Susan says, hugging me and kissing my cheek. She feels like home, too.

"Not sure this party was optional," I say, letting her go and glancing from her to her husband. His face is still stern, and I'm pretty sure he's gritting his back teeth. "But I would have come no matter what."

"Well, either way, I'm glad you did," Susan says, patting my shoulder, and walking inside, leaving me alone with Maddy's dad.

"You two seem to have found your way," he says, his lips twisted and pushed together tight.

"I've missed her, is all," I say.

Okay, I lie sometimes. I lie to this man, because he scares the everloving shit out of me, and because I have now seen his daughter naked, and I feel like he knows.

"Uh huh," Curtis says, blinking when he turns his eyes away from me, stepping in and holding the door as I pass. He shuts it behind us, and I wait for his lead, following him down the hallway to the main room that has been cleared out to make room for tabletops and mingling. Suddenly, my jacket feels tighter.

"I have some folks I'd like you to meet, if you've got a minute?" Curtis says, turning to me as we step into the crowd. There are about twenty of us swimming at the club, and we're all here, but mix in the people with money, family members, dates and such, and it's hard to maneuver around the modest Woodsen home. I manage to follow Curtis through the tables to two men standing by the door. Their suits—they seem to fit right.

"Will, this is Craig and Allan Cumberland," he doesn't need to finish the intro for me to get exactly who they are. I wear their suit. I've *always* worn their suit.

"Nice to meet you," I say, very aware of my grip. I squeeze hard, and I get a smirk from one of them.

"Likewise, Will. I'm Allan, this is Craig," the taller of the two says.

I glance between them and catch a glimpse of Maddy, standing at a table with Amber and her friend Holly. They're all laughing over something, but Maddy's pretending. I can tell; her eyes are on me, and she's watching this conversation.

"Been following your story for a while, Will," Craig says. "You've overcome a lot. It's pretty inspiring."

My mouth falls to a straight line and I look down when a server walks by and drops a napkin at our table for each of us. Prophetic.

"Water for me, thanks," I say before she has a chance to zip off and fetch wine for all of us. She nods, and I catch Curtis's stare, his tight smile.

"I wouldn't say it's inspiring," I say, in response to Craig. "Those things were all kinda my own doing, for the most part. Just trying to claw my way back, I guess—prove something."

"I think you're proving things to a lot of people just by going to the trials," Allan says.

"Maybe," I say, happy that the server returns quickly with my water. I twist the cap and guzzle nearly half of it down, relieved to have something to busy myself with.

"The Cumberlands were thinking, Will...since you wear their suits and all, maybe there's an opportunity for some sit-downs, a few interviews, nothing too big..." Curtis's words trail off while he waits for my reaction. Everyone at this table is watching me drink from a water bottle, and I do my best to smile with my eyes.

"Maybe," I say.

By the way Curtis's face falters, I can tell that *maybe* was not what he was hoping for. He should feel lucky, though. My instinct was an immediate *no thanks*.

"Great, we'll work on some details, run them by you," Curtis says, suddenly attracted to someone on the other side of the room. "We'll catch up with you later. Gentlemen, I went to the Olympics with this guy over here. Come with me so I can introduce you."

They all leave, and I rest my elbows on the table, glad to be alone. Maddy walks up, taking my water from my hands and finishing it herself.

"I hate wine," she shrugs.

I breathe out a laugh.

The room grows busy with shaking hands and ass kissing, and my jacket feels more and more snug.

"You wanna go sit outside with me for a bit? Escape a little?" I tilt my head toward the patio door.

"God, do I," Maddy smiles.

I follow her through the crowd, and she grabs two more water bottles from the bar set up in the corner on our way outside. She slides the glass door shut behind us when we slip out, and I pull two of the patio chairs into a corner, out of the view of the guests inside. Before I sit down, I slip off my jacket and drape it over the back, flexing my fingers and wishing like hell I could pop these cufflinks off, too.

Maddy's knee grazes against mine when she sits, and instinctually, I lean closer. Her fingers trail along my wrist, and my hands open, finally relaxing as she pinches the plain silver link on my left cuff.

"Your dad's?" Her question isn't *really* a question.

"Yeah. Duncan gave them to me this morning. He fixed this up for me, too," I say, laying my other wrist on my knee to show her the watch.

"I figured that was his. It looks like him," she smiles.

She's right. It does.

I reach forward and sweep her hair behind her ear, her eyes glancing to me as her lip quirks up on one side. I slide my finger down to the tip of her nose, then brush my knuckle against her mouth.

"You look beautiful," I say.

Her mouth pulls into a tight smile, her cheeks round and red.

"Thanks," she says, her voice raspy.

Her eyes hit mine, and we stare at each other without breathing for a while, but I can't hold up my façade for longer than a few seconds. I feel my muscles in my face give, my eyes slanting and mouth falling back to that straight line of dread.

I need to tell her about my trip. I need to tell her *something*.

I swallow hard, and her eyes flinch just a little. She's expecting bad news, which if I shared it all, it would be devastating. I smile and shake my head, needing to fix her frown.

"No, it's nothing…nothing bad, anyway, just…I have to go on a trip. I leave early Thursday. And…I'm going to miss more time, so your dad…" I stop there.

Her mouth twists as she realizes my predicament. Missing time will not work in my favor here. Curtis might be inclined to cut me loose.

"My dad loves you," she says.

I give her a wry smile.

"Really, Will…he does," she adds.

I laugh lightly and lean back into the chair, folding my hands behind my neck, cracking my knuckles before shrugging and letting my arms fall to my side.

"Maybe, but this is my second miss. And we have a practice meet next week. I'm already a gamble, Maddy. He's gonna want to cut me," I say.

"Then don't miss," she answers fast.

I open my mouth, the words almost coming out before my brain acts as defense, but I pause with my lips parted, the truth right there, on the tip of my tongue.

I close my mouth tight and shake my head, then look down at my hands, folded in my lap, thumbs rubbing my skin.

"It's not something I can miss," I say, glancing sideways at her. Her face still looks the same—confused, worried…maybe hurt.

"More *paperwork?*" The word is rancid when it leaves her mouth. I don't respond, instead just staring back at her with nothing but apology behind my eyes.

"I have to help a friend," I say, needing to give her something, some version of the truth. I can't have her looking at me like I'm a failure, or like my secrets have anything to do with my DUI, or the bad habits I've avoided now for months.

"Is this friend…someone I know?" She cocks her head, her eyelids falling.

I shake my head and look back at my hands. I need to give her more. Not all, but more.

"It's a close friend, someone I know from State. It's for her kid. He's severely disabled, and he's having these seizures, and…and they don't have any family here, none anywhere, really, that can help. They have a consultation in Cleveland, and I…*have* to make sure they make that appointment," I say, looking up to meet her eyes as I say those final words.

Please don't ask any more questions, Maddy.

"He'll make an exception for you, Will," she says finally, standing and moving so her hands are on the back of her chair, her body facing me. "He'll make an exception because you're the one bringing the sponsors to this thing. But you're going to need to do those interviews."

Her forehead dents, and I know it's because she knows how badly I don't want to talk about the accident, my parents, and my brother.

"I know," I nod, standing and moving toward her. I move my hands so they cover hers, then I lean close and kiss her forehead, holding my mouth against her while my eyes peer through the window, taking in the happy, trouble-free faces inside. I need to turn Maddy into one of those, and I need to make sure she stays happy.

"I'm going to go find your dad, and let him know," I say, leaving her outside while I head in to swim with the sharks.

Maddy

There's a chance I might just stay out here. Minutes have passed, and nobody has come looking for me, so why fix a situation that isn't broken.

I slide back into the chair and kick my heels from my feet, tucking the skirt of my dress under my thighs so I can rest my feet on the empty chair Will left behind. I'm about to rest my eyes and breathe until I can let go of this nagging feeling in my stomach over Will when I hear the sliding glass followed by the voice of my best friend.

"Your position has been compromised," Holly says.

I crack one eyelid open as she moves a glass of wine in my hand then drags her chair next to mine, forcing my feet to fall to the ground.

"You're ruining my Zen," I say.

"Drink the wine. That'll help," she says, raising her glass before sipping on her own. "Why are we hiding?"

I shrug.

"Liar. Tell me," she says.

I laugh.

"It's been a while since I've had to be at one of these kinds of parties, and it turns out…I don't really like them," I say, raising my own wine and sipping.

My friend laughs loudly, and I lean forward to look inside, internally begging that nobody heard her and got clued in to the idea of stepping outside.

"Stop, it's fine. You can't hear a thing in there," she says. I meet her eyes to gauge how truthful she's being, and when I'm satisfied, I lean back and exhale. "I asked Will where you were."

I nod.

"He looked very…*intense*. Everything going all right with you two?" She shakes her shoulders, bobbing her head as if her question is innocent. I know better.

"We're getting along fine, Holly," I say, lips pursed.

She sips her wine, loudly, and stares at me over the rim.

"You…kiss him yet?" Her right brow shoots into her hairline.

I hold her stare, waiting too long to answer, and she moves to the next question.

"You sleep with him?"

My mouth betrays me, instantly reacting, remembering how his kiss felt, wanting more of them, more of his body and the unbelievable way he makes me feel when his hands are on me.

"Maddy Woodsen, you dirty girl!" she teases. "You're blushing. You fucked that boy, and you let him do dirty things."

"Holly, Jesus…shhhhh!" I sit up straight and grab her arms. She shrugs me away from the hand holding her wine and drinks the rest of it down, setting the glass on the ground when she's done.

"Well?" She waits, staring at me. I know what *well* means, and I know ignoring it isn't an option. She'll only move on to blunt questioning after this, using words that are going to make me want to hide in a hole.

"It was unbelievable," I say. I don't smile, though, and that's where I go wrong.

"Huh," she says, turning her head a fraction, eyes still studying me. "Your face says otherwise."

I sigh loudly.

"It was good. I don't know what else you want me to say." I suck at deflecting.

"Maddy, this is the first time you've had sex in four years. It's the second guy you've slept with, and it's the very hot brother of the guy you were going to marry. It's the juiciest shit I've ever witnessed—and I work in a hospital where interns shag in elevators and doctors cheat on their wives and husbands with one another. You can't use a word like *unbelievable*, and then follow it up with a face that looks like you want to weep and vomit at the same time."

Shit, do I really look like I want to vomit? Weep…maybe. I shake my head and sit up straight before letting my face fall into my hands, my fingers at my temples.

"He's got a lot of baggage, Holly. Fuck, we have some of the same damned bags," I say through a wry laugh.

"And…" She shrugs.

I look her in the eye and huff out a breath, blinking slowly, coming to terms with that feeling in my gut, with what it is.

"I feel like I'm hurting Evan," I say, my body deflating with the words. "It feels like a betrayal."

"Honey, Evan's gone," she says.

"Yeah, but Will is his brother!" My hand flies to my face, my fingers pinching the bridge of my nose. "He's the one person on this earth I should probably not fall for."

"But…you…are," she says the words slowly, like she's trying not to scare me when I hear them.

They do scare me, though. They're true. They're truer than true. I was honest with Will when I told him I used to look for him…*wait* for him. My attraction to him came in waves, first adolescent-crush-type attraction, then the more adult kind, and I buried it every time I felt the tinge in my belly, the giddiness at seeing him. I had dreams about him over the years, and I got jealous of his girlfriends. I'd feel the sting, then push it down until I couldn't feel in anymore. Evan was the safe choice, and I let myself fall for him because of it, but there's a part of me—a part of my heart—that always wanted Will more. I question that part because now there's nothing holding it back except for my fear of what other people are going to think about me.

"It isn't right," I say.

"Fuck that," she fires back, and I both laugh and shoot my eyebrows high at once. "Seriously, this world is full of judgmental assholes, and they would all be the first to throw rule books out the window if breaking the rules suited them."

"You're saying being with Will is against the rules?" I grimace.

"No, you're the one saying that," she says, picking up her glass and pointing it at me while she stands. "I'm just busting down that excuse, too. Knock it off and go let yourself be happy with that pretty, pretty man."

Her eyes move from me to her empty glass, and she smirks.

"Refill time. And I'm sleeping here tonight," she says, spinning and heading back inside.

I wait until the door snaps closed behind her before I let her lecture settle in. The thought of being with Will brings a smile to my face. It just happens, on autopilot, and anything that makes me smile like that can't be wrong. Is it going to become a story, though? Is it going to be the thing people talk about, what dominates the trials and the media—Will's interview? Does he need one more thing for the public to judge him about? First, he survived, then he nearly ruined his life. And now…he gets the girl—*his dead brother's girl*.

A chirping sound pulls me out of my messy thoughts, and I shake my head when I realize Will's jacket is still draped on the back of the chair. I pull it into my lap and feel along the pockets, finding his phone just as the call ends. Damn. I hope it wasn't important, or about his trip—the mystery person with the sick child.

I feel the phone buzz in my palm, my body radiates with suspicion. *Poison.* I turn the phone in my hand to see the screen: TANYA. VOICEMAIL. My thumb hovers over the name, twitching. I'm about to give up when another buzz in my palm startles me. The message is right there, in my hand.

TANYA: *He spoke today, Will. At therapy. He said your name, and he said Daddy.*

I'm shaking. My hand feels numb. I hold it with my other hand, ten fingers working together trying to convince each other not to throw the phone through the window—where I can see Will walking toward me right now.

I swallow hard, and a million things run through my head—all of them bad ideas. Will has a son. He has a son he doesn't talk about, doesn't share with anyone. There could be a million reasons why this is a secret he's kept, continues to keep. It has nothing to do with me and him, with *us*. But yet, it *so* does! How can he let me get so close, but keep something so important away from me? From all of us? How does he have a son!

"Maddy?"

He's in front of me before I have time to move, and my hands...they're still shaking.

"I didn't mean to look. I...I was going to bring your jacket inside, and I felt someone calling, and I didn't want it to be about your trip. I swear, Will..."

A deep crevice forms between his eyes, his mouth tightening as he steps closer, his eyes gazing along my hands, to his phone as he pulls it into his own grip slowly. I watch his eyes while he reads. I see the way his pupils scan, his eyes widening, his expression falling. Sympathy and regret and shame—they all mix right there in one look as his eyes move up to meet mine.

"You..." my lips are trembling too much to speak, so I bring my fist to my mouth to steady them, to feel something hard against my mouth to bring back the feeling. "You...have a son."

His eyes begin to water, and mine follow suit. I don't even know why, but the reaction is so visceral. Will has a son who is severely disabled, and needs care and attention. Will is here. With me. Why is Will here?

"He's the one you're helping," I say. His eyes fall closed and his head slumps. "He's who you were helping before...*paperwork*."

Will takes a few slow steps back, sitting in the chair I'd just lifted his jacket from. His eyes remain on the ground, and his hands clasp in front of him, his elbows on his knees. All he can do is nod slowly. He's agreeing with me. My chest twists so tight I can't breathe, so I bring my palms up to my cheeks, forcing myself to inhale deeply and hold it in my lungs.

"How could you not tell me?" I ask, my words coming out a little angrier. My lip quivers again, this time, it's the threat of rage. "How could you be so selfish, Will? What are you doing here? With me? Why aren't you with him—when he clearly *needs* his father? Oh my god, Will..."

I fall into the seat opposite of him, sick with grief. I grieve that glimpse of happiness that I just moments ago talked myself into having. I taste the bitterness of contempt. My body aches with torment, trying to connect the man I was starting to believe in with the one unraveling right here in front of me. I don't know how to do any of it. I don't know how to even look at him.

"How could you, Will? He's your family?"

His head jerks up the moment I utter that word, and I stare at him hard. His eyes dim briefly, as if I cut him and he were bleeding. He closes them for a breath, his chest rising slowly, his brow dimpled with the pains of getting caught. When he opens to look at me again, though, his eyes are resolute. The pain is still there, but something about his expression has shifted—his face tilted a hair to the left, his mouth pulled up ever so slightly on one side, his breathing calm and slow.

Pity.

"He's not my son, Maddy," he says.

The words don't make sense to me. They battle in my head.

"But her message," I start.

He shakes his head slowly, and I begin to mimic him, shaking my own, until his *no* shifts into a nod of *yes*.

"He's not…*my*…son," he repeats.

My mouth waters with sickness. My lips wrinkle, and the tears begin to pool, burning my eyes. I don't touch them. I drown in them. I wait to hear it. I make him say it. If he doesn't, I may never believe it.

"No," I utter.

His nod remains slow and unwavering.

"Say it," I whisper, my throat sore from the pain dying to claw its way out. "Say it!" The second time comes out harsh and gritty.

"He's my nephew," he says, and I fall to my knees on the ground. Will is quick to hold me, but I fight against him, pushing him away.

"You're lying!" I cry. "He's not. He didn't. You are lying!"

I push him so hard he falls back on his ass, sitting with his legs out in his fancy suit, his father's watch and cufflinks on his hands. I know right then he's right. I know that Will has been operating on duty, and I know that I've been mourning a lie.

"He's Evan's, Maddy, and I'm so goddamned sorry," he says, just as I lean forward and throw up every bit of wine I've had to drink.

"Come on," he says, his hands swiftly sliding under my legs and around my back. He carries me around the back of the house, into the darkness, to the small hose bib that my mother uses to fill her pail and water the roses. He turns it on and cups his hands, splashing water on my puked-on arms and legs, trying to rinse away my vomit from my dress.

I weep without sound, nothing but a never-ending rush of tears cascading down my hot cheeks. I'm certain they will leave behind burns, scars that will never ever let me forget how wrong my fucking heart was to choose Evan Hollister.

"You lied to me, Will," I breathe out.

His mouth is a hard line while he washes his hands and lifts my legs one at a time, rinsing them under the water.

"How could you lie?" I ask.

He turns the water off, then looks me square in the eyes.

"How could I not?" he says.

We both stare into one another raw and broken, our breathing labored, our eyes red, our skin blotched and marked with lost hopes and regret and all of the goddamned *what ifs* that don't matter worth shit.

Will looks to the side when we hear the sound of the door opening, and his eyes flash back to me. Without pause, he lifts me in his arms again, carrying me around the side of the house and to the street. He unlocks his car and sets me down in the passenger seat, then rushes to the other side, stopping to talk to someone I can't see.

"She had too much to drink. I'm going to get her out of here, so it doesn't embarrass her," he says.

I hear Holly's voice respond.

"I'll cover for you," she says.

In a blink, Will's in the car next to me, and we're driving to the club. When we get there, Will stops in front of the building, kills the engine, and squeezes the steering wheel in his hands tightly. His jaw clenches and his face grows red as his hands slam against the wheel three times, the pounding sound making me flinch.

"I'm so sorry, Maddy. I never wanted this for you, and I'm just…I'm sorry," he says, getting out of the car, but stopping before the door shuts completely. "Take all the time you need. I'll leave the doors all unlocked. I'll tell you anything you want to know, but make sure you really want to know it."

When the door closes gently behind him, I begin to bawl. I don't stop for hours, and I never go inside the club.

CHAPTER 11

Maddy

There's something to be said about hitting bottom. There's comfort in it, knowing that no matter what comes along, nothing—absolutely nothing—can pull you any lower than you already are.

I thought losing Evan was bottom, and living with the guilt that there was a part of me that didn't want to marry him—that evaded the conversation that last day, before he left, making sure he didn't ask.

That wasn't even close to the depths I've fallen in the last twenty-four hours. I'm so far below bottom, I've burrowed into the earth.

I walked home under the stars. It was after midnight by the time I made it to my parents' house, and they were still busy entertaining sponsors to notice me. I crawled into my mattress bed next to my snoring best friend, and it's like she knew, opening her arm and letting me snuggle up next to her. I never slept, and I'm awake now, the morning light not stopping for me or my misery. I'm wrapped in the blanket my mom saves for guests while I watch my friend tug a travel hairbrush through her tangled red strands.

"You look like Annie," I say, smiling on the side of my mouth that's mushed into my pillow.

Holly doesn't turn around, but she gives me the finger with her free hand. She hates *Annie* jokes. She's gotten them most of her life. She's exactly how I picture Annie growing up, though—if she became a nurse, drank like a sailor, and brought home strange men from the bar.

"You ready to be coherent about whatever the hell happened last night? I know you weren't drunk. And I know you were upset. I didn't have *that* much wine," she says.

I roll so my face is buried into the pillow, and I pull the blanket around my head, blocking all of the light. I don't know why telling Evan's secret makes me feel ashamed, but it does—like I'm admitting I wasn't good enough for him to remain faithful.

"Evan...had a baby," I say, my voice muffled by the mattress and linens.

"What the shit?" Clearly, not so muffled it couldn't be heard.

I roll to my back and kick the blanket down my legs, watching as my friend's eyes move down my body, to the dress I'm still wearing from the night before.

"Girl, it's like, even worse than the walk of shame. You didn't even get to orgasm," she says, sitting on the end of the mattress and tugging the end of my dress down my knees. "At least let me make you look modest."

I laugh, barely, and pull myself up to sit, pressing my palms into my swollen eyes.

"You wanna talk about it?" she shrugs.

The easy answer here is *no*. I don't ever want to talk about it. Evan's dead, and my last four, five...hell eight years may have been a total lie. I want to pretend none of it happened, but then pretending that would erase parts of Will, too. The last several days.

The last eight years I've been noticing him and trying to pretend I wasn't.

"There's not much to talk about, really. I saw a text from the girl to Will, and I sorta jumped to one conclusion, and when he corrected me, I'm not sure what conclusion was worse—the one I had wrong, or the truth," I say.

"I'm only half following you here," she says, pulling her purse into her lap and taking out a packet of mints. She hands them to me, and I take four. Her eyebrow lifts.

"I threw up. My mouth tastes horrible," I say.

My friend hands me two more, then puts her mints away.

I manage to stumble my way into the bathroom and splash water on my face, leaving my dress in a pile on the floor, and putting on a clean pair of shorts and a T-shirt, twisting my hair into a bun. This is as put-together as I think today is going to get. When I step back into my room, my friend has her keys in her hand, and I frown immediately.

"I'm sorry, babe. I'd stay, but I have so much to get done before tomorrow. The hospital has been so busy, and I have two tests this week," she says.

I sigh heavily then move toward her open arms, letting her hug me.

"Look, I'm not sure I understand everything, but I do understand one thing that I don't think you should lose sight of," she says.

"What's that?" I ask, my face muffled against her shoulder.

She pulls back from me, but keeps her hands on my arms, squaring me to look her in the eyes.

"You and Will have been making each other happy. That guy has made you light up in a way I have never seen, and if he's been keeping a secret from you about his brother, maybe it's because he didn't want you to feel the pain it may cause," she says.

I breathe in deep, and her eyes stay open on mine, her face serious.

"Maddy, Will's not the one who cheated on you," she says, stepping into me and kissing my head.

My mouth twists, and I nod slowly. I know she's right, but the fact that Will didn't let me know any of this—that maybe he knew all along—still feels ugly. If the roles were reversed, and a girl he had been with for years was having a relationship with someone else on the side, I think I'd have to let him know. Especially if that girl was my sister.

I walk Holly to the front door and see her off. The rest of the house is quiet. The mess from the party is still scattered around the kitchen and the borrowed tabletops placed around the main room, so I go to work in the kitchen, opening a bag and dropping in napkins and beer bottles, doing my best to set them inside gently, avoiding the clanking sounds.

I'm so quiet while I work that the small tapping on the front door makes me jump. My hand clutches my chest, and my mind races to the obvious conclusion—it's Will. I move to the door silently, still not sure if I'm going to open it and dive deeper into the gaping wound opened only a few hours ago, when the quiet knock comes again.

With a sigh, I set the bag down in the foyer and slip on my flip-flops, not wanting to talk about any of this inside. It takes my mind a second to catch up to the fact that it isn't Will at my door, but instead, his uncle.

"Duncan, uh…hey; I'm sorry I kept you," I say.

His head falls to one side, and his eyes crinkle behind his glasses with his gentle smile.

"I wasn't sure if anyone was awake, even though it's nine, and why waste away a day like this, huh?" he says, his arms stretched out to his sides, a small velvet box in one palm.

I step out on the front walkway to admire the blue sky. It's bright out, a slight breeze tickling the crisp summer leaves of cottonwood trees that line our street. It sounds like the ocean. I turn back to look at him and smile.

"You're right. It would be a waste to miss this one," I say.

His eyes hover on mine for a few seconds, and I can tell he knows things. I get the sense that he and Will are close, so he's probably known things a lot longer than I have. Uncomfortable with that thought, I flit my gaze to his palm, to the small box that's held shut with a rubber band. I nod at it.

"Oh, yes. That's the reason I stopped by, actually. I finished the watch your dad wanted me to take a look at," he says, propping the package flat in one palm so he can slide the band away and open the lid. A golden pocket watch rests surrounded by chain, the hand moving in time around the face. I recognize it as my grandpa's, so I look to Duncan for permission, taking it from the case and holding it closer when he nods that it's okay.

"That one's rare," he says.

"That's what my dad always said," I say, holding it to my ear. I grin at him when the ticks reverberate in my head. "That's why he'd never let Mom toss it or donate it."

"Oh, God. I'm glad she didn't. That watch there goes for about five or six thousand dollars on the auction sites," he says, and my eyebrows react, shooting up my forehead as I hand the watch back for safekeeping. Duncan chuckles, but takes the box firmly in his hand, fastening the band around the lid before handing it all to me in one, safely packed piece. "It's worth even more because of this box, actually."

I chuckle, now holding the box.

"Anything else you want to make me afraid of holding over concrete?"

He laughs in response, and shakes his head.

"No, I think that's about it," he says, stopping with his head turned slightly to the side, his eyes blinking. He has more to say, and I know it's about Will, but Duncan isn't one to force his opinion into things. Where Will and Evan's dad was always bold and loud—quick to brag and forceful with dominating conversation—Duncan is reserved.

"Well…thanks for the watch," I say, holding it up between us. "I'll put it somewhere safe inside and show my dad as soon as he's up. He'll be thrilled."

"Glad to help. It's kept me busy. Let him know I'd be happy to fix anything else, while I'm here. I'm going to have a few days on my own this weekend, but I guess…you already know that," he says, his mouth curved the slightest amount.

Duncan knows things.

I look down to regroup, glancing back at my visitor through my lashes.

"I'll let him know," I say, my words focused on repairs and watches and nothing else. "Thanks for stopping by."

I turn, cradling the box against my chest, reaching for the door, and pushing it open to disappear inside and avoid everything else for a little while longer. But the *quiet* and *reserved* Hollister stops me with one last piece of information.

"He headed out to that lake you two love so much. About an hour ago…in case you were wondering," he says.

I'm starting to think that rather than reserved, Duncan is better described as calculated. I turn my head to one side, enough that I see him in my periphery, his hands in his pockets, his mouth a tight line, satisfied at the bait he's left on his nephew's behalf. I nod once, then push the door fully open, closing it quietly behind me.

There is never a single second when I doubt that I'm going. The moment Duncan told me where Will was, I knew it was his way of forcing us to talk. I'm sure his interest was in his nephew's corner, probably wanting to ease Will's guilt, to force him to have to confront the one person he's lied to, to find closure, and finally clear his conscience. But I think there's also a part of him that knows I still have questions. Duncan has always been so kind to me, and I think maybe he's in my corner a little on this, too.

I put the watch on the counter with a note for my dad, then finish picking up the tables, leaving the rest for my parents to handle when they wake up. I grab my keys, wallet, and phone, and I toss them all in the passenger seat of my car, pulling away from my parents' house a little faster than I should, my speed picking up with each mile I come closer to the truth. For something that hurts so much to face, I'm racing to it at an alarming speed.

Will

I'm not sure how she made it home. I'm not really sure *if* she made it home. I drove by her parents' house, though, on my way to the lake, and everything was calm and quiet. If Maddy were missing, I'm sure there would be visible commotion, which leads me to believe she probably walked.

I don't like that she walked…alone. But I know after the wound I made, I was less welcome than a predator in the dark.

This lake has always provided me with answers. Maybe it just always gives me a place to think—*forces* me to think. I can't be near this water without seeing Maddy, hearing her laugh. She's all around me, and the more places I let her in, the less places I have to hide.

Telling her the truth was the single hardest thing I've ever done. Seeing her face when she realized exactly what I meant, broke me. I instantly wanted to take those words back. I'd rather her hate me, think that *I* was the one who was hiding Dylan, hiding a relationship—I'd rather be the cheater than have her think that someone could have done that to her.

That Evan could have done that to her.

My back aches from this position I've been sitting in for the last hour, so I kick off my shoes and walk to the water's edge, searching for stones. When I gather a few, I throw them as hard as I can, counting the times they skip along the surface. I was the one who taught Maddy how to skip stones. Not Evan.

I pick up another handful, but I pause, closing my eyes, my breath rushing out all at once until I feel it boil to the top, and I let out a growl of a roar, cocking my arm back and thrusting the rocks into the middle of the lake, the stones pelting the ripples left by the breeze.

"I hate you!" I yell.

I yell it out here, where there is no witness but me. I yell at my brother, for leaving me with this. For making this mess to begin with, and for leaving *me*!

My hands find my face, and I rub my palms along my eyes, my energy to do anything waning. I have no idea how I'm going to get on a plane in four days, let alone drag myself through three days of practice. I might not have to if Curtis decides I'm too big of a risk to take…or if Maddy tells her dad what degenerates the Hollister brothers really were.

My feet start to kick at the water's currents, and I lose myself in the swirls I leave along the shore, my feet creating chaos in something otherwise calm and perfect. That's what I am—I'm chaos.

A rock skips by, tumbling along a few of the jagged boulders that stick up through the shallow water, and I jerk my head fast, turning to see Maddy in the clearing of the woods. She pulls another stone from her left palm and thrusts it across the water with her right. It bounces three times, and my lip ticks up on one side with pride.

"You're getting better," I say over my shoulder, not able to look at her fully.

"You're getting worse," she says.

My shoulders shake with my short laugh.

Oh, Maddy, you have no idea how much worse I am.

"How long have you been here?" I ask.

I know.

"Long enough to hear you hate someone," she says. I close my eyes and let my chin fall into my chest while I push my hands into my pockets at my sides. I regret yelling that, because as much as I hate what he did, I don't hate Evan. I fucking miss him.

"I hate someone, too," she says.

My lips shudder at her words.

"I don't want you to hate anyone, Maddy," I say.

It's quiet for several seconds, but I hear the sound of her feet slipping into the water, her steps coming closer, until I can feel her next to me. She's too far to touch, yet all I want to do is hold her.

"Then I need to know it all," she says. "From the beginning."

My eyes open on the water, and I turn just enough to see the place where her legs disappear under the blue. Her skin is pebbled from the chill, and her hands cling to the bottoms of her shorts. I would give anything to pull those hands in mine and kiss them, as if they were mine and only mine—*only ever mine.* But they weren't.

"Her name is Tanya Foster. She lived in my dorm," I say, stopping to let the wave of nausea pass. That's one of the things I still haven't been able to come to terms with in all of this—my role in introducing Tanya and my brother. Tanya was always beautiful—a walking blonde, blue-eyed temptation. I think maybe I'd hoped he'd fall for her. I didn't want him to hurt Maddy, but I think deep down, I wanted him to mess up…to leave her.

"Was she someone you were dating?" she asks.

I shake my head before speaking.

"No, we were friends. We had a few classes together, and I knew her from school. We'd gone to a few parties together, but that was all," I say.

"How did she meet Evan?" she asks.

My chest rises with the slow draw of air, and I look up at the lake, filling my mind with a mix of memories—Maddy *here*, Tanya…*there*.

"About a year before the accident, Evan came to visit me. He stayed for the weekend," I say, the memory so vivid it almost forces me to sit down in the water from the weight of it.

"I remember that weekend. Evan and I…we'd had a fight," she says, and something about the way her voice wavers draws my eyes to look at her. She's staring out along the lake, but her eyes are misted. I hate seeing how much this hurts. I hate that I'm the one hurting her.

I swallow hard before I continue.

"Evan went to a party with us, and they got along. I didn't notice anything more, though. It all seemed friendly, and Evan was with me practically the whole time," I say.

Maddy breathes out a laugh, but I correct her. It wasn't then that he cheated. I'm sure of it. I've heard the entire story of how they got together from Tanya.

"He came to visit a few more times, and whenever I had practice, or had studies or a class, he'd hang out with her. They had become friends, but I didn't start to suspect something until…" I stop, my mind frozen on the night I left Evan with her at a party, when he came into my room hours later, his mouth shut on the subject of her. He wouldn't even tolerate my teasing. I wouldn't know why until weeks later.

"Maddy, I don't want to put these details in your head. It's not fair to you; Evan's not here to answer to them, and the pictures you'll conjure…" I stop at her interruption.

"You have no idea what's already in my head, Will. I *need* these details," she says, her voice a harsh and violent whisper. I turn to meet her gaze, her steely eyes intent on the truth. "I need them to be able to sleep at night. I cannot make up my own questions and answers—it's torture."

I nod slowly, knowing she's right.

"I started to suspect something during his last visit. They had spent more time together—*alone*—and Evan wasn't taking my teasing well. There was this serious feel to everything, and when I confronted him on it, asking him point blank if he had slept with her, he punched me in the face," I say, the memory of that impact still fresh.

"Jesus," Maddy whispers, her eyes fall to my chin, and I see her throat gulp.

"Then…on Christmas Eve," I begin, having to look away from her for the rest of this, if I'm going to be able to tell her my nightmares. "We were getting packed and ready for the trip, and Evan was like this simmering man. He clearly was lost somewhere else, ignoring half of the things I said, not answering Mom's questions when she yelled down the hall, mumbling to himself. He was short with me, and the longer that went on, the more pissed off I became. I think maybe I knew it was something like what he eventually confessed, but that just made me angrier, like he had no right to be mad if he was the one who fucked up so badly, ya know?"

I glance to Maddy, but she doesn't react. Her eyes are locked on the space in front of me, on nothingness, and she's chewing at her lip and her arms folded over her chest, like she's holding herself here and forcing herself to listen. She almost knows it all, so I finish, giving her every last detail of the facts that have haunted me for more than four years now.

"It came to a head when we were boarding. Our parents were finishing loading a few bags, and Evan and I were prepping the cabin when I told him he was acting like a real dick. That's when he told me that he'd 'messed up real bad.'"

Her eyes shoot to mine, and the sadness behind them guts me. I shake my head slowly, wanting to fix this. I know I can't, though. "I asked him what that meant, and he said he'd slept with Tanya, and she called him last week and told him she was pregnant. He was going to do right by her, and marry her. I hit him harder than he hit me the few weeks before. His nose just bled and bled, and my mom yelled about how I was ruining Christmas. My father looked at me with disgust, and Evan just sat there and cried. I hated him so much for that, for just wallowing in his own mess and sitting there like the victim. He told my mom finally that we had been arguing, and it was his fault, but she blamed me—I'm the one who *escalated* things. My dad was furious when we took off. He wasn't focused."

I gnash my teeth and turn my body back toward the lake, away from Maddy. My hands are fists in my pockets, and my insides hurt as if they're on fire. There it all is for her—all of my ugliest secrets, guilt I live with every day. Fucking torture.

Bending down, I pick up another handful of rock, letting the silt filter through my hand until only the flattest, sharpest stones are left. I throw them one at a time, but they're too light to do any real damage. They skim the water once then lose to the current, falling to the bottom again. I repeat this futile act several times, my mind bouncing from my life before I knew everything, to the reality I live with now, to the one I just gave the girl I'd do anything to protect.

"I didn't want you to ever find out," I say, throwing the last handful of stones across the water then bending down to wash the dirt from my hand.

"Why?" she rasps.

My chin falls to my chest and I raise my shoulders.

"Because the ignorance seemed so much safer, I guess," I glance to her. Her eyes don't quite meet mine. "Either way, my brother is gone. And I guess I just thought the lie of his memory was so much more comforting to live with."

Her jaw moves and her lips grow tighter with her swallow, her hands squeezing at her elbows, wrapping around her body.

"I want to meet him," she says.

I take that request in, put it in my mind and play it out. No matter the scenario, her meeting Dylan hurts. That boy has to fight just to stay alive, and her seeing him means her seeing Tanya, and Tanya…she's a victim, too.

"His mom never knew about you," I say, turning to face her. "She still doesn't."

I have kept so many of Evan's secrets.

Maddy's hands loosen their grip, and slowly her fingers slide from their hold on her elbows, falling to her sides as she turns her feet to me.

"I *need* to meet them," she says, her mouth still and quiet, her eyes unflinching as they stare into mine. I breathe with her, and I fight against my instincts. I know it won't make anything better for her, but I also don't think I can keep secrets or say *no* to this girl any longer.

"Okay," I say, nodding lightly. "Maybe when we get back from Cleveland…"

"I'll take you all to the airport," she interrupts.

My head falls to my shoulder, and I pull my mouth in on one side.

"I don't think that's the best way," I say.

Maddy steps closer to me, stopping when we're near enough to touch, her arms folding over her chest again as she lifts her chin and looks me in the eyes.

"I don't care," she says, holding my gaze long enough that I can tell she means every word. She walks away seconds later.

And I let her go.

CHAPTER 12

Maddy

Maybe Will was right. I was a happier person when I was ignorant to the awful truth. I haven't been nice at practice this week. I have, however, been fast. I've matched my best time in three sprints, and my dad keeps gloating about my consistency, about the strides I'm making to peak at just the right moment.

I've never worked harder in the pool, yet every day, I feel like I could do it all again. My muscles just don't seem to grow tired. My body is running on hate, and while it's bringing me results in the one part of my life that still feels right, it's ruining all others. I was mean to Amber in the locker room yesterday, and I heard from one of the other girls that my shortness made her cry. A part of me wants to tell her to toughen up, because honestly, if *I* make her cry then she's going to have her hands full when we face other countries. But that's never been who I am. I've always been the glue. At Valpo, I was the spark that every other girl mentioned in her interviews—the leader, the friend to turn to, the inspiration.

I feel about as inspiring as a motivational speaker high on Sudafed. My insides just feel cold—frozen and jaded. It's cyclical, too, because the more upset I get over how I'm acting, the angrier I get about the reason—*Evan had a baby. Evan cheated. Will lied.*

Will's kept his distance, working just as hard, but swimming opposite hours of me outside of our camp. Our only conversation was yesterday, when he asked me to be here at three today to take him to pick up Tanya and her son for their trip. I promised I'd be here, and then I left before I could simmer in that reality with him any longer. I know he waited while I left; I felt his eyes on me until my car pulled away from the club. It hurts to hurt him, but it stings just as much to trust him and let myself understand.

Will agreed to the interviews, too, and just as I told him he would be, my father was accepting of his "emergency time off." Part of me wants to blow the lid off the emergency to my dad too, but the hate hasn't made me that vengeful yet. I can feel its fingers around my heart, though. I think, perhaps, if telling my parents wouldn't lead to them asking me questions—*consoling me*—then I would. I'm barely okay with the voices in my head for now.

Both Will and Duncan are waiting out front as I roll up to drive him to the airport. Will is carrying nothing more than a backpack, so I don't bother to pop the trunk as I pull up next to them and wait for Will to get inside. He says a few words to his uncle, then gives him a hug before walking behind my car toward his rental, and I shove my car into park and get ready to protest.

"Goddammit!" I growl through my teeth.

"Will, get in the car," I start to yell the second I step outside, but Duncan walks around the back to meet me just as Will shuts the door and cranks the engine on his car.

"Is he seriously trying to leave without me? Why didn't he just go *before* I got here? Gahhhhh," I growl, tilting my face to the sky and folding my fingers behind my neck.

"He needs to drive, Maddy," Duncan says. I lower my chin, my mouth shut tight as I look at him. He reaches forward for my elbows, and my hands unlink, falling until they're in Duncan's. "He didn't think about it until he saw the size of your car. You all are going to need more room, so he needs to drive. He told me to tell you to just park in the spot he leaves, and you can drive our car back here when you're done."

My eyes squint, and I swing my vision from Duncan to the back of Will's head, finally letting go of Duncan's hold and stretching my arms out to my sides.

"Why didn't he just tell me that?" I huff.

"Oh, well, that's because the two of you are acting like children," Duncan says. My eyes close on him more and my mouth curves down. I fold my arms against my chest tightly, like a shield, and tilt my head at his unfair accusation.

"I'm glad you're going with him, though, Maddy," he keeps talking as if my reaction is meaningless. "I think you're going to see a lot of things differently after today. And if you need to talk to anyone when you get back, I'll be around."

His eyes linger on mine, and the tension in my arms and face lessens. With a soft smile on his face, Duncan reaches forward and squeezes my right shoulder, and my eyes go to the touch of his hand. He takes a few steps away until he's again standing on the walkway in front of the club. I glance to Will, to the back of his head, his hands propped on the wheel and his eyes looking at me through the rearview mirror. With a short breath, I turn and climb into my car, circling around and trading spots with Will. I grab my purse and open the passenger door of his car, sliding inside and making eye contact with Duncan one more time. His mouth curves a hint, but it isn't a happy smile. Whatever message he's trying to send with it, though, I raise my hand and press my fingertips on the window just as he lifts his to say goodbye while Will pulls us out of the lot and onto the roadway.

The inside of the car is soundless for more than an hour, and eventually the monotony of the tires over the seams in the highway push me over the edge. I exhale and shift in my seat, giving in and looking at Will. I don't know what I expected…no…that's not true. I expected a fight. I expected him to look just as angry as I feel, to huff at me, and spit out a "What?" so I could yell something. I thought he'd engage, but now that I really look at him, I see how wrong I was.

His hands haven't left their position on the wheel. His eyes are glued open on the road, and even his blinking comes in regular patterns, as if he's counting down to the time between each one, markers for distance traveled and time spent in this car alone with me—*with me and the truth*. He's not going to fight back. He'll just take it, whatever I dish, and it makes me want to scream because Will is not a beaten dog. He's my drive! He was always that person, but what's sitting here with me now—what's left after everything I know now—is just a shell.

I stare at him for miles, at that face I touched and still want to. I watch his chest rise slowly, his seatbelt growing tight with each full breath. His eyes only flit to mine once, and the moment we connect, I see how much he regrets giving in and looking at me. I see how much this hurts—how much *I* am hurting him because I hurt.

"Your car couldn't accommodate Dylan's chair," Will finally speaks.

I flinch at the break in silence, but he doesn't notice. His teeth saw at his bottom lip and his eyes move along the highway ahead of us, flashing to the mirror as he signals for an exit. I recognize the road instantly. We turned this way when I brought him to the strip club—when his body was jerking with nerves and he nearly chewed his fingers to the bone. I thought it was because of how close this area was to the scene of his car crash, but that's not what it was at all.

We turn down a neighborhood street, rows of tiny houses pushed closely together, dirt for front yards, and sparse of trees—except for the few growing wild and covering sidewalks. Cars are parked front to end along the road, and the further in we weave, the faster Will's fingers begin to drum along the steering wheel. He slows the car in front of a small gray house, a long wooden ramp still waiting to be painted or stained stretching along the entire front to the driveway with a gold van that looks to be only a month or two old parked in the front.

Will pulls the car in behind the van, coming as close as he can without hitting it. Our car still hangs out into the street, but a glance around the area doesn't show much traffic, or any other alternatives for parking.

"We're here," he breathes, rolling his hands on the steering wheel then falling forward, and folding his arms on top, his chin resting on his knuckles.

"I won't say anything." These are the first words I've spoken in nearly two hours. Will's head falls to the side and he looks at me through his empty eyes. "To her...to Tanya?"

I look forward at the small house, the cracks as obvious as the homemade attempts nailed, puttied, and painted along the trim in an effort to hold this house together. The mother of Evan's child—*and Evan's child*—live here. Nothing about any of this is good.

"You may have been right about the ignorance. She's better off with the lie..." I say, my eyes shifting back to Will. "Whatever version of the story she has."

His eyes hold mine for a second then move to the house as he pushes away from the steering wheel, nodding.

I follow Will's lead, letting him guide me from the car up to the house, not bothering to knock or ring a bell. He pulls a torn screen door open, then pushes the main door so we can both step inside. My nose is hit instantly with the scent of bleach and lemon-scented cleaners, dryer sheets, and vanilla-scented candles. To the right, the house looks spotless, but to the left are piles of sheets, towels, clothing, and towering boxes of some type of medical supplies.

"She has a hard time keeping up," Will says through an apologetic smile. "I think she wanted to leave the house in a semi-clean state."

I nod and look around me again. She made it halfway.

"Tanya? We're here," he says, his voice loud and echoing around the cramped room. I notice a path is cleared stretching straight from a hallway into what looks like the kitchen, and I remember what Will said about needing room for Dylan's chair. *Dylan.* His name is Dylan.

"Hey, Will. I'm almost done in here. Come on in," a voice calls from the kitchen area. My heart starts to pound, and my fingers feel numb from the blood flowing so fast and hard through my body. Somehow, my legs continue to work and I follow Will into the kitchen. A thin blonde, wearing a plain white T-shirt with the sleeves bunched up over her shoulders and a pair of gray sweats, rushes from the sink to a cabinet, stacks of plates in her hands for one trip, fists full of forks and spoons on her next. She glances up at both of us while she works, and her face looks nothing like the trampy whore I've dreamt up in my hateful fantasies. This woman looks frail, and tired, and…kind.

"Oh, hey! You must be Maddy," she says, running her palm along the leg of her sweats and blowing a tuft of hair out of her eyes while she approaches me. My mouth quivers and my ears fall deaf with the rush of blood to my head, but I manage to reach out my hand to shake hers. "Thank you so much for helping us. Will said you and he were good friends, and you knew how much he hated to fly. I'm just…" she pauses and leans her hip out, running her shoulder against her face as her eyes well up. "I'm just so grateful he's coming with me. I don't think I can get him there alone."

I let her hand slide from mine and look over her shoulder at the piles of things yet to do. Unwashed glasses line the counter. Stacks of files sit in haphazard piles, some with sticky notes jutting from the edges. And underneath it all, layers of dust and stickiness from a kitchen that she probably hasn't been able to clean since the day she moved in.

"I'm glad he can help, too," I answer, swallowing away so many things I thought I knew.

"I swear I'll be ready, Will. I just wanted to get a head start on some of this. I was taking advantage of Dylan napping. I had yesterday off too, and our therapist, Wendy…she helped, even though I know she's not supposed to do housework, but God, I was grateful," Tanya says, her words vomiting out amid her nerves. Will stands with his hands in his pockets, his posture stiff, and his head sunken in-between his shoulders. The only response he can seem to give her is a fast nod, and I can see it affecting Tanya more and more by the second. She starts to rush around the kitchen, moving things, but never really accomplishing anything. Will steps backward until his legs meet a chair, and he falls back and sits.

"I'm going to scoop up the sheets and put them in a bag. I have a laundry service that's going to pick everything up while we're gone. I just need to have it all ready," Tanya says, her voice wavering as she glides by Will, his eyes wide and his mouth firmly shut.

The moment she slips from our view, I step in front of him, my back shielding her from seeing or hearing anything should she come in.

"What is wrong with you? You're supposed to be helping her, but you've gone completely catatonic," I say, and my words do nothing more than draw his eyes to mine. They're still wide, and they're still scared. I kneel down and touch his knee. The feel of him sends a jolt up my arm, and his eyes fall immediately to my touch, softening as his mouth relaxes, the hard line sloping on the ends toward his chin. His hand lands on top of mine, trapping me.

"I'm not sure I can do this." His body shivers and his words come out choppy, almost as if he's breaking a fever.

"Will, that woman is going to fall apart without you. You *have* to get over whatever the hell…" I stop midsentence, words from a minute before finally sinking in: *how much he hated to fly.*

"Oh God…" I say, sliding my hand out from under his, my chin coming up just as his is falling. I reach up, not even thinking, and my hands cup his face. He freezes. His eyes close and the weight of his head rests into my right palm. I run my fingers along his jaw on the left side.

"Is there something you can take?" I ask. His body shakes once, a short breath escaping him in a sad laugh. Right. One year sober.

"Will, Dylan's up! Should we get his things out to the car first? I can get him in the small chair," Tanya calls from the other end of the house. Will's eyes rise to meet mine, and the sheer helplessness reflected in them seizes my chest, and I gasp once, tears threatening my eyes.

I breathe in deeply, letting my eyes fall closed for a moment while I search for courage. Not to do something my heart desperately wants to do, but to let go of the hate that's keeping me from doing what's right.

"Sounds good, Tanya. Will's finishing up the dishes for you, so I'll come in to help," I holler back. My response snaps Will out of his haze, and he starts to stand and push away from me.

"No, no…I'm fine," he says.

I ignore him and pull my phone from my pocket, searching for flights quickly.

"American? Southwest?" I ask.

His hands cover mine, but I fight him off this time, stepping back and holding one palm up while my thumb slides over the screen.

"Maddy, this…none of this, is your responsibility," he says, shaking his head, and I stop with my thumb on the purchase button, looking him right in the eyes.

"It isn't yours either," I argue, my breath catching as it hits me. None of this—me, Evan, Tanya, Dylan, and all the damn ghosts—is Will's responsibility. He chose to carry it. He inserted himself where a blank space was left, and he's been holding worlds together for people when he had every right to walk away.

My thumb falls against my phone, and I hold it up, swallowing.

"I hope it was Southwest," I whisper, a little stunned at the realization of what a mixture of spontaneity and panic can make someone do. "I am probably going to need to borrow some money, too. And…shit…clothes."

Will moves to me swiftly, his hands reaching up but not sure where to touch. There's the barrier between us that came the moment Evan's story unraveled, but I feel like it shifted—just a little.

"Call them, Maddy. Cancel that. I'll suck it up. I'll be fine. It's just a plane ride," he says, but that fear is there still. I see it. "Please, Maddy. Don't take this on."

"If you see the big suitcase in the living room, just bring it to the first door on the right!" Tanya yells.

My eyes are locked on Will's, a silent battle, each of us trying to save the other. But he doesn't see what I see—a man whose soul is so tired that it may not have much fight left in it. My mouth opens to speak seconds before I actually do, and I wait in a sort of verbal limbo, convincing myself past those last few uncertainties.

"Got it!" I respond finally, stepping away from Will slowly, his eyes following my path.

I can feel Will behind me, but I push forward as if I've always been a part of this, as if I was supposed to show up here all along and make this trip with them. My hand grabs the handle of the only suitcase in the room, and I roll it along behind me, stopping at the door on the right. Will pauses a few feet short of the doorway, and I glance to see him standing with both of his arms stretched out, his palms flat on opposite hallway walls and his head low.

"That's the one! Thanks, Maddy," Tanya says, pulling my attention away from Will.

Inside the small room is a hospital bed with rails and monitoring devices, most of them shut off minus one that beeps periodically. A frail boy with brown hair and crystal-blue eyes struggles on the edge of the bed, his fingers curved awkwardly around one of the bedrails while his other arm hugs tightly around Tanya's neck. His legs bend in such a way that I know walking is not possible, and as Tanya lifts him against her, struggling by herself to line him up with his chair, I can't help but flash forward to a time when Dylan is twice this size.

"There," Tanya breathes out, stretching her back and tugging out the band from her hair, refastening it to tuck away loose ends that Dylan pulled out when his fingers grabbed at her. "Step one of about sixty-eight-hundred," she laughs.

I laugh lightly with her, but only for show. My eyes are captivated by the young ones that struggle to meet mine a few feet away. There is so much that is tragic and difficult, and my heart breaks seeing this glimpse of Dylan's battle, but it also beats at everything that is familiar. Evan is there. He's right there, even though he's not here for any of this. I grab at my chest, and when Tanya's back is to me, I turn to see Will—still standing with his arms stretched out. His eyes were waiting for me, and the moment our gazes lock, I understand why he didn't want me to get this far in. It hurts too much—*too much Evan.*

"He doesn't speak, other than a few sounds and *almost* words he's been getting out in therapy, so he probably won't be able to say your name, but he'll recognize you," Tanya says, catching my attention back in the room.

I step forward, closer to her and her son—*Evan's son*. She presses his hand between both of hers and squeezes, and the sensation seems to soothe him, his head shifting from side-to-side while he hums and smiles.

"Dylan, this is a friend of Uncle Will's. Her name is Maddy," she says.

Dylan's head bobs twice and a sound escapes him, almost a yell, but the words are incoherent. His eyes cross paths with mine a few times, and it feels like I'm being painted with his happiness, more cooing sounds escaping his chest as he brings his other hand forward to clap with both of his mom's.

She nods to me, so I step closer and place mine on top of hers so Dylan can touch me. His hand grazes mine a few times, his fingers almost curling around mine once, unable to hold on for more than a blip of a second. The feel of it forces a smile to my face, and when I look up into Tanya's eyes, she's smiling, too.

"I hope it's okay, Dylan, but I'm making this trip with you," I say, glancing from him to Tanya, her eyes growing wide and her smile growing. "I thought you could all use another hand."

When her gaze moves beyond me, to the door, I know that Will has moved from his place in the hallway. I glance over my shoulder, and his eyes meet mine in an instant, speaking nothing but silent apologies.

"I tried to tell her she didn't have to go," he says.

"Yeah, don't feel obligated, Maddy. We're grateful for the lift to the airport…"

"I want to," I interject, turning back to Tanya just before standing and sliding my hands away from Dylan's fragile hold. "I'd really like to help, and I can make up my time. My dad will understand."

Tanya glances to Will for approval, and I turn to face him as well. His focus shifts between us, and his resolve weakens just enough.

"He won't understand at all, but to hell it I can talk you out of something once your mind is made," he relents.

"He will, but you're right about one thing…" I say, moving to the doorway and sliding through, my arm grazing his chest as I pass. "You can't talk me into or out of anything, Will Hollister."

I leave him with Tanya to finish getting Dylan packed and ready for our trip, and I take over finishing the dishes in the kitchen. I cry hard, but I don't make a single sound, and I don't turn my face away from the sink until I know every last puffy, red piece of evidence has been erased.

When we get the car packed, I slide into the passenger seat next to Will and call my father's number. When he answers, I tell him I'm going with Will to help. I tell him it's important, and when he asks for the details, I tell him I can't share any. He's livid, but he's also my daddy. I promise him a new record at the meet next week, and that seems to lighten his mood enough that when I hang up I'm left with only one heavy burden on my heart.

Will's hand rests on the gearshift between us, and without thinking, I thread my fingers through his. His mouth opens and a small breath escapes. It's nothing grand, but that small sound cuts deep. He's breaking himself trying to save so many people, but nobody has ever stepped up to save him.

I'm not sure I'm strong enough to, either. But I can sure as hell get him through the next few hours, in the air—in his worst nightmare.

CHAPTER 13

Will

With every step forward, I want to take six back. I want to run. I've never wanted to run more.

My counselor, after the DUI, told me that I was probably experiencing a panic attack when I drove into that tree. I didn't know what he meant because, well, Jack Daniels does a damn good job of erasing the symptoms of a panic attack. But I'm sober now, and this—*this* is definitely a panic attack.

Everywhere I look, the earth is shaking. Just a little. The colors are brighter, and my forehead will not stop sweating. I can barely focus enough to find my way to the group of seats just outside our gate. Maddy took the lead, checking us all in, loading the luggage, and getting the boarding passes. As difficult as it is to travel with Dylan, his medical condition makes some things easier. We went through a special security area, which meant that there was more time to scrutinize things—*scrutinize me*. For a while, I thought they were going to pull me into a room and test my urine because I look like I'm in withdrawals.

"When you have a panic attack, you will feel like you are dying." That one line from some state-mandated substance-abuse counselor, whose name and face I hardly remember, is ingrained in my mind. He could not have been more accurate.

"Can I get you some water? Or maybe just an aspirin, or something to chew on?" Maddy has been doting on me the entire way to the airport, through security, and to these chairs that I just want to curl up in. I hate that I have become the burden for this trip. We're all supposed to be here for Dylan, but he's been a champ. I have been a massive pain in the ass.

"I don't know, maybe…I guess. No water. I don't want to have to get up as soon as I'm buckled in. But maybe gum? Or candy?" I feel like I want to throw up, but I have to give Maddy something to do. She looks defeated, and I don't like her looking at me like I'm a lost cause.

"Got it. I'll get a little of everything. I've already drained my savings, so this goes on credit," she says through a laugh. "You want me to call Duncan, too?"

"No, I can handle that," I say, sliding my phone into my palm.

I watch her walk away a few steps and I let myself succumb to the shiver that's been building in my spine. Before she gets very far, though, Maddy spins around and rushes back to me, slipping into the seat next to me and throwing her arms around me. Her head falls onto my shoulder as she squeezes me tightly, and I hold my breath the entire time.

"It's going to be okay," she says into the small space where her mouth rests against my neck. I want to believe her. I choose to believe her.

I nod a few times and force my mouth into a smile. It's thin and it doesn't hold up for long, but I think maybe it's more than I could have given her five minutes ago, so that's progress.

With Maddy in the store and Tanya and Dylan resting at the seating area right next to our gate, I pull my phone into my palm and call my uncle. After a few rings, he answers, his voice calm and the reassurances already scripted and spilling from his mouth.

"Will, I'm so glad you called before takeoff. How's the airport? Busy? I heard it was a busy travel day," he starts immediately.

It's a Thursday—an uneventful, midsummer weekday—our flight isn't even full. My uncle is full of shit, but I love him for his effort.

"It's fine, listen…something's come up," I say.

"Will, you can do this. It's just like our flight from Michigan," he interrupts.

"No, that's not it. I'm getting on the plane. It's a different issue," I say, pulling my hand up to pinch the bridge of my nose. "Maddy insisted on coming."

I can practically hear my uncle's smile.

"She shouldn't have, so stop celebrating," I say.

"I'm not celebrating," he chuckles.

"Sure you aren't," I say.

"Okay, maybe a little. And why shouldn't she have? She's a grown woman, and I'm sure Tanya could use the extra help," he says. "You wouldn't let me come, so think of it as if she's taking my place."

"Right…because you and Maddy are so similar," I laugh out.

"She got you to the gate, didn't she?" he says. I pull my mouth up on one side, rubbing my palm along my cheek as I nod.

"Yeah," I breathe.

He's right. My uncle and Maddy are the only two people who have been able to get me this far when it comes to airports. Granted, my flight to Indiana with my uncle also included a near arrest, when I threatened to walk off the plane as we were taxiing, and a close-up view of a Taser from a TSA agent. My uncle assured them I would be fine, and then he proceeded to beg me to "keep my shit together" for the entire hour flight. We almost came to blows a dozen times. I hope Maddy's really up for this.

"So where's the car?" my uncle asks.

"It's in hourly parking, on the north end. I'm sorry, I know you hate driving on the highways," I say.

"Bahhhh, no problem. I have the extra key, and I'll Uber there and take surface streets back," he says.

That trip will take him twice as long.

"I'm really sorry," I say, meaning it. I feel like I need to say it to everyone…for lots of things.

"Don't be. Just use this time wisely. Maybe man up, too, and tell that girl all of those things you've been holding on to for way too long," he says.

I breathe in through my nose and slightly regret the confessions I've made to this old man. He's the only rock I have, though. And I've needed a good rock.

"Maybe," I say.

"Chicken shit," he says, coughing with his laugh as he hangs up the phone.

As if she knew we were talking about her, Maddy slides into the seat next to me the second I put my phone back in my pocket, a smirk on her face and a slant to her eyes that she only gets when she's planning on pranking someone or leaving them in the dust in a race.

"What's that look for?" I lean away and twist in my chair, my guard up, but my pulse slowing a little more.

She turns to face me, bringing one knee up, then plops a plastic bag in her lap from the gift shop she just ducked into, her hands diving into the plastic and concealing whatever's inside. Her grin grows, and she raises her eyebrows once before unveiling her big surprise.

"Pop Rocks!" she says emphatically. I'm not sure how to react, so I end up bunching my shoulders to my ears and raising my eyebrows to match hers. Her smile deflates a little.

"Sorry," I say, taking the grape packet from her hands and tearing the edge open. "You're trying. I'm grateful."

"No, it's okay. I just saw them at the counter, and it reminded me of that time when we were working the snack bar at the club."

I stop with the packet at my lips and laugh at the memory she triggers.

"They came out through Evan's nose," I chuckle.

"He was so upset," she says, pouring a handful into her palm. Her eyes connect with mine, and we both begin to count down from three.

I tilt my head and fill my mouth with the purple candies while Maddy pushes her palm to her lips and eats the red ones. Seconds later, we both stare at one another with open mouths, listening to the crackle, smiling as if I weren't about to climb aboard my literal death trap and she weren't about to see me at my worst. Our lips twitch while be both stifle our laughter, and eventually Maddy gives in, closing her mouth and shaking her head.

"These are truly awful," she says, her mouth bending with bitterness as she swallows them and reaches into the plastic bag for a bottle of water, twisting the lid and gulping down nearly half to wash the taste away.

"I think they're one of those things where the memory is better than the reality," I say, swallowing mine. My words bring her eyes to mine, and her smile softens.

My gaze falls to her arm, and without pause, I reach out for her hand. She gives hers back willingly, and I thread our fingers together, reminding myself repeatedly not to grip so hard that I break her.

"We should get to the gate. We'll board first," I say.

Her hand squeezes mine, and when I look up, she's waiting for me. It's quiet for a few seconds, and I can feel my pulse picking up speed again. Maddy's hand squeezes again.

"Okay," she says.

I wish I felt okay.

Maddy

We're twenty minutes into the flight and I think we might get kicked out—midair.

The attendant keeps *checking in*. That's the word choice she keeps using. Just "checking in on you." I watch her have panicked conversations with the male flight attendant on the other side of the partition, then plaster that fake smile on her face and kneel next to me, as if Will can't hear every word she says about "my friend who seems to be in distress."

He's convulsing in sweats, and when he's not looking down at the focus point—aka the stain I found on the floor between his feet—he's wringing his hands, darting his eyes side to side, and reaching for the in-flight magazine so he can roll it repeatedly. The last time our "friend" came to check on us, she tried to take the magazine away. I think she thought he was making a weapon.

That conversation is happening again, and I see her eyes on the magazine in Will's hands. He's twisting so hard that the spine is starting to split open, so I reach under my seat for my purse, ready to fish out five dollars from my wallet so I can tell air bitch that I am buying the damn thing so if my friend wants to turn it into papier mâché, he can if he wants to.

Her fake smile is waiting for me when I tilt my head back up, but I'm done playing this game with her.

"Hi again," she says—in an accent that I swear to God is fake. She isn't from the South. I bet she went to some workshop once where they told her that if you say something in a Southern accent it doesn't sound as mean. It's actually true, only I've grown numb to her Southern charm and see right through it—right to the core of her cruel intentions.

"Our lead attendant," she stops to gesture over her shoulder to the male attendant cowering behind the partition a few feet away. He raises a hand. *Weakling.* "He has informed me that we are supposed to place severely ill or distressed passengers near the rear of the plane, or, if no seats are available, in the back jump seats with one of us. For safety reasons, I'm sure you understand…"

"No, I don't," I interrupt. I make sure to close my lips and smile. For once, I wish I wore a bright red lip gloss just like she does.

"Your friend here…"

"His name is Will," I interrupt again. I smile…again.

"Right, well, *Will*…"

I can feel Will staring at me, so I turn to him. He looks like he wants to vomit, and I think he's pleading for me not to make a scene, but I know that if I roll over now, they'll take him away from me and put him in the back, or they'll make us both move. And while Dylan is happy now, I know that, too, might not last. I turn the other way, my eyes catching Tanya's before moving a tick to the right, to the ones growing more impatient with me.

"Sandra," I say, taking a cue from her name badge. She glowers when

I say her name. Careful to keep my voice low and calm, I smile again, though I'm sure she can tell it's disingenuous. "Have you ever survived a plane crash?"

Her eyebrows lift, and I think fast. Probably not the best lead in on an airplane where you've already triggered more than a half-dozen security flags.

"No, I mean…I ask because Will? He has. A bad one. Like…the kind that make you swear to yourself you will never set foot on an airplane ever again. Not. Ever."

I wait for her to register my words. She swallows and leans back on her heels, her hand gripping my armrest for balance. I move close and bring my voice just over a whisper.

"We're traveling with his nephew," I nod over her shoulder. Sandra glances and meets Tanya's gaze, and they both nod. "It's an incredibly important trip that Will didn't want to miss. He isn't in distress. He's terrified. His heart is beating so fast that he may pass out from it. I can feel it…every time I hold his hand. But you know what keeps him from falling apart completely? Tearing up your shitty magazine. So rather than make us move and add fire to the flame sitting next to me, how about you take my five dollars, bring *me* a drink, and let my friend here have his way with your high-gloss propaganda."

Her eyes shift from mine to Will's hands, and I move my five-dollar bill into her line of sight. She takes it from my hand and stands, holding it at her hip, her mouth a straight line, and her lips puckered enough that I see the small lines along them that lead me to believe she smokes like a chimney.

"Wine is six dollars, ma'am," she says.

Funny, her accent seems to have vanished.

I tilt my head to one side and let my top lip lift on the right.

"I think you'll spot me that buck," I say.

We face off for a few silent seconds, but eventually she runs my five between her fingers, folding it in half and rolling her eyes in the opposite direction her hips sway before she leaves.

"I'm sorry," I whisper, leaning into Will. His hands continue to work the magazine, rolling and twisting it while pages tear. I settle into my seat and turn my wrist, checking the time on my watch. Seven more minutes have passed, so we're almost to the hump.

"She's totally going to spit in your wine." I don't look up, but I feel Will's arm leaning into mine, and I smile.

"I would," I shrug, and when I feel his arm twitch lightly with his laugh, I smile.

I never look him in the eye, but I keep the pressure of his arm next to mine for the rest of the flight. I drink my wine fast, too. It makes me a little buzzed, but it was also the best way to blow the last five dollars I had to my name.

Will

It's like a switch flips the moment the plane tires skid across the runway. I know it isn't possible, but I feel as though I've held my breath for an hour in the air. My uncle told me that each time I flew it would get better. I didn't get threatened with a Taser this time, so I suppose, yeah…it was better…*ish*.

We hit the ground with little time to spare. Tanya manages Dylan, Maddy finds our luggage, and I do my best not to punch the obnoxious vehicle-registration man between the eyes. I'm starting to think we're having two conversations—the one he's in, where a midsize will work fine for our needs, especially since he just gave away our van—which I reserved—to a family of five who arrived right before us. And then there's the conversation I'm in, where I'm trying not to punch him between his bloodshot, *it's not allergies, douchebag* eyes.

"David," I say, reading the name on his tag and running my hands along the smooth counter. It's void of fingerprints. I bet that's all David does is wipe down this counter all day. He clearly doesn't check paperwork and registrations, otherwise the fuckin' asshole would not have given away our van. I breathe through my nose and flip my head up to face him, mouth tight, tongue held, jaw locked while I resolve myself to be civil. "I appreciate that you're offering a discount. Really, I do. Or actually, no...fuck your discount."

So much for civil.

"I mean, we'll take it, but it should really be bigger since you have just massively inconvenienced a family traveling with a disabled child who—I don't care what you seem to believe, will not fit comfortably in a Jetta. Nobody fits comfortably in a Jetta, David. Have you actually ever *seen* a Jetta? It's small. The seats are miserable. I'm six-four. Me, traveling alone, would not fit in your fucking Jetta..."

"Hey, oh...okay...so, what's going on here?" Maddy glides up next to me and weaves her arm through mine, placing her other hand on my bicep in an effort to calm me down. I jerk from her hold and twist to face her, drumming my fingers on the counter.

"David gave away our fucking van."

Mouth tight, I stare at her. While I grit my teeth she does her best to be my opposite. Moving her hands to mine slowly, running her fingers down my arms to my wrists and exhaling deliberately.

"Okay, well...let me handle this, okay?" she says.

"Have at it," I say, rolling my eyes.

Maddy chuckles then turns to the counter, and the dumbass, leaning forward and resting her elbows on top of the paperwork for the Jetta, clasping her hands in front of her and bringing her knuckles to her lips.

"I'm not gonna lie here, David. This isn't good," she says.

David starts to explain, just as he did with me, but a few words in and Maddy cuts him off again.

"Here's what needs to happen. You need to consult with your manager, quickly, and then you need to either find us the van we reserved, or you will give us two cars for the same price we agreed on for the van."

"Ma'am, it doesn't work that way..."

"Ah...thing is, David, we tried to do things your way. And your way kinda sucked and left us in this situation we're in now. So now, we're going to try *our* way...unless you would like me to go the way of explaining all of the ways you are breaking ADA compliance. I'm sure your local news would *love* to hear about that. Oh, and I could start talking about it real loud right here, too. You know, to make sure that all of the people in line to get their rental vehicles know about how you don't accommodate for disabilities, and in fact go out of your way to make life harder…"

"I'll override the charge," David spits out quickly, swiping his employee card along his computer screen and typing manically, his eyes shifting side-to-side, his mouth twitching in a frown when he sees that the people standing next to us have heard Maddy's speech.

Within minutes, we have two sets of keys, neither for a Jetta, and we're making our way out to the lot toward two matching Buicks. I unlock mine and jog to the curb where Tanya and Dylan are waiting and I help them to the car. It takes a few tries to figure out the best way to fit Dylan's chair along with his and Tanya's bags, but the fit is easier than it would have been in Maddy's car.

I close the trunk and get the address for the Cleveland Clinic from Tanya, then dash around the front to the car Maddy's waiting in. She's already put my small bag in the back and has the engine running.

"We probably could have fit in the Jetta," I say as I get in and pull my safety belt over my chest.

"Probably," she says, her eyes moving around to check the positions of the mirrors and her seat. She twists, resting her elbow on the center console, and her eyes settle on me when she's done. "And you know my car's a Jetta. You fit fine in it."

Her eyes narrow and my smirk grows. I did know that. I also recall how cramped it was when I climbed on top of her in that front seat. I can tell she's thinking about that, too, but I'm not sure I'm supposed to mention things like that with her now—now that Evan's story is out, and Tanya and Dylan are part of the equation. I'm not sure if that means Maddy and I go back to the way things were before, when I was just her friend and the brother of the guy she used to love.

Her eyes blink once when she looks down, then again as she turns to face the steering wheel, shifting into reverse and pulling us out of the parking lot and onto the roadway behind Tanya. I watch her drive; she's chewing at her nails while she concentrates, reacting to my directions, and doing her best to stay close to Tanya's car. I know her dad is pissed that she's gone on this trip. I know him too well, and no matter what Maddy says about promising him a record and him understanding, he thinks his little girl is losing her way. I'm sure there's a part of him that's scared she's following a path that leads her to me, too. Curtis likes me well enough as a family friend from the past, but I'm not stupid. I know why he let me come here to compete. I'm the gimmick—*the comeback story*. Maddy is the champion, and I'm the guy getting in her way.

But she is here. She came more than willingly. Hell, she bullied her way right into the center of this mess. And I can't help but love her a little bit for being so selfless.

"In case I forgot to say it…you know…when I was super manic and crazy on the plane," I pause, breathing out a laugh. Just the sound makes my chest hurt, and it hits me how exhausted I am from surviving the day. Maddy tilts her head and flashes me a soft smile before glancing back to the road. "Thank you for doing this, for…for helping Tanya and Dylan. For helping me. I'm just…I'm just really glad you're here."

She flits her gaze to me briefly, but keeps her eyes mostly on the road. Her lip lifts in a crooked smile as she raises one shoulder.

"I'm happy to help, Will," she says. "Tanya…she's…she seems like a pretty great woman."

She doesn't say anything more, and I know how hard those words were to get out, so I let them be. I flip through my phone apps, bringing up the map so I can guide Maddy the rest of the way in case we lose Tanya on the road. I never mention that I thought I was the reason she came. I sorta feel selfish.

CHAPTER 14

Will

It's almost eight at night, and Tanya and Dylan are finally settled in at the Pediatric Wing. The doctors wanted to be able to monitor Dylan through the night, which is why it was so important for us to get here on time. We have three days—two, really, because I doubt they'll do little more than check us out and fill our arms with brochures and more questions on Saturday.

Tanya is staying at the hospital, which means Maddy and I need to check in at the hotel down the road...which means—*I have no clue what this means.*

We park the car and walk in to the hotel's lobby. I found the place online a few days ago and picked it because it had a decent rating for the price. I reserved two rooms because Tanya and I hadn't planned to room together, and we didn't know if she would have Dylan with her the whole time or not, but now that it's just me and Maddy, I wish like hell this place was booked up with only one room to spare.

Given that we were one of six cars I counted out front, I'm guessing that's not the case. People don't exactly flock to Cleveland to start off their summers. And people here for the hospital are usually booking at the five-star tower across the street. This place does come with free breakfast though, and I notice the leftover bagels and muffins still out for the taking as we walk to the front desk. Maddy grabs something that looks like a blueberry muffin and bites into it, and I stop in my tracks, flinching.

"Did you seriously just eat, like…half of that?" I ask.

"I was hun…" she pauses to swallow, wiping her arm across her mouth, "gry."

I twist my lips, but internally, I'm waiting to watch her reaction—to see if she doubles over or spits out the rest. When nothing happens, I shrug and give in to the growl bubbling in my stomach and grab what I think is a bran muffin, and carry it to the desk. I turn to Maddy while the young girl about to check us in is on the phone.

"Look," I whisper. "I don't want this to be weird. I booked two rooms when we planned this trip. Let's just use them. I'm sure we're near each other."

Still chewing the other half of her muffin, Maddy looks me in the eyes, eventually nodding with a slight movement. The fact that she isn't talking, isn't nodding bigger, or exhaling in relief makes me wish I'd lied, pushed her a little to see how she'd take sharing a room with me. But I don't lie to Maddy—except for that one, awful, horrible big one. This is a fresh start, and friend or more, there will be no more lies from now on.

Once our front desk girl, Clair, is off the phone, she checks us in and swipes my card for the entire cost. I catch Maddy's eyes on the receipt, and I notice the small tick in her lips. Even a budget motel in this part of the city runs two hundred a night, and two rooms over three nights is a small family vacation.

I hand Maddy a key card and lead her toward the elevators. I packed a few of Tanya's things in my bag for her, so when we reach the third floor, I follow her to her room first.

"Three sixteen," I say, gesturing over my shoulder. "Looks like I'm across the hall in three nineteen."

"Oh…" she starts, her brow bunching briefly. She covers it by nodding and folding her arms over her chest, blocking my full entrance into her room behind her. "Good, we're close then."

I lift my bag at my side.

"Your clothes…I could just pull them out real quick, or…do you want them in a drawer?" It's clear she doesn't want me to follow her into her room.

"I think I'll just stick with this," she says, tugging her thin blue T-shirt out from her stomach. "I'm beat from the day, so I think I'll just probably crash, maybe shower in the morning."

"Right," I nod, my mouth closed tight. "Probably a good idea. You want me to just call you or something to wake you up in the morning?"

I'm asking more because I still don't have Maddy's phone number, and regardless of this awkward relationship purgatory we've landed in, I still want it.

"No, I'll be good. Just let me know what time to set the alarm for."

Shit.

"Right…okay, well let's plan on seven? Maybe eight? Let's live a little…sleep in," I say, pulling the right side of my mouth high. Maddy's mouth matches mine, and I want to kiss it.

"Split the difference, seven-thirty," she says, wrinkling her nose when she says the time, like she's telling a secret or being bad.

I chuckle and point my key card at her.

"Deal," I say, tapping the card against the palm of my other hand a few times before nodding and turning to face my door. "This is me," I say over my shoulder, as if it weren't obvious where I was going, and I hadn't just told her my number.

"Good night, Will," she says, and I wait long enough to watch her mouth stretch into the kind of smile that hits her cheeks and holds on to her giggle. Of all of Maddy's smiles, this one has always been my favorite.

My chest warms from seeing a genuine look of happiness stretch across her face, I do my best to smile back. "Good night, Maddy," I say, turning and pressing my card against the reader at the same time she does behind me.

Our doors *beep* in unison, and we both push the handles down and our doors click open. My heart is kicking me from the inside, telling me to wake up and quit being, as my uncle would say, a chicken shit.

"Hey, Maddy?" The words rush out of me before I really have time to decide what comes next. She turns to face me quickly, her eyebrows raised and her body already in her room while I have yet to cross over my threshold. She's trying to speed away while I'm trying to draw things out, but fuck it. No more lies.

"Just then, when I asked if you wanted a wake-up call? It was really just a lame attempt to get your phone number," I shrug.

The same smile from before touches her lips, but this time it makes her blush. She looks down slightly, then peers at me through her lashes.

"Good night, Will," she says.

"Good night, Maddy," I repeat, at least satisfied that I went down swinging.

Her door sounds with a *click* before I finish closing mine, so I give up for the night and twist and hook the latch at the top. Unable to help myself, I rest my head against the door and count to five, then look through the peephole with one last dash of hope in my belly. It bursts quickly when the hallway is empty on the other side.

I turn to face my room—two double beds, a white wooden chest of drawers and entertainment center, a table with a coffeemaker on top, and a window with a view of the Fourth Street parking garage. I laugh to myself, wondering if Maddy's sizing her room up right now, too, then I toss my bag on the far bed and step into the equally plain bathroom to run water over my face. The shower looks tall enough that I might not have to hunch, so I push the curtain back and twist the knob, happy when I feel the water turn hot.

I tug my shirt over my head and walk out to the room, tossing my shirt, along with my jeans, over the arm of one of the wooden chairs near the table. As I turn to walk back to the bathroom, a quick movement under my door catches my eye. A small square of paper, folded in quarters, is flicked underneath, and I hear the sound of the keycard registering and a door clicking closed a second later.

My mouth starts to curve as I step closer to the paper, and my hopeful suspicion is confirmed as I kneel down and pick it up. I see the first three numbers before I completely have it unfolded, and when I flatten it against my chest and hold it out to read, I fist pump with my other hand.

"Still got it," I say, celebrating to no one. I have a weird feeling Duncan can hear me though, and I chuckle at the thought of him eating his nightly bowl of cereal and holding up his hand to give me an air high five.

I carry the note that reads *call me* with a series of beautiful numbers underneath into the bathroom, and I lay it on the counter next to the small bar of soap shaped like a leaf, then I strip off my boxers and climb in for the greatest hot shower of my life.

Maddy

I gave a boy my number once, in junior high. My parents' number, actually. He told me he wanted to invite me to his birthday party, and almost as much as I wanted a call from a boy, I wanted to go to the birthday party. It was at an amusement park, and all of the coolest kids were already invited. The call never came, and I was devastated. I decided to hate the boy for the rest of my life—*Colton Churchfield; I'll never forget.* He works at a gas station now—management. I saw him once when I pulled in to get a coffee and fill up on gas. He looked miserable, and I was overjoyed.

This time, there is no party. There are no hopes of running into Will years later, in a dead-end job. There's just a man. With my phone number. Fifty feet and two doors away from me.

I keep getting up and looking through the peephole, excited at the thought that maybe he's just coming over instead. Part of me wants that. *Most* of me wants that.

My phone in my palm, I leave the comfort of my hotel bed, shoes dumped by the dresser and socks still on my feet, and shuffle back to the door to look again. I stand on the tips of my toes and let my head rest against the wood, pressing my phone between my hand and the door. When it buzzes, I drop it, fumbling as it bangs against the door on the way to the floor, bouncing end-over-end and eventually landing behind the trashcan just outside the bathroom. I pick it up quickly, but stay near the door, pulling my legs in to sit crisscrossed with my back to the hallway just on the other side.

His text is on the screen.

There is something to be said about unlimited hot water.

My lips curl into my cheeks as I read, and I bring my hand to my face to feel my expression, proof that this smile is happening automatically—an instant reaction to the smallest note from him.

Will makes me happy.

I write him back.

I was thinking the same thing about expensive sheets and a comforter as thick as a mattress.

I wait while he types, bringing my knees up and cupping my phone in my hands, like I want to keep his messages a secret for only me. When my phone buzzes with his call instead, I feel my cheeks grow warm, and I scrunch my legs in tighter as I bring the phone to my ear.

"Hey," I say.

"How'd you know it was me?" he chuckles.

"I already gave you a special ring," I lie. "A Fat Elvis song."

"Wow, Fat Elvis. I don't even warrant skinny, movie-star Elvis," he says.

"Fat Elvis is better," I say, stretching my legs out and crossing my ankles as he laughs.

"I think we need to explore this more," he says.

"There really is no debate. His music meant more when he was older. More emotion," I reply.

"You mean more drugs," he fires back.

"Better clothes." That response makes him laugh hard, and I love the way I hear it coming from his chest, like it's deep—*genuine.*

"I liken myself to more of a *Jail House Rock* kinda guy, is all," he says, finally.

"Hmmm," I hum, lowering myself so my head is propped against the door, and I'm now lying on the floor, as close to him as I can be without leaving my room.

"What, you don't think I have moves? These hips—they swivel, darlin'," he says with a slight twang.

"That they do," I respond, pulling a few strands of my hair in front of my face, hiding from the flirtatious words I just said. Will chuckles more, but after a second or two, it's nothing but the sound of his room on one end meeting the sounds in mine.

"Your lip ticks up, like Elvis," he says, breaking the silence just as I feel my blush crawling down my neck and onto my chest.

I punch out a laugh and roll to my side.

"Does not!" I say, feeling my face, my mouth higher on one side. Son of a bitch!

"It does," he laughs lightly. "Always has."

I wait for the quiet to settle in again. I wait to be braver with him.

"Just how many things have you noticed about me, Will Hollister?" The second my question is done, my words are replaced by the rapid pounding of my pulse, but my face—it's still smiling. So hard it hurts.

"Let's see," he says, and I hear him settling into his bed, his voice muffling as his phone presses against his face. "I noticed that you can't stand having your hair pulled up in anything. When we swim, you pull your cap off the second we're done."

"Well that's sexy," I say, covering my face and mentally kicking myself for letting that one slip out.

"Oh, you wanted *sexy* things…" he says, and I open my mouth to say no, but shut it quickly, curious over exactly what he'll say next. "I have lots of those, too, besides the Elvis-lip thing, which yes, Maddy, is so fuckin' sexy."

"Oh," I blush, my thumbnail quickly moving between my teeth.

"Let's see, first, there's the way your legs curve along your quads, the muscle that's there giving them this edge. The athlete part of me likes how hard you had to train to make it that way," he says.

"What does the…" I pause, taking a quick breath, "*man* side of you think?" I ask, now so red that even my arms look flushed.

"Oh, the *man* side…" he growls low, a rumble from his chest. "That part of me likes the ride my hand takes when it starts just above your knee, then glides slowly up your leg to your panties, my fingertips tracing that lacey band that runs along the inside of your thigh and up over your hip."

Holy hell.

"And then there's the way your neck curves into your shoulder, the way your hair tickles your skin and makes you get goosebumps—just like it does when I kiss you there," he says, and my body shivers at the memory of his mouth against me.

"Your eyes do this thing, just before you race, where they haze and close in on their prey. I always imagined what it would be like for you to look at me like that," he says.

"Haven't I?" I ask, waiting a breath while he considers what I'm asking. "Looked at you that way," I fill in. "When we…"

"Maddy, I was so focused on every other part of your body that day, I don't remember what your eyes looked like," he laughs.

"Well maybe next time you will," I say.

"Next time." I can hear his grin in his words.

"Yeah," I breathe. "Next time."

This time.

The quiet comes again, filled only by the sound of his breathing, his breath a long draw that sounds as a warning in my ear. I chew at my nail, waiting…*hoping.*

"Maddy," he says, finally.

"Yes?" I sit up and crawl to my knees.

I hear his door open across the hall, and I stand, pressing my palm and forehead against mine.

"Let me in," he says.

I drop my phone to the floor and unlock my door, his hands running along my cheeks and into my hair the minute he enters my room. He kisses me so hard that he walks me backward several steps before the door slams closed behind him. His hands sweep down my sides to my legs, and he lifts me; my legs wrap around him as he continues to take long strides toward the bed, where he drops me the instant we reach it.

Will doesn't waste a breath, lifting his shirt over his head and tossing it to the floor as he moves closer to me. I lift myself on my elbows and bend my knees as I lower my chin to my chest to look him in the eyes. He runs his hands up my legs and along my knees, pushing them apart enough to put his knee on the bed between my legs. I move myself backward slowly as he crawls toward me—*predator, prey.*

"There it is," he smirks. "That's the look I love. Goddamn, Maddy, when you look like you want something."

His biceps flex from holding his weight, he climbs over me slowly, and I succumb, falling to my back until his elbows rest on either side of my head, his eyes raking over my face as his hands run through my hair and caress my cheek so sweetly I can't help but close my eyes and just feel.

"You have no idea," he says, and I hum, "what?"

Will's lips brush against my cheek, and I feel his tongue tickle my ear, his teeth gently tugging on the lobe as he breathes softly, covering my skin in tiny bumps while my spine rushes with a sensation like morphine—numb and tingly all at once.

"Just how beautiful of a woman you've become," he says into the tiny space above my shoulder. I feel his words travel down my neck, down my body, and I pull my right leg up higher, the sensation settling where his hardness teases against my center.

My eyes blink open, and his are waiting—adoring.

I bring my hands to his face, my cool palms pressing softly against his unshaven cheeks, warm with want.

"When you were eighteen, that summer…just before you left for State," I say, stopping at the sight of his breath catching, his eyes moving just enough that I see this hint of hurt flash behind them. I run my thumb along his jaw, and he turns his face enough to the side so his lips catch my palm. He kisses it, never once breaking our gaze.

"I would have picked you," I confess, my chest lifting with life, my lungs filling with the weight of every single word I just put there between us. I believe it. My heart knows it, and maybe it knew it all along. "If you would have kissed me. A hint, or sign, or…anything. Will…" I let my hands slide down his chest, pausing over his heart. "I would have chosen you."

Seconds pass with his eyes on mine—the only movement the trembling sensation of his thumbs along my own over his rapidly beating heart. His lips fall to my forehead slowly, his eyes closing as he draws near, and I close mine.

"I dream it every night, Maddy. Every single night," he says against me. He moves so his forehead is resting on mine, his body lifted above me, his weight held by his hands on either side of my body. I watch his chest move in and out with heavy, long-drawn breaths. "There is not a single day that has passed since I've met you that I didn't know in my heart you were supposed to be with me."

"You never said anything," I say, touching his face. I lift his chin enough to look at me.

"You were happy. Evan made you happy, and that…" he stops, shaking his head lightly, breathing out a regretful laugh that quirks the edge of his mouth, a small dimple shadowed by his whiskers. "Maddy, there is not a thing in this world I wouldn't have done to make you happy."

His words land on my chest. They dig inside and squeeze my heart and stop my breath. So many things have twisted and turned since Will came back—since he came *home*. Our worlds have been on this slow descent, but they've collided together here and now. Our truths have tangled, and it's clear now as I look at him that there is no going back for us. We will always be everything we've always been for one another. We'll always push; we'll always compete—he'll always be my fire—but not without everything else, we are beyond those things. Not without this.

Will is deliberate as he moves his body flush against mine, my hands searching along his abs and around to his back, feeling every curve and ridge of the muscles that define his shoulders. His arms carry his speed while his back is where his strength is; I could spend hours tracing every bend along his frame. His hands move underneath me, pulling my chest tight to his as he rolls to his back and pulls me so I'm now on top of him. His hands slide up my sides, and his thumbs hook under my T-shirt as he drags it up my stomach and chest. I rise so I'm now straddling him and help him lift it the rest of the way, then slide the straps of my bra down my shoulders just before he takes over, unhooking the clasp in the front and gliding the soft cotton down the length of my arms.

Every movement takes time. I stand and pull away my shorts and panties while he watches, a heavy breath doused in desire leaving his mouth. Will slides off his jeans and boxers, discarding them over the side of the bed before his fingertips reach for mine. He guides me back to him, his hands letting go of mine when I'm near enough that he can touch my thighs. His fingertips slowly snake upward, and I blush as he pauses with his thumbs circling along the top of my legs, where my muscles are the largest. The curves he said he admired bring a devilish grin to his mouth, and he blinks slowly, his mouth hung open as if he's ready to taste. His gaze moves to my eyes, and he looks at me with a rawness that warms my core.

I fall to him slowly, his erection hard against my inner thigh as I move down. His hand wraps around his hard thickness, and he guides himself into place just as I feel the heat of him against my center. As I sink onto him completely, my head falls back, my lips part, and I breathe out in pleasure.

Slow.

Tender.

Every single movement meaningful.

I move above him, my hips working in a steady rhythm that never builds, and that Will never rushes. It's purposeful, meant to make this feeling last as long as it can. It's something we both crave. My head falls forward and my eyes meet his just as my palms fall to his chest to steady myself as I move with him.

I feel him deep inside, and then I lift until he's nearly gone. His fingers glide up my thighs to my hips, pausing as I slide down him again. His hands trail up my stomach, up my ribs, and to my breasts. His fingers stroke my hard peaks like feathers, and I shiver from his barely-there touch.

We move like this, in sync, every movement tender and carrying so many unspoken words. We make love as if it's both the first time and the hundredth—everything new, yet every touch familiar. My body reacts to the pressure of him hitting me inside, and I cry out when the shudders that rush through me become unbearable. I ache for more as each wave passes until I can't hold my need back any longer. I close my eyes and fall down on him hard, again and again until his hips begin to lift to meet me and his hands slide down to my hips, driving me down on him harder.

"Fuck, Maddy," he groans, and I cry out with a new wave just as I feel his warmth fill me inside. Will rolls me to my back quickly, his hands digging into my ass while I grip his shoulders and he rocks into me three more times, his chest shuddering with his final pump.

I lie still while he pushes into me as deep as my body will accept him then lets his head fall against mine again. Our skin is moist, and his breath is hot. My hands reach for his face, my lips craving his kiss, but before I can reach him, Will stops me, backing away enough to look me in the eyes, his cock still hard inside me.

His right thumb runs along my cheek and his mouth curves up on one side. I shift and the feel of him in me makes me tingle in my core, and I cry out, begging. Will's smirk grows larger.

"Give me the look," he commands, reaching down and stroking me just where his cock is still buried.

My lips part and a desperate breath escapes my chest. I shake my head slightly and wiggle my hips, desperate to push him deeper. Just as I do, Will moves back, not leaving me completely, but enough that I feel empty and my body quivers with the slide of his dick inside.

"Look at me," he lowers his chin, "like you want it."

My breathing becomes hard to control, and I try to move my hips closer, but Will only holds me in place, his grasp on me firm. I whimper and stare him in the eyes as he bends down, his mouth covering mine and sweeping against my lips softly until I feel a rough edge glide against my top lip and move to my bottom. He nips at my lower lip, tugging it gently between his teeth and letting go, leaving me hungry and on the edge of another orgasm by just barely touching me.

"Maddy, you know how to look at me," he says.

I breathe slowly through my nose, finally understanding. My mouth curves gradually as my eyes haze and center on his, my focus narrowing until I only see the blue.

Until I own him.

And then he owns me, driving deep inside, again and again while I cry out and cling to him, collapsing beneath the weight of his body as every muscle exhausts and becomes weak from his spell.

All of me is under his spell. I need Will Hollister, and whatever hurt I felt is nothing compared to the things his touch can do to me. I am numb.

I am his.

CHAPTER 15

Will

The first time I felt what it was like to be inside Maddy, to push against her warm and soft body, claim her mouth for mine, touch her the way I've dreamt of touching her for literally years, it was rushed and desperate. It was fucking. It was *amazing* fucking, but it wasn't enough. It wasn't what she deserved.

Last night was about showing her what she means to me. I consumed her. I tasted every inch of her body over three hours, and I made her cry my name a dozen times. We fell asleep with a full moon lighting up the room through our hotel window, and I held her naked body against mine, proud that our flesh was sticky from our sex.

But when I woke up to her asleep in my arms, my heartbeat began to race with the realization of what had happened. Reality came crashing in. Lust can cloud judgment, and last night was selfish of me. There are things in my life—promises I've made in my brother's memory, that I won't break…ever. When Dylan needs me, I'll be there. When Tanya asks for support, I'll give it. And none of that is on them, just like their lives that Evan left them with aren't their doing.

I promised myself that I would be patient, let Maddy really *see* the baggage I carry. If it was meant to be, then at the end of everything, Maddy would be there, and she'd understand. Lying here, the room quiet, miles between us and our goals—her dream and destiny—anything feels possible. It also all feels impossible.

I stroke her hair, tucking behind her ear the same curl—the only one in a pile of twisted yet straight strands that zigzag over her pillow and on my arm. For the last hour, I've thought about waking her, about getting those last bits off my chest and explaining this distorted life I live. My mouth opens, though, and words are caught. I'm unable to make a sound. It's because I'm selfish, and I just want to lay here like this—pretending she was always mine—until I have to give her up.

My phone dings for the third time in just as many minutes, so I carefully slide my arm from under her neck and turn to the small night table on my side of the bed. I rub my eyes to focus them better as Tanya's messages come into view.

Dylan's going in for some blood work. If you're up, let me know.

I breathe in through my nose slowly and turn to the side to see the creamy skin of the girl who owns me wrapped up in a pile of white sheets. I draw my finger along her jaw and she wiggles a little, scrunching her nose, and eventually one eye creeps open.

"Good morning," she says, her voice raspy and her smile crooked.

Skinny Elvis.

"Dylan has a few tests, and I think Tanya could use my help," I say, trying to keep my voice barely above a whisper. It's early yet, and I don't want to completely wake her.

"Oh, well…give me a minute?" She begins to push the blankets down and move to the opposite edge of the bed, but I stop her with my hand on her arm.

"You stay here, get some more sleep. It's probably going to be mostly sitting around," I say, holding her eyes captive. My gut hurts looking at her because there are more things we need to discuss—more things she needs to know—things I should have finished telling her yesterday before I claimed her and took her for mine. But that's not how things happened. My control with her is nonexistent, and when I feel her give, I take. I take before I think, because I've waited to have her for too long.

Maddy licks her lips slowly, but she lays back down in the sheets, her shoulder scrunching toward her head on one side in guilt.

"Are you sure? I could get ready quickly," she says, yawning through the last word.

I chuckle.

"Positive," I lean down and press my lips on her shoulder. The blanket slides down her body as I move toward her, exposing her breast, and the sight triggers the animal inside of me that wants to avoid its responsibilities and instead stay here and take that breast in its mouth, sucking her perfect pink nipple raw until her body writhes and begs for me to sink into her again.

She follows my gaze and her lips curve up slightly as her hands move to my head, gently coaxing me to become the beast, guiding my mouth to her crest.

"Ah," I gasp, curling my chin into my chest in avoidance.

"What's wrong, Will?" she teases. "Don't you like me?"

I groan then breathe out a laugh.

"Maddy," I say, glancing up enough to see her hard peak tempting me. I graze it with my nose and she arches her back, so I lick the tip once, then suck it hard before forcing myself to sit up completely. "If I keep going, I won't stop."

Her bottom lip puffs out and her eyes hit mine as she blinks at me once. I close my eyes, shaking my head while I laugh lightly, then lean forward and pull the blanket up her body, tucking in the sides as she snuggles farther into the pillow.

"You, are bad," I tease, kissing her head and standing.

"You're the one walking around naked," she chirps.

I look over my shoulder as I move across the room, and I wink before kicking my boxers into the bathroom along with my pants.

"Just wanted to make you watch me walk away, baby," I tease.

She moans out a tired laugh, but I know she's not far from falling asleep again. It's not quite six in the morning, and the sun is barely up enough to spill light into our room. I get dressed quickly in the bathroom, then splash cold water on my face, forcing myself awake and washing away those last few temptations lingering in my memory.

I grip the sink on either side and lean close to the mirror, looking myself in the eyes, finally chuckling and shaking my head.

"Okay then," I whisper to myself. I'm going to walk out this door toward responsibility, but I'm also going to hope like hell that Maddy is right where I left her when I return. I won't touch her again until I'm sure she truly understands what she's getting with me. That feeling of faith, though—it's back. I believe in Maddy—I believe in *me* and Maddy. She'll understand, and she'll be here.

She'll be mine.

I get to the hospital by six thirty, and Tanya is kicking a vending machine as I walk from the elevator on the fifth floor.

"Give it hell, girl," I laugh. She twists her head, looking at me over her shoulder then kicks once more, following it up with a single, loud laugh.

"It's stuck," she shrugs.

I nudge my head to the side and she steps to the right as I grasp the corners of the machine and shake it for a few seconds; a pack of Funyuns finally falls down to the hatch at the bottom.

"Oh my god, thank you, Will!" she says, pushing me out of the way and kneeling to reach her hand inside. She grabs the bag and has it ripped open within seconds.

"Hungry?" My eyebrows are high.

She stuffs two rings in her mouth and holds her palm flat against her lips while she chews, lifting a finger with her other hand, the bag dangling in a tenuous grip between her thumb and pinky. The bag shakes, so I reach up and grab her wrist to steady it. I don't like her pushing herself so hard…so hard that she doesn't eat.

"Starving," she says, finally, stuffing two more rings in her mouth.

"You should have called," I smile. "We would have brought you food."

Within a minute, she's crumpling up the empty bag and moving down the hallway. I follow her, and we stop at the water fountain.

"I didn't really sleep at all. I was too busy watching him sleep. They monitored him all night," she says, words spilling from her mouth a mile a minute. She stops long enough to guzzle some water, then stands and runs her arm across her mouth. Her eyes are like saucers.

"Maybe drink a little coffee, did you?" I laugh.

She exhales heavily, her shoulders sagging while her head rolls around in a slow circle as she stretches her neck. I pull her in for a hug and rub the place where her neck meets her back and she sinks into me.

"I have had, maybe, a gallon of coffee—yet, somehow, I still feel like I could collapse right here on the floor and sleep for days," she says, her voice muffled against my chest. "But my brain won't slow down. That…*that's* the coffee's fault."

Her body shakes while she laughs. I let go and she steps back one pace. My hands stay on her shoulders while I look at her—the tired is amplified today. She's been hospitalized for exhaustion twice since Dylan was born, and I fear a third time is coming again.

"Let's get this blood work done and then you are going to lie down somewhere…" She opens her mouth, and I know it's to argue with me about all of the reasons she can't leave. I cut her off before she can. "You can stay here, so you'll be nearby and won't miss any of the non-updates I'm sure you'll get, but I insist on the resting part. You have a family room with a bed. You're going to use it."

She blinks twice, her mouth a flat line, and her chest rises once, exhaling in defeat.

"This whole thing is killing me," she says, her eyes pooling and the whites turning red.

"I know it is, but we've made it here. You've gotten him the best help in the world, Tanya," I say, shifting to walk alongside her and cradling her to my side with my arm.

She wrings her hands in front of her, her eyes wide as we move along the sterile hallway, nurses rushing by with charts and trays with meds piled high. Sometimes I wonder how Evan would have done with all of this—if he would have been present at all. I used to think he would have. I gave him credit, but perhaps that credit wasn't due. Time takes people off pedestals, and it makes golden boys seem less gold.

I let Tanya take the lead, following her into Dylan's room. He's sedated, but he always sleeps peacefully. His hands are curled where they rest on his stomach, and there are wires taped to his body in at least a dozen different places. Tanya sits down in the chair pulled near his head, on the opposite side of the bed from me, and she holds on to his arm, hugging it with her fingers.

"He's my whole life, Will. I wouldn't have it any other way," she says, reaching one hand up to sweep the long strands of brown hair dangling across his forehead out of the way.

"I know," I say, dragging a chair closer from the other side of the room to sit and face her. I press my hand on Dylan's other arm and squeeze once. He doesn't stir at all.

"They have him knocked out. They said it makes the blood draw easier. Less…jerking," she says.

I nod.

"How'd last night go?" I ask.

"No seizures, but we didn't expect any. They're going to monitor him again tonight, and take some readings. The doctor said he'll know more after they run some tests. They'll call me in a few weeks, and maybe Dylan will qualify for a trial, some drug that's supposed to hold off the seizures, maybe make him hurt a little less," she says.

I nod again, then let my eyes move from her to the sleeping boy between us. I spend minutes watching him breathe. Eventually, two nurses come in and begin to fill vials with his blood. Dylan sleeps through the entire thing. I wait for them to finish before stretching out my legs and pulling my phone from my pocket. I felt it buzz while they were working, and my pulse has been racing excitedly ever since. When I see Maddy's name, my mouth forms its automatic reaction, my lip curled higher on the right, my cheeks round like a boy who has just been told he's getting everything he wants for Christmas.

MADDY: *I'm awake. If it's not too far, I'll cab it to the hospital. Maybe bring you and Tanya some real food?*

"You're in love with her, right?"

I close my eyes and let my phone fall with my hands to my lap, but my smile doesn't waver. I open my gaze on Tanya, and she's smirking at me. She nods with a slight laugh.

"It was painfully obvious the moment you introduced her to me," she chuckles. "You can't make eye contact with anybody or anything else when Maddy's in the room."

"That bad, huh?" I don't argue, and it feels good to share this with someone.

"Pretty bad, Will," she says, her head falling to one side and her eyes staying on mine. She studies me for a few seconds, and I grow warm under her gaze.

"What?" I finally ask, shifting in my seat and giving my attention to my phone in the brief pause before she answers. I type quickly, keeping the screen just out of Tanya's view.

ME: *Please come. Forget the food. I'm making Tanya nap.*

"She was around for the accident. She's known you for a while, yeah?" she asks. I hold her stare, and for a second I wonder if she's put this together completely. I finally give her a small nod confirming her question. I feel a sick rush hit my gut, but just as I always do, I pretend. Her life…it's hard enough, and Maddy agreed.

"She was around us both a lot, and they went to the same school," I say, guilt slamming into me from all directions because of how Maddy fits into Tanya's broken puzzle.

My phone buzzes again, and this time I don't even hide how excited I am to get a message from Maddy. It's a small heart image. It's stupid and childish, and I fucking love it.

"She loves you, too," Tanya says, breaking me from my momentary giddiness. I glance up and our eyes lock. All I can do is give her a crooked smile, and hope like hell she's right. "I like her, Will. I like *you* liking her."

I look back down to the phone in my palms, to the stupid heart—pink and cartoonish. I breathe out a short laugh and nod my head.

"Thanks," I say.

Maddy ended up bringing food anyhow, and after we all scarfed down burgers and fries, she insisted Tanya head to the hotel for a little while to shower and get some sleep. Exhausted doesn't even begin to describe her state, so she didn't argue, and I was glad. Maddy and I stayed with Dylan, and Tanya was back after a few hours, refreshed, but still not quite whole. She may never be whole, but she fakes it pretty damn well.

We all ended up staying in the hospital the second night. When Dylan had a seizure, Maddy refused to leave Tanya alone. I tried to explain that those weren't anything new for him, that Tanya was used to them, but Maddy was running on adrenaline, and I know that sometimes it's just better to let her win.

The exhausting marathon day and night has left everyone spent, and while I work to stave off the onset of a panic attack as I lay down on four seats by our airport gate, I worry that I'm really going to have to survive this trip alone. Maddy hasn't let go of my hand once—clinging to my fingers during the drive and through every second of check-in, parting only for security—and only long enough to pass through the X-Ray machine one at a time. Her hand is in mine now, but there's no strength in her grip. Her head is leaned the opposite way, her cheek smooshed against her fist, her body one nudge away from toppling over completely.

My heart is racing, and I'm not sure if it's because of the flight or her. The woman at the gate begins to deliver garbled instructions, and I listen just well enough to recognize that we should be called to board in about five minutes. I swing my feet around, but don't let go of Maddy's hand. She startles, rubbing her face and looking at me, then she gives me a smile and snuggles in against my arm, her other hand hugging over my chest.

My heart is still racing. I am terrified. If this plane falls from the sky, I'll lose her. I won't know. She won't know. We will never be. That…is what terrifies me.

I let my head rest on the top of hers, and I turn slightly to kiss her through her hair. I leave my lips on her, and I let my eyes fall closed so I can breathe her in. My elixir—a potion to keep my heart calm and my head clear.

"I love you, Maddy," I say, the words barely audible. I'm sure she didn't hear them, but her hand squeezes mine the tiniest bit, and I pretend that she did, and that's her way of saying it back.

This plane ride won't be the end of me—*of us*. It can't, because God wouldn't be that cruel. I deserve this, and damned if I don't want it all.

CHAPTER 16

Maddy

My dad did not understand. When I told him I had to fly to Cleveland to help Will, he called me careless. I coaxed him into trusting me, promised him I'd be faster than I was when I left, making light jokes that he did not find amusing. He now expects that speed, and he is not being kind in front of others.

In front of Will.

My dad told me when I rolled in from our trip late Saturday that I better be prepared to work this morning. He didn't call Will, but when we got to the pool, Will was already deep into his warm-up laps. He puts in the work, and he deserves a fair shot at this.

"Again," my dad shouts, his feet straddling the training weights I anticipate he's going to make me tread with as punishment.

He hasn't called any of this punishment, but it's clear that's just what it is. If he knew the whole story—that I didn't just run off because of some new infatuation with Will Hollister, if he knew what Will was busy doing, what kind of man Will was—he wouldn't be barking at me now. The double-standard amuses me while I paddle back to the far wall to take my turns again—to do them faster. All my parents wanted was for me to give Will a pass and not blame him for my pain. That's all they wanted until I started to fall for him and get too close. The fact that they can't trust me, trust that he is still the same boy—man—that my father always admired in the pool, is beyond hypocritical.

I use my anger, pounding my hands through the water three lanes over from the man who has awoken my barely beating heart. I fly toward the wall. I twist and push, and I fly back to where I came from. I'm turning faster than I ever have, and I know it, yet all my dad can do is shout out disappointments.

"Congratulations, and the swimmer from Iowa State just broke your record," my dad deadpans. I match his stare, but he's unfazed and quickly turns to Will. I follow his gaze to see Will breathing hard, holding onto the wall, waiting to take his harsh criticism. "That was good Will. Keep doing that."

My dad tosses a heavy binder on the ground a few feet away and starts walking.

"Maddy, weights."

Not even a full sentence as he rounds the pool and heads inside. I watch through the window as he grabs a bottle of water and turns toward the stairs.

"I thought you said he was okay with you coming to Cleveland," Will says, dipping under two sets of ropes and popping up in my lane.

"I may have overestimated on the *okay* part," I say.

Will looks at me and his eyes droop with a short exhale. I don't want to stick around for him to say he's sorry, because I don't want him to be sorry. I can take my dad's grouchiness. He's not really mad, he just doesn't like me not being his showgirl twenty-four-seven. I get that the idea of him coaching me, of having this family swimming legacy perform well on an Olympic stage, is a big deal to him. He's built it up, and so have I. It's just since Will arrived, other things have started to matter, too. My heart woke up, and I'm not putting it down again.

I strap the weights on my ankles one at a time, then place the others on my wrists as Will does the same and we both tread to the center of the pool and work to hold our heads above the surface for several minutes at a time.

"Your mom *okay* with the fact that you missed camp? Like, *for real* okay?" Will grunts out his question, his arms and legs circling in the water.

"I haven't really seen her. She's been so busy campaigning to save the damned lakeside park," I shrug, dipping down under water to rest my legs. I push up from the bottom and begin to work again.

"She's a fighter," Will says, his lips puckering into a tight smile as he stares at me.

"What's that look for?" I ask.

His head wiggles from one side to the other.

"It's just that I can tell where you get it from—your refusal to give up on anything you want," he says.

"Oh yeah?" I tease, suddenly feeling like I could swim like this for hours, carry these weights for miles, and still win. Flirting with Will Hollister does things to my body.

"*Oh yeah*," he grins.

I laugh at the deeper voice he puts on, but we both stop smiling at the sound of the main door shutting behind our backs.

"That's enough," my dad says, moving to the pool's edge. We both swim over to him and remove the weights.

Will folds his arms on the pool deck and rests his chin on top of his hands while I grip the side and hold on below. My father kneels down and scratches above his right brow, his lips twisted in thought. When he raises his chin, his eyes settle on Will.

"I know you just got back into town, but that interview deal…it's gotta happen this afternoon. It's the only slot they have open before they travel to Omaha," he says.

"Who's it with?" Will asks, and I notice his hands ball into fists. He doesn't want to do this.

"The network. It'll be one of those packages they use between races, kind of with that moody documentary feel. The Cumberlands are pretty excited about it, and they've named you and Maddy as their team for trials." My dad smiles when he mentions this.

"How much did they give you?" I ask, knowing the real reason he's smiling. He doesn't care that Will is getting attention. He told me himself that Will won't see the water after Omaha.

My dad shrugs his shoulders around his neck, his head wavering from side to side.

"They donated a decent package to the program. It'll go a long way in covering the next camp," he says.

"Next camp," I repeat. My dad meets my eyes and his closed-mouth smile grows fast as his eyes light up.

"Wow," I say, knowing without asking what all of this means. My dad's made the staff for the Olympics. "Distance? Sprints?"

His mouth grows tighter, but the smirk is still there.

"Head?" My eyes widen.

My dad chuckles, then rubs his hand along his chin.

"If we do well at trials, it's looking pretty good," he says.

"Wow," I say again, turning to look at the smooth, still water next to me. I also understand without asking what the *we* part means. It's me. If *I* do well, my dad pretty much gets the gig.

"Congrats, Coach," Will says, holding his weight on one arm and reaching to grip my father's hand. There's a pause before my dad reciprocates, and my stomach twists. I know what that's for, too. Will—he's not part of the deal.

I push back from the wall a little, laying back to float in the water, letting water spill over my cap and ears, drowning out some of the noise. I can't cut off the sound in my own head, though. When Will lifts himself from the pool, I let my feet fall and right myself to listen.

"I should probably shower and squeeze in a nap if we're really doing this," Will says. His jaw is working, but he looks at my father with nothing but calmness behind his eyes. He's doing this to help my dad—as a favor because he let him miss out on a few practices—because he invited him here in the first place. I can feel my brow pinching, the wrinkle forming just above the bridge of my nose because none of this is fair. If my dad only knew *why* Will was missing, exactly the lengths he's gone to for everyone other than himself. I have to get Will to tell him.

"We'll set up out here. They want to have the pool in the background, sort of put you in the element I guess," my dad says. "Be here around three, okay son?"

Son. The inside of my mouth becomes sour hearing him say that because I know he doesn't mean it. He's using Will, and I'm heartbroken for two reasons—because Will is going to get hurt, and because my dad is doing something I never thought he would.

Will nods and pulls the end of his towel over his shoulder, rubbing it in his hair, his cap held in his other hand. His gaze lingers on me for a second, and his lip ticks up on the left just a hint, his eyes lowering as he turns and heads inside. I feel warm and adored from just a simple glance.

It only takes my dad six seconds to ruin it.

"You cannot get mixed up with him, Maddy," he says.

My head tilts to the side, and I swim close to the wall again, gripping the sides while my eyes narrow on my father.

"I'm not getting *mixed up* with anything, dad," I say, and he cuts me off before I finish, saying "good."

My eyebrows pull in tight, and my chest burns angry.

"No, not *good,*" I huff, lifting myself from the pool. I step close to him, taking the towel from his hands and wrapping it around my arms while my eyes bore into him. "I'm not getting *mixed up* because it's Will, Dad— *Will.* The same guy you and Mom both told me to give a break to, the guy who you used to always throw in to swim anchor—no matter what the stroke. Will was always your man, and Dad…he has…"

I look down and bring my thumb and forefinger to the bridge of my nose. I'm in such a weird paradox, and I have no idea how I got here. I breathe out a laugh and shake my head.

"Will has brought me back from the dead, Dad," I say, glancing up to meet his scowl. His mouth is pulled tight and his forehead is wrinkled— he's looking at me like I'm crazy.

"You weren't *dead,* Maddy. You're being dramatic, but what exactly *are* you and Will?"

I swallow hard and close my eyes.

"I was not living, Dad. Evan died, and I made this impulsive decision to just put it in a box and never love anyone again," I say. "I go to school. I live with Holly, and I hope like hell she never meets anyone for real so I don't have to live alone. I'm thinking about continuing on to get my practitioner license, because school is something I have figured out, and when you're in school, you have this sort of built-in excuse for being alone. I can lie to myself and say *that's why I don't date*. I can lie to people who try to fix me up."

I breathe in deep, flapping my arms against my side with a heavy exhale. "I don't date, Dad. I haven't since Evan died. I haven't done more than flirt with cute doctors, then run away when they actually looked interested. I'm a goddamned mess, or at least I was…until Will found that girl I used to be."

"Maddy, you're just infatuated with this memory; it's nostalgia, and it's normal. Will is a good friend—hell, I love that boy…"

"He's more than a friend, Dad. He's that and so much more to me you have no idea. There are things…" I stop and take a sharp breath. I can't share pieces of Will that aren't mine to share. That's for him to do, but my dad just needs to understand how special Will is. "The man Will has become would astound you, Dad. And if you really loved him, like a son, you would dig a little deeper to find out exactly what all of those things are. And you'd let him compete on fair ground, with you behind him—with you *really* pushing him. I see you hold back. You let him slide today. You know he's capable of more, but you don't want him to succeed. If Will wins, he's in. That's…"

I stumble back a step and watch my father's shoulders sink.

"If he wins, you have no choice," I say, my eyes slowly sweeping up from the ground between us, my mouth open—stunned.

"I'll talk to him before that. He won't, Maddy," my father says, his eyes flashing just as mine do at his words. He didn't mean to let all of that come out.

"You can't take that from him!" I shout.

"We're in the hole—" My father fires that response, and I scrunch my face in confusion. I wait while he walks around the pool to the opposite end, bending down and picking up the binder he dropped several minutes ago. He flips it open as he walks back to me, holding it flat in both palms. I look from his eyes down to a delinquent bill clipped into the rings, pressing my finger on the paper and sliding it to the other side to see the next bill underneath. Statement after statement—mortgages, second mortgages, threats to cut power, liens, bankruptcy papers.

My bottom lip falls open, and I gasp as my eyes flit to my father's. His cheeks hang low, dragging his mouth with them, and the sadness in his eyes is the most honest look I think I've ever gotten from him.

"I need to coach this team, Maddy. I need to be successful, and I need to bring big sponsors to the table. I do this, our business will rebound just because of the fame. Without it?" He pauses, flipping the book closed in his hand, the pages snapping shut. "This club is closed by winter."

"How did this happen?" My mind is spinning with everything—with Will, with my parents' debt, and the idea that a place I identify as home could be ripped away from us.

"Time, less kids swimming," he shrugs. "It's always been hard, and I think you know that."

I nod because yes, I do.

"It just got harder, and then…" My father stretches out his hands, his financial burden held in one and the other empty.

"Daddy, I'm so sorry," I say. "Has Mom tried anything? Maybe something public, with the city? Like a takeover, partnership…whatever…"

"Why do you think she ran in the first place?" My father's mouth quirks up on one side and his chin lowers to his chest as he pulls the binder in close.

It's quiet between us for several seconds while my mind works to process what's happening. I spin it a dozen ways in my mind, and there isn't a single way that everyone wins. I keep coming back to Will, though, and how many times he has put everyone else first. The funny thing is, I bet if my father asked him to step away, he would. But Will has sacrificed enough.

"You have to let him compete," I say, my eyes snapping to his.

His head shakes, but I fight on.

"You have to, Dad. Will deserves this," I say, breathing out a desperate grunt through my nose.

"His DUI, Maddy…the recreational drug use, and the drinking. He's like one of those rock stars or child actors that your mom tells me about when she flips through tabloids in the grocery line, and sponsors don't want to jump on board with big risks," my dad argues. "I need to bring in the money. The greatest coaching in the world is meaningless compared to dollar signs. Will is a risk I can't afford—at least not past the trials. His story buys him a shot, but one race…that's all the risk people are going to want to take."

"But that's not Will's whole story," I defend.

His mouth closes tight, and he breathes in through his nose, his chest lifting slowly, like he's building a shield against any argument I can throw his way.

"He's doing this goddamn interview for *you*, Dad!" I finally let that out, because my father has to see—he must know this is the last thing Will wants to do. "He's going to walk through the most horrific moments of his life on camera, because you asked him to, Dad. That…*that* has to count for something!"

"That makes the Cumberlands happy," my dad shrugs. His face is growing pale, and I think it's from shame.

My mouth curves in disgust.

"They want his story on primetime, because the world loves gossip," I shake my head, walking away from my father.

"Maddy, I love that boy like a son," he says to my back, a last-ditch effort to cover up his own desperation and greed.

I pause with my hand on the handle for the door, and I speak my words, unable to turn and look at him. For the first time in my entire life, I can't look at the man I've idolized. I'm ashamed of him.

"No you don't. But I love him, and maybe that will be enough to change your mind," I say.

I step inside and shut the door behind me, then fight my instinct to rush up the stairs and take Will by the hand and beg him to just run away. We could run away from it all, and our lives would be amazing. But there would always be unfinished business. I'm supposed to win. He's supposed to race for real.

I just need to find a way to make that happen so it doesn't ruin life for everyone else.

CHAPTER 17

Will

The lights are always hot.

That's the one thing I remember from those interviews after the crash. I remember that, and I recall how fast the questions came. I was the human form of a speed bag, the reporters pummeling just fast enough that I had time to catch my breath and say words at their next intrusive question.

"How are you coping?"

Words, words, words.

"Are you in any pain? Will you ever swim again?"

Words, words, words.

"You must feel a tremendous amount of guilt. It's natural; can you share a little about that?"

Words, motherfucking words!

I know why Curtis is pushing for this interview—I bring buzz, and that gets airtime, which equals revenue. As painful as the interview is, I feel like I owe him for this shot, and if it can help secure him as head coach—*a coach*, at the very least—then one afternoon of misery on my part isn't so unbearable, especially when I look at it in context with the big picture of four years of grief.

I have one nice suit, and I've worn it once already since I've been back in Knox. Either my muscles have doubled in size from a few weeks of workouts, or that panic I thought was reserved for airplane rides is starting to bleed into other areas of my life. Either way, this collar is fucking tight. I slip behind the counter at the club's small snack bar and tug my tie loose, fumbling because, well…fucking panic, when I feel her cool hands glide over mine and take over. I let them.

"Thank you for doing this," Maddy says, her thumbs dusting across my knuckles. I stop her and work my fingers through hers, nodding lightly and blinking once. Bringing her hands together, I press them between mine and turn her wrist to kiss the inside. She sighs. She's worried about me, but she doesn't realize how many interviews like these I've survived.

I let go of her hands and she goes to work retying my tie, a little looser, so I can breathe.

"There are probably going to be some questions…some *things*…that you don't want to hear. I've done dozens of these, and they like to talk about Evan, about his *path to greatness* getting cut short. It just…it might be hard to hear," I say, partly preparing myself to hear the awful regurgitation of events I'm only now starting to overcome. For Maddy, this will be the first time she has to hear the story knowing about Tanya. It makes it hard to sit quietly and listen without choking out a laugh every time they compliment his great character.

"I'm staying," she says, her eyes focused on her hands at my neck. Her mouth is set in a hard line. I figured she would stay, but I felt like she at least deserved the warning.

"They're ready," Curtis says. Maddy walks away the second her father walks beside her, and we both turn to watch.

"She's just mad because she thinks you're forcing me to do this," I say, giving my attention back to him, his brow low and his eyes not blinking until his daughter steps outside.

"Yeah, probably," he says, shaking his head and turning to me, our feet squared with one another as I stand straight. He puts a palm on either shoulder and brushes out twice before patting and squeezing. When he's done, though, he doesn't let go, and the way he looks me in the eyes feels off, but then again, so does everything in my life.

I reach forward with my right hand and pat his arm, squeezing and nodding to let him know I'll be okay, and his mouth curves into a tight smile.

"I'm happy to help, Curtis. You taking a shot on me...that means everything, and if I can help you in return, I'm glad," I say.

His cheeks tick higher, and while his mouth smiles, his eyes dip and look sad. His hands fall from my shoulders. I nod to him one more time before sliding around him and moving to the deck area, which is now covered in lighting equipment and a play-back station on a cart. The chair I'll soon be sitting in is centered on the TV screen. Maddy is sitting in one of the chairs by it, her feet pulled under her legs and her hands in her lap, twisting.

I stop just long enough to run my hand along her back and bend forward to kiss the top of her head. She grabs my arm as I walk by and her hand slides down from my elbow to my fingers, clinging to them until I step completely away. That one touch fills my lungs, and I know I can do this.

The Cumberlands are standing nearby, and as I slide into the tall chair and raise my chin to let the nervous college-intern guy clip a mic to the inside of my tie, I see Curtis move between them, the same look on his face as before. I wait for his eyes to hit mine, and when they do, I smile and give him a thumbs up. He reciprocates, but the hard line on his face doesn't change at all. I know the look—it's guilt. He thinks he's making me do this, but what he doesn't get, what no one gets, is *I* make myself do these things. I was allowed to survive. I owe the universe many favors.

"Will, it's a pleasure to meet you. I'm Donna Morris," a tall woman says as she reaches her palm forward to shake mine. We shake, and her grip is strong. My lip ticks up on one side.

"Former swimmer?" I ask.

She chuckles and nods. She looks to be in her late forties, maybe early fifties.

"I had my time. College, but never the big stage. I wasn't as good as you and Maddy Woodsen," she says, pausing before sliding into her chair to glance up at my eyes. "Or your brother," she adds.

That's obligation speaking. Evan was talented for a college swimmer, but he was never Maddy. Death makes people greater than they were.

I nod politely and glance over to Maddy, her thumbnail between her teeth and her eyes intent on the TV screen.

"We'll start slow, some general questions about your training and workouts here, then move into a little bit of your history. The questions will sound weird because this airs with next weekend's race, and portions with the trials, so we'll be pretending it's the future, sound good?" she says, not really looking at me. She's focused on the stack of cards in her lap with subjects she's been told to bring up—the gory ones people tune in for.

"Whatever," I shrug, shifting in my seat enough to put my feet on the ledge below and folding my hands in my lap. *Future*—how does that sound? I glance back to Maddy and think the word in my head, my mouth following my thoughts, curving up as my chest warms. I haven't looked forward to a future in quite some time, but I do now.

I catch a glimpse of my uncle near the far back just beyond Maddy, and he holds up a hand. I nod to him, glad to see where he is—just in case I need to look someone in the eye that I know, without doubt, is in my corner.

The lights adjust, and Donna runs through a few sound checks. I lift my hand to loosen my tie, but catch myself, knowing I can't touch a thing now that I'm miked up. *Prison* begins in three, two, one…

"America loves swimming dynasties. The Hollister brothers were well on their way to becoming one, until tragedy struck. Four years ago, on Christmas Eve, the Hollister family—made up of father Robert, his wife Nan, and their two college-aged boys, Will and Evan—boarded a plane to make a trip up north to a cabin in Wisconsin. It was an annual tradition, a flight Robert had made dozens, if not hundreds, of times over his life as a pilot. This trip…would be their last. Weather, a glitch in the mechanics, and the slightest shift in direction were all blamed in the FAA report, and for months, the sporting world mourned the loss of one of its most promising swimmers."

My eyes shift to Maddy, her body curled tighter in the chair. I can't see her face, but for a small glimpse of her profile. She shouldn't be hearing this, no matter how badly she wants to be here for me. No one should hear this story, yet people keep telling it.

"Will Hollister, the oldest brother—and while often not as *flashy* as his younger brother Evan, certainly just as talented in the pool—survived. He endured months of rehab, and when his physical road to recovery seemed to straighten out, his mental one took a turn. Rumors of drug use, evidence of alcohol abuse, a car totaled when it ran into a tree just outside of his hometown, between Knox, Indiana and the nightlife of Indianapolis. The headlines told the story of a lone survivor busting at the seams. *Survivor*…perhaps that's the key word, though, when talking about Will Hollister."

"What a difference a year makes. Tonight, the last Hollister will take to the water again in a match-up against some of the best swimmers in the Midwest. The meet is just a *friendly* arranged among some of swimming's legends, recently anointed as the lineup of coaches charged with leading the US Men's and Women's Swimming Teams to the top of the podium later this summer. It's a practice-run, of sorts, before the real trials happen the following week. But for Will Hollister, the trials begin with this race…they began when he started training again, living in Michigan with his uncle, his only living relative. They began…when that plane took off from an icy runway on a journey that would forever change one of the greatest swimmers in Indiana State University history."

I feel it coming before she asks. It's like I've rehearsed, though I haven't—I've just been asked these questions enough.

"Will, how have you been coping with the attention? I'm sure you feel the pressure—even here," Donna says, turning to look me in the eyes. I know the cameras are on me now. I smile, mouth closed, hands clasped in my lap. I am the epitome of calm on the surface. Inside, I am numb.

"This place has always been home. The Shore Club is where I started, it's where Evan and I trained, where we first met Maddy and Coach

Woodsen. It just seemed right to train here—if I was going to really give this a shot," I say, exhaling when I feel the focus shift back to Donna. She winks at me, a sign that my answer was good. I know it was—it's what they all want to hear.

"And how do you feel about your shot? It's been a while since you've competed, other than a few small meets leading up to your time at training camp. Do you think you can still find that fire that once drove you?"

I run my palm over my cheek, thinking about her question. I've answered this before, but she's asked it differently. And this time—it's not the same. Before, I wasn't sure I'd ever find the water again, and now that I have, I need to find the fire to win. My mouth ticks up on one side at that thought, and my eyes shift to her.

"I think when you're a competitor, that drive is always there. I just had to wake it up again, remember what it felt like and use it. It kind of comes back to training here, too. Coach Woodsen…*Maddy*…they push me. They always have. And maybe that need to win carries a little more weight than it once did, too," I say.

"Uh huh," she hums, leaning forward on one arm, closer to me. Her eyes move from one of mine to the other, and I can tell she's legitimately interested in my story. It's probably because she's a former swimmer, but it sets me at ease a little, and I feel the weight on my chest lift enough that I no longer feel the need to rip my tie from my neck.

We settle in to a pattern, and the questions come as I expect. We talk about Evan; we talk about how hard it was for me to grieve, the guilt I felt, and the pillar of strength Duncan has been for me over the last four years. And then she mentions Maddy.

"You two…you're close," she says, her lip curling as she delves into uncharted waters for me and interviews.

"We're friends," I correct, my eyes warning hers.

"I can imagine you both lean on one another, especially here. It must be hard not to miss your brother at something you all probably talked about doing together." The tone of her voice lifts at the end, trying to pull me in with her fake empathy.

"Like I said, we're friends," I say, forcing my voice to remain calm and my body to stay disciplined rather than squirm under Donna *Has-been's* glare and innuendo. I don't give a fuck if she's right—me and Maddy, that's our business. And sharing what we are happens on our timeline.

"Evan would like that you both remained close, wouldn't he?" she says, crossing one of her long legs over the other and settling into her chair. Donna was probably a mediocre swimmer, but she's a great tabloid reporter. I've reached my limit with her. It's happened to me before, but it's never been over questions about Maddy. Usually it's pot use, my DUI, losing my license—I can't handle the way the reporters beat my worst moments to death, asking me question after question on the same indiscretion. But I'd do rounds of those questions before I sit here and put that spotlight on Maddy. I don't like where she's leading this.

"I don't really care," I finally say, crossing my leg over my knee and folding my hands on top of my ankle, tapping my thumbs together while I wait for her to try to salvage this.

She blinks rapidly, flipping through the cards in her lap before looking up at me with one eyebrow quirked.

"You and Evan…did you…get along?"

I smirk and chew at the inside of my mouth. I'm done. All I do is shrug.

Her glare narrows as her lips part. She finally blinks a few times, looking up at her cameraman, drawing a line with her finger across her neck. When he drops his headphones around his neck, I stand and drop the mic pack from my pocket, leaving it in a pile of cords on my empty seat.

"Will, we're not done," she says.

I tilt my head and twist my lips, my eyes catching a glimpse of Curtis and the Cumberlands behind her. They've gotten enough juice, and they know it. I let my gaze fall to Donna, still perched on her chair, waiting for me to come back and fulfill my duty. I've given enough.

"Actually, we are," I say, walking toward Maddy, who is now standing near the door, next to my uncle.

My heart is angry—it's pounding against the walls of my chest, and I can barely contain my desire to scream. But I see her. Maddy's face is calm, she's sure and safe—she's home.

"Come on," she says, tugging my arm toward her as she takes steps to the front door. "Let's get out of here."

Responsibility…promises—that weight is pulling at my back, clawing at me and reminding me that I should go back, finish what I promised and find a way to make everyone happy. But I'm tired. I'm so tired, and I don't trust my decisions anymore.

I let Maddy lead, unknotting my tie from my neck as we walk through the parking lot to her car, on our way handing my jacket and the tie to my uncle. He doesn't ask questions, and nobody follows us, or begs us to stay. They're done with me, and I'm done with them. I'm not pretending for Evan anymore. I just need to set the story straight for one more person.

"They're going to start talking about us…romantically," I say the second I shut the passenger door.

Maddy turns over the engine and fastens her seat belt before twisting to look me in the eyes.

"Let them talk," she says, her expression resolved. She's done, too.

"You and Evan…they're going to talk about that, too," I say.

"I know," she whispers her response. Her eyes linger on mine for a few seconds before she leans back in her seat, checks her mirrors, and pulls us into reverse.

Evan's perfect legacy…it ends here.

Maddy

The boy I used to chase—his speed, his drive—that boy is gone. The anger and resentment—the fumes that Will has been using to push himself in the pool, through life—it's all gone, too. He has carried it all for years, and he's finally hit his limit.

He hasn't asked where we're going. I turned right onto the highway, and I'm pretty sure he knew. These secrets, sorting out who needs to know what, who can handle what truths—it's killing him. It ends now…here…today.

I find the familiar street easily, turning from the highway and winding down the neighborhood road lined with houses and dirt lawns, cars parked in yards, and dogs chained to stakes out front. I stop near the gray one, the ramp in front—Dylan's ramp. The van is parked outside, which means they are both home. I haven't gotten to know Tanya well, but I know enough from her spirit to be sure that she and Dylan are never—*ever*—apart if she's at home.

I park quickly along the curb and turn to Will, his eyes locked straight ahead, just as they've been for the last hour.

"This part is for me to tell. This isn't yours, Will," I say. His head leans toward me and his hand slides over mine, squeezing.

"It's all mine, Maddy," he says.

"No, you've just gotten used to convincing yourself of that. It's really not," I say. His eyes flit to mine, and they are filled with defeat. We need to clear the air completely so I can help him find the champion that lives inside of him. And when I'm done here with Tanya, I intend on telling him all about the odds he's up against in the pool. His fire is out, but I aim to light a new one.

"You visit with Dylan. Your heart needs it," I say, his lip quirking up at my suggestion just before he nods.

We both cross the dried-grass lawn, and I knock on the door before nerve leaves me and doubt steps in. My hands tingle at my sides, and I flex my fingers in and out, my purse feeling like a tourniquet on my arm. I can hear the footsteps on the other side of the door, and I know she lives here alone—she's cautious.

"Tanya, it's Maddy and Will," I say.

The door handle unlocks and when I meet her gaze, her mouth pinched on one side, flat on the other, I get the sense that she knows why I'm here. She doesn't hesitate to open the door wider to let us both inside.

"Thank you," I say.

"Of course," she follows. She steps up on the tips of her toes and hugs Will, kissing his cheek.

"Dylan's in his room," she says, her sightline shifting to me.

"I'm going to go say hi," Will says, leaning toward me and planting a single kiss on top of my head before turning to head down the short hallway.

I scan around the space that was buried in organized clutter just a few days ago. Boxes are still stacked as tall as I am, but they've all been pushed against the far wall. Laundry piles are gone, except for one last stack of towels, and a quick glance toward the kitchen shows she's been working hard in there, too.

"I had a little help," she says, shrugging and quirking her lip as she sits down on the opposite end of the sofa, turning her knees toward me. "I get a cleaning lady once a month, and she helps me get back on top of it."

She breathes out a laugh.

"It takes about thirty days for it to all fall to shit again," she chuckles.

I smile, and we hold our eye contact for a few seconds, reflecting pleasant melancholy faces at one another.

"Is Will okay?" she finally asks.

My chest shakes with a sad, quiet laugh, and I glance down to the table in front of us, a few boxes and papers strewn on top.

"I don't think Will's been okay for a long time," I say, glancing back to meet her eyes.

She tugs her mouth in on one side and nods, agreeing.

"He had a rough interview today," I say, her brow lowering as she listens. "The reporter brought up me…Will got protective."

Her head moves slowly up and down, her mouth still tight, but curving in recognition. Will being protective is nothing new to her.

"That man…he just wants to help. He's protective of Dylan, too. He'd do anything for him. I'm too over my head not to accept it, and I hate that I have to because I see what it does to him. But Dylan needs a team. Hell," she leans back, pinching the bridge of her nose between her fingers while she laughs. "Dylan needs Will to be his team captain. That boy is a fighter, and he needs someone to show him how to keep fighting. I kinda…"

She stops, leaning forward and turning to face me more.

"I kinda can't think of anyone more perfect to teach someone how to fight than Will," she says.

My eyes drop to my knees, and my cheeks push high with my smile. She's right.

"Just when I think he can't be more amazing," I chuckle, twisting my head to look at her sideways. I raise my eyebrows, no need to finish my words.

"I know," she agrees.

I look down again, considering the gaps she's filled in—the ones I owe her. I turn as she moves closer, pulling one leg up to tuck under her body. I face her, feeling more at ease and wanting to show her respect. She props one elbow on the back of the couch, resting her cheek against her fist, and she studies me with her kind, tired eyes.

"You love him," she says.

I smile at the mere mention of the word.

"I do," I say. My lips pucker with my smile and my cheeks flush.

"He deserves that…so do you," she says.

I glance up and quirk a brow.

"Thanks?" I say it like a question, a tiny nervous laugh leaking out.

She continues to stare, and my mouth starts to tingle from the effort to maintain my expression. My eyebrows pull in, and suddenly my mouth relaxes. My breath escapes and my shoulders sink.

She knows.

"How long were you with Evan?"

Tanya's eyes lock to mine the moment she speaks. I hold her gaze, blinking when she does, speaking with my eyes. After several seconds, she looks down.

"Oh," she says.

Her chest shakes once, and she reaches up to run her wrist under her right eye.

"I'm sorry," she laughs nervously, barely a whisper. "I'm not sure why I'm reacting like this. It's not…it's not really a surprise. I knew for sure when I saw you. Evan…he had your pictures on his phone. He said you were friends, but a girl can tell."

She rests her face on her arm along the sofa back, and she blinks away the remnants of tears.

"It wasn't your fault," I say, grabbing her hand in mine on instinct. We're both sisters in this twisted, tragic circumstance.

"It's not yours either," she says, her gaze flitting up to me briefly. Her eyes are red, and I feel gravity pulling me down hard, guilt like a weight tied to my insides. My own eyes begin to sting. I run my thumbs under them, pausing when I look up to see Tanya doing the same. We both start to laugh, quietly.

"Boy, Evan Hollister was a real prick," she says through a mix of mad laughter and tears.

"It's starting to seem so, yes," I agree.

Tanya's right hand forms a fist, and she presses it against her mouth as she glances away.

"How did you find out about me? From Will?" she asks, glancing at me sideways.

I nod *yes*.

"You must have thought I was awful," she says, her eyelids sweeping closed, her knuckles still flush against her lips.

"For a little while, yes," I admit. "But Will told me everything. I didn't hate you after that, and when I met you…and Dylan."

She sucks in her bottom lip, her eyes opening on me before she turns to look over her shoulder, down the hallway.

"He's an amazing kid," she says. "He's hard…oh god, is he hard. And there are days," she pauses, shifting her posture and moving her hand open, pressing the palm against her chin. Her eyes stare back out into the room, and I see her slip away to someplace else, the corner of her mouth drawing down, her chin denting—as if she's going to be sick.

She is going to be sick.

"Come on," I say quickly, sliding my arm behind her back, carrying her weight and moving with her quickly into the kitchen. I turn on the faucet while she leans on me, and I start to cup water in my open hand, splashing it on her neck and forehead. She's breaking out in a sweat, her normal pale skin is growing paler.

"I'm going to throw up," she coughs, not able to move herself quickly enough as yellow, acidic bile drips from her lips.

"Tanya, that doesn't look good. You might have the flu, or food poisoning," I say, switching into my nursing mode.

"No, I'm okay," she says, coughing again and spitting out more vomit.

"When was the last time you ate?" I ask, turning the water on higher before bending down to open up the cabinet in search of a switch for the disposal.

I stand back up and put my hand on her back, rubbing in circles while she rests her chin on her folded palms, the water running in front of her and her eyes squeezed shut.

"I'd feel better if we at least saw your doctor, or maybe urgent care…I don't want Dylan to catch something if you're contagious," I say.

Tanya's body starts to shake, and I press my hand to her harder, kneeling down to look her in the eyes. I rest my head on my hands next to her, both of us bent over the edge of the sink, and her eyes flit open to mine.

"You can't catch cancer," she says.

Her words sink in quickly, followed by the crashing train they carry along with them. I lift my head just as she does, and we both stand.

"You being so tired…it wasn't just *you being tired*…was it?"

She breathes in slowly through her nose, then exhales swiftly. She doesn't answer or shake her head. I don't ask any more questions. We simply stare at one another, understanding how cruel fate can be.

After nearly a minute, Tanya breaks our gaze, her hand wrapped around the edge of the counter to steady herself while she cleans the sink and runs a towel along the counter surface with her other. I reach to help, but her hand stops the instant I move to take the towel from her.

"I know you want to help, but I need to do what I can do on my own, Maddy. While I can," she says.

"While..." I repeat that key word, my eyes glued on Tanya's profile. Her eyes close again, then open on me.

"This is my second fight. Ovarian. I had a hysterectomy. De-bulking surgeries. Chemotherapy," she says. I don't blink. I've been around this—I've seen this. I know what she's saying before she says it. She isn't giving up, but she's going to lose anyway.

"When did you find out?" I ask.

"A few months ago," she says. "It's...it's everywhere."

We both pause when we hear laughing mixed with a loud, happy groan echo from the hallway. Her eyes begin to tear and she covers her mouth while she shakes in front of me. I pull her into my arms and hold her frail body—one that I previously thought was small from not eating, from exhaustion.

"Does Will know?" I ask, feeling her shake her head against me.

"I can't do this to him again," she says.

"He'd want to know. You're his family," I say.

She steps back from my hold, her mouth pinched tight, her eyes again blinking away tears.

"The stress of it all last year almost killed him," she says.

I freeze on that thought, my focus blurring out. The car accident—Will's bottom. It was her cancer.

"He's still going to want to know, Tanya," I say, refocusing on her face. "All of the hidden things have been killing him, too."

"After trials. I just...I just want him to have this," she says, and I can tell she loves him when she speaks. I don't even really care if she loves him the same way I do. It's nice seeing people love him. He needs more of that.

"After the trials," I agree.

Tanya looks down to my hands, limp and lifeless at my sides, and she pulls the one closest to her in her own. I look at how similar we are—our skin, our size, the small wrinkles—mine from hours in the water, hers from life.

"Please love him, Maddy. Will...please love him," she says.

I remain quiet, eyes on our rigid yet tenuous hold on one another.

"He deserves someone to love him, Maddy. Give that boy a reason," she says.

I look up and into her waiting stare, the red gone, replaced by a clear green and white, her mask in place for just a little while longer, and I lift my chin slightly. She shakes my hand in her grasp, her lips pulling into a tight smile as she nods with satisfaction.

"I will say this about Evan Hollister," I say the moment I see her eyes begin to slant again, sadness trying to take over. She raises a brow in question at me. "He had excellent taste in women," I say, biting my lip until her mouth curves into a grin, her lips part, and a laugh of madness escapes.

"That he did," she says. "Impeccable, if I dare say so myself."

CHAPTER 18

Will

She never left.

Maddy...she stayed.

I blew her dad's interview. My temper, it's been in check for way too long, and I just couldn't handle being the doormat any longer. Maddy was my line—the trigger.

She insisted on staying with me. I know it's because if she goes home, to her parents' place, she has to deal with the aftermath of me walking out. It isn't fair to her, and before she has to, I'll make amends with her dad. Or I'll quit before I sink his chances. Maddy's peace of mind is what's important to me.

She's peaceful when she sleeps. We got back to the club at around seven, and Duncan had made spaghetti. Maddy crashed on the sofa with her bowl half eaten. I took a photo with my phone because I want to remember her forever, just like that. I'm making up for all of those moments I missed, that Evan got and wasted. I bet Maddy fell asleep in their dorm studying sometimes. I bet she got drunk at parties, and wore sexy little costumes on Halloween. And I bet she spent many nights in his bed, or he in hers, curled up with his arm around her. The envy guts me. It always has, but somehow it feels even worse now.

That's how I win over it, though. I make my own memories—better ones that erase the ones I've imagined and grown jealous of, and ones that have been tarnished and ruined for her. I will treat her like the queen she was meant to be.

"Will," my uncle whispers, twisting the dimmer on the small light in our kitchenette. He's been sitting at the table for the last hour, tinkering, while I've been sitting on the floor across from Maddy, staring at her.

I nod to him and climb to my feet, pausing to click off the TV before moving to the darkened kitchen.

"I can't wake her," I whisper.

"It's fine," he smiles, glancing past me to where she rests. "You take the bedroom, and I can go sleep in the office across the way."

"No, no," I shake my head. "I doubt I'll sleep anyway, and if I get tired, I'm fine on the floor."

His eyes crinkle at the corners as he looks at me, and his mouth pinches, suppressing a laugh.

"What?" I whisper.

He keeps quiet, picking up the day's paper that he has yet to read from the table and folding it under his arm before reaching up to pat my shoulder as he passes.

"Welcome to the world of smitten, my boy," he teases, the chuckle rumbling from his chest.

"I think I've been smitten for quite some time, old man," I say.

"Ah, yes…indeed you have," he winks, nodding for me to look over my shoulder. I turn around to find the most beautiful pair of brown eyes staring at me over the back of a tattered sofa.

"You smitten with me, Will Hollister?" Maddy asks, her voice crackling with sleepiness.

The bedroom door shuts behind me, and I glance back to where my uncle just was, and I smirk before turning my head sideways to look at her.

"Yeah, Maddy. I'm pretty smitten," I say.

She stretches her arms out so I walk toward her, the greatest feeling in the world the one that comes with her arms wrapping around my waist. She rests her cheek against my stomach and holds me quietly for several seconds, and I'd be content to stand here like this for days.

"What time is it?" She twists her head, her chin in my belly while her wide eyes blink open at me. I slide my hands up her cheek then bend down to brush my lips against hers.

"Not quite ten," I whisper.

She smiles against me. I feel it.

"Midnight swim," she says, stretching her arms out to her sides.

"At ten?" I quirk my brow, and she giggles, twisting back around on the sofa and getting to her feet.

"No, at midnight. That gives us time to make a few phone calls," she says, her eyes squinting while her lip curls on one side.

I hold her stare for a second, but give in to her crazy idea quickly, shrugging my shoulder and raising my brow. "Okay," I say. I think that's part of being so *smitten*—no idea of hers is ever going to be too crazy for me to do again.

Midnight swim was Maddy's invention. It started the first year we all met, when she insisted that Evan and I stay with her in the clubhouse for a sleepover. Her mother stayed, too, and we all snuck downstairs at midnight to swim without her knowing. The rules were you had to whisper, and no clothes were allowed. That summer, we had maybe a dozen sleepovers and midnight swims, sometimes with the other kids from the club. The midnight swims stopped the next year—when bodies began to change.

I don't think the whisper rule still needs to be in effect, but I'm curious how Maddy plans on handling that second one. I'm kind of rooting to keep it in play.

"Who are you texting?" I ask, sliding my hands around her hips and resting my chin on her shoulder to watch her thumbs move rapidly.

"Holly," she says, "and Amber, and that sweet boy she's been hanging out with at practice. Maybe she can ask some of the other swimmers, too."

"Another boy, huh?" I tease, and she twists to face me quickly, glaring with one brow higher than the other.

"I'm not surrounding you with a bunch of hot women, Will Hollister," she says.

My eyes dance around hers, and I hold my smirk at bay.

"Because of the second rule?" My eyebrow ticks up to match hers.

She never responds, but her eyes haze over the brief seconds she stares at me before returning her attention back to her phone.

For the next hour and a half, I think of nothing but how erect I am and how I'm going to handle skinny dipping in front of others with Maddy Woodsen pressed against my side.

In my shit life, there have been a handful of major things that I have been, and continue to be, thankful for. Beyond surviving—*twice*—I'm thankful for my talent. I'm among a few elite swimmers, and given my personal circumstances, I know that innate talent is maybe the only reason I'm in the position I am today. Second, I'm thankful for my hair. It sounds vain, but that's not my reasoning. I'm grateful because it's just the right length, texture and thickness to require absolutely no effort on my part to look decent at all times. Evan used to spend minutes, sometimes nearly thirty, sculpting with gel and product. I put on a hat, and like magic, my hair dries and I'm done.

There are maybe a dozen other things—some big, some small—that make up this list, but tonight I add a new one. I think maybe it goes on top.

I am thankful that the Shore Club pool is dark enough on the far end that if a man were to tread water in it, anyone standing farther away than ten feet can't tell if he's naked. This wins because I am naked. Maddy? Not so much. Amber? Nope. Holly? She has her phone camera rolling video.

"Will, come on…you have to laugh. It's kinda funny?"

"Nope, still not funny," I yell toward the deck where the girl I love stands, perfectly dressed in a suit and perfectly dry with our guests.

Maddy pranked me, letting me strip down to nothing just before everyone arrived by daring me to cannonball into the center of the pool. There are a few things that make even the most mature man turn into a teenager again, doing dumb shit because his cock tells him to. Naked in a pool with Maddy Woodsen? That's one of those things.

"Come on, Will. So far my viral video is hella boring," Holly shouts, following it up with a whistle and a cat call. I give her the finger, and she tells me to fuck off.

"You saw that?" I lower my hands to camouflage my parts, my legs treading furiously, and my muscles growing tired.

"Yeah, well your middle finger must be bigger than…*other things,*" she deadpans.

I flip her off again.

"I never said we were all skinny dipping, Will," Maddy giggles.

"You kinda alluded to it," I say, resting my limbs and sinking under the water.

"Come on, everyone will turn around, and I'll hand you a towel. I'm starting to feel bad," she says, but the laughter still sneaks through her words.

She can't tell, but I'm smiling, too. I was embarrassed for about fifteen seconds, but then I started to realize how much fun I was having. I haven't had fun in years, and I haven't felt weightless in forever. No obligations dragging me down, or a running list of things I can and can't say to people. And honestly, if it weren't for the fact that I've been treading water for several minutes, I'd be fine with walking around, balls out and dick hard for everyone to see.

"Here's the deal, Maddy," I say, swimming a little closer while my girl kneels down near the water's edge with a towel held in her hands. I glance over to Holly, who is still holding her phone out hoping to capture the million-dollar shot. She leans her head to the side and makes eye contact with me, and I wink. Her mouth raises sinisterly on one side, and she shifts her phone camera to Maddy. She gets where I'm going with this.

"I'm not coming out of the pool, like…at all…until you take that bikini off and come in to get me," I say, swaying my arms and legs and pushing back a few feet to where I started.

Maddy's hands drop and the towel falls to the deck.

"Will, I didn't mean to hurt your feelings. I'm sorry…just come out," she says, standing and crossing her arms over her bare belly. She's blushing—I can tell, even in the dark, by the way her hands slide over her skin and try to guard her.

"Oh, my feelings are fine, Maddy. But I just want you to know that if I cramp up and drown, that's on you. I'm not budging," I say, slowing my hand movement down and letting my body dip below the water again.

"Will, come on," she laughs.

"Water's fine, Maddy," I tease, leaning back and kicking my feet twice, splashing everyone standing near the edge.

She holds my stare for several seconds, finally kicking her flip flops from her feet and scooting the towel away from the edge with her toes. She steps forward, and bends down to sit on the pool's edge, letting her feet and legs dangle in the water, but not taking her suit off.

"Lose the bikini, Woodsen," I say, splashing her once with my hand. She squeals when the water hits her, pulling her legs up.

She stares at me again, but I can tell she's growing bolder. She's going to do it, and cold water or not, I'm hard as a rock.

"You're such a pig, you know that, Will Hollister?" she says, standing and reaching behind her back. She pauses, pointing a finger to her friend. "Camera off, Holly. I don't need any *TMZ* video showing up during trials."

Holly keeps her phone held high, until Maddy steps forward and dips her foot in the water, kicking up a splash at her friend.

"Hey! I was shutting it off. That's how my operating system works, I hold the phone over my head and count to ten," she jokes.

"Uh huh," Maddy says, her mouth pulled in on one side.

"It's off; it's off," Holly says, tucking the phone in her bag and kicking her own shoes from her feet and sliding her shorts down her hips.

"What are you doing?" Maddy asks, her hand still holding the straps behind her back while she tilts her head in question of her friend.

Holly tugs her T-shirt over her head, then slides the strap of her swimsuit top down her shoulder while eying her friend.

"I'm racing you," she says, sliding the second strap down before reaching around her back and unsnapping her suit.

My eyes blink wide, and now I'm not sure how to proceed. I'm not sure I'm even needed, because in seconds, Maddy and her best friend are in a full-out, sorority-porn-style race to strip down in front of me, a guy named Nick, and incredibly shy Amber. Both naked and staring at each other, the two of them start laughing hysterically when their eyes meet.

"We do this together," Maddy says.

"Oh fuck yes!" I tease, holding my fingers in my mouth and whistling loud.

Within seconds, both rush at the pool, jumping toward me and splashing wildly, kicking their arms and legs while we all laugh so hard that we don't hear the others join us. The pool deck is a pile of stripped away clothes and suits, and for the next twenty minutes we all make silly dares, jumping in and out of the water just long enough to catch glimpses of things. We act like children, and make sex jokes, and live like drunken college kids running on nothing but this natural high that somehow we all must have needed. When it wears off, I swim to the pool's edge and toss everyone their suits, modesty hitting us all at once. Regardless, though, a new closeness settles in—a comfort that I feel in my chest and see reflected in Maddy's eyes.

"Midnight swim," she smirks, paddling around the water near me after slipping her suit back on. I tug on her loose strap, her hand gripping it quickly but not before I can bring her close to me. Our eyes lock and I reach behind her neck, tying her suit the rest of the way for her.

"This was a lot more fun than it used to be," I say, my voice low. I peek over her shoulder to where our friends are climbing out of the pool on the other side, reaching for their towels and drying their bodies and hair.

My gaze slides back to hers.

"It was more fun for you because I have tits now," she says, her mouth pinched in a crooked smile.

"You had tits then," I say back quickly, and she pushes from my chest, splashing me. I grab her fast, though and pull her back in my arms.

I hold her against my body, and she turns so we're both facing the front of the pool. We wave goodbye to our friends, and Holly holds up her phone.

"I'll have it posted by morning. I'll split the profits with you, Will," she jokes.

"Awesome," I say back, grunting when I feel Maddy's elbow in my gut.

"She's kidding," I whisper against her ear. My lip brushes the side and I linger there, tracing it once with my tongue before pulling her cool skin between my teeth. Maddy hums and leans her head to the right, welcoming me to taste more of her.

I do. I kiss her neck and shoulder and eventually work her bikini top back off of her body, caressing her breasts until she whimpers and begs me to take her inside.

I do that, too. We don't make it far, stopping at the small snack-bar nook where we both used to sneak sodas and ice cream pops from the refrigerator. I press her body against the counter, bending her over and untying one side of her bikini bottom, jerking the material to one side so I can slide inside her.

Our sex is hard and fast, and my hand covers her mouth to muffle the whimpers that escape her lips every time I push against her. When the pressure becomes too hard to hold back from, I press my mouth against her bare back and muffle my own moans. Her body is flush against the counter, her arms spread out to the sides and her fingers grip the edges of the granite while I fill her with every inch of me until there's nothing left but our exhausted bodies and bliss.

I round up her clothes and the bikini top we discarded and lead her upstairs, whispering once inside. I make us a small bed and tug her body in against mine, under an old quilt that we probably used to build forts when we were young.

"Where'd you find that swimsuit, anyhow." I smile through the words I speak against her ear, and I feel her shiver.

"I haven't worn it since high school. It was in the supply closet, in an old box," she says. Her voice is raw and weak, the early morning hours and our love making catching up to her.

"It still fits perfectly," I grin, ticking her arm with my fingertips.

"It's kinda tight, actually," she says.

"Like I said…fits perfectly," I say, my mouth tugging up on the side near her skin. I kiss the space where her shoulder curves into her neck and she nestles deeper into me.

We lay together, my eyes on the profile of hers, my hand tracing the perfect lines that sculpt her muscles. My mind is calm and my heart is steady. My world, it feels right, and I don't know what I did to deserve it. I doubt I do, but I'm taking it. I'm not giving any of this back.

"You know you're going to have to win, right?" Maddy says.

I don't answer right away, instead just continuing to trace patterns along her skin. I'm not surprised by the thought. Maybe a little at hearing Maddy acknowledge it. It means that her dad has probably said something to her. It makes the hurdles more real. I knew that my role here began and ended with the money, and now that I walked out on an interview securing big-time cash flow, well…

"I know you're going to think I'm giving up when I say this, or that I'm making excuses before I even try, but honestly…from my heart, Maddy…I'm good with whatever happens. I'm satisfied having come here, having trained here with you—with your dad—in this place that…" I let my palm fall flat along her arm and breathe out, shaking my head slightly. "Maddy, do you know how hard it was to come back here?"

"I can't even imagine what it's like for you to be here after everything that's happened, Will," she says.

For a minute, I allow her to think that's where it starts and ends, that the accidents are what kept me away. But the more seconds that pass, the more unsettled it feels not to be raw and honest right now. Losing my family left an enormous emotional scar, one that I will never get rid of completely, but my heart was broken long before that plane went down.

"Do you remember when I left for State?" I ask, my eyes memorizing every freckle on her shoulder blade, every tiny hair along her neck.

I feel her quake with a small giggle against me. I memorize the feel of that, too.

"You didn't want to go," she says. "You thought they were just taking you on the team to lure your brother."

I nuzzle into her hair, hiding my embarrassed smile even though no one can see it.

"Do you remember what you said?" I close my eyes, wondering if these moments are locked away as tightly in her mind as they are mine.

"I told you that you were better than your brother," she whispers, her voice cracking with the words. I feel her swallow. "I meant it, you know."

She turns into me, and I let her, my hands finding her face, then sweeping back her hair. Our legs tangle and we push apart just enough to look each other in the eyes.

"I can tell you every single thing about that moment, Maddy. We were on the other side of the Swim Club parking lot, where your dad had those old wooden benches carved out of logs. The air was humming with the sound of June bugs and the sun was half below the horizon, storm clouds covering one side of the sky and orange filling the other. Everything smelled like cedar, except for your breath. That smelled like cinnamon, because you'd just finished eating a bite of my mom's cobbler. You were wearing that purple T-shirt we got for free for completing the presidential fitness testing at our high school. Your hair was down, but it was crinkly and wavy on the ends from swimming with a ponytail all afternoon. And," I stop, because saying this next part terrifies me. As close as Maddy and I are right now, I'm not sure if it's as real for her as it is for me. Evan is always there—even when he doesn't deserve to be.

"Maddy, I know you wanted me to kiss you that day. For just a second maybe, but it was there. I stopped questioning, and you stopped talking, and it was quiet," I say, encouraged that she isn't flinching right now, or denying anything. Her eyes are set on mine, and her mouth is soft. "I got up when we heard Evan pull the car into the parking lot, but I kicked myself all semester for not having the balls to kiss you then and ask you to be *mine*."

Her hand moves to my face and she inches up higher against me, her eyes fluttering closed and her lips dusting my mouth.

"I remember," she breathes.

I let my eyes close with her touch, relishing it. But Evan…he's still always going to be there. Maybe even more for me than her. I think the only way to move past it is to weave our stories together, to make sure she knows all of my details so I can learn to live with what they shared.

"I came home early for Thanksgiving," I say. I feel her muscles tighten against me, her face shift in my hands, but I keep my eyes closed and my head down against her. Her eyes make me weak, and I tuck things away, because I'm too afraid of losing what's in front of me.

"I came home with plans of following through with it, kissing you like I should have before I left. And when I came to your house, you and Evan were sitting on the couch together, holding hands…" I stop, shaking my head and pulling my lips in tight. "Then later that night…" I swallow hard. "I saw you both together…at The Mills. That's when I knew you were never going to be mine."

Her lips find mine again before my eyes can open. She kisses me hard, her hands weaving through my hair and her body inching forward until the space between us is completely eaten up with her response to my doubt.

I kiss her back, and I soak up the taste and feel of her, even though I know it's not enough. I take this for now. I take her kiss, until our lips are raw and our bodies are exhausted. Our eyes are barely able to stay open, and the sunset looms only an hour or two away—our wake-up call to jump into the competitive waters and push our bodies to the max again.

"I know it's going to take you a while to believe it, and I know our story…it isn't how these stories are supposed to go," she says, her face almost panicked. Her lips quiver, and a familiar fear washes across her face, making her pale. I recognize it, because it's the same anguish that takes away my courage, makes me believe I don't deserve things. This is where we run. We both do it; when we're afraid that safety net will be gone—*we run.*

Please, Maddy…please don't run from this. I know you feel it.

I hold her head in my hands, my forehead against hers, and I let myself beg for it. Because I need to hear it. I don't think I can come back from this now—I'm too far gone.

"Please," I whisper.

"I love you, Will Hollister," she says, and I let my lips dust hers just at the sound of those words.

"It has been forever, Maddy. That's how long," I say against her skin. "I have loved you…forever."

I pull away just enough to look her in the eyes.

"I loved the idea of your brother," she says. "And the safety that came along with letting myself fall for him. But my love for you is deeper than that. It's the real kind of love. It's not about ideas or fantasies. It's just something my heart can't help. And I know with every single beat of it that whether Evan cheated or not, I'm with the man I was truly meant to be with. My story with Evan—it doesn't matter. This is the only story that does. Our story."

My body is exhausted, and my eyes fight to stay focused on her angelic face, but I do just long enough to tell her I love her more. I say the words a dozen times—a dozen different ways. I could never say it enough, and I don't think I'll ever grow tired of hearing how those words sound falling from my lips to land upon her ears.

"I love you so much, Maddy, and I'm going to win. I'm going to win for you, and fuck anything else."

CHAPTER 19

Maddy

We're not the only ones dragging. Amber and the guy she brought with her last night, Nick—they're dragging, too. We're all slightly pissing my father off because with a key meet staring us down in days, *dragging* does not make for much *winning*.

It's temporary, though. I think maybe after the failed interview and my refusal to answer my father's phone calls, or come home for the last twenty-four hours—my dad is starting to realize that his best shot at turning around the sinking ship that is this Swim Club might just be riding on the shoulders of the only star swimmer *not* dragging in the pool this morning. Of all of us, Will should feel pressure the most, but this morning it's like he woke up a new man.

Reinvigorated.

Hungry.

Driven.

My father's routine with him is the same. He tells him he's done well, offering praise for his turns, his starts, his strokes. The difference today, though, is Will tells him "it isn't good enough."

We have one more set of sprints, and my father is pairing us. It doesn't matter much who he pairs Will with, because I know anyone is going to lose—I will lose. But I know that if anyone is going to push Will the hardest, it's me.

Nick steps up on the blocks next to Will, but I nudge him before he gets set.

"Let me have a crack at him," I tease, winking at Will. He smirks at me, but pushes his goggles to his face tighter, dangling his arms, his shoulders rippling and his back muscles flexing as he leans down.

"Bring it, Woodsen," he says out of the side of his mouth.

I glance to the other end of the pool, my father's weight leaning on one foot, ankles crossed and clipboard tucked against his chest. He isn't amused—he thinks I'm goofing off, not taking this seriously. But my mom showed up today, and a quick look at her face tells the opposite story. Her arms are crossed over her chest, but she's smiling. It's the same face she used to make when me and the Hollister boys would race as kids—prideful.

"Go on the sound," my father shouts, his words short and his tone un-amused.

The timer clicks off, beeping to signal go, and Will and I fly into the water. His jump on me is almost a body's length by entry, but I make up some ground with my powerful strokes. I put in two for every one and half of his, grabbing hold of the wake left behind his feet in the lane next to me. I push with my head down, not breathing but once, and only to fuel my arms to continue the frantic pace I'm putting them through.

I feel his water slide past me, the rush of his kick leaving me in the dust, the water calming, but a stroke later my fingers hit the wall.

My father is staring at his stopwatch, and my mother is hooting with her arms in the air. I glance to Will, and both of us tug our caps from our heads. We smile from the rush of speed, but Will's eyes are crinkled in a confused look as he moves closer to the ropes.

I'm about to ask him how that felt when I feel my mom's hand rest on top of mine at the edge of the deck. I turn to see her knelt down near us, an open-mouthed smile plastered on her face and pushing her eyes wide and high.

"Maddy, that was a full *point three* faster than you've ever swam. That was incredible!" She stands and cups her mouth, turning to my father who is still frozen with the watch in his hand, staring at the time.

I feel Will's hand cup the back of my head and move me close enough so he can kiss my forehead and hold his against mine.

"That's my girl," he grins.

I laugh lightly, still in disbelief, because I felt like Will was absolutely smoking me in the water, but then my head does the math and I glance up to take in my father's expression again. The watch now back in his pocket, he's concentrating on a few notes he's writing on the clipboard, his eyes pinched in, making a deep wrinkle between them. Will still beat me, but I could feel his movement in the water the entire way. Our race shouldn't have been that close. While I swam a personal best, Will swam a personal worst. He did it days before a race.

Will pushes away from the wall and floats backward, his ears under the water and his eyes open on the sky. He winks at me as he drifts out of my reach, but his smile falls the moment his face tilts, and I can tell he's weighed down with what just happened and what it means. What I want to tell him is it doesn't mean shit! It means he saw a dozen sprints today after putting his body through weeks of stress. Sometimes we're tired. This little showdown in the pool doesn't count for anything other than making my mom feel good she saw me swim fast. The race that counts happens Saturday, and then the Saturday after.

Everyone's exited the water, and I pull myself up to stand near my parents, my mom still glowing over my time, my father continuing to work out whose side he wants to be on. Will showed weakness just now, and the number-cruncher who is getting pressure to drag Will down should be tittering like a happy, evil fool. He's not, though. He's caught in-between, and I can't take watching him wade in limbo any longer.

"What's wrong with you?" I ask, my voice hushed, but angry. My dad's eyes snap to mine, and my mom's smile falls fast, her brow lowered as she glances between us.

"Not here, Maddy," my father says, nodding over my shoulder. I turn to see Will still floating, pushing himself to the other side of the pool. It wouldn't matter if he could hear or not, though.

"He knows what you think of him," I grit. "Of his odds and the benefit it brings to the table. He's not stupid, Dad. But he's sure as hell hurt."

My mom's head falls to one side and she glares at my father.

"Are you undermining that boy, Curtis?" she spits out.

"No!" My father raises one hand, trying to stop our train of conversation.

"The fact that even now—after the interview, where Will was obviously protecting me from speculation and rumors—you still can't see how much more you have to gain with him on your side rather than just being good enough to hold open the door, Dad..." I start, stopping when my mom's hand slaps hard against my father's chest.

"He's like a son to us, Curtis. You love Will!" she says, no longer guarding her volume.

I turn to see Will now holding himself at the pool's edge, his arms stretched out and his eyes on us and our conversation. I turn back to face my father.

"He deserves this, Dad. Probably more than any of us," I say. My father's jaw works, his cheeks moving as he grits his teeth. "He deserves it more than me. Definitely more than you. He deserves it more than Evan ever did, Dad."

My father's eyes flutter closed at the mention of Evan's name. It isn't something he's put on. My dad had dreams of coaching both of these boys to their highest levels. But Will is so much more worthy.

"He can't do this without you. I can push him. But nobody can bring out what he needs to win like you can," I say.

My father doesn't respond, but the tightness in his face eases, until he's left with nothing but sad, sloping eyes and cheeks that weigh down his mouth.

"Is this about saving the club?" my mom finally says. "This…dump?"

A laugh escapes my mom's chest as she turns with one palm up, showcasing the eight-lane pool, cracking deck, and fence covered with awnings held down by twisty-ties.

"It's all we have, Susan," my dad shakes his head, his eyes lost on the ground a few feet away.

My mom laughs once more.

"No, Curtis," she says, leaning toward me and pressing a kiss to my cheek. "No, it's not even close to all we have. And when it comes to priorities, it doesn't even make the list."

My mom walks around the edge of the pool, stopping at Will on the other end, bending down, and pressing a kiss to his head. She looks up to catch our stare one last time, and nods—a warning to my father. I look back at him to find his face unchanged, but the sadness reflected in his eyes stronger. His chest lifts slowly as he blinks, his gaze moving from the door my mom just closed to the man waiting for his help in the water. He's quiet for several seconds, and I let his mind work out whatever fog I see passing behind his eyes, until he finally throws the clipboard to the ground between our feet and moves past me.

"Fuck it," he says, kicking his shoes from his feet and tugging his shirt over his head. He's wearing workout shorts, and he turns to me handing me the contents of his pocket before turning back and diving into the pool. He swims toward Will, who glances from me to this strange version of my father swimming toward him. All I can do is move back a few steps to the bleacher seats, gathering my father's things with me so I can watch.

For two hours, my father bends Will's body in the pool, analyzing every single position, from the place where his hand enters the water, to where the beads leave his toe from every kick. He never asks him to swim fast. He's resting him—forcing him to think beyond brute force and power. He's building strategy and fine-tuning the machine.

He's leaving limbo behind and swimming in the light.

And neither of them are going to lose. I feel it in my gut.

The noon sun blazing down on them, my father finally forces Will from the pool. I meet them both by the main deck near the door.

"I can just leave your things inside, by the kitchen, if you want to run upstairs and shower off. You might still have some spare clothes up there," I say.

My dad takes his things from my hands and balls them up in his dry shirt.

"Maddy, if I *do* have clothes up there, I can guarantee you they don't fit anymore," he chuckles. I smile with him.

My father's body isn't what it was when I was a kid. Time has made his belly thicker and his shoulders less prominent. But the swimmer is still there. I saw him in the pool today.

"I love watching you work," I say.

My father sorts through his things in his shirt, finding his keys and glancing up at me. His mouth draws into a tight smile as he shakes his head.

"I missed it," he says.

"Missed what?" I ask.

"Believing in something," he answers fast.

I stare into his eyes, and they're clouded with uncertainty, but for the first time in weeks they look happy.

"I don't know what we're going to do about the club," he says, taking a sharp breath through his nose and drawing his shoulders up high. I feel Will step inside behind me, and my father's gaze leaves mine briefly. "Every day. That. We do *exactly* that after every workout. If you feel like putting in more, you call me—I'll come. I don't want those arms hitting the water a single time without my eyes on them. You're going to be damned near perfect, but the only way I can be sure of that is if I know what's behind every stroke."

"Yes, sir," Will says, stepping close and holding his palm out for my dad to take. My dad grips it, watching how they shake, and stopping their movement with his other hand on Will's. He lifts his chin and the two men look at one another as reflections of past and present.

My dad pats Will's arm twice with his palm before letting go of their grip completely and making his way to the door. He pauses just before pulling it open, turning with his eyes down before flitting them up to meet mine, one side of his bottom lip caught in his teeth, a poor attempt at masking a look of amusement.

"You two better get used to racing like that, too. Now that I know that *point three* is out there, Maddy…I'm gonna want more," he says, chuckling as he spins and lets the door close behind him.

"Have I mentioned how much it sucks to be Coach's daughter?" I say, my eyes squinted and my stare still on the place where my father was. I feel Will lean into me and kiss the top of my head.

"Just about every day since the moment I met you," he says, his hand sliding down my arm and gripping the tips of my fingers, urging me to follow him up the stairs. "Let me shower and buy you lunch. Since you don't have a cent to your name and all."

I blink a few times then look up at him as he walks up the stairs backward. I start to giggle, a little hysterically, and Will's brow pulls in as he draws me close to walk alongside him.

"I wasn't kidding about any of that, just so you know. I really am broke now," I say, my eyes still wide, the reality of my life at twenty-two, not a cent to my name, truly hitting me.

Will stops at his room door, tipping my chin up with his finger until our eyes meet.

"I'm paying you back for the ticket, Maddy. I insist," he says.

I open my mouth to protest, but close it quickly, twisting my head slightly to the side while I wince.

"I am going to let you," I laugh out nervously.

Will's mouth pinches in, trying to keep his smile at bay, but it breaks through. His lips curve up and he leans in, pressing them against mine, and I don't know what kind of kiss I love more—ones like this, where I can feel him smile against me, or the kind where he's lost in me, whiskers rubbing me raw.

I trail behind Will as he pushes the door open, and the smile on both of our faces comes slamming to a halt. Tanya is sitting on the sofa, Duncan holding her hand in both of his. I already know why she's here, and I know in just a few minutes, Will is going to, too. The time Tanya thought she had left has shrunk considerably, and Will is going to have to carry weight through the water once again.

Will

"Where's Dylan?"

There is so much wrong with the scene that I walked into the moment Maddy and I stepped through that door. Dylan being missing is only a fraction of it, but I know that part has an answer. I think I'm going to need to tackle the easy things first with this one.

"His therapist is at the house. She offered to stay. I trust her," Tanya says.

I nod, blinking away from her red eyes. My hand instinctively covers my face, my fingertips scratching lightly along my saturated skin. I smell of chlorine, and my skin is pruned. My legs twitch from exhaustion, but I'm too afraid to move forward and sit on the sofa next to her. I know what she's going to say, and I just feel like if I can stand here on the cusp of my world falling apart for a little while that maybe it will pass by me, and for once, I won't have to deal with the hurt that comes with bad news.

"I'm sick, Will," she says. It's the same way she said it last time—a year ago, before I drove my car into a tree. I wasn't the man I am today then, though—I wasn't equipped for it, as if I could ever be equipped for the uncertainty that something like this comes with.

I feel the familiar sting hit my eyes, and I push my forearm against them both, keeping the tears where they lie—on the edge of falling.

"It came back," I say.

"They aren't sure it ever really left," she says.

Maddy steps in close to me, and I don't hesitate to grip her hand in mine. It isn't fair to her, but for the next few hours at the very least, I'm going to need to lean on her. What she learns, though, might mean I lose her for good.

"I'll quit. We'll start chemo again. I'm here this time, so I won't have to fly in. You won't have to rely on your mother…I know you can't count on her, and she's far away…"

She looks up slowly, her eyes leveling me. She's looked so tired, more than she should—how could I not have noticed.

"It's past that," she says.

My hand covers my face again instinctually, and I let my tears smear against my palm while I let my face contort underneath, my teeth gritting while my body twitches with the need to sob.

"It happened again," Tanya says, and I look up, trying to understand what she's saying, but when I do, I realize she isn't looking at me, she's looking at Maddy. "Last night, I threw up blood."

Maddy's eyes close.

"You knew?" My heartbeat begins to pick up, and my fingers work loose of their grip with Maddy.

"I got sick in front of her, Will. It's only been a day, and I begged her not to tell you. I wanted you to race first," Tanya says.

My hands twitch at my sides as I walk backward until my body slams into the closed door. My eyes flit from every pair in the room, and I feel like I've been in the dark.

"We were going to tell you, Will. Tanya was going to tell you as soon as trials were done," Maddy says, glancing from me to her, her mouth moving long after the words have left it, as if she's trying to find more words to give me, even though there aren't any.

"Don't take this out on her, Will. This was me," Tanya says.

I press my back harder into the door.

"I'm just afraid that I can't take care of Dylan now. I thought I'd have *months*, but I'm stumbling. I haven't been able to stay on my feet for more than a few minutes at a time since you left my house. I think the trip took all I had left. I'm weak, and tired, and…" Her body shakes as a cry escapes her chest. She sucks her top lip in and closes her eyes as my uncle moves closer, putting his arm around her body.

"We're your family, Tanya. We'll help," he says, swinging his vision to me.

My eyes are wide and my mind is racing with all of the wonderful things that were so nearly in my grasp. I'm going to have to give them up.

I can't be both a father and the man I was only minutes ago. I suppose I should be thankful that I ever got to be that man at all, however fleeting that time was.

"Of course," I say, void of emotion. I stare at my uncle's hand on Tanya's, the picture blurring the longer I stare until I blink it into focus and look Duncan in the eyes.

"And you'll still compete," Tanya says.

I laugh lightly because I'm not sure whose lie is worse—Tanya for asking what she knows I won't do, or me for the answer I'm about to give.

"I'll still compete," I say. There isn't a single person in this room who believes me.

Maddy

I was never around for those moments in Will's life—the ones that sent him down spirals. I have nothing to compare this moment to, but my instincts are screaming at me to fight his demons for him. He barely processed the news before excusing himself into the back room to change, then walking back past each of us and out the door, keys in his hand.

"What happened to waiting until after the trials?" I ask, moving to sit on the coffee table in front of both Duncan and Tanya.

"I fell just trying to get Dylan to his chair this morning. It took me two hours to get us both up and out the door, just so I could make it to my doctor appointment where he could tell me that the chemo isn't working this time," she says.

My heart stops beating, sinking in my chest, and a wave of nausea leaves my neck sweaty and my face pale.

"I'm so sorry," I say, my mouth overcome with the sour taste of guilt and helplessness. I need to keep in perspective what *she's* going through. "I didn't mean…"

"It's okay. You're looking after Will, and I'm glad," she says.

The three of us sit quietly for several seconds, my mind running through the small list of places Will could be—my parents' house, the lake, a bar somewhere off the sixty-five.

"You know he's quitting, right? That right there—what we all saw—that was Will quitting," I say.

"Then don't let him," Duncan cuts in quickly.

I jerk my attention to him, but he doesn't back down, looking me right in the eyes, his mouth a hard line and his shoulders square with mine while his hands still hold on to Tanya. His lip eventually raises on one side, and I exhale.

"You've always been able to get that boy to do just about anything," he says, his words trailing off with a soft laugh. "You know he didn't even want to swim in the first place?"

I tilt my head to the side and scrunch my mouth. Duncan laughs out hard, his belly shaking as he throws his head back.

"He was fixin' to quit, mostly just to piss my brother, his dad, off. Robert wanted swimming to be this great bond between his two boys, but he pushed them to compete against each other constantly—Will hated it. He was going to give it one last *hoorah*, come check out this new Swim Club his dad had heard about and see if maybe there would be something there that would make swimming fun again. Turns out…there was."

His eyes settle on me, wrinkling at the corners with the soft curve of his mouth. My heart is beating so hard I can hear it echo inside my body; I can *feel* it pulse at my fingertips and toes.

"Go on…go get him. Go make sure he doesn't regret anything, and get him to give swimming one last shot. You and I both know he was born to do it. I'll get Tanya home, pack my things up and stay there for a little while…until we can decide what needs to happen next."

My breath is coming hard and fast even though I haven't moved in several minutes. My nerves are kicking me, begging me to go find him, but my mind still isn't sure that I can say the right words to make Will believe that choosing himself—for just a little while—isn't selfish.

I stand anyway, taking my keys in one hand and my wallet and phone in the other. I'm not sure where to find him, though there's a voice in my head whispering that Will is where he always goes—where *I* would go.

"I don't know what to say. If I find him, I'm just not sure how to begin." My head falls against the door, my eyes looking down at my hand on the knob.

"You say *please*, Maddy. That's all it's going to take," he says. "That's all it ever does."

I leave without turning around again, knowing that my reflexes will want to stay and help Tanya, too, if I look at her again. Duncan's right. I'm the only one who can get through to Will, and Tanya was right to tell him. Will has so much to swim for, and I'm going to make sure every member of his family is there to watch every moment when he does.

I leave Tanya with Duncan and rush to my car. My tires kick up gravel, spinning freely as I leave the lot, the back end of my car fishtailing as I swerve onto the thankfully empty road. I don't bother to go home and ditch my swimsuit. If my gut is right, I'll need it.

I pass a few cars as I speed along the country highway, turning hard when I almost miss the turnoff for Peterson Lake. Will's car comes into view quickly, so I pull up next to it, jump out and pick up a handful of rocks without hesitation.

"I should have known it was all too good to be true," he says, not bothering to look over his shoulder. He knew I'd come.

I toss one of my rocks, and it skips six times. I smile and stop walking, marveling at something I've never been able to do before.

"Did you see that?" I ask.

He turns to look over his shoulder, lifting his mouth up on one side.

"I sure did," he says, looking down and dropping the few stones left in his hand into the water. He bends down to wash his hands off, his feet splashing in the water as he walks back up the shore. I throw another rock, and Will follows its path from my hand. It sinks right away.

"Should have quit when you were ahead," he says, pulling his lips in tight, his eyes on the ripple left behind.

"I'm not sure I like to hear you talk like that," I say, letting the rest of my stones fall to my feet.

I step close to him, our toes almost touching, and I reach for his hand, taking the fingertips in my right, then reaching for his other hand with my left. Will threads our fingers together, bringing our tethered hands between us, linked.

"You know what went through my mind first? When I saw her…before she even said anything, but I knew…I just knew she was sick again." he says. "You know what I thought?"

I shake my head *no,* and curl my fingers through his, squeezing, before meeting his eyes.

"I thought," he stops to swallow, looking to the side briefly before coming back to me. "I just got Maddy, and now she's going to leave."

A short breath pushes through his nose and his eyes tilt in desperation. "How awful am I? Tanya is dying, and she needs support—and there's Dylan, and my uncle…he can't do what I can do for them. But all I could think about when I was faced with that was how I would surely lose you," he says, his eyes fighting to stay open on me.

"You're not awful," I say, moving closer, freeing my hands from his grip to wrap my arms around his body and press my face against his chest. "You underestimate me, but you're not awful."

I feel his chest sink as air escapes.

"You can't say that now, Maddy. You can't answer that—*this*—now. It hasn't sunken in yet," he says.

"It has," I say. "And I can."

I burrow into him more, and when I feel his chin fall on top of my head, I let myself believe that Duncan is right—that I *can* get Will to do anything. I also let myself believe that I am, in fact, prepared for all of the things I'm about to say I am. I'm not—I'm nowhere *near* prepared. But I know enough to know that walking away from Will would be far worse.

"Maddy, there's a reason Tanya lives far away from her parents, why she doesn't accept their help. They're terrible people, and Dylan can't end up with them," he says.

"Okay," I say, feeling the wave of change that reality will bring to Will's life hit my chest. I take the impact, and I remain standing here. I can survive it.

"I'm going to be his guardian. The insurance money from the accident, it's barely enough for Dylan and me," he says, and I turn my head to look up at him.

Our eyes meet.

"Okay," I smile.

He starts to smile, too, but it doesn't stick. That sense of hopelessness is strong, and his eyes wilt.

"Dylan is four right now. His disability—it's lifelong. I'm committing to him for life, Maddy. However long that is for him," he says.

My eyes don't lie, and I know Will sees me working through that last fact. It's something I thought about the first time I met Dylan, about his needs, the constant demands. Tanya has been his advocate, and now Will is going to have to step into that role.

"I understand that this is a permanent thing, Will," I say. The thunder of my pulse rattles my body. Uncertainty threatens my resolve, but the other side of that is a life without Will—a life where *I* didn't try.

"I'd like for my parents to meet him," I say, bypassing the question in Will's eyes. I don't even address doubt, and I skip over the out he's giving me. It isn't an option, just like his not competing isn't either.

Will's head cocks to the side and he moves back a pace to look me in the eyes.

"When I held his hand, something happened to me, Will. Dylan is a very special kid…and his family," I say, pausing with my tongue held between my teeth, my smile growing genuinely. "His family is bigger than you think…and so is yours."

CHAPTER 20

Will

I can't get over that nagging feeling, that I shouldn't be doing any of this—that I should be back in Indianapolis making arrangements, sorting through things, moving Tanya and Dylan into a better place where we can all stay until it's just Dylan and me. I wear it, though—that feeling—and whenever Maddy sees the proof of it on my face, she steps in to argue all of the reasons in favor of me staying right where I am, right here…with her.

I'm not even worried about racing the younger and stronger guys I watched file in to the locker room here at Valpo a few hours ago, each of them with a dream of their own—one more fine-tuned and less rife with obstacles, in comparison to my own. I've put in the work with what time I had, and Maddy believes in me. Somehow, I've earned Curtis in my corner completely. I shut my eyes and all I hear is his voice telling my arm exactly where to go—"precision movements for maximum output."

Whatever will be will be. It's this moment that's about to swallow me whole, though, that's consumed my sleep and waking dreams.

I've swam with Maddy's father for extra hours every day, every second my mind split between two places—in the water with him and on Dylan, and exactly how this moment would go. I finally gave up, realizing that one part of the day I would be able to prepare for, while the other—introducing Maddy's parents to Dylan and Tanya—would go how it's going to go despite all of the preparation in the world.

"They're going to love him, Will. They'll love her, too. The history…it won't matter," Maddy says, reaching her arm around my neck as she steps up behind me where I sit. I pull her over my body until her face is looking at mine upside down.

"Spiderman kiss?" she smiles.

I let her cup my face, and I close my eyes, feeling her mouth on mine. She rights her head and walks around me, sitting on the small footrest across from me in the main lobby. There are athletes milling around, along with a dozen television cameras and reporters. My entire body beats in anticipation of the people noticing and asking about Dylan and Tanya. I want to protect them from having to feel that scrutiny.

I begin to count to ten in my head, breathing in slowly, in search of rational thought.

"Nerves again?" Maddy asks.

I forget the counting and suck in a quick breath, holding my chest full and exhaling hard, my eyes on my one steady thing.

"Your parents loved Evan," I say, looking Maddy square in the eyes. "I'm just preparing myself for that look."

Her eyebrows fall.

"What look?" she asks.

"The one that comes with shattering what's left of their illusion of my brother," I grimace.

Maddy scoots forward and reaches for my hands, so I sit up and give them to her. She turns both palms over in her lap and begins to trace the lines with her fingers.

"People love magic tricks, and things like palm readers and all of that hokey stuff," she says, and I curl my right hand around her finger, catching it.

"Are you about to tell me that my baby line says I'm going to have seventeen kids?" I tease, not able to sell it well, because my heart's just not ready for funny.

She flattens my palm back out and scowls at me, jokingly.

"Boys don't have baby lines. That's for girls," she says, "and no. I'm just saying we all love an illusion. But really…what we want to know is how the trick was done in the first place."

She curls my hands into fists this time, pulling them to her lips and kissing my knuckles on each side. I smile at her softly.

"I don't think this is quite the same, but I appreciate your faith," I say, splaying my fingers on either side of her face as I lean in and kiss the top of her head. My eyes scan above her as I do, and I see my uncle pushing open the main glass door. I lean back and my gaze falls to Maddy's, and she turns where she sits to follow my sightline beyond her.

"I guess it's show time," she says.

"Time to reveal the man behind the curtain," I say.

I stand as Maddy does, but I pass her, not wanting to put the burden of this awkward introduction on her. I catch Susan's gaze from across the room, and wave her over, knowing she'll find Curtis.

"How are you feeling?" I ask Tanya. Her features haven't changed much, other than a little noticeable weight loss in her face.

"I'm good, Will. Your uncle has been very helpful," she says. I kiss her head, and when I feel her back I can tell that her body has lost more weight than is evident in her face. Her shoulders are more frail, and the muscle tone she had only weeks ago in her back is dwindling.

"I'm glad. Did you all find a place?" I ask, looking from her to Duncan.

"We found a good two-bedroom near the hospital where we can pay month-to-month," she says, no celebration. Month-to-month means that at some point that lease will cease to be necessary. I nod in response, not wanting to say anything about this is positive or good. It's just essential, and I leave it at that.

I feel Maddy at my side again, her hand working its way into that familiar place of strength, and I ready myself for whatever will be.

"Deep breath," she whispers in my ear, and I turn, one part of my family behind me, and the other standing before me.

Both Curtis and Susan are trying not to stare, but Dylan is hard not to look at. He's trying to communicate, but his sounds come out in hoots, and his curled hands fight to wave and clap. Tanya holds on to his chair behind him, both to stand as one with her son and to steady herself.

"Susan, Curtis…I wanted you to meet my family," I say, my choice of words getting a bit of a flinch from Curtis and fast blinking eyes from Susan.

"Oh, I didn't know you had more than Duncan, Will. I'm so glad they could make it," Susan says, her mouth pinched at the sides trying to put this picture in order as she turns to shake Tanya's hand. I don't mean to time it like this, but the second they touch, I fill in the blanks.

"Dylan is my nephew, and Tanya is his mother," I say. Susan's head swivels toward me, her hand now grasping Tanya's, but her movement stilled. "She's…she's like a sister to me," I add, lowering my head slightly and looking at Susan with a raised brow.

Our eyes connect, and I watch the pieces fall in place for her, every stage shifting quickly—from shock to betrayal, and from anger to pity, and eventually that heartbreaking place where we all end up when we realize everything Evan missed and how hard it has been on those he left behind.

"Tanya," Susan swallows, her eyes trailing back to our guests. "It is…I'm sorry," she stammers, reaching up with her other hand to rub away the emotion threatening to unravel in her eyes. "You'll have to forgive me, but this is a surprise to me."

"I know. I can assure you that it is for me, too," Tanya says, her expression soft and honest as her eyes flit to Maddy. She glances to me next, and I nod, encouraging her on, and Maddy squeezes my palm, wrapping her other hand around my bicep.

"So this young man, he's…" Susan begins.

"Evan's," Maddy fills in, her voice breaking at the mention of my brother's name. That small emotion she just emitted hurts, but I remind myself that she hasn't known about Dylan for long, and as much as I *know* she's mine, she was also Evan's for a long time. Betrayal hurts regardless.

Susan's bottom lip puffs out, but she sucks it in quickly, holding onto that quivering urge.

"I see," she swallows.

"Evan's," Curtis repeats, standing behind his wife, his hands on her shoulders. I wait for him to look me in the eyes, and when he finally does, I nod.

"Dylan, can you say nice to meet you?" Tanya encourages. My nephew makes a few sounds, and with Tanya's lead, it's possible to recognize the sounds Dylan makes to be the words she asked for.

He reaches his hand forward, and without hesitation, Susan takes it between both of hers. I watch her body shudder at the contact, like touching something important and discovering it's real for the very first time. This is how my heart reacts to Maddy.

"Dylan, you look so very much like your father," Susan smiles, and I can't help but follow suit. There are so many things that she could have said, but none of that matters to Dylan, or Tanya. My resentments, the heartbreak Susan and Curtis feel on their daughter's behalf, the betrayal that must eat away at Maddy—it's all real, all valid, and we recognize it. But just not here—not in front of the innocents.

"He really does," Maddy says, echoing her mother's words.

Curtis nods in agreement behind his wife, and his eyes slide to mine with a new layer of understanding behind them.

I carry a lot of anchors in that water, Curtis. And I'm going to need every bit of help I can get to unload them for just a few seconds.

Maddy

I did not shave a third of a second off my time again, but I swam fast enough to win my heats easily, and I breezed into first place in both the one hundred and two hundred free races. Funny how winning can still feel like a disappointment, though, when you know you have more to give.

"I'll get the record at trials," I say, sliding into the space on the bench next to my father.

"Damn straight you will, and before I'm done, you'll be beating this guy in the water," my dad winks, nodding toward Will.

We both look on while he stretches his arms, leaning over and letting his limbs swing. His body looks ready, but I can still see his head is caught in so many other places.

"Where's Mom?" I ask, trying to loosen my father up. He's clasping his hands together and swaying where he sits, and it's beginning to affect everyone sitting next to him. I lean into him, and he catches on, glancing down at where my arm touches his and shifting his position while flexing his hands.

"I guess I'm nervous, sorry," he says. "Your mom's in the family section with Duncan and…"

His lips part, but nothing escapes except for a heavy sigh.

"Evan's family," I fill in for him. My father bites the tip of his tongue and his mouth stretches out in forced smile.

"Yeah," he says, blinking as he looks away from me.

We both watch on in silence, letting the shouts around us fill in the quiet while Will stands behind the heat before him, pacing. He never listens to music like so many of the other guys do, and I wonder if it's because he already has plenty of noise in his head. He talks to himself, closing his eyes and imagining the start, nodding where every stroke goes as he visualizes the race.

"She…the girl…" My dad struggles for what to call her.

"Tanya," I answer.

He breathes out a short laugh, pulling his lip up on one side.

"She didn't know about me either," I answer before he asks.

My father's lips pull together tight as he nods, his eyes on the activity in the pool, but not really focusing on any one thing. I struggle to say more, wanting to explain how I found out, how much it hurts, but how I also feel like everything has been pushing me toward Will anyhow. None of it makes sense, and my heart is a messy place. That's what stops me. I'm sure those questions will come from my parents—about how Evan and Tanya met, how I found out, how old Dylan is, what his struggles are.

I'll need to tell them about Tanya's cancer, and I'll need them to understand Will's commitment, because I don't plan on going anywhere, but I can't lie to my father. I can't say I'm not scared, because he would see right through me.

I am terrified.

I'm not afraid to love him. That part…it's easy. But I'm terrified that I won't be strong enough, and that I will let him down. I just don't think the man about to fight through the waters trying to drown him can handle one more disappointment.

My father stands, his hand resting on my shoulder, but his eyes still on his swimmer—the one he was always meant to push the hardest. My heart is overjoyed to see him stand behind Will again. I cover my dad's hand with my own, and we make a silent deal to pick up the rest of the conversation about Evan later. For now, we give everything we've got to the other Hollister brother—the one nobody saw coming.

"Time to explode, Will. You have to explode out of this—that's your edge," my father yells. His hands form fists at his sides while his swimmer steps up to the blocks.

"Eighteen!" my father begins to shout, and I stand up next to him and begin to yell along with him.

This is the number we chase—the one Will chases. The US record in the fifty is barely a breath above eighteen seconds, and if you can even dance with the decimals that come after that number, you buy yourself respect.

My father has been daily drilling this number into Will's head. He's inscribed it on his cap, and we all repeat it in our minds here now. I glance back to where my mom is standing with her arm linked through Duncan's, and Tanya stands behind Dylan's chair with her hands clasped together and her neck straining with her held breath. So many people want this for him, but Will has to want it for himself.

Things begin to happen in slow motion as the bodies lined up along the pool all still, minus the occasional finger twitch in anticipation of the starting sound. The beeps begin, and my eyes sweep closed with the first two as I breathe in hard and fast, filling my chest as I know Will is. When my eyes open, they're all in the air. Will's start was mediocre. My father swears, leaping down from our team section to the deck below, cupping his mouth, following along the distance of the pool while he shouts. His words are meaningless to any ears but the ones he's speaking to—claw, smooth, dig, push…sixty…sixty-five…seventy. My father is counting the strokes. He knows exactly how many it should take. Meanwhile, his eyes are scanning in those last few seconds for places where they can fit one more, take one away, find the edge.

Nineteen.

The clock stops on Will's lane just as his hand touches the wall. He swam the fifty in nineteen seconds flat. He came in second in his heat, and he'll swim again today, but that number—*nineteen*—is going to become one more anchor that he needs to shed.

"Goddamnit!" My father's face is red, his eyes bunched as he covers his mouth with his hand and relives the last twenty seconds over again in his head, searching for what went wrong.

"It was the start," I say, and my dad nods.

His eyes meet mine, holding my stare until his palm falls away from his face. It wasn't a loss, but to us, it feels like one. To Will—it *is* one. I look over to the pool's edge where he's climbed out, but remains kneeling, his eyes set on the lane he just left. His elbows are on his knees, and his chin is balanced on his fists, his jaw set tight and his eyes like sights for a sniper.

Those demons of his—they slow him down.

CHAPTER 21

Will

Second twice.

There's a wall I can't seem to get over. I didn't even lose to the same guy each time, which means that on any given day, I'm slower than any other man I face in the pool.

I don't feel much like celebrating, but Susan insisted on having everyone to their house. I took Duncan, Tanya, and Dylan home, yet nothing about that small house they live in felt like one. It made me sick to leave them there, though I know that they'll be moving soon—to another place...that won't feel like home.

I've been sitting on the porch stoop outside the Woodsens' house for ten minutes, and I just can't seem to get myself to go inside to join the laughter. I feel the door shift open behind me, and I turn enough to see Susan's profile slip through the screen door.

"There are better hiding places than this, you know," she jokes.

A breath of a laugh escapes my nose, and I glance up as she sits down next to me.

"I was planning to come in soon," I say, not sure if I really was.

It's been years since I've sat alone with Maddy's mom. She was always the one to comfort me when I lost meets when I was a teenager, so I guess it's fitting that she's the one sitting here now. She lifts my elbow and slides her arm through mine, matronly, patting the top of my forearm with her other hand.

"We've come a long way from a popsicle making this all better, haven't we," she says.

I chuckle and nod, then turn to her with my nose scrunched.

"I hate to break it to you, but the popsicles never really worked either," I admit.

"That's because you take it all too seriously," she says.

I laugh at first, but as I study her face, I realize that her smile is soft, and she isn't joking.

"It's the only thing I can control," I shrug. "Swimming? That's all me—and if I win, that's on me. If I lose, it starts and ends with me."

I feel her shake where our arms touch, and I glance to her face to see her laughing quietly.

"Oh, Will…" she says. "Honey, you can't control a damn thing. But I promise you this…"

She tugs on my arm, encouraging me to stand with her. I pull my tired legs in and obey, letting her hold me by the shoulders, our toes facing so she can look me in the eyes.

"The sooner you realize that this life is just a ride, and that there are good parts there to enjoy, to balance out the crap that makes you sick, well…you might just find yourself creeping closer to that eighteen number you all seem so obsessed with," she winks, her lip ticking up higher on one side.

"Your daughter is a lot like you, you know?" I say, following her lead as we head inside.

She glances over her shoulder, speaking from one side of her mouth.

"Why do you think she's so fast?" she says.

I chuckle as we enter the main room, and Maddy's eyes find mine through the dozen other people here. I slip my hand in hers and revel in the squeeze she gives me back. I taste the sweetness of the cider and hold it in my mouth long enough to feel the tickle of the bubbles on my tongue.

I make sure to notice the colors of other people's eyes when we shake hands, to listen to the timber of their voices when they tell me I had a great race. I let the sound of Curtis's laugh settle in my own chest, and I try to replicate it in my own way.

I live in the moments. I force myself to every second for the entire evening. I want to find the joy, but somehow, when each precious thing passes, I sink right back to the bottom where nothing but failures and duties live.

Maddy's touch grows tender in my hand, and she frees from my grip, sliding her fingers up my arm to the tight muscles of my neck. Her thumb and fingers press lightly, and I succumb to her efforts, closing my eyes and breathing through my nose. I nearly relax when the clanking sound of a spoon on a glass jolts me to attention. I glance around the room to find Curtis standing on one of their dining-room chairs, a little drunk.

"I wanted to make an announcement," he says, his smile crooked and his body wobbly. Susan rolls her eyes and steps up next to him, holding her hand on his lower back. "Thank you, sweetheart," he grins.

She raises her brow and shakes her head.

All eyes move to Curtis, and his jolliness shifts as his hand covers his mouth and his chin sinks to his chest.

"I want to thank you all for training here," he begins, pausing, his eyes blinking at the floor. I look to Maddy and she glances at me, her head falling to the side, and my heart sinks. I'm not sure what news Curtis is about to deliver, but I know enough from the things I've survived to brace myself.

"This Swim Club…it has been my life…*our* lives. Maddy, Susan, me…*Will,*" he looks up, nodding toward me. "I think people are born competitors. I am one. I married one. Our daughter, Maddy—she's a lion. There is no one fiercer than her when it comes to those waters outside."

"Where is he going with this?" I whisper to Maddy.

Her hand squeezes mine harder, and when I look at her, her eyes set on her father, the tears pooling in them, I feel that sense of loss wrap its claws around my insides again.

"I wanted you all to know the honor you hold," Curtis says. "You will be the final group of swimmers to train here…"

Gasps fill the air, and Maddy's strength falters next to me. I reach around her and hold her against me, my stomach sick.

"Don't…no…" Curtis shakes his head. "Don't be sad," he says, raising his head, a genuine smile on his face as his eyes scan around the room, finally settling on mine. His mouth curves more when our gazes meet. "Don't you dare be sad," he says, as if these words are meant for me. "I have had so much joy running this place, working with you all. I have loved helping you compete. And I intend to see it through to the very end, through trials and at the Olympics. My dream lives on with each of you…it's just the mortgages that need to stop."

A few people laugh lightly, and Curtis smiles as he looks down at Susan, reaching to hold her hand.

"Let's raise our glasses to toast," he says, lifting his champagne, the real stuff for him. "To one more race…to the Shore Club and memories. And to that god-forsaken, bloody-hard-to-get, goddamned eighteen!"

"Here, here," several people shout, raising their glasses and drinking their liquid down in gulps. I hold my eyes on Curtis's, each of us looking at one another through the celebration. I need to find the joy, and I need to get that number for him. I need to win if I want to swim for him past the trials.

I need to stop the bleeding.

"Let's get out of here," I say to my side before tilting my glass back, draining it and setting it down on the edge of the dining-room table.

I look to Maddy, and she does the same, nodding to me and meeting my stare.

She doesn't ask where we're going as I drive back toward the Swim Club, passing it, and continuing on to the only place left that I think might ease the growing hole in my heart.

The sun glints off the rustling leaves as I wind through the country road to Peterson Lake, and it still hasn't quite set when I shift the car into park and exit, walking around to Maddy's side in time to take her hand.

She's wearing a white sundress and sandals, and I'm wearing my dress pants and the button-down shirt I've probably worn out by now. As we near the end of the trail, Maddy halts me and pulls her shoes from her feet, her smile hitting my eyes like honey on the tongue. She walks backward, her lip quirked on one side, her fingertips linked with mine as she lures me down to the water, a slight breeze making zigzags along the shallow surface. I kick my shoes off near the edge, and we both stop where the ground becomes wet. I look to the outcropping where our tree still stands.

"They still planning on tearing that down?" I nod toward the rope swing, and Maddy turns to follow my gaze.

She shrugs lightly.

"My mom hasn't said, but I know they're looking to put some houses up here," she says.

I breathe out a short laugh, shaking my head as Maddy turns.

"It all goes away, doesn't it?" I say.

Her fingertips dance along the tips of mine, and as I look out over the water, I feel her looking at me.

"Not everything," she says, bending down and picking up a small, flat stone. She opens my palm and sets it inside, wrapping my fingers around it, curling it between us.

My lips tug up at her sweetness. I open my palm and shake the rock down to my fingertips, holding it up and squinting at it with one eye.

"For old time's sake?" I say.

She holds my gaze, her mouth a smirk.

"You're on, Hollister," she says, looking down and holding her hair out of her vision as she scans the water, flipping over rocks with her toes. She finds her perfect stone, then lifts it up for me to inspect.

"Seems heavy to me," I grimace, baiting her.

Her eyes squint as she rubs her thumb along the rock's edge, holding it between us.

"That's you being a chicken," she says.

"Chickens first, then?" I say.

"Be my guest," she says, taking a step back, giving me room to throw.

I stretch my arm across my body, still feeling the tightness from racing today, then I glance around the water for the perfect direction. Rocks jut up in some places, so I want the longest runway possible. Cocking my arm back, I look at her one last time.

"What's the wager?" I ask. "Strip club again?"

She purses her lips and lets her head fall slightly to one side, her eyes narrowing on me.

"Liked it that much, did you?" she teases.

I shrug, laughing hard enough that my chest rumbles. I feel lighter, and I know that's because of Maddy.

"How about this," she begins, one eye closing more than the other, her hip shifting her weight to one leg. "You win, I'll do a swing with you…in my white dress," she says, one brow quirking up.

My lips pull up in a tight smile, smirking at the visual in my head.

"But I win," she interrupts my fantasy. She steps closer, looking down at the rock in her hand, shaking it in her palm a few times before glancing back up to me, now inches away from my body. "Then you have to hit eighteen. Saturday. You race like your life depends on it, and you hit that number."

My breathing becomes ragged and my heart starts to race. What she's asking for feels impossible, but if I promise her I'll do it, I'll find a way. I love her for asking—I love her for challenging.

I wink at her and hold up my opposite hand, waving her to take a few steps back.

"Deal," I say, cocking my arm and letting my stone fly across the water, skipping five times before finally diving into the depths for good.

My heart is still beating wildly, both because of her challenge that I do the impossible, and because I've made it hard for her to win. She's only skipped a rock more than five times once, and for the first time ever, I want her to win. I think I need that pressure—from her—to pull this off.

Maddy's eyes stare straight ahead, and her mouth remains unchanged, the hint of a smile still painted on her lips as if she knows a secret that makes her just a little better than the rest of us. She brings her stone to her lips, kissing the flat, harsh edge, then brings her arm back, slinging the rock side-armed along the water.

I move my lips with the numbers as I count silently, and my heart slows down when I pass five. The rhythm is back to normal when I end at seven, and in a blink, Maddy is standing in front of me again.

"Those years when you were gone?" she says, the Elvis lip twitching—taunting me to kiss it. "Someone practiced skipping rocks," she says, a slight waggle to her head.

I bite my bottom lip and squint my eyes at her, feeling nothing but the moment for real this time. All of those other times—everything I try—I'm not able to keep the demons at bay, but when I'm with Maddy there is nothing else.

"I hope you practiced jumping from rope swings, too," I say, giving her exactly a half a second to catch on and stiffen her muscles in panic before I lift her over my shoulder and run up the hill. Her feet kick and her hands pound at my back, but her laughter fills the in-between—it fills up all of the blank space.

"You lost fair and square, Will Hollister," she shouts between howls, trying to jerk loose of my hold. "This is cheating!"

"If I'm going to swim fifty meters in eighteen seconds, I'm going to need some motivation, Maddy. Time to see how that gorgeous fucking dress looks when it's wet and clinging to your skin!" I shout, wrapping one arm around her waist and gripping the rope in my opposite hand as I kick off from the cliff's edge.

Maddy shouts my name, and the sound of her voice echoes off the canyon wall, around the lake, through the trees, and right into my heart. I tug her close and her legs wrap around mine before I let go and send us flying out above the water. She lets go just as our toes begin to kick at the surface, and she rises up through the water quickly, splashing her arms wildly at me, making wave after wave, until she's close enough that I pull her to me again.

I never get to see how the dress looks wet against her skin. I imagine it, but I don't have time to look because my need to kiss her is too great. My mouth craves her, and when our lips crash together, it's like breathing for the first time—it's weightless.

It's my joy.

I found it.

CHAPTER 22

Maddy

"Are there always this many people at a press conference?" I clear my throat after I speak, extra nervous now that I hear the rasp in it. I've been fighting a cold all week. It won't matter in the water tomorrow. I can convince my body it isn't sick for two minutes. But speaking to a crowd, to lights and cameras? I'm not so sure I can muster enough energy for that.

"No idea. My first one, really." My father shrugs with his response as I work to straighten the knot on his tie. His movement forces it askew again, and I let my hands fall in defeat with my sigh.

"Sorry," he grimaces, pulling both ends loose and holding them out for me to try again. "You know your mom can't tie them either."

"I know," I say with a roll of my eyes, pausing with my eyes giving him a sideways glance. I laugh lightly and tug both ends of his tie, forcing them straight.

"You had interviews and stuff when you and Mom went to trials…and at the Olympics," I say, tugging one last time, satisfied that at least I no longer could see the half of his tie that's hidden in the back.

"It was a different time. We had the press, guys with notebooks, and maybe *a* camera. Today's world is on people's phones, though. Have you looked at that podium?" he asks.

I glance through the curtains, where the spotlight shines down on the wooden stand with a single mic, the surface covered in cellphones.

"That's how they do it now," my dad says, shaking his head.

I walk with my dad to the edge of the stage, a few other swimmers filing into their rows of seats. Only a few of us will get questions—me...*Will.*

"Can he handle this?" my dad asks.

Will was a different man all week. He was driven like he was that first time I saw him race when we started camp weeks ago, but his spirit was lighter. He still got lost in the moment—and those things he fights for, they'll probably never go away. His brother...his parents—they're his ghosts, and ghosts don't leave. They only fade.

"We talked a lot last night, about the questions he knows are coming," I say.

"Can he talk about Evan? Without feeling defensive?" My father quirks a brow at me, his hand gripping the rope near the stage curtain.

I smirk at him, realizing as I do—*Elvis lip.*

"He'll say nicer things about Evan than I will," I say.

My father puts his arm around me, urging me to step toward the stage with him.

"You and me both, sweetheart," he says, a rumble of a laugh coming from his chest.

I step up on my toes and kiss my father on the cheek, then find my way to my seat. My palms are sweating—I wish instead of this press conference I would just swim extra laps for the public while people filmed me. That's what I'm good at. Cameras...they're...invasive I guess?

"You look pretty," says a deep voice next to me. I glance up and catch the UCLA logo on his shirt and enough of his smile to recognize flirting.

"Pretty fast," I say back. He laughs, so I turn my head away, not wanting to engage more conversation. I wore my pink dress with buttons on top and a flair just above my knees. It was supposed to be for my graduation, but since that's not happening for another six months, I figured I'd break it in. Holly told me it made me look smart.

I tuck the skirt under my legs and sweep my hair behind my ear, my palm shading my eyes from the lights while I look out to the few people behind the cameras. Holly came with my mom. She said she wanted to support me, but I know my friend better than that. She wants to ogle the male swimmers.

She can—every one, but this one.

My head falls to the side, and his blue eyes are waiting.

"You got this," I mouth.

His lip ticks up and he raises a thumb.

"That Will Hollister?" my UCLA friend asks me.

"That's him," I say, finally meeting my flirtatious friend's eyes. He looks like every other guy here—broad chest and shoulders, arms filling his sleeves, thigh muscles about to rip through his pants. They're bred this way, and they all come out the same, but it's that stuff inside that separates them. Will…he has just a little bit more than they do.

Mr. UCLA ends our conversation there, but I count the times he glances down our row to Will. I'm sure there's a part of it that's Will's story—his survival is hard to believe unless you see him sitting in front of you. But there's also an edge of fear with the way my neighbor's leg bounces, his hands twisting in his lap. The more he looks at his competition, the more my Elvis lip twitches, until I can't help but laugh to myself.

Will…he has that extra something, and this guy—he's dead in the water.

The questions come at him like bullets, and Will handles every single one with grace. He memorializes Evan, and he speaks with reverence about his parents, recounting the first time they came to my parents' club, the practices his dad drove he and his brother to, the way his mom would always try to make sure they both felt like winners—even if one of them lost.

Nobody asks about me until the end, and when the question comes about our friendship, a hint of innuendo in the reporter's tone, Will says exactly what I told him to if that question were to come up.

"You'll have to ask Maddy about that."

His response gets some teasing "oooohs" and some laughter, but after a few minutes, the reporters move on to my dad and the rest of the coaching staff. It's clear that there's a division there, too—some people ready to embrace Will, hoping to see him dominate in the water, others not. My father leaves no question about his loyalties, telling the room that our best shot at a medal is with Will swimming anchor, and that response makes my friend sitting next to me squirm in his seat. My instincts tell me that he's a freestyle sprinter, too.

For a while, I think I might skate by, but eventually the floor comes around to the *Star* and *Tribune*. My hometown papers have watched me grow up, and they've covered my swimming from high-school championships to US titles at Valpo. While I'm surprised to see the familiar faces here in Omaha, I'm also flattered that my story is worth it. I'm grateful for this platform, because as much as Will intends on outright winning every race he swims, leaving no question up for debate—I also see no harm in adding just a little insurance.

The microphone squeals when I lower it, and I notice several people in the room hunch their shoulders at the sound.

"Sorry," I say, holding my hands out and slowly backing them away from the mic, as if I'm balancing a house of cards. I smile out to the cameras and my friend and mom, who I know are somewhere behind the lights. "That's what you get for talking to all the boys first, though. I had to make this thing a girl's height," I laugh.

A few people snicker with me.

"Maddy, it's John Tucker, from the *Star*. I covered you at nationals last year," the first familiar face begins.

I offer him a closed-lip smile and brace myself.

"Nice to see you, John," I respond.

His questions are basic—nothing I haven't answered in one-on-ones before. My training and preparation, what I think my chances are, how much my parents have influenced my swimming life—questions I answer by rote, the words coming out ready to print, perfect sound bites.

His counterpart steps in with a few more questions, picking up on a few things my dad answered earlier—about the impending closure of the Shore Club, and how this week was its last hoorah. The local papers care more about this angle, so I give them the heartfelt answers they deserve—words I mean.

"No place will ever feel the same," I say, glancing over and catching my dad's sad smile.

I start to worry that I waited too long—that my opportunity was slipping by as the *Tribune* reporter hands away the mic—when the public's insatiable appetite for gossip and romance comes to the rescue.

The reporter, the same one who finished with Will, stands tall, waving her hand in desperation for the microphone. I don't recognize her, but I can tell she's with one of the entertainment outlets—the sports reporters all have a different look about them, less...*polished*. She stands, brushing a wave of blonde hair over her shoulder as her eyes lower toward me and her smile creeps up. She's probably expecting me to evade romance rumors, too—which she'll simply turn into juicy gossip that won't have anything to do with how we swim tomorrow. I'm about to do her one better.

"Hi, Maddy. Sheila Vargas, Z-TV," she says. I give her a closed-mouth smile, raising my brow, welcoming it. She looks giddy. "Will told me I should ask you about the rumors that you two seem to be forming a...*special* bond, so let me just put it out there—are you and Will Hollister...dating?"

I look down to my hands, folded near the mic, and I start to tilt my head because as ready as I am, the blush still hits me hard. I wait for my cheeks to feel it, for the smile to be unstoppable, and then the wave of attention passes enough that I can talk without messing this up.

"We train so hard, Sheila. Hours in the water, and the hours out of the water are all spent on mentally preparing yourself for something that for most of us lasts less than a minute—that might last *eighteen seconds*," I say, that last part for Will and my dad. I don't even have to look to know they're both smiling. "When I first started competing, it was Will Hollister pushing me to be my best."

I glance over my shoulder to find his eyes waiting, his head tilted slightly, his uncle sitting next to him for support.

"I love him something fierce, Sheila," I smile, turning back to face the reporter, her eyes glowing with the gem of a story I just gave her. I hold her gaze on mine for a few seconds, and she lowers the mic, satisfied and probably already mentally putting together the six-o'clock package I just wrapped up with a bow. I'm about to sprinkle it with glitter. "We're in this together, and if Will doesn't swim for Team USA, neither do I."

I step back when I finish, my eyes glancing down at my hands as my fingers drum once on the wooden surface. I can't avoid Will's gaze as I walk back to the seat, but I avoid my father. I went off script for that, and neither of them are going to like it. It means Will's just going to have to win. It just so happens, though, that I have an incredible amount of faith in him.

Will

I'm starting to think Maddy's aim may have been to incite fear in my bones, to make me feel the death threat of her father at my heels in the pool. The moment she made that public comment yesterday, I felt Curtis's eyes on me in a way I never have. He hasn't said it, but I know the threat is real—if I fuck this up for his daughter, I can kiss my balls goodbye.

There's a part of me that knows Maddy wasn't serious. If something happens, and I am on the bubble—the guy they choose, or don't choose, for alternate—I don't really believe that Maddy would turn her back on her dreams in protest. But then there's that other part of me that knows that Maddy doesn't lie—not to my face. She looked me in the eyes when she walked away from that microphone, conviction in the sway of her hips and smug confidence in her grin. She told me the rest was up to me.

I'll give her this, I haven't thought about Evan, or Dylan and Tanya, until right now, and only because I can see my nephew on the screen for the camera. They're panning to my family.

My family. Only two of them are related to me by blood, yet they all have this piece of me.

"You ready, son?" Curtis says, his hands fists that knead at my shoulders.

Son.

My head falls, my eyes look at my feet, water on the ground tracked in from the race before me. It all comes down to this—to eighteen seconds.

I tilt my head and look at him sideways as Curtis moves to stand next to me.

"Explode, right?"

He nods, reaching his fist forward to pound against mine.

"You got this," he says, just like his daughter. I wait with the other sprinters. I won my heat, but my time wasn't the best. I'm in lane two. But lanes aren't going to make the difference for me today. I could be swimming in a separate pool from everyone all together, alone…in the dark, and it wouldn't change what I need to do to get myself to the games.

I know I'm supposed to clear out my thoughts of anything but his words, but my head is full. It's crowded in there—responsibilities running into memories—the past tangling with the present, guilt melting into pride, a dash of anger thrown on top for good measure. I doubt my mind will ever be quiet again, but I'll learn to use it. I better learn fast.

I don't hear them call us out, but I follow the guy in front of me. He's lane three, and I can tell by the smug smile he gave me before he slipped his goggles on that he thinks that means he's better.

It doesn't mean shit.

I'll beat him first.

We all line up behind our blocks, and I bend down to stretch out those last few nerves. It's the same every time—a little trick my brother taught me that I will probably do until I'm too old to dive head first into the water any more. You visualize that monkey on your back, and you swing until he can't hold on any longer. He always falls in the water.

I step up on my blocks, and I feel everything. I feel the air in this building—however slight it blows—against my face. I feel the grit beneath my feet, and the buzz in the air from everyone's collective anticipation. I feel the steady rhythm of my heart, the pound gaining speed with each drum until I hear it hit the rate my arms need to move to. I breathe in long and deep—one last taste until I get to the other side, and then I let the noise in my head take over until it's deafening and only one single thing rises to the top.

Maddy.

"Take your mark."

I recognize the words. My body obeys, and I coil into position.

Maddy.

The beeping sounds. My heart threatens to break rhythm. One. More. Breath.

Maddy.

The reaction is automatic. It's innate. I explode, and I don't have to look to my right to know that lane number three's shot at making the team is over. I don't care about him anymore. I don't care about lane four, or five. I care about eighteen. I care about that perfect line, the way my arm comes out, goes in, digs, pulls, grabs…and does it all again. I care about left. I care about right. I care about twenty. Twenty-five.

Boom-boom. Boom-boom.

The sound in my ears has become thunder. My legs punish the water. Bedlam lives behind me, peace straight ahead—I cut through it like a sacred sword—sharp and precise.

Thirty. Thirty-five.

The explosion is behind me, and I've long forgotten the feel of the air. All I feel now is the smooth silk of the water as it caresses my face. I disrupt it…break it—the calm gone with my arm, the perfect line, tight across, low down, fast through—above all else, fast.

Maddy.

Seconds slow, yet my breath feels endless. I don't look left. I don't look right. I know that the storm around me is thick and furious, and every single lane is occupied with someone who feels just as worthy as I do—no doubt, more. But they're still not going to win. They can't have today. Today is mine, and doubters can go to fucking hell, because I'm done serving my sentence. I'm done feeling like I owe the universe. I don't owe anyone shit.

I swim for me and that beat that's picking up pace. My arms follow it—chase that sound. I drive faster.

I race…for her.

Maddy.

My fingertips graze the wall, collapse against the slick surface and the wave I've carried behind me comes crashing into the back of my head. My mouth gasps, and my lungs fill with sweet air. I know before I turn. My heart feels it before I see it.

It doesn't make it any less sweet.

Eighteen.

EPILOGUE

Six months later...

Will

I've always loved coming out here before sunrise. There's a peacefulness to the water—no ripples, no sound other than the chirping of crickets and the occasional toad. Man, nature, and the elements.

Maddy mentioned it before bed last night, those times when we were in high school and she and I would wake up at four or five, just to get our laps in before anyone else. She never invited Evan to those swims, and I always kept them a secret.

That—it's just ours.

Always will be.

I'm not here to swim this morning, though. This just seems to be the only place I can think—where I can really find the guts to dare for impossible.

I get to the ground, sliding my shoes off behind me and rolling up my sweatpants, testing the water with my toes first. We put a new heater in at the Shore Club last week, but I still haven't tried it. My mind can't make sense of the snow my eyes see on the ground around us to get myself to dive into the water.

"Just a leg," I whisper to myself, dropping my foot in slowly.

The water still bites, but the heater is definitely working. I follow with my other foot, grinning over the brim of my coffee cup, like a proud father, while I wiggle my toes in the water I now own a share of along with my uncle and the Woodsens.

The Shore Club couldn't close. More than just what this place means to me, to Maddy and her family, to Evan's story—the good parts—this place still has a lot of work to do. I have work to do here.

My future became incredibly clear on that Olympic podium, a silver medal around my neck, the weight of the world somehow lifted from my shoulders. I have so much to give this swimming world, and I'm just getting started.

I approached my uncle with the idea first, knowing that my savings wouldn't be enough. I was prepared to have to convince him, or to have to find alternative investors, but I think maybe the idea of family has grown to mean something more to him, too. He and my aunt never had children, and she died young. Tragedy brought me close to him again, but that special bond that only comes from blood found its familiar place and imprinted itself on both of us. He was just looking for a way not to go back to Michigan.

Tanya died two months ago. People say that death is easier when you have time to prepare for it, but I think those people are full of shit. It felt just like I knew it would—like the devil had his way with my heart and then shoved it back in my chest, and I was expected to find a way to continue to live—to breathe and go on every day with the things on my plate now.

A year ago, I might have given up.

I might have driven my car off the edge of the world.

I didn't have Maddy then.

I sip the steaming coffee before setting it next to me, leaning back on my palms, my feet circling in the water and my eyes watching the sky move from a deep royal-blue to violet. Morning—and the colors that go with it—makes me think of her.

Before Tanya's passing, we worked out the paperwork to make sure I would become Dylan's legal guardian. Maddy finished school, but instead of taking the job at the hospital, she applied to a special program at State to work with kids like Dylan. I saw something happen to her the first time she met him and he held her hand. My nephew has so many things to overcome, but love isn't one of them. Love just pours from him, without words, and with limited gestures. It's in his essence, and it makes me believe in things that I've damned and doubted since the day I lost my brother and parents.

It took some work to fix the Clubhouse, but using the lobby space along with the upstairs, we were able to make it livable for Dylan, me, and Duncan. I think my uncle often fancied the office space, with the "just-right light," so it was just a matter of blowing out a few walls to make the studio apartment's bathroom shared.

We added a wall downstairs, and though it's tight, we have enough room for the three of us, more often four when Maddy stays the night, to gather for dinner at a table, and for Dylan to be able to easily maneuver his electric chair from his new bedroom to the kitchen and bathroom.

I've found the routine of things, and I've found comfort in it. But I still wait for the hour when I get to see her face—every day. Sometimes, it's midnight after a long day studying, or putting in hours with the hospital's special therapy programs. Other times it's mornings like this, when she puts on her suit and we make silly bets neither of us mind losing, and we race for nobody but ourselves.

She is my joy.

She always has been.

"Either the heater's working, or you're tricking me—seeing if I'll dive in and catch a cold." Her voice soothes my soul, a song starting behind me, then wrapping around me completely. I keep my eyes on the sky—her favorite color coming next—and I point up.

"Oh, you know how I love the orange," she says, kicking her shoes off, rolling up her jeans and sitting down next to me.

She shivers a little when her feet plunk in, and she wraps her arm through mine, laying her head on my shoulder to look up at the sky with me.

"Coffee?" I ask, holding my cup out for her to take.

"Mmmmm, yes please," she purrs.

I watch her sip, her eyes blinking to stay open from the fog of the drink, to stay on the quickly disappearing stars above.

"Thank you," she says, smiling as the cup's edge leaves her lips.

I take it from her and set it back down next to me, and I lean back a little more on my left palm, careful not to disturb the place she's cradled on my right arm.

Maddy won two golds at the Olympics, but my story was the one on the front page. Sports can be sexist like that. The press also never seems to get tired of exploiting my story. I don't know how many times people can read about the boy who survived, only to come in second, but I guess at least one more time.

Between the two of us, Maddy's the real survivor. She's the strong one. I protected the lie, but she's the one who had to overcome it, to come to terms with what my brother had done. She never once put that hurt on Tanya or Dylan, but there have been times in the last few months that she's gotten angry. She'll find something that reminds her—a photo or old yearbooks—and it just opens up the vicious circle for her. Evan's scars have made it hard for her to believe that good love—*true love*—is real.

But I know it is. I'm looking at it right now, watching it look up at the stars.

I've been wandering the world half a man, and Maddy, she made me whole.

"Marry me," I say.

Two simple words. They fly from my lips with little warning and little fanfare. I suppose it's rude that I didn't say them like a question, but I simply can't. The only answer I can take from this woman is *yes*, and I won't quit saying them like this until she concedes.

I've asked twice already, and both times she's said *no*. So I won't ask anymore. I'll just speak it like the truth it is.

Her eyes blink slowly once, and I marvel at the way the orange above mixes with her brown to turn her eyes gold. She doesn't flinch, and her breathing remains steady, as if she didn't hear me at all. I'd think maybe she didn't, but I know how loud I was. I left no doubt. It's been weeks since I've asked, since she told me I wasn't ready, but I know I am.

I wait with my eyes on her for nearly a minute, finally resolving to repeat this routine in two days, when I know her morning is free again. I don't sigh. I'd hoped for her to accept, but I'm not discouraged. I'm empowered, because every time I ask, the words get easier to say. This time, they were nearly effortless.

I rest my weight back again, watching the peach-colored clouds shift to white, the sky around them growing more and more vivid in its blue. It's going to be cold today, with more snow maybe tonight. I'll need to shut the pool down completely for the next month, but I just wanted to test the heater. Classes will begin in the late spring, and then I'll get to teach. My heart is steady, and my mind is calm. I'm exactly where I'm meant to be.

"Yes," she says.

It takes me a second or two to realize I didn't imagine her word. My mind halting on the to-do list I'd just begun, my head falling forward again, tipping to the side.

Her eyes blink again, and her lip tugs up on one corner. Fucking Elvis!

"Ye…yes?" I stammer, nowhere near as cool and calm as I had pretended I would be when I fantasized about how this morning would go.

Maddy nods, her smile growing.

"Yes, Will Hollister. I will marry you," she says.

Her eyes dazzle, and my heart stops, just for a moment, almost as if it's etching a memory of this moment on my insides, as if *right now* is anything I could ever forget.

I turn to face her, lifting her body into mine, her legs falling over my own, our bodies pressed close together while my hands graze up her arms to her cold cheeks, pink from the morning chill. I lean into her, stopping when my forehead rests against hers, holding my kiss until I can just be certain I'm not dreaming.

It's my smirk that gives me away.

"You're totally going to throw me into the pool, aren't you?" she asks, and I nod against her, biting my lip, but unable to stop the devious laugh that puffs out from my chest as I squeeze her to me tightly and push off with my legs, dumping us both into the water.

She screams when her head breaks back through the surface, and in typical Maddy fashion, her arms swing wildly, pelting me with balmy waves that still sting in the cold Indiana air. I let her hate me for just a second, and then I grip her wrists and drag her kicking toward me, my hands smoothing down her soaked sweatshirt, pressing her into me for warmth.

"I can't believe I signed up for this for life," she says, her voice quivering and her lips vibrating from both laughter and the cold.

I cup her face in my hands and kiss her hard, holding her head against mine for a second or two more, finally helping her from the pool, and then chasing behind her for the locker-room showers.

Once the hot water penetrates our skin, I pull her naked body to mine again, and I kiss every spot I missed the first time. I never tell her that I can't believe she signed up for this either. I don't share the millions of times I doubted deserving what she's given me already. I keep all of those voices away from my head and heart. I lock them out, and I promise myself never to let them back in. It's taken me years to defeat them. I couldn't do it on my own. I needed joy.

My joy.

Maddy.

Maddy...and eighteen seconds.

THE END

ACKNOWLEDGEMENTS

I had this heavy idea, and it lingered. I gave it a name eventually—Will Hollister. I think I have tortured Will more than any character I have ever constructed, and I am inspired by his ability to persevere. More than Will, though, I am inspired by the *real* fighters—the people who are knocked down so far it seems impossible, who face adversity, even when it's more tragedy, but yet find a way to climb again—to rise above. This book is for them. Whether it feels like a hill or a mountain, your climb is brave. Even if you fall on the way back up.

There are so many people I need to thank for Hold My Breath. My home and heart always comes first. My husband is the reason I write. He is my joy, the thing that pushes me. And I am grateful for him every single day.

I'm rarely in a writing cave. Life is too precious to miss pieces of it, so I try to stay disciplined, never missing the important bits. But it doesn't mean I don't multitask. There are many practices, tournaments, batting lessons, school pickups, etc. where I am carrying my laptop, opening it between innings or squeezing in some editing during game breaks. My son never thinks I'm weird, and he's usually pretty damn proud. That feels good. Love you to the moon, buddy.

Now for the girls. My beta squad: Ashley, Bianca, Jen and Shelley. You are truth, encouragement, honesty, praise, more honesty (LOL) and love all rolled into a group of kick-ass readers that I will hold hostage for as long as you let me. (Actually, probably longer. Stop reading for me and I will hunt you down.) I'm so thankful for the time you give my words. And the people I bring to life are better because of you all.

Tina Scott and BilliJoy Carson, my words end with you. You are the fine finishing. I come to you a Honda and you send me away a Cadillac. Thank you ladies for being the best editors ever!

Ninjas! Oh my gosh, I can't believe I got so lucky. You all are the best readers, and your support and undying dedication to shouting from the mountaintops fuels me. Bloggers—each and every one of you, no matter the size—I am honored every single time you share something of mine, you review, you post, you suggest, you tag. You are my rock stars!

There are dozens of other names I need to shout out, and I'm sure I'm forgetting someone, but know this—I am beyond grateful for your time. Whether it's answering my crazy nursing practice questions (Theresa Nelson, you are the best!) or just telling me to keep writing because you're excited for the book, every word you send to me is meaningful. You all make me believe in miracles and magic.

Let's do this again, shall we?

ABOUT THE AUTHOR

Ginger Scott is an Amazon-bestselling and Goodreads Choice Award-nominated author of several young and new adult romances, including Waiting on the Sidelines, Going Long, Blindness, How We Deal With Gravity, This Is Falling, You and Everything After, The Girl I Was Before, In Your Dreams, Wild Reckless, Wicked Restless, The Hard Count and Hold My Breath.

A sucker for a good romance, Ginger's other passion is sports, and she often blends the two in her stories. Ginger has been writing and editing for newspapers, magazines and blogs for…well…ever. She has told the stories of Olympians, politicians, actors, scientists, cowboys, criminals and towns. For more on her and her work, visit her website at http://www.littlemisswrite.com.

When she's not writing, the odds are high that she's somewhere near a baseball diamond, either watching her son field pop flies like Bryce Harper or cheering on her favorite baseball team, the Arizona Diamondbacks. Ginger lives in Arizona and is married to her college sweetheart whom she met at ASU (fork 'em, Devils).

Ginger Online

@TheGingerScott
www.facebook.com/GingerScottAuthor
www.littlemisswrite.com

BOOKS BY GINGER SCOTT

Read The Complete Falling Series
This Is Falling
You And Everything After
The Girl I Was Before
In Your Dreams (spin-off standalone)

The Waiting Series
Waiting on the Sidelines
Going Long

The Harper Boys
Wild Reckless
Wicked Restless

Standalones
Blindness
How We Deal With Gravity
The Hard Count
Hold My Breath

Made in the USA
Middletown, DE
09 October 2022